# Praise for
## *Crime of Privilege*

"A whodunit set in *Lifestyles of the Rich and Famous* . . . fast-paced with lots of sharp turns . . . you'll lose yourself in it."     —*The Guardian*

"Nuanced and emotionally convincing . . . A subtle, well-paced thriller."     —*USA Today*

"[A] tale of moral redemption . . . Fans of John Grisham and Scott Turow especially will love this engrossing story of murder involving high society."     —*BookReporter*

"A slick, satisfying conspiracy novel where revenge tastes best served with a highball."     —*Milwaukee Journal-Sentinel*

"*Crime of Privilege* is a privilege to read."     —*Hartford Books Examiner*

"[S]pot-on characterization, a protagonist whose humiliating past compels sympathy, and a host of unexpected suspects. The novel's moral complexity will appeal to readers who enjoyed works as diverse as Tom Wolfe's *Bonfire of the Vanities,* Nelson DeMille's *The Gold Coast,* and any number of contemporary thrillers." —*Library Journal*

"A sheer pleasure to read . . . George must find his own moral compass, in a summer read notable for credible characters and unpredictable twists." —*Publishers Weekly* (starred review)

"A page-turning, puzzle-solving adventure." —*Booklist*

"Walker maintains his dry, sometimes biting humor and moral edge . . . a convincing portrait of misbehavior among the rich and powerful." —*Kirkus Reviews*

"*Crime of Privilege* is not only a first-class legal thriller, it is an astute examination of our society and how we are corrupted by power and money. The rich are indeed different; they get away with murder. . . . A finely nuanced tale." —Nelson DeMille

"*Crime of Privilege* is wonderfully written, and Walter Walker has a great talent, the God-given kind that can't be taught or learned or acquired, and the reader knows it from the first paragraph of the book. The characters are complex and interesting yet also emblematic of all the players in the class war, which is the stuff of all epic stories. I love the protagonist, and I also love the portrayal of the world of the very rich. There is something about the very rich that is hard to describe, but Walter Walker got them in the camera's lens perfectly."

—James Lee Burke

"A gripping, chilling tale that pits privilege against pride, with a not-entirely-innocent man caught in the untenable middle."

—Chris Pavone, *New York Times* bestselling author of *The Expats*

BY *WALTER WALKER*

*CRIME* OF *PRIVILEGE*

# CRIME OF PRIVILEGE

## A NOVEL

## WALTER WALKER

BALLANTINE BOOKS
TRADE PAPERBACKS
NEW YORK

Published in the United States by Ballantine Books, an imprint of Random House, a division of Random House LLC, a Penguin Random House Company, New York.

BALLANTINE and the HOUSE colophon are registered trademarks of Random House LLC.

Originally published in hardcover in the United States by Ballantine Books, an imprint of Random House, a division of Random House LLC, in 2013.

LIBRARY OF CONGRESS CATALOGING-IN-PUBLICATION DATA
Walker, Walter.
Crime of privilege : a novel / Walter Walker.
pages cm
ISBN 978-0-345-54837-5 (Trade paperback : acid-free paper)
eBook ISBN 978-0-345-54154-3
1. Upper class—Fiction. 2. Murder—Investigation—Fiction. I. Title.
PS3573.A425417C75 2013b
813'.54—dc23        2013004332

Printed in the United States of America on acid-free paper

www.ballantinebooks.com

9 8 7 6 5 4 3 2 1

Book design by Barbara M. Bachman

*TO ANNE, all these years*

Crime of Privilege *is a fictional work about invented characters and the glamorous world they inhabit. Although much of the action of the novel takes place on Cape Cod, where I have a home,* Crime of Privilege *is no more or less than an imagined story.*

*CRIME* OF *PRIVILEGE*

## 1.

ALMOST EVERYONE HAD HEARD OF THE FAMILY'S MANSION on Ocean Boulevard, but very few had been there. A large part of the reason I had agreed to go to Florida, to spend my spring break with McFetridge, was simply to get inside. We were staying at his parents' place, down the road in Delray, but every night we were invited to a party or a gathering somewhere, and this was the crowning event, cocktails at the iconic Spanish Revival house on the beach, where, it was promised, the Senator himself would be present.

I would speak to him as a guest of a guest in his house. *Senator, yes, George Becket here. I admire your work on . . .* What did I admire his work on? Any liberal cause, I suppose. I was twenty-two and filled with grandiose ideas. And then I was there, in his house, surrounded by people wearing silk and linen for a supposedly informal gathering where everyone acted as though it was normal for men in white jackets to park your car and women in black pinafores to serve champagne in crystal flutes carried on silver trays; and I had no opportunity to say anything more than, "Hello, Senator, thank you for having me."

I had entered in McFetridge's wake and we had been greeted by several family members who were not so much stationed in the foyer as conversing in its vicinity. I stood to the side while McFetridge went about kissing women's cheeks and shaking men's hands.

McFetridge seemed to know everyone. He knew them from a sailing race he did each May between Hyannisport and Nantucket, from Christmas-week ski trips to Aspen, from clubs to which his parents belonged, from prep school. "Nan . . . Eastie . . . Harlan . . . this is my friend Georgie."

I had gone to prep school, too, but not Hotchkiss, St. Paul's, Groton, or even Milton. In my brief exchanges with his friends, I found myself mentioning the dominance of my school on the athletic fields, courts, tracks, and pools of New England. We didn't even play their schools. We played Andover, Exeter, Choate, Deerfield, and beat them all. I caught looks that said, *You want to talk about that?* And I would scramble for something else to say. "You guys always had a good crew team, didn't you? Going to Henley this year?" Sometimes I would be ignored, sometimes abandoned. George thought he was having a conversation one moment; George was all by himself the next.

I wandered through large rooms with red tiled floors, nodding at everyone who caught my eye and smiling at those who seemed to be wondering who I was. There were pictures on the walls, pictures in bookcases, pictures on shelves and on top of the grand piano. Pictures of members of the family with the pope, Churchill, Desmond Tutu. I wondered if Desmond Tutu had the same picture in his house. I wondered if the pope did.

Eventually I found myself standing next to a striking young woman who seemed similarly out of touch with everyone else at the party. She had thick black hair that swept past her shoulders and green eyes that probably sparkled when they weren't so glazed with drink. Kendrick Powell, she said her name was, and she was a student at Bryn Mawr. I had been there once, for a mixer, and I knew just enough about the school to keep the conversation going. And then one of the cousins appeared holding two very large cocktails in his hands. Palm Beach Specials, he said they were, and he had just made them.

He handed a drink to each of us and then he was gone, and we were left sipping fancy combinations of liquor and fruit juice out of tall frosted glasses. "Are you part of the family?" she asked, and I told her no, I was a friend of a friend. She looked as though she had to consider that, whether it was worth her time to continue talking to me if I was only a friend of a friend of the family, and then the friend himself appeared. Paul McFetridge, with his dangerous smile and his air of knowing exactly what was going on, delivering yet another Palm Beach Special to the already intoxicated Ms. Powell. He rather absently handed me one as well, and now I stood with a Palm Beach Special in each hand, feeling rather like McFetridge's butler, his man George, as he shouldered his way between Kendrick and me. Elliot was here, did she know Elliot? She didn't know Elliot. Wonderful squash player, Elliot. She didn't play squash.

I finished one of the drinks in a single long swallow and put the glass down on whatever surface I could find. It was immediately scooped up by one of the waitstaff, who was gone before I could even say "Sorry."

And then McFetridge, too, was gone, replaced by two more of the cousins, Peter Gregory Martin and Jamie Gregory, and I was pushed to the outskirts of the conversation once again. It had been Kendrick and me. Then Kendrick and McFetridge and me. Then Kendrick and Peter and Jamie, and I was left with no one to talk to, nothing to do but hold my place while Peter chatted her up.

What had they talked about? What do rich girls discuss when they are at the homes of even richer people whom they do not know personally, but whom they know all about? Peter had offered her things. You ever Jet Ski? We've got a couple, you want to go out on the ocean with us? Maybe tomorrow. Oh, wait, there's a polo match. Have you ever been to a polo match? Jamie, half a head shorter, had chimed in, telling her what a hoot they are, spread out a blanket, get a couple of bottles of champagne. What did I have to offer? I had no place to go tomorrow. No place to go even while they were talking to her.

Maybe that was why I agreed to join the tour when Peter and Jamie offered to show Kendrick the rest of the house. They said, "C'mon," and I went. Tagged along. Not to have done so would have meant standing alone.

## 2.

THE THING ABOUT THE SENATOR WAS THAT DESPITE HIS FLAWS, and he had many of them, he was an incredibly nice guy. He was also very polite. When he saw what was happening—when he opened the door and stuck his head into the room, saw that the girl was not protesting, saw that her eyes were open—he simply pulled his head back and shut the door. This was no place for him.

The thing about me was that I wasn't doing anything, which was both my saving grace and my ultimate shame.

I had thought we were going to look at pictures, such as the ones I had seen already. Oh, my, look. There's Jacques Cousteau! Willy Brandt! James Earl Jones! I had been thinking that we were going to visit rooms where important people had gathered: statesmen and politicians, artists and actors and writers and singers, educators and generals, industry leaders and social activists. That we were going to stop to admire mementos given by one celebrity to another. But instead we went directly to the far end of the house, down a long hall and away from the rest of the revelers to the library. Where it was quiet. Where we shut the door behind us.

Except the door did not quite shut before Peter stopped in his tracks and looked rather blearily at me. He was a fairly large man, his face pink, his eyes light blue, and for a moment he seemed uncertain who I was or what I was doing there. And then it came to him, I was

McFetridge's friend. "Georgie," he said, as though he was responding to a quiz.

"Yes?"

"Why don't you go and get us another round of those specials?"

I still had one in my hand. I didn't need another round. I had done nothing but drink since I arrived. I looked at Kendrick. Her glass was empty except for the ice. She had drunk two to my one, and neither Peter nor Jamie seemed to have anything. I tilted my glass to my mouth and for the second time drained everything in it in one very long swallow. "Okay," I said.

When I left, Kendrick was standing in a corner of the library, staring at a painting. When I returned, she was on the couch. Both shoes were off. Her feet were up on the cushions. Her knees were up and her black dress had slid a fair way down her thighs.

I had four red drinks and was clutching them together so that extraction of any single glass had to be done quite carefully. "Oh, *thank you!*" she cried as I bent at the waist to give her first choice. I turned then to Peter, who was positioned down by Kendrick's feet, one haunch on the couch cushion, one leg extended behind him, almost as if he was ready to start a sprint. "Put them over there, Georgie," he said, waving to a credenza that was under the painting I had seen Kendrick admiring.

The painting turned out to be a Winslow Homer. I was pretty sure it was a Homer. A seascape illuminated by a spotlight that did little more than emphasize how dark and dusty the painting was, as though nobody had paid attention to it for a very long time. Kendrick was drinking. Peter and Jamie had taken up positions on either end of her. And I was staring at the Homer. Ah, the patina provides a palpable sense of the perils of pursuing a large *poisson* in a small boat on the open sea after dark.

I think the Senator looked in when Peter was still half on the couch and half off. When he was still wearing his blazer. When it was possible to look from the door to the couch and not be absolutely positive what was going on.

But what was going through my mind?

Was *anything*? Was I just there, holding the remains of my third

Palm Beach Special? Kendrick, by this point, had had at least three, which was why she was in the condition she was, more or less spread-eagled on the couch in the library, saying nothing, doing nothing, while Peter and Jamie moved their hands over her. While I stood by, a half-smile on my face.

Was I smiling?

I try to imagine that I wasn't. But what else would I have been doing? Peter wasn't paying any attention to me, but Jamie kept looking up and grinning almost maniacally. What are you supposed to do when someone grins at you like that? When you barely know him? When you are a guest in his family's house? Like the Senator, I was being polite.

I think now I should have slapped that grin off Jamie's face. Now when I see his picture in a newspaper or a magazine I remember the way he looked at me and it literally makes my stomach turn. Sometimes I gouge his face out of the picture, leave just a hairline and a body, usually clad in a sport coat, a white shirt, a loose tie, khaki pants. Even when I do that you can still tell who it is, by the hairline and the family uniform.

Back then I didn't slap, didn't gouge. I just watched. It was only when I thought Peter was going to hurt her that I stepped in. *Hurt her*. Jesus, what was I thinking before, that she wasn't being hurt? Hurt, harmed. I didn't want him to do physical damage to her. Permanent damage. Go ahead, abuse her. Foul her. Debase her. But don't hurt her.

Jesus, Jesus, Jesus. What was I thinking?

Peter was looming over her, looking like a Cape buffalo eyeing its prey. He had one hand on the back of the couch, one hand on the coffee table. She was leaning back. To lean back meant tucking herself into the corner of the couch. Was she trying to escape or was she relaxing? One bare foot was on top of the couch. A narrow foot at the end of a long, slender, well-tanned leg.

Why do I remember that part? Was that what I was looking at?

Kendrick wasn't saying anything. Had she not paid attention when Jamie kneeled on the floor behind her head? Did she not care when he put his hands on her shoulders, when he started rolling his wrists to make the transition from black cloth to bare skin? Wasn't he making little cackling sounds like a roulette ball makes when it drops into a slot?

Peter was stroking her ankle, her shin, sliding his hand up to her knee, sliding it back down her calf. Couldn't she have pulled the leg away? Especially when his hand, on the third or fourth passage, went over the apex formed by her knee and slid down her thigh? The front of her thigh. And then around the side, to someplace where the black dress had bunched. Peter's hand disappeared, then came into sight again as it traced its way along the back of her leg to the crux of her knee. Where it lingered. Where it twisted and turned in a gentle little screwing motion designed to open the angle between calf and thigh. And all the while he was talking to her, complimenting her, murmuring something about her perfume. He recognized her perfume.

If you are just standing there and a girl, a college girl, who seems to know so much more than you about things that count, isn't protesting that two men are touching her with increasing intimacy, is it up to you to tell her she should be? Is it up to you to ask if she is all right when she isn't saying anything about the one man's hands down the top of her dress and the other man's up the bottom of it?

Was it enough for me to be on alert in case she got hurt?

Peter's hands went under her buttocks, lifted her up, and came out from under her dress with her panties, black silk underwear with a filigree front on which was embroidered an intertwined set of vines. I didn't know that detail when he took them off her, when he tossed them back over his shoulder. I knew only that the panties were black. And small. With a front panel that you appeared to be able to see through.

I waited for her to say something. She didn't. I didn't.

Peter took a red candle out of a brass candlestick.

She didn't say anything and I didn't.

His blazer came off. His pants and boxers went below his knees. He took her legs and put them on either side of his waist. He held the candle in front of him and moved forward, grinning at Jamie. And Jamie grinned back.

She didn't say anything and neither did I.

It was only later, when he dropped the candle and I realized what he meant to do with the brass candlestick, that I acted.

"Hey, that's not cool," I said, putting one hand on Peter's shoulder. I was still holding what was left of my drink in my other hand.

Peter twisted his head predatorily, looked at me as if my opinion meant nothing. How did I know what was cool? He had gone all his life without taking advice from me, or the likes of me. Who was I to tell him what was cool in his family's house?

I squeezed his shoulder, tugged on his striped shirt.

Peter was big, but he wasn't strong. I squeezed harder, pulled more. My fingers were digging deep into his flesh.

He could have swung the candlestick at me, but Peter was not interested in fighting. He just kept looking at me, his pink-and-white face slightly flabby and dissolute, his pale blue eyes seeming not quite to recognize me or understand my message.

I was trying to smile while I squeezed. It wasn't a real smile, my lips never opened, but it served its purpose. I was telling him it wasn't my house. Not my party. The girl wasn't my friend. But guys don't do this sort of thing.

I just wanted him to stop, that was all.

# 3.

THE PLACE I LIVED MY SENIOR YEAR AT PENN WAS FOUR BLOCKS from campus. It was a house with antique oak floors, built-in bookcases, a leaded glass front window with a window seat, three bedrooms and a bath on the second story, another bedroom and a bath in the basement. It was trashed most of the time. McFetridge wouldn't wash dishes or put food away. Ellis took a vow that he would not do McFetridge's cleanup for him. Tuttle was oblivious.

On any given day, pizza boxes, beer cans, soda cans, and newspapers covered the chairs, the couch, the coffee table, the dining room table, the kitchen table. If we needed the space, if we wanted to sit down, we pushed the clutter aside.

One problem with throwing out boxes or cans or containers was that any one of them could be a repository of scraps and butts of marijuana, and there were times when those roaches had to be stripped down and consolidated into re-rolled joints. These times usually occurred around 10:00 p.m., when someone made a hoagie run. It was spring of senior year and the only one who was still studying was Ellis. He was hoping to become a doctor.

It was not likely that anybody would ring our doorbell at 9:30 in the morning, but there it was. Ellis was off at class; McFetridge was out; Tuttle wasn't going to get up for anything or anyone. The bell rang and rang until I had to come down from the second floor to get it. I did not even brush my teeth. I should have at least done that.

A grown man was standing on our front porch. He wore a plaid shirt, jeans, running shoes, a gray jacket that was unzipped. Could have been a neighborhood guy, come to complain about the music, the junk in the yard, the lights that stayed on all night. Except he had an air of authority about him. If he had flashed a badge, I wouldn't have questioned it. But what he showed instead was a cardboard tray holding two coffees, a couple of small containers of cream, stir sticks, and half a dozen packets of sugar.

"You George Becket?" he wanted to know.

I told him no.

Very slowly, a smile spread across the man's mouth. It was not a wide mouth and the smile did not have far to go, but it was there. "I'm not a bill collector, kid," he said.

I figured he wasn't a coffee delivery guy, either. He was probably five-feet-ten, but looked taller, just by the way he carried himself. His hair was dark, cut short around the ears, combed carefully from left to right on top of his head. His eyes were as dark as his hair, his features narrow. There was, from what I could see, not an ounce of fat on him. Indeed, he seemed almost spring-loaded, as though he could bounce up and hit his head on the ceiling of the porch, come back down and not spill a drop of the coffee.

The longer we stood there the more sure he became that I was George Becket. Perhaps he had seen a picture. Perhaps it took him a while to realize that the tousle-haired, sleepy-eyed guy in front of him was, in fact, the same person who had appeared in a coat and tie for a fraternity or graduation photo.

"I've got a little something to talk to you about, Georgie," he said. He gestured to the porch, where perhaps he expected there to be chairs. He recovered fast enough to keep his hand moving until it ended at the top step. "We can do it out here."

I could have, I suppose, simply closed the door in his face. But I was not thinking clearly. I moved to the top step and sat down. I had nothing on but jeans and a gray athletic department T-shirt that had the number 46 on its chest. I shivered in the morning air and tried to place myself in as much sunshine as possible.

The man handed me one of the coffees, let me take a cream and a sugar and a wooden stir stick, and waited until I had mixed and stirred and sipped.

"My name is Roland Andrews," he said. "I work for a man named Josh David Powell." He let the name sink in before he continued. He wanted to see what kind of effect it would have. "I believe you know his daughter. Kendrick."

I gave a lot of thought to my next move. I, of course, had no idea what Mr. Andrews did for Mr. Powell, but I had my suspicions.

"She said you were very nice to her."

Nice. I helped clean her up. I walked her out of the party. Put her in her car. Kept her panties in my pocket.

I sipped my coffee and tried to buy time. How much time can you buy when a man on a mission is sitting right next to you, watching every breath you take, every flick of your eyes, every twitch of your face?

"She said you were there when she was raped by Peter Gregory Martin."

*Raped*. It was a word I had been thinking about for two weeks straight, ever since we returned from Florida. I had even looked it up. "Illicit sexual intercourse without the consent of the woman and effected by force, duress, intimidation, or deception as to the nature of the act." Webster's *Third New International Dictionary*. I had carried that definition around with me for a few days, telling myself it did not apply to what Peter and Jamie had done. There had been no force, duress, intimidation, deception.

"I don't exactly remember it that way," I said.

"Which part don't you remember, son?"

I wondered if I could say I didn't remember any of it. But Kendrick had told him I had been there. She had told him, told someone, enough to track me down. Had I given her my last name? I must have told her where I went to school. She said Bryn Mawr, I said Penn. Just a few miles apart. See how much we have in common?

Had she been sober enough to remember any of it? She had been sober enough to drive. She had had a little sports car. A red one. An Alfa Romeo drop-top. With a stick shift. And I had let her get in it, get behind the steering wheel, go off down the gravel driveway and out the gate to Ocean Boulevard. But so had the valet. A smiling young black man, to whom I had given five bucks.

He should have said something.

"I was just there in the room when she was fooling around with those guys."

The man's breathing became more shallow, as if somehow I had just insulted him, the man who had brought me coffee, the man who had called me "son." "Fooling around?" he said, his voice barely above a whisper. "Is that what you call it?"

I didn't answer. There was nothing I could say that was going to bring this conversation to a pleasant end.

"Do you know who Mr. Powell is, George?"

"No."

"You ever hear of CPA Properties?"

"No."

"CPA stands for Coltrane Powell Associates, out of Delaware. It's the largest developer of commercial properties in the Mid-Atlantic region."

I didn't know CPA. I didn't know the first thing about developers.

"Delaware, Maryland, eastern Pennsylvania, southern New Jersey." He delivered the names of each place directly into my ear, as if he fully intended the accumulation to cause me to break down, beg for mercy, promise a lifetime of cooperation if only he would stop hitting me with geographic areas.

I said nothing, tasted my coffee, which tasted like nothing. My bare feet began to rattle on the stairs. I told myself it was just because I was cold and tried to hold them steady, press them down into the old wooden planks.

"Mr. Coltrane is dead."

Mr. Coltrane. Who was Mr. Coltrane, and why was that of any interest to me?

"Which makes Mr. Powell virtually the sole owner of CPA and a very wealthy man. A very. Wealthy. Man."

Did he just jab my knee with his finger? Was that what that sudden weight was? Was that why my leg went numb? I tried to kick it out. It wouldn't move.

"More wealthy, I would venture to say, than even your friends the Gregorys. The difference is . . ."

I waited for him to tell me, waited for the numbness in my leg to clear. Both happened at the same time.

". . . his money was earned during his lifetime."

Yes, of course. The Gregorys had to go back two generations for theirs. Back to Peter's and Jamie's grandfather. I wondered what he had done to get my leg to spasm like that.

"Not so many people know about Mr. Powell's money, which makes it a little easier for him to operate. Doesn't get in all the right clubs as easily as the Gregorys, but he's under a lot less scrutiny, if you know what I mean."

Did I? A lot less scrutiny for what?

"Mr. Powell wants something done, he's in a position to get people to do it."

"People like you, you mean?"

It was a childish swipe and Mr. Andrews easily deflected it. "Know what I did before I went to work for Mr. Powell?" He did not expect me to answer. He paused just long enough to build suspense. "I was Special Forces."

My leg almost spasmed on its own, without him even touching me.

"There were things I learned there that make me a valuable person to a man like Mr. Powell."

"Learned how to go around intimidating college kids, did you?"

Mr. Andrews took a long time to respond. He spent that time searing me with his eyes. It was impossible for me to look back at him. I glanced, looked away, glanced back, and looked away again. "I learned," he said, his words coming out slowly, each seemingly hanging in the few inches of air between us, "a lot more than that, pal."

I had little doubt that he did. My hand was now shaking in counterpoint to my feet and I chose not to even try to raise my coffee to my lips. "What is it you want, Mr. Andrews?"

Very slowly, he reached inside his gray jacket. I thought about throwing the coffee at him. I would throw it directly into his face and then roll away. Throw, roll, run. In fact, I could not even move.

"I want you to talk to the Palm Beach County state attorney." Mr. Andrews was now holding an envelope that he extended into that very small gap between us. "Round-trip airline tickets, five hundred dollars expense money." He nodded at the envelope. "Instructions on whom to call and where to go." He pushed it closer, so that it was touching my chin, then he traced it up my jawline. "I want you to fly down there and tell the state attorney the truth about what happened at the Gregory home week before last."

There were cars going by in the street, one after another, a steady stream heading west. Drive off in that direction, you could just keep on going, get on Highway 80, take it all the way to California, where nobody would have heard of Josh David Powell and CPA Properties, and where they might not even care so much about the Gregory family.

The envelope came to rest against the side of my face. "Georgie? You still with me?"

I pulled my head away. The envelope followed. My ear was practically against my shoulder when I said, "Look, Mr. Andrews, the truth is, I didn't really see what went on. Kendrick was really drunk. They all were. We all were." Suddenly my words were flowing and I seemed to have no more control of them than I did the cars in front of me. I didn't know where they came from or where they were going, they just appeared, one after another. "She's a beautiful girl, that much I remember, but I hardly know her. Okay? I hardly knew anybody at the party and so I was just kind of wandering around by myself. I was talking to her, talking to some of the Gregorys, looking at all the stuff on the walls, and then I ended up in the library and there she was on the couch, fooling around."

"You keep saying that, don't you, kid?" The corner of the envelope carved into a spot beneath my ear. It pinned me as if it were a dart. "Peter Martin was penetrating her with foreign objects!"

*Jesus,* I wanted to say, it was only one foreign object. I stopped the second one. But I didn't say anything at all. For a moment or two I may not have been breathing at all.

Mr. Andrews swung around so that one of his legs was below mine, his foot on the stair below where my feet were. He was practically surrounding me, so close I should have been able to smell the coffee on his breath as he hissed, "That girl's in therapy now. Probably will be for a long time."

I thought of telling him the things I had been telling myself. Kendrick knew what she was doing when she went to the party in her fancy little sports car and her tight little dress. She knew what she was doing when she got drunk, when she went into the library with those guys. Who would go into a closed room with Peter and Jamie, for God's sake?

I said none of that and yet Mr. Andrews seemed to have heard it all. "You really are an arrogant little shit, aren't you?"

The last guy who had said something like that to me had gotten a fist in the face. But I wasn't doing that now. I was just trying to move my head to keep Mr. Andrews away, keep his teeth away, keep them from ripping the skin from my skull.

And then suddenly he pulled back, as though he couldn't stand being near me any longer. "I don't know how you justify it," he said, "but what Peter Martin did to Kendrick Powell was something you wouldn't accept from an animal. And he's going to pay for it."

Rich girl, tight dress. If she was so drunk that she allowed what happened to happen, then she couldn't really be psychologically scarred, could she?

"So, she's going to sue him?" I said, because I had to say something, because I wanted to know if this girl who was so humiliated was going to exchange her humiliation for money.

"Sue? No, George, she's not going to sue." He spoke as if only an avaricious weakling like me would think of such a thing. "Like I told you, the Powells have every bit as much if not more money than the Gregorys. No, what Josh David wants is to bring them in line, once and for all." He waited for me to lift my head again. He wanted to make sure I was listening to every word. "The Gregorys have been getting away with this sort of outrageous behavior for a long time, and Mr. Powell's determined to put an end to it. Expose them for what they are. Let the world see they have to play by the same rules as everybody else."

"And I gather you need me to do that."

He waved the envelope.

I looked down at it, looked up and saw McFetridge come walking along the street. Mr. Andrews saw that, too, and the envelope disappeared.

McFetridge wasn't just walking, he was sauntering. He had spent the night with one of the girls from Tri Delt, and he had his socks sticking out of the pockets of his jacket to prove it.

The sauntering slowed as he saw the stranger next to me. His eyes darted between us. McFetridge was six-feet-four, a tennis player, and used to using his size to his advantage. He was trying to figure out if he needed to do that now. "Hey," he said softly as he turned onto the cement walkway leading to the steps.

"Hey," I said, and did not otherwise move.

"Hey," said Mr. Andrews. He did not move, either.

McFetridge stopped. "What's going on?"

"This is Mr. Andrews. He used to be in Special Forces."

Funny how you can use a person's accomplishment in such a snide way. With that one remark, the die was cast.

"Yeah?" said McFetridge, staring down at the older man. No doubt McFetridge was feeling full of himself, having just gotten laid, this being his front porch, it being spring semester of his senior year.

"Kendrick Powell's father sent him to talk to me." Craven, that's what I was. Looking for help.

"Who's Kendrick Powell?" McFetridge said.

"She was at the party at the Gregorys, down in Palm Beach."

McFetridge nodded. He had heard the story. "You want to talk to me?" he said, addressing Mr. Andrews like he was issuing a challenge. "I was there."

"Were you?" said Mr. Andrews. His tone was every bit as challenging as McFetridge's. It was, in a way, like watching two Thoroughbreds about to start a race, each one leaning forward, waiting for the gun to go off.

"Were you in the library with Kendrick and Peter Martin and Jamie Gregory?"

"Yeah," said McFetridge, moving his feet apart, squaring up his stance. I remember looking at the socks sticking out of his jacket pockets. I remember thinking they looked like little bunnies. I remember thinking he was about to get annihilated.

"Nothing happened," he said.

"Is that right?" Mr. Andrews's eyes narrowed. "You were all just standing around? Admiring the Winslow Homer?"

There. She couldn't have been that drunk if she recognized the Winslow Homer. Unless she had been there before. Or unless Mr. Andrews had.

McFetridge's eyes clouded just enough to make me think he either didn't know about the painting or didn't know who Winslow Homer was. But he recovered nicely. "Hard to say what we were admiring, we were all so drunk."

There, see, Mr. Andrews? Just like I said. You can go home now. Leave the two of us alone.

But Mr. Andrews didn't go home. He pretended to think through what McFetridge had just told him. "So then you don't remember if nothing happened," he said.

"No," McFetridge said, knowing he had just been played and not liking it. His head dropped lower, bull-like. He had not had a haircut all year. It had been the subject of much discussion among the older set down in Palm Beach, and now his hair was dangling down in long, looping spirals as he tried to press his point on the ex-soldier. "I do remember. Nothing happened."

Mr. Andrews gazed up at him as if in all his life he had never met such a clueless moron. I have tried many times since then to piece all those elements of his expression together to form some semblance of the overwhelmingly unflinching look of contempt that Mr. Andrews bestowed on McFetridge, and I have been unable to do it.

McFetridge faltered. His movements were all slight: a shift of his weight, a lift of his head, a baring of his lip; but none of them was quite complete before Mr. Andrews popped into a standing position in front of him. The stairs were a help. They put the shorter man on direct eye level with the taller, they allowed Mr. Andrews to smirk right in his face, promising without saying anything that if McFetridge so much as hinted at another act of aggression he would slit him from hip to shoulder, pull out his guts, stomp them into the planks of the porch.

"Well, I guess there isn't anything more you can tell me," Mr. Andrews said, and the two men continued staring at each other until finally McFetridge was reduced to blinking, to glancing down at me, to saying, "Well, unless you need me for anything, Georgie, I'm going inside. Shower up."

He had to step past Mr. Andrews to get to the door. He did it by going around me. He tapped me on the shoulder as he went. A slight tap. It could have meant many things. It could have meant farewell.

Our visitor turned his upper body without moving his feet and watched McFetridge enter the house. McFetridge looked back and Mr. Andrews nodded mockingly, as if paying respects that they both knew were not due. Then Mr. Andrews looked down at me.

I was sipping my coffee again, trying to appear as though nothing strange had just taken place, as though my reinforcements had not just fled the field.

The envelope appeared again. Directly in front of me. Held as steady as if it were resting on a table. "All you have to do is tell the truth, son," said Mr. Andrews. "That's what makes it so bloody easy."

# 4.

How drunk could she have been if she managed to drive away? That Alfa had to have had at least five gears. She had to have been able to coordinate the clutch and the stick shift, maneuver it out of the driveway, turn in the right direction on Ocean Boulevard, find her way home.

Peter and Jamie had left after I stopped Peter from using the candlestick. He had looked at me and then down at the girl. I had a sense that he couldn't believe what he almost had done. Or maybe he couldn't believe what I had done.

Kendrick lay sprawled on the couch, her black hair splayed out in three different directions. Her left arm was over the back of the couch; her left knee was tilted against the cushions. Her dress was pulled up so high that she was fully exposed. I could see every inch of her tan mark from hip to hip. I knew exactly how small the bottom was to her two-piece bathing suit. I knew precisely the color of her skin before the sun touched it.

"I gotta take a piss," said Peter, and then he pushed his way into me, making me back up, as he took a circuitous path out of the room.

His cousin looked at the girl, reached down between her legs and rolled his finger slowly across the arch. She did not react. He rolled his finger back and forth and then thrust it inside. Kendrick bounced a little, but that was all.

"Hey!" I said.

Was I moving in slow motion? I know I stepped forward, regained the ground I had lost from Peter's push, but I know also that Jamie slid his hand from side to side and then pulled out his finger, jammed it into his mouth and was gone before I reached him, scampering out of the room, the door closing behind him, leaving me standing over a nearly naked girl whose green eyes seemed to be staring at absolutely nothing.

Suddenly I was afraid. What if someone else came in and saw this, saw her, saw me? What would I say? That it wasn't me? That it was Peter and Jamie? And what about her, why wasn't she saying anything? Why wasn't she doing anything?

"Kendrick," I said. I must have put my glass on the coffee table because I reached out to her with both hands and tried to pull her into a sitting position. "Kendrick, c'mon. You have to get up. Here, let me get your dress down."

She did as I wanted, sat up like a doll that had to be held in place. I was tugging the dress, trying to pull it down to her thighs, tilting her one way and then another. I had to put one arm around her shoulders, use the other to pull down the dress, then switch arms and pull on the other side. Her face was pointed toward the floor so that when I stepped back to see if I had gotten everything I still had to keep my hand on her, make sure she didn't fall forward. I didn't know what to do about her breasts. She had a bra. It seemed to be a very flimsy bra and it seemed not exactly in place. I settled for straightening out the straps of the dress.

I asked if she was all right.

"I think I'm going to be sick," she said.

I looked around, feeling panic of a whole different kind than I had a few moments before. There was a maroon wastebasket with some kind of old-world map on its sides. I leaned Kendrick into the cushions, told her to hold on, ran to the wastebasket, and got it back to her just in time. I turned my head away so I didn't have to see.

I had one hand on her, one hand on the bucket, my head twisted over my shoulder. I heard the sounds and almost instantly smelled the odor. I did not want to retch myself. I waited until she was done, tilted her back again, and ran with the wastebasket to a window. I undid the latch, shoved up the window, threw the entire basket into the bushes. Then I ran back to Kendrick. Her legs were straight out in front of her. She had vomit in her hair. "Shit," I said.

"Shit," she said, and started to laugh.

Was it a laugh? It wasn't a real laugh. It didn't last more than a note or two.

I looked around the room, trying to figure out how I was going to clean her up. My eyes went to the drapes, maroon, with gold figures on them. If I could get her over to the windows, I could at least use the cloth to clean her hair.

"Can you get up?" I asked, but I wasn't waiting for an answer. I was already pulling her to her feet. "Okay, that's it. Stand. Now lean on me. We're not going far."

The vomit, I feared, was getting on my sport coat. I would throw it out the window, too. No, I would use the drapes to blot it, then find a sink somewhere with running water. This was a twenty-room house. There had to be running water somewhere.

"You're so nice," Kendrick said.

"Yeah, I'm a saint," I said, maneuvering her step by step. I got her to the windows, turned her around, guided her into a sitting position on a windowsill. "You okay there?"

She nodded.

"I'm okay," she said, and got to her feet. She took one step, caught herself, and then staggered across the Spanish tile floor to a closed door.

There were three doors in the wall on the opposite side of the room from where I had intended to do my emergency cleaning. She went directly to the one in the far corner, the one that was behind and to the left of the Senator's desk. Her head was slightly bowed and she did not walk in a completely straight line, but she knew where to go.

Which may explain how Mr. Andrews knew about the Winslow Homer.

She opened the door, hit a switch, and illuminated a small bathroom, a powder room, an antechamber with a toilet and a sink and a mirror over the sink and a rack with towels.

How drunk could she have been if she was able to go directly there?

The door closed and I could hear water rushing from the faucet into the basin. I sat on the windowsill, just as Kendrick had done, looked out the window, where the map-covered wastebasket was ensconced in a green-leafed bush with inch-thick branches and where the smell of vomit was mixing with the fragrances of jasmine, hyacinth, and gardenias, and wondered what to do. I settled for closing the window.

The water kept running. Long enough for me to think I should go in there and check on her. But then a different door opened. It was the one through which we had entered, through which Peter and Jamie had exited, and it brought with it the distant sounds of the cocktail party that I had almost forgotten was taking place.

The woman holding the door, her hand on the doorknob, her arm stretched out fully in front of her as she leaned in, was one of the Senator's sisters, famous enough in her own right for me to know who she was.

"Oh, excuse me," she said. It was her house, her family's house, but she was requesting forgiveness for intruding. And then she realized that I was all alone. "Is everything okay in here?" she asked.

There was someone behind her. She obviously was going to show that person the library, or something in the library, and with that realization my eyes darted to a black object on the floor. I had been sitting there doing nothing for minutes and only now did I notice Kendrick's silk-and-mesh underwear in a tiny, tangled bunch on top of a burnt-umber tile.

"Hello, Mrs. Martin. I'm sorry." I pushed off the windowsill with my hips, took a step toward the little black mound. "I'm just waiting for my friend Kendrick." I thrust my hand toward the door of the bathroom, thrust it harder than I needed to, harder than anybody in his right mind would have done, but I was taking another step and trying to get Mrs. Martin to look that way, to notice the noise of the rushing water, to not notice the cloth on the floor. "She isn't feeling too well."

"Oh, dear," said Mrs. Martin, and looked back at her companion. Then she looked at me again and by this time I had made it all the way to the underwear. I was standing in front of it. I had one shoe next to the other and was posed as rigidly as a West Point cadet while Mrs. Martin asked, "Do you think she needs some help?"

"Oh, no, Mrs. Martin, she'll be all right in a minute." And when my hostess seemed dubious, I added, "I think she's embarrassed. That's why I'm sort of standing guard."

See? See how I'm standing?

"Oh," she said to me. Then she looked at her companion again. Then back to me. "Maybe we'll return in a minute," she offered.

"Gosh, if you would. I'm sure it won't be long and I know she'll feel so much better if she thought nobody knew."

Nobody knew she was drunk, shitfaced, puked on herself. Nobody knew she had just been fingered, fucked, *screwed with a candle* by your son, Mrs. Martin. Your deplorable son and your repulsive nephew.

## 5.

I CALLED BRYN MAWR. IN THOSE DAYS YOU COULD DIAL THE SCHOOL'S main number, get a school operator, ask for the student by name, and you would be connected to the student's room.

"I'm sorry," the operator said after putting me on hold for half a minute, "Miss Powell is no longer attending Bryn Mawr. She's withdrawn from the school."

"But she was just there a few weeks ago."

"That's all the information I have. Her number has been disconnected."

I wondered if I should call information in Delaware. If the Powells lived in Delaware, they probably lived in Wilmington. Maybe Dover. Those were the only cities in Delaware I knew. But Powell was a common name and if Mr. Powell was as wealthy as Mr. Andrews said, he would have an unlisted number.

I thought of calling CPA Properties. *Hello, can I speak to the owner? To the owner's daughter?*

In the end, once again, I did nothing.

# 6.

THE WATER HAD BEEN SHUT OFF AT LAST. THE DOOR HAD BEEN flung open. She had come out of the powder room without looking at me and gone along the line of bookshelves, heading back into the heart of the party.

"Kendrick?"

I ran to head her off. Sprinted. She put her hand out for the door handle and I got there first.

"Get out of my way," she said. Her green eyes were not as glazed as before. They did not seem to be normal, but it was hard to tell what was going on behind them because they were looking right through me.

I tried to get her to focus on me, dipping my head to get on eye level with her. "You okay?" I asked.

"What do you think?"

What did I think? The theme of the evening. The thing to which I keep coming back, even now.

"I think you probably had a little too much to drink."

"Fuck you," said Kendrick Powell, defying me to say anything more.

Her skin was somehow pale beneath her tan. Her hair was slightly wet, but all the signs of sickness had been removed, along with all traces of eyeliner and lipstick. She still looked beautiful, but dangerous, like a jungle cat that could strike out at any time. I wanted to put my hand on her bare arm, tell her everything was going to be all right. But it seemed like such an inappropriate thing to do, to touch her after she had been touched so much.

I got out of her way.

She walked straight out of the library, past Mrs. Martin, who was waiting on the other side of the door with not one but two friends, both older women wearing pale greens and pinks and giant diamonds on their left hands. Was Kendrick's head held high or was she hanging it in shame? Why do I think now that she was doing both? She took three, maybe four, steps and then her foot slipped, her ankle rolled, and I realized she was barefoot.

Mrs. Martin and her friends went from staring at Kendrick to looking at me in horror. What had I done to the poor girl? Kept her in a closed room with her shoes off? Sent her stumbling out in a stripped-down, almost disheveled, state, trying to be brave, trying not to reveal her abject level of humiliation? Oh, young man, how could you?

I thought to run back into the library to get the shoes. They were little more than sandals, really. Small heels, thin straps, probably didn't weigh a pound between then. How do I know what they weighed? I never picked them up. I didn't pick them up before Mrs. Martin gaped disbelievingly at me, and I didn't pick them up afterward. I followed Kendrick instead, followed her through the sea of people in yellow sport coats and blue blazers and Lilly Pulitzer dresses with patterns of shells that looked like flowers and flowers that looked like shells, followed her all the way to the front door. Where was McFetridge? Where were the Gregory boys? Didn't Kendrick know anybody at the party? Why was I the only one standing under the portico with her, waiting for her car?

She hadn't even called for it. She just appeared, stood there barefoot, her arms at her sides, and one of the smiling young black men in white jackets went and got it for her.

"You sure you're okay to drive?" I said.

"Fuck off," she said.

*Fuck off, fuck you,* the last four words she said to me; and she told Mr. Andrews how nice I had been to her?

The Alfa arrived. Its engine throbbed and what might have sounded like music somewhere else was almost unseemly in front of the Gregorys' front door. The young man leaped out, held the door, and Kendrick, placing her right hand on the trunk for support, hobbled around the back of the car and got in the driver's seat without so much as looking at him. The valet shut the door gently but firmly; Kendrick put the car in gear and was off, the pebbles in the driveway spattering in every direction.

She drove away and I stood there.

"Can I get you a car, sir?" the smiling man asked. Not "your" car, but "a" car. He seemed astute enough to know I didn't have one of my own.

I gave him the five bucks that was loose in my pocket and went back inside, where a crowd was gathered around the grand piano. One of the Senator's buddies, a radio talk-show host up on Cape Cod, was playing and singing "Goodnight, Irene." But he changed the lyrics, spiced them up, directed them to one of the older ladies, who started to dance, to move her hips, until she realized how risqué his version was, and then she called out, "Ohhhh," in a throaty voice that made everybody laugh as she raised her hand to her face in feigned embarrassment.

Then the Senator himself began to sing, "We were sailing along . . ." The pianist found the right notes on the keyboard, took up the accompaniment. ". . . on Moonlight Bay. We could hear the voices ringing, They seem to say, 'You have stolen her heart, Now don't go 'way!'" The Senator reached out to grab the hand of his sister, the one who was married to the movie actor, and twirled her toward him. The crowd shook their highball glasses appreciatively as she spun in close and twirled back away again, her dress blowing outward, showing off a pair of legs that were quite commendable for a woman her age.

The verse was finished, repeated, and everyone around the piano joined in. A few brown-spotted hands were clapping and bracelets were jingling as the voices sang, "You have stolen her heart . . . ," and this time when the Senator's sister spun back to him, it was he who changed the lyrics, his voice booming out in a passable baritone that made all the others drift off, "We were strolling along. . . ." His right arm slipped around her waist and his left hand took hers and held it chest high as he sang, "On Moonlight Bay." He looked over his shoulder, grinning at us, grinning wholeheartedly, a grin that said, Look! Look what I can do! Can you believe it? And then he adjusted his position, moved in slightly behind and to the side of her, and the two of them began gently waltzing away from the piano, "We can hear the voices singing, 'You have broken my heart, please go a-way!'"

The guests roared. Fingers tapped on the heels of palms as the brother-and-sister dance team continued across the floor. It was all great fun, so much so that I almost would have forgotten the incident in the library if it were not for the small ball of cloth in my pocket.

## 1.

WENT INTO POGO'S FOR DINNER. BAD NAME. I'M NOT EVEN SURE how good the food is, but for years I went there three or four times a week. I could eat at the bar, a lovely slice of veneered log in which the natural contours provided cutouts that allowed a man to sit comfortably in whichever of the twelve long-legged, spindle-back chairs happened to be available. I liked that veneered log. I liked the television behind the bar. I liked the post-middle-aged people who worked there and knew just enough about me to ask how things were going without inquiring too deeply.

I suppose certain aspects of my life were obvious. I wasn't married and I didn't live with anyone, or I wouldn't have been in there eating dinner as often as I did. I usually wore a suit, particularly if I stopped off on my way home from work, so I had to be a professional. I never dined with clients—or, for that matter, anyone else—so I was unlikely to be involved in business. I didn't have an accent, or at least not a Boston or Cape Cod accent, so I was not originally from the area. I liked to watch whatever sporting event was on TV and I made appropriate noises in support or condemnation of the Red Sox, Celtics, Bruins, and Patriots, so I had to have been around for a while. And I liked to have a Manhattan, or a couple of beers, or a glass or two of wine, or even an occasional martini, so I was a man of party potential without being an alcoholic.

Of course, the Cape is a small place between October and May, and sooner or later a person in my position was bound to come into contact with one of the employees outside the restaurant. Jury duty, a domestic dispute, an unlawful detainer action, a kid in trouble, even a moving violation, was going to get one of them into the courthouse at some time or other; and I tended to be in one of the county courthouse buildings eight to ten hours a day. So at some point somebody was going to run into me.

The first time I recognized anyone from the restaurant was when a waitress named Meg appeared on one of my jury panels. Judge Wilkerson dutifully introduced me as the deputy district attorney representing the people of the Commonwealth and asked the courtroom full of citizens if any of them knew me or the defense counsel or the defendant in the case. Several people raised their hands, but none of them identified me and none of them was Meg. I had merely turned to the audience, let them see me, not searched their faces. It was only when Meg was called to the jury box that I realized she was there. I looked right at her, she looked right back at me, not a sign of recognition was passed.

The case, as I recall, was a break-in, the defendant a Brazilian. It was not a big deal to anyone but the victim and the accused. When it was my turn to question the prospective jurors, I addressed Meg. "Ms. O'Brien, do I look familiar to you?"

"I'm not sure. Should you?"

"You mentioned you work at Pogo's restaurant in Osterville. I happen to eat there sometimes. I wonder if you recall ever waiting on me?"

Meg was a hard-faced woman with dun-colored hair, who wore her restaurant uniform with the hem of her skirt an inch or two higher than the other waitresses did. If I had to guess, I would have said she was about fifty, divorced, had raised or was raising two kids on her own, lived in a rented house, and depended on her unreported tips to survive. She was also none too bright, as evidenced by her answer to my question. "Not really. You usually eat at the bar, don't you?"

The defense counsel exercised one of his challenges to take her off the jury, and later, when I ran into her at the restaurant, she asked me why I had brought up the fact that she knew who I was. "I wasn't gonna say nothin'," she said.

I told her I appreciated it, but it could have jeopardized the prosecution if anyone found out she really knew me.

She shrugged. "I figured the guy was guilty as sin anyway, or you wouldn'ta been chargin' him. And if he wasn't"—she shrugged again—"then I would have given you a raft of shit next time I seen you. So I figured the pressure was really on you."

Somehow, in her mind, that all made sense. I tried to follow it through, but got only so far. In any event, she was off the jury, the Brazilian got convicted, and from that point on whenever I sat down at the bar I was addressed by John the bartender as Counselor.

In March, the main dining room was closed. There were about twenty patrons scattered in booths and at tables throughout the pub, which had logs burning in the brick fireplace and was where I always ate anyhow. I was alone at the bar, sipping a Manhattan and reading through the printed list of daily specials that was tucked into the menu, when a man came in and sat down next to me. There were three seats to my left, eight to my right. There wasn't any need for him to do that.

"How's it goin'?" he asked John.

"Goin' good," John said, as if it was none of his business, and slid him a menu, a black paper place mat, a set of silverware wrapped in a white napkin.

I turned my shoulder. I wanted to eat alone, watch the Celts. They were playing Phoenix, as I recall. "I'll have the clams, John," I said.

The bartender hesitated. I wasn't sure if he cut his eyes to my neighbor, but it took him a few seconds to murmur, "I wouldn't. Not many bellies, from what I could see."

"What do you like?"

"Scallops look fat. Swordfish is good."

"Fine. Give me the scallops."

"Plate or roll?"

"Plate."

"Squash, french fries, chowder okay?"

"Whatever you say."

John took my order back through the swinging saloon door to the kitchen without writing anything down. The man next to me, a man with sparse white hair that tufted on the crown of his head and could have used a good clipping at the back of his neck, said, "He obviously likes you."

"It's just because I come in here all the time."

"Sure. They only cheat tourists and drunks." He was smiling. He had made a joke. He wanted me to know he didn't really think they cheated anybody.

I turned away again.

"My name's Bill Telford." He was holding out his hand. He wanted me to shake.

The man had come in and seated himself next to me, told me a joke, and now he wanted me to be his friend. I wanted only to watch the game, eat dinner, go home. I shook his hand and did not give him my name.

"They need a real center," he said, looking at the screen, not seeming perturbed in the slightest by my lack of manners. "Way back when, they had the second-worst record in the league. Got screwed in the lottery and the best center in basketball went to San Antonio. 'Magine what it would be like if we had gotten him?"

"Tim Duncan." I shouldn't have said anything.

"That's the fella. What did we get? A bag of mulch."

"Chauncey Billups. He's a good player."

"Yeah? Then why didn't he do anything for us?"

"They traded him away after a couple of months."

"Maybe that's where we got the bag of mulch."

He was right, but I felt no need to say so.

John returned with my cup of chowder and looked at Bill, who nodded at what I had and said he'd like a bowl of the same. And a glass of water. This was not going to pay John's greens fees come May and he said nothing. He just plunked ice cubes in a glass, squirted in some water, plopped it on the bar, and stomped back to the kitchen.

"Don't come in here much," Bill said, looking around as though this restaurant, which could have been most anywhere on the Cape, was a very foreign venue.

The man was probably in his seventies. He wore a zippered fleece jacket and appeared to have a sweater and a collared shirt under that. His voice was not unpleasant and there did not appear to be anything wrong with him. He just wanted to talk. "Live over in Hyannis. Off Ocean Street."

I watched Paul Pierce heave in a twenty-five-footer for the Celts. Nothing but net. Hyannis was all of five miles away. Buffered only by Centerville, where I lived.

"Don't know if you recognize my name, but I've got a case with you fellas."

I froze. This was one of the reasons I did not go out of my way to tell people what I did.

"Perhaps you've heard talk about it around the office. Heidi Telford? My daughter. Murdered nine years ago." He was not looking at me. He was looking at the screen. But he was concentrating on me. "Wianno Club, just down the street from here. That's where they found her, anyway." I could sense him shrugging, telling me he didn't think that was where the murder had taken place.

I knew who Bill Telford was now. *Anything New* Telford. He was something of a legend, periodically calling, occasionally showing up, always asking the same question: "Anything new on the Telford case?" Everyone tried to avoid him, pass him on to the next-lowest person down the line, let him get told by secretaries, paralegals, summer interns, that no, there was nothing new about the case of the pretty young girl who had her skull crushed and was found on the sixteenth fairway of an ultra-exclusive private golf course.

From what I understood, it wasn't that anyone had anything against Mr. Telford. He was unfailingly polite, never pushy, just persistent. If anything, the people in the office felt sorry for him. But there was nothing to report.

"I like to check in," he said, reading my mind, "just to make sure Heidi's not forgotten."

"I know, Mr. Telford."

"Do you?" He seemed to brighten at that. I still wasn't looking at him. I was still looking at the television screen, but what I was seeing wasn't registering.

"So somebody's still working on it?"

All I knew was that people talked about Anything New Telford. That didn't mean anyone was working on it.

He seemed to consider my silence. "Whenever I come up with anything, I pass it along, you know. The police, well, they didn't seem equipped for an investigation like this one, if you know what I mean."

I did not. After a moment or two, I told him so. "Police here deal with murders just like any other police department. We probably have two to four every year. One year we had nine."

"You're talking about the County of Barnstable, not the town. Town of Barnstable has maybe one per year."

He was right. I didn't argue. In my job we dealt with the whole county. And I didn't get the murder cases, anyway.

"We have almost a quarter-million people in the county," he said, "if you count all the way to Provincetown. Got a fairly high welfare population. A lot of people unemployed, especially in winter. Frustrated fishermen, construction workers. Not a lot to do. People get to drinking, shacking up with women who aren't their wives or men who aren't their husbands. Feelings get bruised. Secret of the Cape is that it's not always as nice as it looks to people who only come here in the summer."

He got his chowder. He was silent for a while and I glanced over. His eyes were closed, his lips were moving. He was, I saw, praying. I looked away.

"In the off-season," he said, as if sprung back into the real world, "you got people here that maybe shouldn't be here, maybe don't want to be here, and plenty of bars and package stores to fuel their frustrations. Mix in the drug smugglers that come in off the ocean, the drug dealers and drug users living in converted cottages or winter rentals, you're bound to get some violent crime. That's what you see mostly, isn't it?"

Yeah. Sure. It wasn't worth arguing over.

"Of course, you see some of that in some of the villages of the town of Barnstable—Hyannis, Marstons Mills, maybe. But what you don't see very often is that kind of crime in the hoity-toity places: Hyannisport, you know, or here in Osterville, for that matter. Places where the big-money people have their summer homes."

He spooned up his chowder. He spooned it away from him, the way you are supposed to do it, the way nobody does. "So," he said, taking his napkin from his lap and dabbing his mouth, "a college girl's body is found on a golf course in Osterville, the local police are programmed to think, well, she must have been murdered by somebody from Mashpee, Yarmouth, Truro, anyplace but here."

"And you don't believe that's what happened to your daughter?"

"No, Mr. Becket, I don't." He ate some more, sparing me any slurping sounds. I found myself liking Bill Telford just for the way he approached his chowder.

"My daughter was an exceptionally pretty girl. A bright girl. Size you up in a jiffy. She was going to Wheaton College. Do you know it? Didn't know anything about it myself until they came and got her. But it's a wonderful institution, and they recruited her right out of Barnstable High on her guidance counselor's recommendation. Didn't give her quite a full scholarship, but made it possible on my salary. I was an insurance adjuster, Mr. Becket. My job was to go out and assess damage, mostly on homeowners' claims. I'd go into some of these multimillion-dollar properties here in Osterville, do my work, then I'd say to the homeowners, these people who had done so well in life, what can you tell me about Wheaton College? To a person they said good things. They were all familiar with it, all had somebody in the family or knew somebody who had gone there, so I said, that's it. Whatever it takes, my daughter's gonna go there."

All I had done was ask him whether he believed his daughter had been killed by someone from outside Osterville. I wasn't going to ask anything more for fear he would start telling me where he bought his clothes, gassed his car, went to the grocery store.

"Point is," he continued, not caring that I wasn't asking, "Heidi was meeting her share of rich and successful people at Wheaton. Maybe not famous people, I don't know, but she had learned how to handle some of these kids who had a lot more than she did. Went to mixers at

Brown, dated boys from Harvard. So I don't see her as being overly impressed by somebody just because he came from a famous family."

Heidi Telford died when I was still in law school. Her death was old news by the time I started in the Cape & Islands district attorney's office. All this talk about Heidi and her dates and famous families meant nothing to me. I tried to make that clear by scraping the bottom and sides of my cup for the last bits of chowder. Then I started casting my eyes about for John.

"Being an insurance adjuster gave me the opportunity to do some investigating on my own, Mr. Becket. Or at least gave me some of the skills I needed to do it. And whenever I came up with anything, I'd bring it right to District Attorney White. I expect you know all that."

Now I had to answer. He was waiting, looking right at me, seeing that I was not watching the game anymore, that until the rest of my food came I didn't have anything to do except listen. "I really haven't been involved, Mr. Telford."

"Nice fella, Mitchell. Takes what I give him, tells me he'll have someone look into it. I never hear anything more."

"Maybe because he doesn't have anything to tell you."

"Except I'm telling him things. I talk with Heidi's friends, with her friends' friends, and even friends of those friends, and whenever anybody says anything, no matter how small, I write it down, pass it along. Then I follow up. Ninety percent of the time I find that the people whose names I pass along never hear word one from the police or anybody else."

"Mr. Telford, why are you telling me all this?"

He put his spoon down. He wiped his lips one more time. He fixed a pair of blue-gray eyes on me. "Because, Mr. Becket, I been hearing good things about you."

"Like what?"

"Like you're a straight shooter. Don't appear to be obligated to anyone or anything but the truth. You see something that's not a crime, you stand right up to your boss or the police chief or whoever says it is and tell 'em so. You see something that is a crime, you go after it."

I choked on my Manhattan.

Mr. Telford's eyes narrowed with concern. "You want some water?"

John never gave me water because I never drank it. I started hacking, trying to clear an air passage. John came running from somewhere. So did one of the waitresses. Somebody was pounding me on the back. It took a few seconds to realize it was Mr. Telford.

"I'm okay," I gasped. "Something just went down the wrong way."

John and the waitress, whose name was Fiona, both glared at Mr. Telford as if my travail was his fault. I had to tell everyone all over again that I was all right.

When we were left alone at last, when John had gone back into the kitchen to get my dinner and Fiona had wandered off to do whatever she had to do, I said to Mr. Telford, "Look, I don't know where you're getting your information from, but I'm just an assistant D.A. I'm not even a first assistant. I'm assigned cases, I work on those, and that's all I do."

"I heard you backed down Chief DiMasi. I heard he wanted to prosecute some colored boys for running a bicycle-theft ring and you said no."

"First of all, they were from the Cape Verde Islands, those kids. Second, they were stealing bikes, but it wasn't anything so sophisticated as a ring. They were just stealing them and selling them. And third, I did prosecute them inasmuch as I got them to plead to misdemeanors."

"And sent to a diversionary program."

I shrugged.

"When the chief wanted them sent to prison as felons."

"The chief can be aggressive sometimes."

"About teenagers with no connections stealing bicycles."

He was not far off the mark. But he was also just a guy sitting next to me in a restaurant. I was glad when John came out and put my plate in front of me. I was even more glad when Mr. Telford picked up the check John had put in front of him and took out his wallet.

"All I'm asking," he said, as he got to his feet, "is if maybe you could do some checking yourself. See if these little things I'm givin' District Attorney White are going anywhere other than the circular file." He put a five-dollar bill down on the bar, then looked at the check again, then selected two more dollars to put on top of it.

"You see, sometimes"—he hesitated, his hand covering the money as though he were holding his place until he got the phrasing just right—"sometimes I'm afraid Mitchell may not want the information I'm giving him. Sometimes I wonder if Mitchell isn't a little too close to some of our better-known residents."

"Meaning anybody in particular?"

"Meaning the Gregory family, Mr. Becket. Very much in particular."

## 2.

EVEN NOW THERE ARE TIMES I LIE AWAKE AT NIGHT, UNABLE to sleep, playing and replaying the events of that distant night in Palm Beach, thinking about how the lives of so many people were ruined by what took place in a period of no more than one hour, imagining what might have occurred if only I had acted differently. What would have happened if I had pulled Peter off her? Knocked Jamie away? Tried to raise Kendrick to her feet, shake her out of her stupor?

Was she in a stupor? She had not said anything. She had made noises. They had sounded like . . . moans. Is that what they were? And if they were moans, were they indications of pleasure or the fact that she could not formulate words?

She had formulated words later. "Fuck you," she had said. "Fuck off," she had told me. And she had driven that car. Without her shoes. Without a purse. When young women go to a cocktail party at a place like the Gregorys', don't they bring purses? If she had left it there, wouldn't the Gregorys have found it? Somebody in the Gregory family had to have known who she was. Somebody had invited her.

I get lost sometimes, conjuring up things I do not know, or that I know only in part. And then I can't get to sleep at all. I lie there until the sun comes up, not sure if I am remembering things as they actually happened or if I am just remembering what I imagined on other nights that I have lain here like this.

And now Bill "Anything New" Telford tells me what a straight shooter I am, how I am not obligated to anyone or anything but the truth, how I see a crime and go after it. Stand right up to the people in power.

Poor Bill Telford.

## 3.

LIKE ME, MITCH WHITE WAS NOT FROM THE AREA. THAT SHOULD have been a point to bond us, outsiders in a provincial legal setting in which many of the regular players could trace their local roots back for generations. In fact, it only made District Attorney White highly suspicious of me. He knew how I had gotten my job.

The same way he had.

In the ten or so years Mitch had been D.A., he had tried hard to adapt to the culture. He had the requisite sports memorabilia around his office, but one had the sense he could not withstand a grilling about Bobby Orr, Carl Yastrzemski, or maybe even Larry Bird. He bought a table for the Boston Pops concert that was held on the town green every summer, but people who were forced to sit with him reported he never seemed interested in the music and spent most of the time scanning the other tables for celebrities, officials, and people to whom he could wave. He did not have a boat, did not golf or fish, did not seem to care about the beach.

Among the things Mitch had clearly never mastered was the art of dressing like a native. He was prone to short-sleeved dress shirts, even when he wore a tie. In the summer he liked to wear seersucker suits that could not have cost him $200 and tended to show both wrinkles and the damp spots of perspiration that came from sitting in a leather chair. He had a mustache that no doubt was meant to distract viewers from his underslung chin and wore dark-framed glasses in which the lenses were fitted into frames shaped liked oxbows. His arms, sticking out of his short sleeves, were remarkably thin. On his left hand he wore a very prominent gold wedding ring. I might have been overly critical, but to me everything about him screamed Not From Here!

Nevertheless, each time Mitch was up for reelection he ran virtually unopposed. I had no involvement in the process, but it seemed to me that the decision was made as to who would be district attorney before the matter went to the voters, and as long as Mitch didn't piss off the wrong people, the job was his.

That did not make Mitch a secure man, however. And among his insecurities was me.

There were twenty-three prosecuting attorneys in our office. A couple of them were stationed in Falmouth, a couple more in Orleans, and then there were a few on the islands, Nantucket and Martha's Vineyard. The rest of us were located at the main office in the "new" building at the courthouse complex just off Route 6A, on the bay side of the Cape in the town of Barnstable. I was relegated to the basement, down the hall from the jail cells. I had been there by myself for years and had come to think of it as my private domain. For a period of several months before my meeting with Bill Telford I had been sharing my office with a woman named Barbara Belbonnet, whom I would have thought quite attractive if her primary interest in life had been something other than making arrangements to have her children picked up after school. Barbara was neither a bad person nor a bad attorney. It was just that her husband had left her with two kids and moved off-Cape, and she had gotten the job with the D.A.'s office because her father was an Etheridge and somebody owed him a favor and told Mitch he had to hire her.

So there she was one day, following behind a couple of staffers pushing a desk and carrying a computer, telling me she was sorry, but she was a new hire and this was where she was told to go. I was not given the option of complaining. "Welcome to the dungeon," I said.

It turned out to be no different for Barbara than it was for me. In general nobody other than an occasional secretary or messenger ever came to see either one of us. If we were wanted, someone would call

over the intercom and direct us upstairs, usually to one of the first assistant D.A.'s, Reid Cunningham or Dick O'Connor.

It was not that Mitch himself openly avoided me. He would greet
me with a "Hello" and use my name on those occasions when he happened to see me in the hallways or at an office birthday, Christmas, or
farewell party. "Hello, George, how's it going?" he might say, although
he would not wait for an answer. He would respond to my questions if
asked, but mostly he steered clear of situations where I would have the
chance to ask. He knew my connection but wasn't sure how deep it
ran. His own, apparently, wasn't deep enough for him to find out.

By sequestering me in the basement, Mitch was able to limit my
exposure to whatever was occurring in the office. He couldn't keep me
from talking with the other lawyers or going on coffee breaks with
them, but he kept my workload restricted to matters that generally did
not require interaction. Here, George, here's twenty-seven drunk driv-
ings for you. You be the OUI specialist. As for Barbara, she was given
the domestic disturbances. The small ones. The pushings and shovings
and throwing of plates. The ones nobody else in the office wanted to
go near. Here, Barbara, you take these. You have a problem, we'll be
right upstairs. Better yet, ask George. That way, you won't even have
to come upstairs.

I wondered sometimes if anyone would even say anything if I didn't
show up. But I did show up and I worked hard, in large part because I
had nothing else to do. My fellow prosecutors did not, as far as I knew,
have anything against me personally, but they recognized my lowly
status in the office, my office in exile, and understood that friendship
with me was not going to advance their careers. Besides, most of them
were married and I no longer was, which limited opportunities for
social interaction outside the office.

Strangely—to me, anyhow—some of my better friends were the
defense counsel I opposed in court on a regular basis. Guys like Jimmy
Shelley, Alphonse Carbona, Buzzy Daizell; guys with senses of humor
about their place on the legal food chain, guys who took their victories
where they found them: getting a felony reduced to a misdemeanor,
getting a not-guilty on five counts even if it meant being hit on another ten; securing a Colombian client.

"Colombians are near and dear to my heart," said Buzzy one time. "They pay in cash." That was defense-counsel humor.

Sometimes these guys would invite me out for a beer, or to attend a cookout, or even to a Red Sox game. But I had to be careful. It would not look good if I appeared to be too close to any of them, and while I was relatively sure that there was almost no offense that would cause Mitch White to fire me, I did not want to be ostracized any more than I already was.

In my eight years as his employee, I could remember being in Mitch White's commodious corner office only three times. Once was on the day he hired me. Once was on the day he found out my wife was divorcing me. And I cannot remember the third occasion. Maybe it was when he told me I would be getting all my assignments directly from Dick O'Connor, but mostly I was going to be the office's "Operating Under the Influence" guy.

My visit after my conversation with Bill Telford was, therefore, my fourth to Mitch's inner sanctum. It took just two calls to his secretary.


MITCH GREETED ME WITHOUT getting up from his desk. Like every other male in the office, he worked without his suit jacket when he was not in public. Unlike every other male, Mitch kept his tie in a knot pulled tightly to his neck. Even though I had put on my suit jacket for this visit, he made me feel I was a little more casual than the situation required.

"Yes, George." *Yes, George, I'm a busy man. See all these papers on my desk?*

"Last night I talked to a guy who indicated he was having a problem with our office."

The wheels on his chair made scuttling noises as the D.A. pushed himself back from the edge of his desk. He used his hands to position himself at exactly arm's-length distance. *George from the basement is telling me this?*

I nodded, confirming the question he had not actually vocalized. "He feels we're not paying attention to a very serious matter."

Now I wasn't just from the basement, I was George with friends in high places, conveying a criticism of his operation. He gripped the edge of the desk until his fingers blanched. "Who we talking about?"

"Bill Telford."

"Anything new." It was hard to tell if he was making a statement or asking a question, but the color returned to his fingers. Anything New Telford wasn't quite as much of a threat as, perhaps, others were.

"He says he's been handing in stuff on his daughter's murder for some time and nobody is following up on it."

"There's no case, George. No suspect, no file, nothing for this office to do except pass along what we get to the police." He lifted his hands about six inches, dropped them quickly to the security afforded by the edge of the desk. Having done that, he waited.

"If I read him correctly, he seems to be of the mind that we're not doing anything because the Gregorys might be involved."

The name. The magic word. Mitch White's muddy brown eyes popped from their sockets, his pupils magnified by his ugly oxbow glasses. And then, within the space of a second, his expression changed. *But wait,* it seemed to say, *the Gregorys are your ticket, too, George.* Now he saw me sitting before him not as a threat but as an ally. I had come not to attack him but to warn him. And to work with him. We had done it before, right? The time that young Kirby Gregory had gotten arrested for driving with a .20, we had made it go away—he and I.

"That's a lot of horse manure," he said, raising one eyebrow tentatively, making sure I agreed.

"I was wondering if I might take a look."

Now both eyebrows went up, and then they softened. Of course. George Becket, friend of the Gregorys, checking on the Gregorys, what better solution?

"This goes back," he said, sitting up straight, pulling himself into the desk, "almost ten years, you know. Bill and his wife, Edna, are fine people, and the murder has devastated them. They still keep Heidi's room just as it was, you know that? Kind of creepy, I know, but that's how much they were affected."

He peered through his lenses. Did I see how difficult this was?

"Bill quit his job. I don't know, he may have lost it, but this search for the killer became an obsession with him. Always coming up with some theory or other."

Mitch stopped talking for a moment. His fingers began to beat on the desk. A rhythmless sound like typewriter keys clacking.

"After a while they all seemed to revolve around the Gregorys. There was a party that didn't really happen. A pickup at the general store that nobody is quite sure actually took place. You know the kinds of things I'm saying. A horrible thing happens in the Gregorys' neighborhood and all of a sudden conspiracists are everywhere, feeding the grieving parents information that doesn't really have any factual basis. All that does is make us have to be extra-careful on our end. Pressure like the kind Bill puts on almost makes you push back harder than you otherwise would. You listen, sure, but after a while you grow pretty skeptical and you just say, okay, show me what you've got, but I'm not carrying the water for you just because some right-wing nut who has it in for the Gregorys says one of them was seen talking to a pretty blonde girl on the night Heidi died. Heck, that's what the Gregorys do. Probably isn't a pretty blonde girl on Cape Cod who hasn't been talked to by at least one of the Gregorys."

He gave a modified laugh. It sounded like a steam heater. His mouth laughed, his chest laughed, his eyebrows stayed put, elevated above his glasses. Like his mustache, they were too dark for his pale skin. The image they presented distracted from his message.

Still, I smiled, because that is what he wanted me to do. Eight years we had barely spoken to each other and now, in a matter of minutes, we were so inextricably intertwined that we could make little in-jokes about our mentors. If things kept improving like this, I might soon get out of the basement. Maybe even get invited to the Pops concert. Sit at a round table and help Mitch look for celebrities.

Hey, there's Regis Philbin.

## 4.

"Don't we pay for all the things we do, though?" Who said that? Hemingway. Lady Brett to Jake Barnes, the protagonist in *The Sun Also Rises*.

What had she ever done to compare with what I had?

Better yet, is what she said even true? Or is it true for some but not for others? Was Peter Martin paying now that he was a doctor in San Francisco, living in Pacific Heights, attending opening night at the opera in black tie? What about Jamie Gregory, now a Wall Street banker, living in a landmark four-story townhouse in the Village?

The one who really paid was Kendrick, and all she did was get drunk.

Kendrick. Her father. Her mother. And, oh yes, George Becket, living by himself on the Cape, working out of the basement office of a political hack, lying awake at night thinking about how different things might have been.

# 5.

CELLO DIMASI WAS SAID TO HAVE BEEN A FINE BASEBALL PLAYER. He went to an obscure college in Connecticut but made it onto the Hyannis Mets in the Cape Cod League, which bills itself with good reason as the premier summer collegiate league in the country. He played two years for the Mets as a catcher who couldn't hit, had a bad arm, but handled the pitchers well and excelled at blocking the plate. There is a picture on the wall in Muggsy's showing him upending a guy who stood six-feet-four and went on to play five years for the Baltimore Orioles. The guy is literally flying through the air, and Cello, his head down, his squat body hunched and tilted forward, has both feet planted firmly on the ground.

Cello never fulfilled his dream of signing with the pros, but he made a lot of friends in the area. After college, he ended up on the Barnstable police force, and after twenty years on the job had worked his way through the ranks to the position of chief.

Like Mitch White, Cello had a cadre of supporters, but they were most definitely not the same cadre. Cello's group were people like "the Macs," McBeth and McQuaid, people who ran the building trades, put on fishing and golf tournaments, coached youth sports, went to Muggsy's for breakfast and took their cocktails at Baxter's on the waterfront during the off-season when the tourists weren't around.

I knew the chief only in terms of discussing cases. There had been the bicycle-theft incident over which we had been at odds, but for the most part we were able to work things out to our mutual interest. The Kirby Gregory matter might not have had such a positive outcome for her if the Breathalyzer results had not been made questionable by a failure to locate the calibration records of the device. On the other hand, Michael McBeth's nephew was able to walk with a reckless even though he had spent the night puking his guts out in a Yarmouth jail cell.

The chief greeted me as though I had come to cut another deal.

"Georgie!" he said, calling to me through the bullet-proof window of the utilitarian reception area of police headquarters off Phinney's Lane. "C'mon back. Maddy, buzz the good counselor through."

Maddy buzzed, I pushed open a metal-plated door, the chief stuck out his hand, and we shook with the force of a couple of pile-drivers. I had been the victim of Cello's crushing handshakes in the past, and I knew from my years playing football that you got hurt less when you met force with force. "C'mon back. Take a load off your feet," he said, for Maddy's benefit. Maddy, if I was not mistaken, was married to one of the guys who did building inspections for the coastal commission, guys who made sure new construction was not too close to the water or didn't have too many bathrooms or nonnative plants in the land-scaping, guys who could make life miserable for a lot of people if they felt so inclined.

The chief's office had fake wood paneling and bookshelves that were filled with trophies from youth sports: soccer, swimming, base-ball, basketball. I couldn't imagine the chief or his kids having much to do with basketball, given the fact that the chief was about five-feet-seven and two hundred forty pounds, but you can't argue with tro-phies.

He went behind his desk, which was strewn with various objects—a coffee mug, a wrist brace, a woman's shoe, an aerosol can, a flywheel—but he did not sit down. He was wearing the dark blue uniform of his force, looking like a man ready to spring at the sound of an alarm.

"What do you got?" he asked. He did not do it in an unfriendly way, just a businesslike way. He and I were neither friends nor enemies, although the rules of our engagements required us to appear to others to have a certain camaraderie.

"You still working on the Heidi Telford matter?"

"Heidi Telford," he repeated. "Anything New? It would be a closed case if it weren't for that poor bastard. What do you got?"

"Just the poor bastard. He's kind of glommed on to me now. I told him I'd look into it."

"What's to look into?" The chief still hadn't sat. Neither had I. We were talking across his desk as if it were a stream that could not be forded. "Girl got her head bashed in and then got dumped on the golf course. Thing about that course is, you got a fairway runs right along West Street. You go down that street two, three o'clock in the morning, you're gonna be the only one there. Stop alongside the road, pull the body out of the backseat, run it out to the fairway. You're gonna be gone less than a minute and that body's not gonna be found till dawn."

"Less than a minute? How much did she weigh?"

The chief squinted at my impertinence. Then he regrouped. He still was not sure why I was there, what I was trying to do. "She wasn't a big girl. Hundred and ten, hundred fifteen pounds at the most. Maybe less, I don't remember. And maybe it would have taken a couple of minutes, get her out of the car, across the fairway, into the trees where we found her." He slung his hand from one side of him to the other. "Point is, other than us guys patrolling the place, you're just not gonna find any traffic out there at night. Only people live on West Street are rich ones who are so old they fall asleep at nine o'clock at night. What do you got?"

"And what did she get hit with?" I asked.

"Probably a golf club. That's what the medical examiner figured, anyway."

"Okay, so correct me if I'm wrong, Chief. The girl's found on a swanky golf course, her head crushed by a golf club. That doesn't sound like she got picked up by a transient."

"Who said she was?"

"Well, what do you think happened?"

Perhaps it was the tone of my question. Perhaps I should have shown more deference to the chief of police. In any event, Cello Di-Masi exploded. "How the fuck do I know? If I knew, I'd arrest somebody, don't you think, Counselor?"

I smiled. I said I was sure he would.

He grumped, like maybe it would be best if I just got my overeducated ass out of his office, out of his police station, took my bleeding heart out to save the colored kids who steal honest people's bikes.

My smile did not seem to be working. I used to have a good one. Now I get the feeling people regard it as something I just drop over my face, like a page on a flip chart. Still, what do you do when you're trying to placate someone like the chief? I tried words. "Mitch White thought it might be a good idea if I took a look through the file."

"Mitch White, huh?" The message was clear: Mitch White, another Ivy League prick like me.

I slowly lifted my hands, palms up, as if there was nothing I could do, Mitch was my boss. Smile, speak, roll over like a dog with my paws in the air.

The chief hitched his belt, made the leather creak. He was not wearing any weapons, but the belt was black and three inches thick, the kind that could hold a gun, a truncheon, a foot-long flashlight. Somehow hitching it, making it creak, passed for a sign of dominance.

"C'mon," he said, and led me out of the office and down a corridor in which the walls were made of cinder blocks painted light green. We had to walk a good hundred feet and every time we encountered someone, the person would squeeze his back to the wall and say, "Chief," as we passed. The chief did not acknowledge anyone by name, just nodded as he steamrollered toward our destination, a green door with a wired window at the far end of the corridor.

He grabbed the brass handle, shouted, "Door," and somebody in an adjoining room buzzed it open. He did not look back, just flung the door wide and let me catch it on my forearm before it slammed shut again.

The department's file room was virtually a warehouse, with rows of adjustable shelves that looked as if they had been built from an erector set. There was a little desk just inside the door, but nobody was at it. "Clancy!" the chief bellowed, and an ancient cop in a faded uniform that looked nearly as old as he scuttled out from the stacks.

"Right here, Chief."

Cello DiMasi flung a thumb in my direction, again without looking at me. "This here's Assistant D.A. Becket. He wants to look at what we got on the Telford case."

The old man turned to me with an expression of concern. Worry, maybe. Possibly fear. "The Telford case, sure. Right this way." He made another turn and hurried down one aisle with his shoulders curled forward and his hands splayed in front of him as if he were sweeping for mines. We followed, me first and then the chief, and Clancy took us all the way to the end of the aisle, where he began scanning the shelves, looking over once or twice at the chief as if to tell him not to get excited, the files were right here somewhere.

Like Clancy, I looked at the chief. Unlike with Clancy, the chief did not look back at me. He was still seething over whatever insult he thought I had dealt him. I was in the process of replaying our conversation in my head when Clancy let out a cry of relief and hauled two cardboard boxes from the back of a shelf, where they had been obscured by a whole series of other files. The boxes had the name *Telford* written on them in black Magic Marker, and the old man dropped them onto the floor in triumph.

The chief looked down, poked them with the rounded toe of his shiny black shoe, and said, "Lemme know if you find anything us dumb cops overlooked." Then he spun around and left me to do my own digging.

Once the chief was gone, Clancy began fawning over me. He had a nice desk and chair for me, he said. He could bring the boxes to me. He offered me coffee, claimed he had just made a fresh pot. I picked up one of the boxes, nodded to him to pick up the other, and told him all I needed was his desk and chair.

I HAD COME TO the police station with the idea that it was going to take me hours to go through the evidence. It took forty minutes. Then

I went back and went through it again, sure that I had missed something.

The contents of one box consisted almost entirely of photographs, pictures of a blonde girl in a sleeveless summer dress sprawled on her stomach under a maple tree just to the side of a meticulously groomed fairway; close-ups of the back of her head, looking not so much crushed as carved open like a melon; close-ups of her face after she had been rolled onto her back, her eyes closed, her features expressionless, somehow unreal, as if she were not a person at all but a model of one. There were scores of shots from the autopsy, including about a dozen of her naked body lying on a metal table, but I chose not to look at them. I was interested mostly in the way she appeared on the golf course.

The dress was of no particular quality that I could discern. It was blue, patterned with what appeared to be little red roselike figures. She wore no shoes and of course no stockings. The photos at the scene did not show whether she was wearing underwear, but in the second box there was a sealed clear plastic bag with a pair of pink-and-white striped bikini briefs. The autopsy report, also in the other box, said she was wearing the briefs but no bra. I went back and looked at the pictures of her lying supine on the coroner's table. It was hard to tell from that position, but she did not appear to be a woman who could regularly go braless without attracting considerable attention.

I did not need to speculate about her legs. Her knees, just below the kneecaps, showed grass stains.

A good-looking girl, twenty years old, had either been on her knees voluntarily or had been dragged across a lawn. I studied the pictures yet again. There were none of the golf course itself. It was depicted only as the location of the body. One shot was taken from the road, looking through one set of trees, across the fairway to a thicker copse where Heidi's body lay. Another was taken from just beyond the first set of trees, on the fairway side, showing about one hundred feet of grass. Another was taken at fifty feet from the body, yet another at twenty-five, and then several at ten feet. I could not tell from any of them if there was a drag path.

I had to assume there wasn't. Surely, if there was evidence that she had been dragged, the police would have recorded it.

What the photos did show was that there had been plenty of foot traffic in the dew-laden grass. I pulled out the police report and read that at 5:45 a.m. on Tuesday, May 26, 1999, a groundskeeper named Rinaldo DaSilva had discovered the body on the sixteenth fairway. He had been driving a golf cart pulling a fantail rake behind it when he had first noticed what he described as "a pile of blue." He had thought, for some reason, that it was a pool cover that had blown onto the course from somebody's home and so he had not gone to it right away. When he did realize what it was, he panicked. He got out of his cart and ran to her side but did not touch her, thinking that it would be wrong, inappropriate, something he shouldn't do. Instead, he stood over, shouting down to her, "Lady! Lady, are you all right? Lady, wake up!" Then he ran to the street, thinking he might see somebody, some friend of hers, somebody who could help him. He admitted he was not thinking very clearly.

He ran back to her, forced himself to kneel down, to part her hair. He had seen that her hair and neck and back of her dress were bloody, but he hadn't seen where the blood had come from until he separated the tangle of hair and saw what he thought was her brain. Then, he said, he fell over, fell backward onto his hands and did a crab-walk to try to get away from her. He thought he went about fifteen feet before he collapsed. Then he got to his feet and ran to the street again, shouting for help as loud as he could.

A man named Lowell Prentice came out of his house in his bathrobe, demanding to know what was going on. Rinaldo DaSilva pointed to the trees. Prentice followed Rinaldo back to the body, apparently hobbling with considerable difficulty because of some knee condition that required him practically to drag one foot behind him. Once there, he didn't know what to do, either. The two of them seemed to accomplish little more than trampling whatever evidence might have existed.

According to the medical examiner, Dr. Rajit Pardeep, Heidi had died from intracraneal and intercerebral bleeding after having been struck on the back of the skull by a narrow, dull-bladed metal object. Given the fact that she had been found on a golf course, Dr. Pardeep surmised she had been struck by a golf club. He found no semen in her body cavities, no evidence of sexual molestation. Her stomach contents were thirty-three percent liquid, which he attributed to alcohol, and her blood alcohol level was .12, enough to be intoxicated but not falling-down drunk.

The investigation report was prepared by Detective Howard Landry. I knew him only by name. He worked serious crimes and I didn't. His presence on the case meant that, at least initially, nobody was trying to sweep this under the rug.

May 26, 1999, he had been called at home at 6:10 a.m. and arrived at the scene at 6:42. Other officers as well as EMTs from the fire department were present, and Heidi Telford had already been pronounced dead. Barnstable police had put up yellow tape to seal off the area, but Landry confirmed my suspicion that irreparable damage had been done in terms of failing to preserve evidence of footsteps or drag paths. He could find no blood spatters on or around the maple tree beneath which the body was found.

He made a preliminary determination that the body had been brought to its resting place from the scene of the killing, and so he checked the roadside for tire marks in the dirt. Whatever was there had been obscured by what he called "first responder" vehicles. Since he did not otherwise identify them, I assumed he meant police patrol cars responding to Mr. Prentice's 911 call.

In sum, neither Detective Landry nor anyone working with him found any clues on or near the sixteenth fairway of the Wianno Club golf course except the body itself.

Landry's report traced the events of Heidi's last day. It was Memorial Day, and she had had her first weekend of work in her summer job as a lifeguard at Dowses Beach in Osterville. She had gotten off work at five, driven home to Hyannis in her Jeep Wrangler, and arrived in particularly good spirits. Her parents attributed that to her really liking her job.

She had spent about an hour and a half doing "the usual things," according to her parents: ate, showered, changed. At around 7:30 she had gone out, telling her mother she was going to walk down to Main Street, which was only a quarter-mile away. On a summer night, Main Street, Hyannis, is probably the most active stretch of road anyplace on Cape Cod, with the possible exception of Commercial Street in Provincetown. Stores, bars, and restaurants are open, and tourists flood them all, along with the sidewalks and the vehicle travel lanes. Locals tend to stay away from Main Street at such times, but this was the very end of the holiday weekend and most visitors would have gone home.

What the Telfords thought was peculiar—disturbing, even—was that Heidi had not been wearing the blue dress with the red rosettes when she went out. She had been wearing white shorts, white sandals, and a yellow Izod shirt, which, her mother insisted, she never would have worn without a bra. She was a D-cup, her mother said. She wasn't the kind of girl to show off.

Her mother remembered that she was carrying a rather large purse, a rope or hemp purse with two brown leather handles that you could sling over your shoulder and let ride on your hip. She had not thought anything about it at the time. Afterward, she wondered if her daughter had been carrying the dress inside the purse. But, she said, she couldn't think why she would do that. She had just finished her sophomore year at Wheaton. All she had to do was tell them if she was going out on a date.

Landry appeared to have done a good job canvassing Main Street. Within two days he had presented her picture at every bar and restaurant. While she was known to some of the waiters, waitresses, hostesses, and even a few of the bartenders, nobody had seen her that night. Landry expressed a lack of surprise. He noted she was twenty years old and not old enough to drink legally, and she had eaten before she went out.

He thought he might have better luck with sales staff and shopkeepers, but his interviews with them had also failed to produce anyone who had seen her at any time after she left her parents' home.

He met with friends, co-workers, high school classmates, college classmates, former boyfriends, and came up with no one who had any idea why someone would kill Heidi Telford or even want to. The most common response, repeated several times by different people, was that she "was not that kind of girl." With no clues, no weapon, and not even any rumors to follow, Landry essentially gave up. His report was still labeled "Preliminary," the file was still labeled "Open," but the last thing I saw with a date on it read 2000, and there was no sign that anything had been added to it since then.

Whatever the things were that Heidi's father had been giving to District Attorney White, they had never even made it into the police department's boxes.

## 1.

ENJOYED MY FIRST MONTH OF LAW SCHOOL. I PLAYED PICKUP basketball in the gym three afternoons a week, met some guys who asked me to join a flag football team that played on Saturday mornings, drank with classmates at the 21st Amendment on Friday afternoons, and tried never to miss a lecture or homework assignment. And then Mr. Andrews found me.

I was living in an apartment a few streets from the National Law Center at George Washington University. I had not been there long, had not given anyone my new address, but there was Mr. Andrews, looking taut and wired in jeans and running shoes and that same gray jacket he had worn in Philadelphia six months before.

"George," he said, and stood there, silently demanding that I invite him in.

My place was on the third floor of a building that sacrificed comfort for character. I had a small living room that led to a smaller dining room, off of which was a kitchen that was just big enough for one person at a time. The living room converted to a bedroom at night. The dining room was used full-time as a study. I had yet to have anybody there as a guest, and so my computer, my books, and my desk lamp were all positioned on the dining room table. When I ate, I simply moved to a different part of the table. I had two chairs.

I looked at the chairs, looked at the couch that had been left by the previous tenant, and wondered where I would put Mr. Andrews. I wondered why I had to put him anywhere at all. I said, "What do you want?"

The man stared at me long enough and hard enough that I somehow knew what he was going to say before he said it. My lower lip began to tremble. I bit down on it to make it stop. He didn't even blink. I put my hand on the door frame and gripped it tightly so that I could lean forward and not use all my willpower just to stand up straight. And still Mr. Andrews did not say anything more. I had to ask him.

"What happened?"

"Drug overdose."

"Is she all right?"

"She's dead, George. Is that all right enough for you?"

I stepped away from the door. Fell away, ended up on the couch. I lost a small segment of time, but then Mr. Andrews was standing over me and I was leaning forward, my forearms on my knees, my hands dangling. "I'm sorry," I said. I may have said it multiple times. I wondered why I was saying sorry to him—he was just a messenger, an employee, a hired hand—but I had to say it to someone, and he was there.

"They got to you, didn't they?"

"I went to see him. I did what you asked."

"Oh, you went to see him, we know that. I doubt very much you did what I asked."

"I answered his questions."

"So what are you saying, George, the fucking state attorney for Palm Beach County didn't ask the right questions?"

"He asked what happened that night. I told him there was a party at the Gregorys' and a bunch of us had gotten completely drunk—"

"Very bold of you. Went way out on a limb, did you?"

"It was true. I had, Kendrick had, some of the cousins had. What he kept asking about was the Senator. Whether the Senator had gotten drunk. Whether I had seen him with Kendrick. Whether the Senator had done anything inappropriate."

"He didn't ask about Peter and you didn't tell him."

"It was the Senator he wanted to know about." I sounded as if I was whining. I didn't mean to whine. I wasn't going to whine. If he was here to punish me, then I was going to take it. *Go ahead, Mr. Andrews. Smack me. Beat the shit out of me, if that's what you've come here to do.*

But Mr. Andrews did not do that. He didn't slap me, he didn't kick me, he didn't grab me by the shirtfront and throw me through the dining room window to the sidewalk fifty feet below. He just stood over me and waited for me to explain.

I had time to gather my thoughts. Gather them up, have them split apart again. "Look, Ralph Mars, the state attorney down there, told me it was a very sensitive matter because of who was involved. He said he had to be careful the claims weren't just politically motivated. That was all he seemed to be interested in."

It was not good enough. Mr. Andrews twisted my words in his mouth and spit them back at me. "*Politically motivated?* A girl gets violently raped and you claim that all the prosecutor cares about is whether her complaint is politically motivated?"

"He wanted to know if the Senator had come into the library when Kendrick was in there with us. He wanted to know if the Senator had participated in any way."

"*Participated?*" He was twisting again, making everything I said sound foolish.

"I told him the Senator just stuck his head into the room and I didn't think he really could see anything other than, you know, there was a girl in there with a couple of guys."

"A girl who was being raped."

"Well, see, it wasn't all that clear. Even to me."

"What wasn't . . . clear . . . Georgie?" He used the diminutive like I was a child. Like I was an idiot.

"Like whether she was . . ." I didn't want to use the word again.

"*Participating?*"

"The thing is, she wasn't saying anything. She wasn't doing anything to stop them."

"She was passed out, you perverted little creep."

"She wasn't passed out," I argued, my voice rising. And then I cut it off.

"What was she doing, Georgie, while people were shoving things up her vagina?"

It was a candle. I had stopped Peter from using the candlestick . . . Peter's dick maybe, although I hadn't seen that for sure. And his finger. And Jamie's finger.

"Look, I didn't get Kendrick drunk. I didn't invite her into the library, and I didn't get her to lie down on the couch, take her shoes off, put her leg up."

He bent at the waist, moved his face close to mine. "And you didn't do anything when those scumbags began shoving shit inside her, did you?"

Don't say a word. Don't say anything, George. Let him hit you if he wants. Whatever it is he does, just take it. Take it and keep your mouth shut.

Mr. Andrews, however, still did not hit. He straightened up instead, pivoted as though he could not stand breathing the same air I did, and walked to the dining room table, where he looked at my books and my notebook. "Quite an accomplishment, you getting into this school, Georgie. How do you suppose that came about?"

"I had good boards."

The man kept his back to me. "That so?" He picked up my notebook and flipped through it. "I happen to know that before you went to see Ralph Mars, you and your good boards had been turned down by every law school you applied to. You had given up any thought of going anywhere and all of a sudden, after a half-hour talk with a state attorney, there they were, acceptances from Boston College and GW, one school where the Senator lives and one where the Senator works. Pretty remarkable coincidence, don't you think?"

"What I think is remarkable is that you seem to know so much about my life."

"Oh, you can bet on that, Georgie." Mr. Andrews turned with deliberate slowness. He held my notebook as if he were calculating its weight, and then tossed it behind him, showing no sign of caring when it hit on the edge of the table and slid to the floor. "Mr. Powell has lost his only daughter. Mr. Powell is one pissed-off, vengeful, resourceful sonofabitch who can buy things that aren't even for sale. And Mr. Powell is going to burn your life down around you, my fatuous little friend."

He put his hands behind his waist and rocked forward onto the balls of his feet as if he were very much going to enjoy the fire. "I can guarantee you that things are going to start happening now that never would have happened before. And they are going to keep happening in every aspect of your life until you get to the point that if you so much as buy a losing lottery ticket you're going to think Mr. Powell rigged the game against you."

Mr. Andrews kept his eyes on me as he walked to the door. He stopped when he got there. "You've gotten yourself caught up in a very nasty war here, Georgie. And I daresay, I think you've chosen the wrong side."

# 2.

"CHUCK, CHUCK LARSON," AS HE ALWAYS INTRODUCED HIMSELF, was the Senator's man. He would say his first name, then his whole name, then pause to see if you recognized him. It was not an unreasonable expectation. He was at least six-feet-five, at least two hundred and ninety pounds, and he had been a stalwart on the offensive line for the Washington Redskins for many years.

Chuck had a broad red face and sandy hair that was getting thin but was still long enough to form curls. He had the kind of face that was built to smile, that made you think the only thing that made him sad was not smiling. When I told him about my visit from Mr. Andrews, the outer edges of his pale blue eyes became a mass of crinkles and the lines at the corners of his mouth turned into grooves.

"Oh," he said, "I am so sorry, George."

"Like, I don't know," I said, because I really didn't. "He was threatening me without actually threatening, if that makes any sense."

"Well, they're feeling bad in that family, George, you can understand that. Girl they gave birth to, loved and raised, did everything they could for, something like this happens and they've got to make it somebody else's fault." He nodded his big round head at the tragedy of it all. He bathed me in sympathy as he explained, "Otherwise, the universe is in chaos. You have to find a reason something happened so you can restore order. Usual thing is finding it was somebody else's fault."

He was sitting on my couch, the same place where I had sat when I received Mr. Andrews's guarantee of how bleak my future was going to be. Chuck's job was to tell me that wasn't so. He was wearing a short-sleeved collared shirt that was white but had faint red stripes spaced several inches apart. He was wearing blue jeans that had to have been purchased in the Midwest for use as work clothes, and tan lace-up boots that you might see at a construction site. This was pretty much the way he had dressed when he had first come to see me in Philadelphia, back in the spring, shortly after the visit from Roland Andrews.

Roland appeared. Chuck followed. Except this time I had called him.

"It's almost as if he was telling me he was putting a curse on me, you know?" I laughed lightly, because guys like Chuck and me knew there was no such thing as a curse.

"You know," he said back to me, "I once broke my helmet. It was just a snap for the chinstrap, but I borrowed someone else's and ran onto the field. Didn't fit quite the same, but it was still a helmet just like the one I always wore. First play, I'm supposed to trap the D-end. Dude blows right by me, flattens our quarterback, who lets the ball go fluttering away like a homesick brick. I sure looked bad on television, on the game film, in the coaches' eyes, QB's eyes. I blamed it on the helmet."

"What are you telling me, Chuck?"

"That we get knocked out of our ordinaries and it can bother us in ways it never should. Ever see that movie *Pumping Iron*? Arnold Schwarzenegger, there, he's in some Mr. Universe contest or something, and he wants to throw his opponent off his game so he hides the guy's yellow shirt. It's just a shirt the guy warms up in, but the guy freaks. You watch him come completely apart and, naturally, he loses the competition. Arnold had gotten in his head, see?"

"And you're saying this guy Andrews wants to get into my head by making me think Mr. Powell's going to cause bad things to happen to me?"

"Sure. And once he's got you in that position he'll come back to you, say, 'Okay, now tell me something bad about the Gregorys and I'll make everything all right for you again.'"

"Lift the curse, huh?"

Chuck's broad shoulders rose an inch or two and crashed back down again.

"But you're saying his threats are all bullshit."

"That's right," Chuck said.

And I believed him because under the circumstances he knew a whole lot more than I did.

## 3.

I<small>T TOOK A WHILE FOR THE NEWSPAPERS TO CATCH ON. THE FIRST</small> reports were matter-of-fact: Kendrick Powell, twenty-one, of Wilmington, Delaware, was found dead of an apparent overdose in a Midtown hotel in New York City. Then *The Wilmington News Journal* identified who she was and ran a respectful article on the unexpected passing of the daughter of one of the city's more prominent citizens. A day later the Florida newspapers picked it up and expanded on the story: "Gregory Accuser Found Dead in Hotel Room."

The *New York Post* took it from there. *The Washington Post* and even *The New York Times* were obliged to follow. The *New York Post*'s article was lurid, carrying an old picture of Peter looking half crazed as he exited some unidentified drinking establishment and referring to a "wild party" at the Gregory mansion without providing any specifics. The others had short articles that appeared to have been written by someone who did not really want to touch a keyboard. Kendrick was identified, her father was identified, and in a last paragraph it was noted she had filed a criminal complaint against Peter Gregory Martin, nephew of the Senator, and that the Palm Beach state attorney had declined to press charges, citing a lack of corroborating evidence.

After that, one of the national television networks hurriedly put together a half-hour show of investigative journalism that was long on titillation and short on facts. The network had come up with a few photos of its own, including one of Kendrick as a preteen equestrian in full riding garb, another of her father standing next to the mast of some gargantuan sailboat, and yet another of her mother dressed in a formal gown and accompanying her latest husband to a New York City gala, so they were able to refer to Kendrick as a beautiful young socialite victimized by the depredation of the Gregorys.

Josh David Powell, a beefy man with an unruly head of graying hair, was featured prominently in the show, saying there was no doubt in his mind that his daughter had been raped by Peter Gregory Martin and that the authorities' failure to act on it had sent her into a state of depression that led to drug use, drug dependency, and now this, the fatal overdose. The show cut first to a still photo of a bunch of pills spilling from a jar and then to a video of a body on a gurney covered by a white sheet being wheeled from a building to an ambulance.

The show then caught Mr. Powell in a close-up, looking particularly wild-eyed as he declared that he had reason to believe that it was not a self-inflicted overdose. Even now, he announced, he had investigators working to prove that.

There was a snippet of an interview with Ralph Mars, state attorney for the Fifteenth Judicial Circuit, in and for the County of Palm Beach. Mr. Mars, looking Hollywood handsome and, unlike Mr. Powell, with every hair on his head combed neatly into place, gazed with complete sincerity at his interviewer and explained that he could fully understand Mr. Powell's emotions, but his office had looked into the matter and there just wasn't any evidence to support the accusation.

The television reporter, a perky brunette whom I would wager was not hired because of her investigative acumen, was then shown standing on the street in front of the Gregory home on Ocean Boulevard wearing a low-cut blouse and tight slacks as she explained to the viewers: "In fact, on the evening in question there was a full-blown party going on here at the Gregorys' storied waterside estate, attended by some sixty or so members of Palm Beach society, and not a single person has come forward with the evidence Ralph Mars says he needs."

*Cut back to Mr. Mars:* "We'd prosecute a Gregory just as fast as we would prosecute anyone else. But there simply was no evidence."

*Cut to Mr. Powell, his shirt unbuttoned to mid-chest, his eyes puffy, his hair matted as if he had just swum up from the bottom of the ocean:* "That's a load of crap and he knows it. My daughter went to Humana Hospital and they confirmed that she had been raped."

*Cut to perky brunette, still on Ocean Boulevard, this time with documents in her hand:* "In fact, Kendrick Powell did not go to the hospital until the day after the party, when she was taken by a female friend who was staying at the Powell home about a mile and a half from the Gregorys' here in Palm Beach. A spokesperson for the hospital has informed us that it is against hospital policy to release patient records or even to confirm whether someone was a patient. Josh David Powell, however, readily provided records (*pause, wave sheets of paper at the camera*) that show that both the doctor who examined her and a rape counselor believed her story." (*Cut to the pages, lying in V-formation; close in on top page, scan down, then highlight and magnify the words "vaginal bruising."*)

*Cut to Mr. Mars, now in shirtsleeves and tie, leaning forcefully across his desk:* "Look, there was evidence that Ms. Powell had been involved in some sexual activity. But there was no proof as to who it was with or whether it was consensual. And let's be honest here, the type of accusation that is at issue is one that our police department deals with every day. If it were not for the family of the person being accused, I have no doubt we would not be having this conversation."

*Cut to perky brunette, sitting at a studio desk that looks very much like a real anchorman's desk:* "Kendrick Powell did not return to her studies at Bryn Mawr, not even to complete the second semester of her junior year. She appears to have kept a low profile until she checked into this hotel (*cut to gray-walled high-rise with modest awning and glass door just off busy Lexington Avenue in New York City*) three days before her death. *Back to brunette:* As for Peter Gregory Martin, he remains a second-year medical student at Northwestern University in Chicago. Both he and members of his family declined to be interviewed for this segment."

# 4.

CHUCK, CHUCK LARSON, HAD ASSURED ME I DID NOT NEED TO worry. I worried anyway.

Every day that I walked to or from the classroom building at George Washington I would look down alleys, between parked cars, over my shoulder, for any sign of Roland Andrews. When I ate in restaurants I always faced the door. I stopped going to the gym and quit the flag football team. I stopped having conversations with strangers after I met a woman on the Metro whom I thought was asking too many questions. I stopped socializing with my classmates, and gradually developed the reputation that I was a rather peculiar fellow. I couldn't find fault with their thinking. Especially when I lay in bed unable to sleep at night.

After a month of this self-imposed exile, I allowed myself to be talked into returning to the 21st Amendment for Friday-afternoon beers. I was the subject of a lot of questions, to which I did not give answers. This apparently made me mysteriously attractive to a woman from my section named Marion, and that night I ended up back at her apartment.

She was several years older than I was, divorced, and obviously pleased that I found her attractive. Which I did. She had long, flowing dark hair, spirited eyes, and a figure that some of my male classmates had commented on at least once a week since school began and that I got to discover all on my own. I am sure we had a good time, but I had drunk so much beer that most of what happened was but a blur. I woke up at some point with her sleeping soundly beside me. Rather than stick around till morning, I dressed in the dark and snuck out. Afterward, we only said "Hi" in the hallways.

In December I took my first semester exams. I thought I did well. Why not? With the exception of my one experience with Marion, I had, since Roland Andrews's visit, done almost nothing but study. In the week between Christmas and New Year's I got my grades: an A in criminal law, an A in torts, a B in real property, a B in contracts, a D in civil procedure.

As soon as I returned to school for the new semester I went to see my civ pro professor, a septuagenarian who always wore suspenders and a bow tie, a man whom I had no reason to believe knew me as anything other than a name on one of his class rosters. We were in his office, just him and me, and I explained as deferentially as I could how well I had done in my other classes, how equally well I thought I had done in his. He got out my blue exam book and spent no more than a minute glancing through it.

"Civil procedure is not an easy subject," he informed me. I agreed. I told him that I enjoyed it.

He flipped the notebook onto his desk. "The grade looks appropriate to me."

I probably sputtered.

"Mr. Becket, I do not expect this D will ruin either your life or your legal career." And then he looked at me knowingly beneath great white clouds of eyebrows.

If he had pointed out flaws in my reasoning, my citations, my writing style—one flaw, any flaw—I might have understood. If he had urged me to use this barely passing grade as a springboard, a motivational moment, a learning experience, I might have accepted it. But instead I immediately began thinking of Roland Andrews and Josh David Powell.

I do not remember arguing with the professor; I do not remember thanking him for his time or his comments. I remember only staring at him with a feeling of utter betrayal, and him staring back at me with what I was sure was utter disgust.

MARION INVITED ME TO A PARTY. I was surprised. We had barely spoken since I had snuck away from her apartment. She had gone out with other guys, I knew. I had heard them talking. One had even bragged about what a fantastic time they had in bed. But she wanted to go out with me. I agreed because I had not had a date, a planned-ahead date, in about a year, not since I had gone to Palm Beach, and because I had some vague idea that I might be able to make up for sneaking out on her the last time we were together.

One problem was that I didn't have a car and the party was outside the district, in Old Town Alexandria, down the Potomac River and into Virginia a few miles. Not a problem, said Marion. She would pick me up in her car, which turned out to be an Audi coupe, a going-away present from her former husband.

We went and we had fun, partying in a townhouse that had been built before the Revolution and now belonged to a third-year student who had made a fortune at a private equity firm before he attended law school. We danced and drank. Marion knew everyone, and I knew almost no one, except by sight. I overheard one of the other women ask how she had managed to "snag" me. I heard another tell her I was so "mysterious," and ask what I was really like. One woman actually said she and her friends thought I didn't like girls, but she was clearly drunk. I laughed and joked and danced with everyone who asked me.

When it was time to leave, I was the one who ended up with the keys to Marion's car. Her driving was not an option. She could barely walk. I helped her into the passenger seat, got her buckled up, and took my position behind the steering wheel.

It was necessary to drive three blocks west to Washington Street, turn right, and then just keep going straight until the road became the George Washington Memorial Parkway. From there we had only to go past National—or Ronald Reagan Airport, as they were now calling it—and continue on into the District. Even a drunk guy could do that. We made it a block and a half.

The red light came on behind us, accompanied by some other-worldly blipping sound. I immediately pulled over. "Oh, Christ," gurgled Marion, and she struggled to sit all the way up in her seat. She wasn't going to fool anyone. I still had aspirations for myself.

"Yes, officer?" I said, powering down the window.

The cop was middle-aged and portly, with bad skin. While I was looking at him his partner somehow managed to creep up on Marion's side of the car. The partner was a sinewy fellow, also middle-aged, and he was bent at the waist, his hand on the butt of his gun, looking through the window from Marion to me and back again. Two middle-aged cops riding in a patrol car and performing traffic stops in a neighborhood like this did not bode well.

I asked Marion for the registration and she was unresponsive. I reached in front of her, intending to go into the glove box, but the cop next to me screamed in my ear, "Freeze!"

I froze.

"Keep both hands where I can see them," he said, his voice still louder than it needed to be, and somehow I knew that he, too, had his hand on his gun. "I'm gonna open this door, and I want you to sidestep out with your hands away from your body."

I was only part of the way out of the car when I heard the other officer opening Marion's door. I was not completely out when the cop on my side grabbed me by the back of the shirt and slammed me up against the side of the Audi.

"Put your hands behind your head, asshole," he said.

*Asshole?*

He was breathing hard as he put his foot between mine and kicked me on each instep. I gathered he wanted me to get my feet apart, and I tried to comply. He smacked me in the back of the head and told me not to fucking move.

On the other side of the car, the sinewy cop had Marion out of her seat but was unable to get her to stand up straight. Her hair, her one great vanity, was tumbling all over the place, covering her face like a veil. He tried to push her against the car the way my cop was doing to me, but she slithered down and he had to plaster her against the side with both hands. "Roy, we got a problem over here," he called out.

"Put her on the ground," my guy told him.

With some effort, the sinewy cop got Marion lying facedown on a strip of grass between the road and the sidewalk. She lay there and didn't move. He then looked to see what he should do next, and the cop behind me told him to leave her alone, check the glove compartment, see if the registration was there. It took the sinewy guy about a minute, but he came up with a card in his hand. "Lars Bjorklund," he read. "Darien, Connecticut."

"That you?" my cop said. "You don't look like a Lars. Guys named Lars are big guys with big heads and stupid looks on their faces."

I had not seen enough of my captor to ascertain what would constitute a stupid look to someone like him, but the whole event was taking on a surreal aspect. Why hadn't he asked me if I had been drinking? Made me walk a straight line, touch my nose, say the alphabet backward?

"Yeah," the cop said, seeming pleased with his knowledge of Scandinavian physiognomy, "you don't look like a Lars. You look like Prince Charles. Is that who you are? You some kind of prince or something?"

Why would he think that? What had I done besides drive someone else's car for a block and a half? I tried to tell him the car belonged to Marion, that I believed Lars Bjorklund was her ex-husband.

"So we find her license, it's gonna say her name is Bjorklund, is that it?"

I knew it wasn't. I couldn't remember what it was. Something Italian.

"And if we call up there to Dairy-Anne, Connecticut, they not gonna tell us this car's been stolen, are they?"

Before I could answer he grabbed me by the collar and the belt and manhandled me over to the strip of grass where Marion was lying, her eyes blank and unblinking so that I couldn't tell if she was seeing anything or not. "Get down," he said, and roughly pushed me first to my knees and then to my stomach. I was now staring at Marion from about two feet away and she still had not blinked.

There was a tremendous crushing sensation in the middle of my back and I knew that Roy the cop was kneeling on me. I made some kind of noise from deep in my chest as air rushed out of my lungs, and then suddenly the whole area in which we were lying was lit up with headlights.

A car stopped, then another, then another after that. The cop bellowed at the cars to move on, but they didn't. Doors began opening, footsteps began sounding on the asphalt.

Roy was stuck then. He was surrounded by law students—six, eight, ten of them.

"Good evening, Officer," said a calm, cheerful male voice. "May we be of some assistance here?"

"You'll be in the back of a patrol car in two minutes, you don't get the hell out of here."

"I'm sorry, sir, but I'm counsel to these people." The speaker did not say he was our lawyer.

The cop lightened the load he had put on me, giving me the chance to turn my head. The speaker was, of course, one of the partygoers, a third-year student, a guy people had been talking about as having already secured one of those coveted associates' positions with one of the premier D.C. firms. Behind him, one of the other students was taking pictures with a flash camera. She took a picture of me, then took several shots of Marion lying on the ground, glassy-eyed, with the sinewy cop standing over her.

"Hey," my cop shouted, "you can't do that. Cyrus, get that camera away from her. And you, all of you, get outta here before I call for backup and have you all arrested."

The third-year student held up his hand with such authority that Cyrus stopped moving. When he was sure he had Cyrus's compliance, he said to my cop, "On the contrary, Officer, as long as we are standing back a significant distance and not interfering with the conduct of your official duties, we have a right peacefully to gather and observe the proceedings. *People v. Baldwin*. Supreme Court, 1984."

Both cops were silent.

"My father argued it," the third-year said. "He is now United States deputy attorney general."

"I don't give a damn what your daddy does," said the cop. But it was clear that he did.

"Oh, I concur with that sentiment exactly, Officer. I only mention it because he lives right here in Old Town, and if you will allow me to, I can call him and have him here within just a few minutes so he can give you not only the cite to *People v. Baldwin,* but he can bring the published opinion, show you where—"

"You're already interfering with our official duties," the cop said. But lights were going on in the homes lining both sides of the street, and out of the corner of my eye I could see the cop swinging his head from one lighted house to another. This was not what he had anticipated. He knew even better than we did that anyone could be living in Old Town: Supreme Court justices, cabinet officers, elected officials. It was that kind of place.

The cop got off me altogether, pushing down with his hand on my shoulder harder than was necessary as he stood up. I stayed where I was and waited to see what would happen next.

"With your permission, Officer," the third-year student said, "I would like to have one of my colleagues attend to Ms. Bettinelli, who appears to be in some danger. My colleague is an Army medic who served in Bosnia." He pointed to a rather dazed-looking fellow with short hair. "And if you would prefer not to have him approach her, then we really should call the EMTs. In fact"—he pulled out a cell phone—"I can do that right now, if you wish."

Roy hesitated. From my position on the ground, the left side of my face in the dirt, what I saw was a pack of drunken law students. Roy must have seen it differently. He said, "You got a medic, send him over."

The dazed guy lurched forward in a relatively straight line, dropped down onto one knee, gently turned Marion's head, and then used his thumb and forefinger to apply pressure to the sides of her mouth to force it open. I was lying right next to him. I didn't see anything but teeth. "There's signs of vomitus," he announced gravely. "She's got to get to a hospital."

"That's where I was taking her," I called out in a sudden wash of inspiration.

"Oh, gosh," said the third-year, and everyone was quiet for a moment as if contemplating the dangerous possibilities of this traffic stop.

"She still has a pulse," shouted the erstwhile medic as if he had done something miraculous to discover it.

"Cyrus," ordered the cop in charge, "see if there's vomit."

Cyrus, who had made it back to the patrol car, returned to Marion, reconnoitered a position where he could get down on his hands and knees and move his head between hers and mine, got down so low his head was on the grass and his hat fell off, and tried to peer into her mouth. His picture got taken in that posture, too.

"Oh, God, Cyrus," said the other cop, "sit her up, would you?"

Cyrus and the student each took Marion under the shoulder and twisted her and rolled her until they could hold her torso in some semblance of a right angle to her legs. There was no sign of vomit on her lips, her chin, her sweater, at least none that I could detect. There was, nevertheless, a round of murmurs from the gathering of students. It grew stronger until the cop, perhaps thinking that none of this was going to be worth the effort of filling out forms and making court appearances, not to mention responding to media and department inquiries, gave up. "All right," he said without bothering to look himself, "I'll accept what you're saying. Go. Take her to the hospital. But," he added, straightening up and kicking me with the side of his foot, "this one's not driving."

"No problem," said the intrepid third-year, and within seconds I was bundled, pushed, and folded into the backseat of the Audi, my legs behind the driver's seat, my hips behind the passenger's seat. The cop leaned in the car then and looked directly into my face as if intent on remembering it. "I understand you got some powerful friends, boy." He waited a beat. "I just want you to know you got some powell-ful enemies, too."

Did he say "Powell-ful"? Did I really hear him say that? I could not be sure, but before I could formulate the question he was gone and the other students were loading Marion into the front seat like a large sack of cement, and then the third-year himself got behind the wheel, strapped himself in, made sure Marion was strapped in, called "Thank you" to the cops and "Bye" to his friends, and wheeled onto the street.

We went a block and a half to Washington and turned right, heading for the Parkway. I was too stunned to say anything, and then I noticed our driver trying to catch my eye in the rearview mirror. "How did I do?" he asked.

"Fantastic," I said. I was about to express admiration, gratitude, wonder at what had just taken place, when he derailed me with a laugh and a quick glance into the seat next to him.

I knew it was coming the instant before it happened. There was a movement, then a tumble of dark hair, then one dancing eye peering around the curve of the seat back. "And how did *I* do?" said Marion.

## 5.

LEFT GEORGE WASHINGTON IN MAY AND NEVER RETURNED. I TRANS-ferred to a school in Boston. I had hoped to get into Boston College, but even with a strong letter of recommendation from the Senator, I wasn't able to overcome the D I had gotten in civil procedure.

The school to which I went was fine, and while it may not have had the same prestige as GW, it allowed me the freedom not to fret quite so much about who was watching me, grading me, pulling me over in the middle of the night. Two years later, I graduated, sat for the bar, hung around my mother's house in New Jersey awaiting the results, and when I was sworn in as an attorney I got a call from Chuck, Chuck Larson, telling me to apply to the Cape & Islands district attorney for a job.

## 1.

"ANYTHING NEW?"

"You know, Mr. Telford," I said as I watched him climb onto the long-legged chair next to mine, "if you don't stop coming here, I'm going to have to."

I wanted him to know I was not joking. "I like this restaurant, I like sitting at the bar, I like having John mix me a Manhattan. I like, most of all, that I'm not working when I'm here."

Bill Telford kept his eyes on the television as he completed his personal seating arrangement. The Bruins were on, game seven of the first round of the playoffs, and while Mr. Telford dutifully watched, he didn't say anything pithy or knowledgeable, the way a real hockey fan might.

John asked him what he wanted, and he said he would like a nice cup of coffee. This got barely a grunt out of John.

I turned back to my meal, steak tips over rice.

"I didn't hear anything from you," he said.

"I didn't have anything to report."

"I heard you went to see the chief."

I dropped my fork, let it clang against the crockery. The two of us sat there staring at ten men slapping a disk up and down the ice, pausing in their pursuit only long enough to slam one another into the boards and occasionally grab one another by the sweater.

"None of my stuff was there, was it?"

"Mr. Telford, you obviously don't need me. You know everything already."

He got his coffee, turned the mug so that the handle was to the right, and poured in a fair amount of sugar. "Just wanted to confirm it."

"So I was, what, an experiment? A mine canary? If you've got friends in the police department, why don't you just ask one of them if anything's going into the files?"

Mr. Telford stirred his sugar into his coffee, being careful not to let his spoon crack against the sides of his mug. "I wanted you to see for yourself."

"Why?" But I knew I was asking a question to which I probably did not want the answer.

"Because, Mr. Becket, you're a decent guy and my last hope."

He fixed me with his blue-gray eyes and let them linger, even when I looked away. Perhaps he realized a commercial was on the television screen and there was nothing else to capture my attention. I tried focusing on my food, which did not seem as appetizing as it had a few minutes earlier. I decided I was, indeed, going to find a new place for dinner. Maybe I would even start cooking at home. Get microwave meals, sit by myself in front of the television, eat off a tray table.

"Mr. Telford, I'm just someone doing a job, that's all. I've got no pull in the office, no say. I sit in a little dungeon in the basement and I do what I'm told, okay? So if you think I'm your best hope, you might as well forget it."

"You talked Mitch White into letting you look at the file."

"Honest to God, Mr. Telford, you're so much more on top of things than I am, why don't you just use all these other resources you have, go about your business, and leave me alone?"

Did I say that too loud? Is that why John looked up at me from down the bar?

But Mr. Telford was unperturbed. "My resources," he said, "as you call 'em, are mostly people like me, support people who lived here all their lives doing the jobs that allow other folks to come down and have a good time for a few weeks every year. I want to get a plumber to my place seven o'clock in the morning, I can do that. I want to plant a cactus in my yard, I got no doubt I can get somebody to look the other way. But that only gets me so far. It doesn't get me into the files."

"Both the district attorney and the chief of police know who you are. They know the case isn't solved and the file is still open."

"Sure. They see me coming, they smile and say, 'Hi, Bill,' 'Sure thing, Bill,' 'Get right on it, Bill.' Then they never do anything." He sipped from his mug, put it back on the bar. "Which you just proved."

I tried to go back to watching the game, but he stayed where he was, his head hanging slightly, holding on to the mug handle like a tired swimmer. I finished my drink, pushed my plate forward, signaled to John that I was ready to go.

"I don't know what's been goin' on in your life, Mr. Becket," he said suddenly. "But I'm willing to bet something has."

"Yeah, the Bruins are getting the crap kicked out of them, the Celtics lost last night, and I'm glad baseball is under way so the Red Sox can prove that winning last year's championship was a total fluke."

"Guy like you," he said, "young, good-looking, talented, you clearly could be doing something more than sitting in the basement of some backwater prosecutor's office."

I thanked him for his observation and he nodded as though my thanks were genuine.

John sidled over. "You done with that meal, Counselor? You want a doggy bag or anything?" I shook my head and made a little check mark in the air. He cut his eyes to Mr. Telford, indicating he knew exactly why I wasn't eating, why I couldn't enjoy my drink and the game in solitude. Guy comes in, orders a coffee, ruins everything for everyone. All that was expressed in one side glance.

Mr. Telford waited until John went back to the kitchen with my plate before he spoke again. "You know, it's funny. My Heidi wanted to do so much with her life and didn't get the chance, and here you are, you got the opportunity to do wonderful things, and what do you do instead? Sit around watching other guys play games on television."

I grimaced. Kept my mouth shut. The guy had lost his daughter.

"Do that much longer," he said, "you won't have any other options. Maybe you could take up fishing. Stand out on the jetty every night with all those guys, got nothing else to do."

"Look, Mr. Telford, I'm sorry for your loss. I really am. But that doesn't give you the right to track me down, try to make me do what you want by insulting me."

"Why do you suppose none of the tips I been giving Mitch are in the police file? Why do you suppose they never followed up on any of 'em?"

"Maybe it's because the stuff you're giving them isn't really helpful."

"The stuff I'm giving them is about the Gregorys."

That was the moment when I could have left. Should have left. John had emerged from the kitchen and was at the cash register at the end of the bar, totaling me up. I could have gotten off my chair and walked down to where he was, given him my money, gotten out of the restaurant without another word passing between Mr. Telford and me. But that is not what I did. Instead, I looked around.

There was an overweight couple a few seats down the bar in the opposite direction from the cash register. Behind us, there was a table occupied by a family and the parents were making a fair amount of noise telling their two kids to sit, be still, stop kicking, eat their french fries.

I looked back at Mr. Telford. His head may have been hanging low, but his eyes were piercing right through me, almost daring me to leave. Go ahead, George, get up and go. Go join Mitch White and Cello DiMasi in whatever circle of hell is reserved for those who choose not to do the right thing, who cover up for people who really don't give a damn about them.

John appeared in front of me, a slip of paper in his hand. I ordered another Manhattan. John got a funny look on his face, but he took the paper back and went to do what I asked.

"All right, Mr. Telford, tell me what it is you think you've discovered."

"Let me start by asking you something," he said.

He made me look at him. The blue-gray eyes, I saw now, had dark rings around the irises.

"You're a lifeguard," he said, "working Dowses Beach here in Osterville, and you want to grab something on your way home to Hyannis, a snack or whatever. Where you likely to stop?"

How would I know? I wasn't a lifeguard. Except there was really only one way to go from Dowses to Hyannis. Leave the beach parking lot, take East Bay Road to Main. Turn east.

He pointed in that direction. "It's just down the street." We were on Main. "Next corner, really."

I made him tell me.

"The Bon Faire Market."

I knew it, of course. An upscale grocery that had once been a house. Either that or it was so old that it had been built in a day when markets were made to look like houses. If you wanted French cheeses, sculpted cuts of meat, jams that cost nine bucks a jar, fruits and vegetables that looked like works of art, Bon Faire was the place to go.

"Owned by the Ross family," Mr. Telford said. "Nice people, but they know their clientele. You can't blame 'em. They're not going to push the most famous family on the Cape out their doors by talking about them."

My drink came, and with it my revised check. It felt like a secret message: Get out of here, George. Drink up and go before the crazy old man ties you to his car and drags you bump, bump, bump through all the torturous streets and potholed lanes of our precious little seaside community.

"They got fresh-baked cookies, those flavored waters, little energy bars, you name it. So the police check and, sure enough, one of the Ross family girls—Rachel, her name is—had a memory of Heidi going in there on her last day. Thing is, she can't remember anything else." Bill Telford raised his mug to his lips and took a sip. He made a face, which I assumed was because the coffee was not to his liking. But then he said, "You probably want to know why that's important, Heidi being in there. Well, it's one of those things that only her mother and me would know about, and it took us a long time to put it together."

"You think she met one of the Gregorys in the store."

"Well, by God, it didn't take you long."

He seemed more put out than appreciative.

"Look," he said, "the Gregorys come down here in the summer, come down from their fancy schools, and they get any girl they want. My daughter and all her friends knew that. Still, it was kind of a thing for them. Good that one of the Gregory boys hit on you—bad if you went along with it. Because, you know, the locals knew these kids weren't interested in them in the long run. So we just had a little restriction in our house, same as a lot of other families around here. You can go out, you can date, you don't allow yourself to get picked up by a Gregory." He wanted me to tell him I understood.

What I was tempted to say was that I knew full well what the Gregorys did with pretty girls. What I actually said was, "Because you felt they were only interested in one thing and you didn't want your daughter to be known as one of the girls who gave them that thing."

"It's true," he said indignantly, as if I was arguing with him.

But I wasn't arguing. I was thinking of Kendrick Powell lying on her back, her leg on top of the couch back, while Peter leered over her, his cock in his hand. Except I hadn't seen his cock, had I? I had seen the red candle, I had seen his fingers, I had seen Jamie's finger disappearing inside her. I shivered and drank quickly to try to hide it.

"This is how we put it together, my wife and me." Mr. Telford wiped his mouth as if smoothing the path for what he was about to say. "That dress Heidi was wearing, it was an Ann Taylor dress. Paid more for it than she ever did for any of her other clothes. It was probably a style she picked up at school, quality without looking too sexy, you know what I mean?"

I didn't know if I did or not. I had not looked at the dress that closely, not thought about it that deeply, didn't know too much about dresses in the first place. My wife, when we were married, kept most of her dresses at her apartment in Boston.

"Thing is," Mr. Telford went on, "what was she doing wearing that dress? Like I told you, it wasn't what she was wearing when she left the house. Second thing, okay, we found some pictures of her when she had worn it before. It had a red belt. Or at least she wore it with a red belt. And red sandals. Accessories, my wife calls them. Both the sandals and the belt are missing. They weren't in the house and the cops never found them. So it makes sense they were in that bag she was carrying when we last saw her. All of it: the dress folded up, the red belt, the red sandals. And she obviously changed someplace outside the house. Question is, why would she?"

It was his turn to look around, look at the fat couple, at the rambunctious kids behind us, at a new group of post-middle-aged, none-too-fit folks who had just come in and taken a table in front of the fireplace. Then he leaned in closer. "This is the part I'm not real comfortable talking about, Mr. Becket. But my daughter was what you call 'well endowed.' You know what I'm saying?"

It was important to him that I understand there was nothing salacious about what he was telling me. It was just a fact to be recognized. Recognized and reckoned with.

I nodded.

"When they found her, she didn't seem to have been sexually molested, but she wasn't wearing a bra. Okay, we look at the pictures, the pictures of when she was wearing the dress before, and she was definitely wearing a bra then. The other thing is, the cloth of the dress, it's good, sturdy cloth. It's not like you're going to be able to see all the way through it."

"Just enough to see that she's well endowed and not wearing a bra."

He sat back, embarrassed. But this, apparently, was his point.

"Maybe whoever killed her took off the bra."

Mr. Telford shook his head. "The way that dress was, it didn't make sense. We're back to the part that's hard for me to talk about, Mr. Becket, but it was like, you'd have to peel the dress down from the top, take off the bra, and then pull the dress back up, you know, to get it the way it was when they found her."

I flashed back to Kendrick, to what I had tried to do when I was dressing her.

When I focused again on Mr. Telford, he had both hands on the bar, his fingers folded tightly together. "Look, maybe this is just something that only a parent can feel. But that dress is the clue. The dress and the bra."

"You're saying she put on a dress because she was going someplace she didn't want you to know about. It was a conservative dress, which tells you she thought she was going someplace nice. And she took off her bra because she didn't want whoever she was going to see to think she was too conservative."

"She was twenty years old, Mr. Becket. I see my other daughter, she thinks she's gettin' dressed up when she puts on a denim skirt."

"I'm just trying to make sure I understand the clue you're talking about, Mr. Telford."

"Yeah, you're understanding, all right. More than Mitch White. I give him the photo, tell him the same thing I'm telling you. Ask, 'Who would she do all that for, Mr. White?' He just stares at me."

"And you were trying to tell him she'd do that for the Gregorys."

"Well, they fit the bill perfectly, don't they? And here's one more bit of information for you. That was Memorial Day weekend when it happened. What goes on around here on Memorial Day weekend? That race over to Nantucket. The one they call the Figawi. Who sails in the race? Well, the Gregorys do. Some of 'em, anyhow. And what happens at the end of the race? Parties. Parties on Nantucket, parties here. You're an attractive girl like my daughter, you run into a Gregory, he invites you to a party, you're gonna be sorely tempted, don't you think? Even if your parents wouldn't approve?"

I stared at my drink, wondering if I should finish it off or ask the next question, the one that could get me in a whole lot of trouble. I did both. "I don't suppose you found out which Gregorys were in town that weekend?"

"Their boat's called *The Paradox*. I found out who was registered as the crew. Six people. Five of 'em guys."

There was no exit now. "You want to tell me who?"

"Ned Gregory was the captain. It was his boat. Crew was Jamie Gregory, girl was Cory Gregory, there was a boy named Jason Stockover, another one named Paul McFetridge, and then there was Peter Gregory Martin."

My Manhattan surged back up from my stomach, got caught in my throat, didn't seem to want to go back down again.

"You know him? Peter Martin? He was the one who was accused of rape down in Florida that time. They never proved anything, but people said the only reason he wasn't prosecuted was because he was a Gregory."

My skin was burning, my chest was constricted, and yet my whole body was so cold I began to shake. I gripped my empty glass around the stem and held it tight just so the old man could not see my hand rattling.

"I took the names, I give them to Mitch White, give them to Detective Landry. What happens? They go, 'Hmm, hmm. We'll look into it, Mr. Telford.' Never hear anything more. So I do my own work. Start going to Bon Faire on a regular basis. Get to know the Ross girls; they get to know me. They know about Heidi, of course. They ask me what's going on. They're interested, and I can tell they're concerned because, like I said, they're good people. And finally one day I'm in the store alone with Rachel and I ask her, that last day she remembers Heidi being in there, was Peter Martin there, too? And she tells me the truth. She tells me he was."

"Same time?" I surprise myself by getting the words out. They seemed to have escaped through a corner of my mouth.

"Well, she's a little evasive there, but I can tell they were. See, what you gotta understand is that Rachel knows Peter. She probably knows the whole family, but, well, she's a little chunky, so she's probably not on their radar. Anyhow, she's already told the police she can't remember anything else, but now here she is admitting Peter was in the store. And what she's really doing, Mr. Becket, is she's being honest with me while still being loyal to them."

"You told all this to—"

"Yep." Bill Telford drew a five-dollar bill from his wallet. "And now I'm telling you." He slid the bill under his coffee cup, inclined his head in the direction of John the bartender, and said, "That ought to smooth his feathers a little bit." Then he got to his feet, looked up at the television screen, where the Bruins were getting shut out, and said, "Those three guys they got in the trade for Thornton are about as worthless as hazelnuts."

## 2.

THAT THIRD-YEAR STUDENT WHO HAD SAVED US FROM BEING busted was named Tiel. I never saw his name spelled out, but I assumed it was T-i-e-l. His father did not live in Old Town and was not deputy attorney general of the United States. There was no *Baldwin* case, either—at least none that held what Tiel had claimed.

He and Marion had wanted to celebrate what they had managed to pull off. I just wanted to go home. After much protesting, they dropped me at my apartment and continued on to Marion's place, where Tiel proceeded to spend the night with my date.

Marion liked the fact that I wasn't bothered about Tiel sleeping with her. She thought it meant I was kinky. And I thought that was why she called me when she moved to Boston.

She was working for a well-known firm and hating every minute of it. She had heard I was on the Cape and wanted to know if she could come down for the weekend.

Sure, I said. Come on down.

Within a year we were married.

# 3.

"Yes, george?"

Mitch White seemed put out that I was coming to see him a second time.

I took the seat I wasn't offered and told him that I had looked through the Telford files.

"Make any great discoveries?"

The district attorney almost smiled. At least that is what I think was going on beneath his twitching mustache.

"Only that none of the stuff was there that Bill Telford claims to have turned over."

"What stuff? A picture of his daughter in the dress? Is that what you're talking about?"

"He said he gave it to you."

"Which is why I took it. But Detective Landry and those guys, they already had pictures."

"So what did you do with it?"

"Hey—why are you talking to me like that?" Mitch White's eyes flashed behind his glasses in a way that was meant to remind me of who he was.

"Just . . . the picture was part of a point Mr. Telford was trying to prove."

"What point?" He put his hands under his pectorals and cupped them there. Then he stared.

I looked around Mitch White's office rather than look at the spectacle he was making of himself. I wondered how a man like him could make me feel like such a loser.

The district attorney's hands flew up in the air, extending over his head, compelling me to look back at him. "C'mon, George," he said. "After nine years, that's all he's got? And you think that's good enough for me to what? Convene a grand jury? I'd be the laughingstock of the community."

I didn't tell him he already was. I just said, "Well, I got the impression Mr. Telford had to build up a lot of good faith with the girl in the store, the one who finally told him about Peter Martin being there."

"What, did the girl get jilted by the Gregorys? Is that what's behind this? She couldn't remember before, but now she does?"

"I don't know, Mitch. I'm only asking because Mr. Telford says he's supplied various items to the investigation, and from what I can tell, the files haven't even been opened in years."

"You know what the first thing he wanted us to do was? See who bought golf clubs. Medical examiner says the girl must have gotten hit by a golf club. Okay, nobody has any reason to argue with that. So Bill Telford thinks it's a good idea for us to canvass the Cape, get a list of everyone who bought a single club in the thirty days after Heidi's death." Mitch White flung himself around in his chair in agitation. "What, we go to every golf course, Sears, Walmart?"

"We don't have a Walmart."

"Yeah, well, you know what I'm saying. I tell him we can't do it, don't have the manpower. So he comes up with these lists. Says if you're gonna use a club to make the wound Heidi had, it can only be one of these clubs. I forget . . . three, four, five irons, I think he figures. Flat heads. Then he says okay, if the person knows about the Wianno course, it's only going to be a nice club, a Ping or something. Then he says, and he's not going to be buying it at a Sears or a Kmart. That's the other place I was trying to think of. So all right, we indulge him. Detective Landry goes to the shops at all the golf courses, private and public, in about a ten-mile radius. And that's a lot, believe me. We come up with a couple of doctors, some university chancellor, the travel editor of *The New York Times*—"

"Any Gregorys?"

Mitch White stopped talking and went back to staring. After about ten seconds, he seemed to have a revelation. His forehead tilted back, his chin, what there was of it, lifted up. "No," he said. "No, George. There was no evidence of any Gregory buying any golf club that we were able to find."

His expression had lost the agitation, the sense of annoyance, he had shown before.

"So when Bill Telford goes around saying he's handed in all this stuff, the only thing he's really talking about is a picture of his daughter in a blue dress with a red belt, red sandals?"

"That's right, George." It was clear now: Mitch White thought I was putting him through some kind of exercise.

"What about a list of the people on the Gregorys' boat in the Figawi race that year—did he give you that?"

"Oh, yes. He gave us the list." He pumped his head in a show of assurance.

"What did you do with it?"

"It's around somewhere."

"Did you contact any of them? The people on the list, I mean?"

And just that quickly Mitch wasn't sure about the rules of the exercise anymore. If I was asking these questions on behalf of his friends and mine, why didn't I already know whether he had contacted them? He rolled his chair back from his desk, extended his legs out in front of him, put his elbows on the arms of the chair, and folded his hands about chest high as he stared that question at me.

I tried to look back as innocently as I could.

After maybe thirty seconds Mitch began speaking in measured terms. "Look, I'm sorry for Bill Telford and his family, I really am. I'm sorry for all the victims and their families on the Cape and Islands. I hope I can bring the perpetrators of their misery to justice. I hope I can do that every time. But I can't go off on every wild-goose chase every one of them wants me to go on. Bill, he didn't have much for us in the beginning. Didn't understand how his daughter could be dressed like she was. Didn't understand how she could have ended up in Osterville when she was walking into Hyannis. Gave us names and phone numbers of everyone she knew, told us all the places she might have liked to have gone. Even dug out old credit card receipts to show where she'd gone in the past. Police did the best they could and they came up with nothing. They searched for her bag, the clothes she was wearing when she left home, the weapon that was used. Nothing. Unfortunately, crime on the Cape didn't stop with this murder and we've had to deal with other things, too. So, simple fact of the matter is, it became time to move on."

It was unclear whether Mitch was trying to convince me or was rehearsing for someone else. Either way, I was listening dutifully. Seeing that, he opened his hands and flared them, an indication of hopelessness.

"We didn't close the case, but we're tapped out. Something comes up that's viable, fine, we'll look into it. We don't like having a citizen's murder go unsolved. It doesn't look good for us; it doesn't look good for the Cape in general."

Mitch sat up straight, pulled his chair back to the desk so he could make sure that all our attention was focused on each other, that it was just him and me, talking in our private tunnel. "Bill wants to do his own investigation; we're not going to stop him, as long as he doesn't break the law himself. Okay, Bill, let us know if you come up with anything. Years go by. He's out there. He's in here. He's over at the police station. He's got nothing. At some point he comes up with this Gregory theory. Well, I'll be damned! Good God Gertie! The Gregorys—what a concept! I mean, you know every bit as well as I do, George—"

Here, he paused.

"—the Gregorys are fair game wherever they go. It's the downside of being who they are. So now we've got this poor old guy, can't come up with anything else, so he fastens on them? Gets some poor clerk in a grocery store, nine years ago thought the world was going to be at her feet, now here she is, fifty pounds of brownies later, realizes she's not going anywhere, least of all to a Gregory wedding, and suddenly she remembers something? You know what I'm saying?"

I didn't tell him.

"Okay, well, let's assume that her sudden restoration of memory is one hundred percent accurate. What have we got? Heidi Telford, young, beautiful, and maybe just becoming aware of her own sensuality, talks to a kid from a famous family, then a couple of hours later sneaks out of the house. Mr. Telford puts it all together and decides she had to be going to a party at the famous family compound. Teases the boys with her boobies hanging out—he's not saying that, but you know that's what he means, all that bra talk and stuff. They want the boobies, she doesn't give them up, they hit her over the head with a golf club and kill her. You like that story, George? Like it in terms of buying it? Think anybody would? The Gregory boys can get any titties they want. They don't have to go hitting people over the head. They're done with some girl for whatever reason, they just call a cab, send her packing. Hell, the worst of them would just open the side gate, tell her to walk home."

He laughed. A little *heh, heh*. It was a typical Mitch White laugh, with no real humor behind it. He thought this was the kind of thing guys thought was funny. When I didn't laugh, he stopped.

"So you see, George," he said, wiping his mouth uneasily, "I wasn't going to inflict an investigation on them. Certainly not on the basis of what Telford came up with."

I wondered if looking at Mitch White was like looking in a mirror. If that was what made me hate him as much as I did.

## 4.

I WENT FOR A RIDE. I GOT MY BIKE OUT FOR THE FIRST TIME THAT spring, pumped up the tires, oiled the brakes and the Derailleur, and loaded it onto the rack on the back of my old Saab. I drove east on the Mid-Cape Highway to Exit 9A and turned south. In half a mile I was at the Rail Trail.

This time of year there were hardly any vehicles in the parking lot, and within minutes I had the bike off the rack, my helmet secured, my shoes locked into the pedals, and I was cruising the smooth pavement that covered what had once been a railroad corridor. This was not a hard ride. In fact, it would be difficult to find an easier one, but I could go twenty-two miles to Wellfleet, turn around and ride back, and feel I had a pretty good workout.

I cruised past river swamps, cranberry bogs, an abandoned lumber mill, ponds that would soon be teeming with swimmers and small sailboats. I rode faster and faster because there was virtually nobody else on the trail: an inline skater, a woman with a dog, a man with some sort of baby carriage affixed behind his bike.

It was good, I told myself, to be doing something other than thinking. And then I realized that was exactly what I was doing. But I wasn't brooding. No. I was doing something positive. Yes. That's what I was doing. I was preparing myself for something in the future. The Pan-Mass Challenge, 110 miles from Sturbridge to the Cape Cod Canal the first Saturday in August. Preparing meant going forward, and that was good. Go forward, George. That's good. That's good. Keep pumping. Get in shape. Raise money. Children's cancer fund. The Jimmy Fund. Pump your legs, raise money. Forget old man Telford and the Gregorys and Mitch White and your lost wife and anybody else you can think of forgetting.

Except I wasn't really raising money, was I? I was contributing it. I had pledged $2,500 back in January, the minimum for the one-day ride that I was planning to do. Riders were supposed to get sponsors, send out solicitation letters, hit up friends and relatives, but I hadn't done that. I didn't have anybody I thought I could ask. Try my colleagues at work, maybe; make things awkward for everyone, those who gave and those who didn't. *The guy in the basement wants me to give him a hundred bucks. Look out for George, he's asking people for money.*

How much would I raise? Whatever. It wasn't worth it. If I was going to pay $2,000 of my own money, I might as well pay $2,500. Pump, George, pump.

I was beginning to tire as I reached Nickerson State Park. Drop down. Pass through the tunnel beneath Route 6A, go back uphill and head toward Orleans Center. It wasn't much of a hill. I pushed myself harder. Go faster, George. What are you saving yourself for?

Guy my age ought to have friends he could call on. I had dozens of friends in college. A whole fraternity full of friends.

And I hadn't seen a single one of them in twelve years.

# 5.

I STILL HAD THE TELEPHONE NUMBER OF THE APARTMENT IN New York City.

When I called, a woman made the word "hello" last about three seconds.

I told her who I was and she made the silence last even longer.

I told her that I was Paul's roommate at Penn.

"Oh, yes." She still did not know. She was only pretending. Being polite. Mrs. McFetridge was always polite.

At the graduation party, I had seen her talking to my mother. Or, rather, I had seen my mother talking to her. Talking and talking and talking. I had drifted over to perform some kind of rescue operation, but when I got close enough I realized my mother was telling her all about my friends the Gregorys, who had been kind enough to have me to their house in Palm Beach. Mrs. McFetridge had grown up with the Gregorys. She had known some of the Gregory sisters and wives at least since Miss Porter's School. And here my mother was, name-dropping, no doubt making up a few disparaging comments in her ef-fort to be *en famille*. I hesitated now to bring up anything that would remind Mrs. McFetridge of that painful moment. I told her instead that I had been a guest at her place on a few occasions when Paul and I spent the weekend in New York.

She responded by saying, "How nice of you to call." Perhaps she thought I was soliciting for the alumni fund.

"I was wondering if you could tell me how I could get in touch with Paul."

"He doesn't live here anymore."

Of course he didn't. He was thirty-four years old. But I just murmured as though that was my bad luck.

"He lives in Idaho. He's sort of an adventurist."

I did not know what an adventurist was. She did not know who I was. Two people heaving information into the dark.

"Um, can you tell me where I can get hold of him in Idaho?"

"Well, I don't really know. You fly to Boise and then you wander off in the woods somewhere until you get to a river. I believe he's what is known as a river guide." She said the last two words going uphill with "river," resting at the peak, then going downhill with "guide."

Mrs. McFetridge's son had gone four years to St. Paul's before going four years to an Ivy League school. Eight years of very expensive education and now he was a river . . . guide. I did not have the feeling Mrs. McFetridge was overly pleased to be telling me that.

"He likes to be outdoors," she added. "Skis all winter, rafts all summer, heaven knows what he does in between."

"Is there a phone number where I could reach him?"

"Well, I don't know. Why don't I take your number and I'll have him call you if I hear from him? And if you should get in touch with him through another source, perhaps you could have him call me."

"Ah, yes, of course, Mrs. McFetridge."

# 6.

I KNEW CORY GREGORY A LITTLE.

I had met her once. We had been sitting at a big round table in the middle of the floor at the British Beer Company on Main Street in Hyannis—some of the defense guys and me—when she walked in with a couple of her friends. About five-feet-four, with short, somewhat muscular legs that she was showing off in a pair of white shorts that stopped halfway down her smooth brown thighs, she was not what you'd call classically beautiful, but she caught your attention.

She had, in fact, just come off a tennis court, but there was nothing other than her clothes to indicate that. Her shoulder-length brown hair, perfectly highlighted, did not have a strand out of place. She looked cool and smooth and, if anything, probably smelled of talcum powder. Her cheekbones were high and prominent, her jaw was strong, and you knew right away who she was. She might not have been Cory, exactly, but there was no doubt she was a Gregory.

Buzzy Daizell grabbed her wrist as she went by. She went ice cold for an instant and there was a feeling that all kinds of things could happen and then she recognized who it was and said, "Buzzy!" just like any other girl and bent down to give him a hug. I watched as her arm, thin in comparison with her legs but just as tanned, just as smooth, briefly encircled his neck and shoulders, and for one moment the electricity was so strong that I felt almost as though it was wrapping around me.

She straightened up again and looked at the rest of us with an expectant smile on her face. Her lips parted and she flashed teeth that were slightly too long and blindingly white. The woman was a collection of imperfections, put together in one exquisite package. I got to my feet. So did everyone else at the table. We had never done that for any other woman we had whistled down, called over, grabbed, or greeted when she walked past.

I introduced myself, shook her hand, forced myself not to say I knew her cousin Peter, and waited while the introductions went around the table. She waved her hand at her friends, wanting us to meet them, too, and this time we all nodded and immediately forgot their names. It was decided that they would join us, we would all squeeze in together, four women and four men. Cory took a chair between Buzzy and Alphonse, and I ended up with three girls on my right and Jimmy Shelley on my left. Since Buzzy was talking to Cory, Jimmy had no one to talk to but me. Since the three girls with Cory were bunched together, they talked among themselves. Occasionally I got in a few words with the girl immediately next to me. So, where you from? Really? I was there once. Just here visiting? Ah. How did the tennis game go? Aha. Oh, yes. Oh, my. She would answer my questions and then go back to huddling with her friends.

They left after one drink. I could not say I really knew Cory Gregory.

I did know Buzzy, though, so I tried calling him. I was in the dungeon when I made the call and Barbara Belbonnet was sitting at her desk. For once, she was not on the phone herself, which meant she heard everything I said, most of which went along the lines of, "I just want to talk with her. . . . No, I'm not going to ask her out. . . . We've got a mutual friend, that's all, and I'm trying to find him."

It turned out Buzzy, for all his bravado, did not have Cory's number. He had met her at a charity auction. They had stood in a group drinking champagne and now, whenever he saw her, he said hello and was lucky enough to have her remember who he was. So no, he couldn't help me other than to tell me where she lived, which everyone knew was on Sea View Avenue in Osterville. But there was a guard at the gate, and don't even think about trying to get past him just because you claim you want to see Cory.

I hung up and found Barbara watching me. "You want Cory's number, why didn't you ask me?"

"You know her?"

"Only all my life."

Of course. Barbara was an Etheridge. Etheridges knew everybody on the Cape.

"You know, George, there's lots of things I could tell you if you'd only ask."

Because Barbara was tall, because she had perfect posture even when she was sitting, she was able to look at me over the top of her computer screen. And I was able to look directly back at her. Her face was so often worked up in emotion that it was hard to remember it was startlingly pretty when, like now, it was in repose.

"Want me call her for you?"

# 7.

I T WAS ARRANGED THAT I WOULD MEET HER AT BREAK A'DAY, A coffee shop across the street from Pogo's. The meeting was to be at 10:00 a.m. on Saturday morning. I got there at 9:30 to make sure we got a table. Break A'Day was not a large place. In the summer, Break A'Day had tables with umbrellas outside on the patio, but this time of year the seating was only on the inside and it was crowded with locals and weekenders. There was a counter for twelve and another twelve tables that would seat two to four people, depending on how much you were willing to be jammed together. Nine-thirty on a Saturday morning, it turned out, was too late. All the tables were taken and the waiting list was forty minutes.

The hostess was a small woman with a round face and dark skin, her hair pulled back in a careless ponytail. Her name tag said Di. I gestured for her to move closer. She did not, but she allowed me to lean forward enough to whisper in her ear. "I'm meeting one of the Gregorys here at ten. It's a business matter, and I really need one of the tables, preferably in the back or one of the corners."

Di made a noise with her lips, pulled her head, rolled her eyes, all of which was meant to show my request was inappropriate; famous people came in here all the time, and we could wait in line like everybody else.

I leaned in again. "You don't want there to be all kinds of commotion, people coming up to her, trying to talk to her, clogging things up while we're standing around waiting. So if it would be at all possible to kind of move us up if something opens—" I tried to slip her five dollars and she reacted as if I were trying to hand her a toad.

A couple got up from a table along the far wall. I looked. Di looked. She lifted a clipboard, called the name of the next people on the list, and directed them to take their place. At this point, I had not even given her my name and was not sure what I should do. She walked off with her clipboard to greet some new arrivals. Two more times she called out names to replace departing customers and then she walked by me and threw her arm toward a newly opened table in the far corner. "Take that one," she said, and I had what I wanted.

At 9:55 a large black man entered. There was nothing unusual about that, in and of itself, except this man was ebony black, wore a blue topcoat, had a shaved head and a diamond stud in his ear, and in general was not the kind of fellow one usually saw on Cape Cod, at least in the off-season. He looked around the room, looked at each and every person sitting there, looked no longer at me than anyone else, then turned and left. By bending various ways, I could see him outside on the patio, talking on a cell phone. Then I could see him walk to what looked like a large Jeep, get in behind the wheel, shut the door. But it was not a Jeep. It was a Hummer, and it did not move.

At exactly 10:00, the door opened, the people waiting for their tables parted, and Cory Gregory, smiling and saying, "Hello. Hi. Hi. Hi," made a beeline straight to my table. "Hi, Georgie," she said, grabbing my hand and kissing me on the cheek before I was halfway to my feet. I melted back into my chair.

She was dressed rather mannishly, wearing a pair of what we used to call "white ducks" for slacks, a white polo shirt, and a blue pullover windbreaker. On her feet were a pair of two-tone suede shoes that would not have been out of place in a bowling alley.

"I love this café," she said, picking up her menu, bouncing around in her seat.

And I loved her. I didn't say that. But I felt it. I also felt the burn on my cheek where she had kissed it. Cory Gregory had kissed me. And now she was sitting directly across from me at this tiny table, where anytime I wanted I could reach out and lay my hand on top of hers, maybe slide it along her forearm, feel that slender but no doubt powerful wrist honed by chip shots and spinnaker raisings.

"This is so exciting," she said, leaning across that very same tiny table, bathing me in breath that was imbued with honey, locking brown eyes on me that said I was the only other person in the universe despite the fact that everyone in the little café was looking at us, "to hear about Paul. I didn't know you knew him."

Paul. Of course. McFetridge. She didn't know I knew him. She had met me one time, across a table, in a brew pub, and she was surprised that hadn't been revealed.

"We were roommates in college," I explained.

She was listening, I'm sure, but she was also taking off her windbreaker, pulling it over her head, getting it caught in her hair. I had the briefest glimpse of her breasts poking through the cloth of her polo shirt, breasts the size of sparrows. Delicate little things.

"Fraternity brothers," I gasped.

"Oh, at Cornell."

"No. Penn."

The slightest furrow appeared in her brow. I had the irrational fear that we might be talking about two different Paul McFetridges, and I quickly played my trump card. "He and I went down to Florida one time, hung out with your cousin Peter."

"Oh, Petey. He's such a big bear."

With that, the image of Peter Gregory Martin looming over Kendrick Powell filled my mind. I stopped feeling so giddy.

"That's what I used to call him," she said, "Big Bear." She was the one sounding giddy.

The waitress appeared next to us, pad in hand. "Good morning. My name is Maxine." She looked at Cory with frank curiosity. "All the muffins are fresh this morning," she told her, ignoring me. "Corn and bran are the best." She said "cahn" for *corn*.

"I'll just have coffee," Cory said, handing back the menu without even glancing at poor Maxine. "Decaf."

I ordered coffee and both the muffins Maxine had suggested.

"That it?" she wanted to know.

I nodded and she went away disappointed, apparently having been laboring under the impression that a Gregory and her companion would be issuing multiple orders for eggs Benedict, eggs Florentine, eggs with oysters and big chunks of lobster.

"So," Cory said, smiling at me, just at me, only at me, "what is it you can tell me about Paul?"

"Well, no. I've lost him. That's the thing."

I stopped because Cory appeared confused. Her distinctive features molded to ask what "the thing" could possibly be.

"I tried reaching him through his mother," I said. "I got the impression she hadn't seen him in some time."

I stopped again because Maxine was already back with the coffees, a pot in each hand. I waited until she had finished displaying her ambidexterity and meandered off. I watched as Cory filled her cup to the brim with cream, lifted the cup toward her mouth, and the mixture slopped onto the table. "Whoops. Umm. Ahh," were some of the sounds she made before she put the cup back down.

"Mrs. McFetridge," I said, feeling a little more uncertain about my love than I had a minute ago, "said he was off in Idaho somewhere, working as a river guide."

"You're kidding!" Cory said, thrusting her upper body forward, her voice soaring.

That movement, the jolt against the table, not only spilled more coffee but seemed to bring the general hubbub of the café to a halt. Cory, however, was oblivious.

"You know," she said, "he always liked the outdoors, but . . ." Like Mrs. McFetridge, she did not want to appear too judgmental. "In a way, that kind of explains everything."

"Explains what?" I said, purposely keeping my own voice low.

"Well, he hasn't been around here since . . . I don't know, years. And he used to come regularly. He used to do the Figawi race with us."

"The one to Nantucket?"

"Yes, we do it every Memorial Day. At least one boat. Sometimes my uncle enters his boat, too, but Paul used to always be there and I bet we haven't see him since—"

"Nineteen ninety-nine?" It was a guess, but not a wild one.

She moved her lips, counting to herself. "You know, it could have been. I really don't know. It's been a long time." She took another somewhat sloppy sip of her coffee. "A river guide, huh?"

"I was just wondering if anything happened the last time he was here. I mean, I know he loved to come to the Cape and he loved the race and he was good friends with Peter. . . ." I ran out of reasons why I might be asking these questions and hoped she would pick it up from there.

She did. "Well, I'm six or seven years younger than those guys and I'm trying to figure out the last time I saw Paul, whether I was in college or at Putney."

Our muffins arrived, my muffins, with appropriate fanfare. "Here's your muffins," said Maxine. One plate, two muffins, banged into the middle of the table. Cory absently picked the edge off the bran muffin and began to nibble at it.

"Didn't you guys used to have parties at your house after the race?"

"Well, usually, yeah. There was always something going on." She must have liked the bran muffin because she took another piece.

"And was there a party the last time he was here?"

"That's what I'm trying to figure out. The race back from the island is on Monday and there's always a post-race party in Hyannis and then people tend to wander over to our house and stay the night, so, yeah, there could have been. But, see, 1999 was the year I graduated from Putney, and graduation was the week after Memorial Day, so I probably went right back to Vermont that day. . . ."

She was drifting off, so I gave her what I had, twisting it only a little. "Nineteen ninety-nine was the last time I heard from him. He said he was coming up here to race on *The Paradox*—"

"I don't like that name," she said. "I told Ned I wasn't going to race on it anymore unless he changed it—"

I talked over her, tried to get back on point. "He told me Peter was going to crew and Jamie and you—"

"Peter? Well, that should be easy to figure out, because he hasn't raced in years, either. Let me see, he was just like a first-year med student at Northwestern when he had that trouble down in Palm Beach and I know he was up here after that went away. So what is it? How many years is med school—four? So, 1996, '97, '98, '99. Yeah. And after that he didn't come anymore. He was an intern or whatever out in San Francisco and said he couldn't get the time off. So if Paul was sailing with him, the last year it could have been was 1999." She seemed pleased to have figured that out and ate more of my muffin.

I was pretty sure I was no longer in love. It wasn't fair, I realized. She was answering my questions without guile or subterfuge, taking me at my word as to the reason for my interest. And yet something about the way her mind meandered, the way she bopped about in her seat when a thought occurred to her, the way bits of bran muffin stuck in her teeth—I wondered what it would be like waking up next to her in the morning. I wondered if she would be attractive at first light, if she would expect me to get up first, open the curtains, run the shower till it was hot, water the plants.

Cory drank more coffee and smiled at me. It was a genuine smile, a lovely smile. The bits of bran muffin had disappeared.

I said, "So Peter, I can understand. But I'm wondering if something could have happened that weekend that affected Paul."

Was I being too direct, too obvious?

"Like what?" Cory said, still smiling.

"Look." Emboldened by what I had gotten away with so far, I set off on a new lie. "That was the last time any of his old crowd heard from him, that weekend of the race. After that he seems to have taken off out west, almost as though he was trying to get away from everything in his old life. Sort of *escape,* maybe."

She was still regarding me as if she and I were the only ones in the café, but the look of confusion had crept back into her eyes.

"So there was your cousin Ned, your cousin Peter, your cousin Jamie—"

"Jamie's my brother."

"Sorry." Cory's appeal took another slight tumble.

"Okay, the three of them, plus you, Paul, and a guy named Jason Stockover—"

"Who?" She blinked, thought about it, then sparked again. "Oh, Jason, I remember him. He was so cute. Okay, it *was* my graduation year, because that was the last time he ever came and I had such a crush on him and then I never saw him again. So, okay, 1999 it was."

"You know what happened to him? Know where he is?"

"No. Like I said, we never saw him again. He went to Deerfield or Dartmouth. One of those green schools, because he had a dark green baseball hat with a white *D* on it." She finished, and there was a new clouding on her brow.

I had to ask what was wrong.

"You know, it's kind of funny because we had such a good time. But you think about it and there were, what, six of us, and three of them never sailed again. I mean, like I said, Peter has an excuse, but our two friends, to just never hear from them after that . . ."

"Which is why I'm asking if something happened."

And suddenly Cory Gregory was not having such a good time anymore. "George," she said, not Georgie but George, "what is it you do? For a living, I mean."

"I work with Barbara Belbonnet. I thought she told you."

"You're a district attorney?" She seemed shocked. Her hand went to the center of her chest.

"Assistant. I'm an assistant D.A., like Barbara."

Now her hand started grabbing around her hip, both hands did, she was getting her windbreaker. I started to speak again and she stopped. "No, George. You seem like a really nice guy and all, and I'm sure you only want to get hold of your friend, but we have to be really careful who we talk to and what we talk about. So I thank you for the coffee, but I'm afraid this conversation is over."

I reached across the table and saw the same ice coldness come over her that I had seen when Buzzy grabbed her in the British Beer Company. "Don't," she commanded. "I'm going to leave now and, I swear, if you so much as get out of your seat I'm going to press a button and a guy is going to come flying through that front door and it is not going to be pretty. Understand?"

I told her I did.

She stood up, did not put on the windbreaker, just tucked it under her arm. She started forward, hesitated in mid-step, said, "Thank you," again and walked out of the café.

My date with Cory Gregory was at an end.

# 8.

CORY GREGORY WAS NOT THE FIRST WOMAN TO DITCH ME ON Cape Cod. Marion had left me with a three-bedroom house, a two-vehicle carport, and a third-of-an-acre yard.

The first time she came down the Cape I took her to the dunes at the National Seashore. I had gotten a fire permit, and we went to Marconi Beach and walked far away from the guarded area to a spot where we could lay out a blanket and have nobody within a hundred yards of us. As it grew dark, we dug a pit and filled it with driftwood. Then we spent hours huddled next to the flames while she told me all of her frustrations and I told her none of mine. Later, when ours was the only light on the beach and there was nothing else around us but millions of stars in the sky and the sound of waves crashing on the shore, we made love in the sand and she proclaimed it the most perfect moment of her life.

By the time she went back to Boston on the Sunday of that weekend she had determined to leave her big-city job with its preposterously large paychecks and seventy-hour workweeks and move in with me. She would apply to all the firms on the Cape; somebody would want her. Or she would get a job with a government office, like I did. Or she would just chuck the law altogether and open a tea shop. Wouldn't that be great, never having to worry about billable hours again?

I did nothing to encourage or discourage her. I liked Marion. She was smart and funny and fun, and I had been lonely, especially during the winter months.

So I let her make her plans and tell all her friends, and I didn't complain when she never gave her notice at work. I didn't complain when we bought our house and she only came down on weekends. I didn't even complain when she started skipping weekends.

## 9.

MUGGSY'S WAS NOT NEAR THE WATER AND WAS NOT ON ANY of the main roads that visitors used. It was in Marstons Mills, and you had to know where it was to find it. Either that or you had to stop for gas at the two pumps outside and notice that the shingled structure behind the pumps had a neon sign that said *Eats* in tubular cursive. Then, if you were so inclined, you were in for the best five-dollar breakfast you could find on the Cape.

The owner was the cook, and he didn't seem to care if people ate or not. He had tattoos on his forearms, perpetually smudged glasses, an unkempt mustache that no doubt discouraged fastidious diners, and he ran the place more like a social club than a restaurant. He would come out from behind the counter and sit with the guys who came in regularly to drink coffee, eat coffee cake, joke about people who were not like them, and mock those who were like them over their golf games, fishing mishaps, and spending habits.

That same Saturday morning that I met with Cory Gregory, the guys with whom Muggsy was sitting consisted of not two but three Macs, and one police chief wearing civilian clothes. There was no waiting list for tables, as there had been at Break A'Day. In fact, there was nobody in the place but the cook and the four men, all gathered around one table.

I could hear them talking when I was in the parking lot, which was hard dirt and still contained potholes from the recent spring thaw. I could hear them laughing. I could hear three or four guys trying to get their smack across by shouting over the others. When I walked in, they all shut up.

"Morning," I said, and got a couple of silent nods, none of which was from the chief. I stopped just inside the door and smiled at them. It seemed the best thing to do. The Mac I did not expect to see was an old guy named McCoppin, very tall, with a full head of snowy white hair that stood out because of his bright red V-neck sweater. I knew who he was because he had once been on the Board of Assessors. He did not know me and looked away so he would not have to talk to me. The other two Macs probably said my name, or something close to it, in a manner that indicated they had no reason to talk to a guy like me and I had no reason to be there in their little clubhouse. The chief folded his arms.

"You want something?" Muggsy said. Because he was the owner, he could have been asking if I wanted coffee, orange juice, scrambled eggs with a side of ham. But it didn't sound like that.

"I wanted to speak to the chief for a moment, if I could." I pointed softly at Cello DiMasi, in case someone did not know who the chief was.

"It's my day off, George. Can't it wait till Monday?"

"Sure. But it's only a quick question and I drove all the way over here to ask it." I was still smiling.

McBeth pulled a rolled-up copy of *The Herald* out of his pocket and spread it out on the table. Everybody but the chief looked at it as if it was really important to see who won the lottery, which Boston city councilor was accused of which impropriety, and whether the Red Sox's new shortstop was too sensitive to perform in Fenway Park.

"All right," said the chief, "I'll give you three minutes," and then he led me outside, away from his friends, who had started debating whether the city councilor really had taken a bribe or was conducting his own investigation when he was videotaped stuffing cash into a computer bag.

He walked all the way to his city-issued SUV and leaned his back against the engine compartment. He folded his arms.

He said, "Yeah?"

I said, "Tell me if this list of names means anything to you: Ned Gregory, Jamie Gregory, Cory Gregory, Peter Gregory Martin, Jason Stockover, Paul McFetridge."

"Sounds like the list Old Man Telford was peddling."

"What did you do with it?"

"Gave it to Detective Landry."

"What did he do with it?"

"You'd have to ask him."

I nodded. The list had not been in the files, at least not that I had seen. I said, "Is he working today, by any chance?"

"Not today. Not any day."

"How come?"

"Took early retirement. Moved to Hawaii."

"Where?"

The chief silently considered whether "Hawaii" was enough. It was very clear I annoyed him. Like Mitch White, however, he was unsure of my connections. He settled his internal debate with a shrug of his shoulders. "Not one of the famous islands. The other one."

"Kauai?"

"That's it."

"When did that happen?"

"About six or seven years ago."

"So the list wasn't something Bill Telford just came up with recently."

"Wasn't recently, wasn't right away, neither. It was just something Anything New came up with somewhere along the line. He was always trying to come up with something."

"Did Detective Landry follow up on it?"

"I believe he did. Couple of people he couldn't find. The ones he did talk to, they said there wasn't any party at the Gregory house that night, and none of them had seen anyone matching Heidi Telford's description."

"And you believed them?"

"Me?" The chief laughed. "I didn't have nothing to do with it. It was Detective Landry's investigation, and if he didn't feel there was anything to Bill's latest theory, well, that was his call." He pushed himself away from his vehicle. "Now, you done with me? Can I go back inside, talk to somebody I want to talk to?"

"One more thing. After Landry left, who took over the investigation?"

"Technically, that would be Detective Iacupucci. But, seriously, kid"—he paused in his departure long enough to poke me in the chest—"what's to investigate?"

# 10.

CHUCK, CHUCK LARSON, WAS ON THE PHONE. "YOU SHOULDNA scared Cory like that, Georgie." He sounded sadder than I had ever heard him.

"I didn't scare her, or at least I didn't mean to. I was just asking questions."

"Yeah, but about what?"

"I was trying to locate McFetridge. You remember him."

"You wanted to know where someone was, you shoulda come to me, Georgie. I can pretty much always help you with that. What did you want to find Paulie for?"

"He was my roommate, for heaven's sake. At one time he was my best friend. I just wanted to find him, talk to him, see what he's up to."

"Yeah, but you were asking Cory questions about stuff that happened a long time ago."

"Because it turns out that was the last time she saw him."

In court I have learned that it is best not to stick to a script. You ask a question, get an answer, pick that answer apart. It was different when you were the one being questioned. I didn't want be picked apart, to say things that were going to spawn whole new areas of inquiry.

"She says she had the feeling you weren't just asking about Paulie. See, what you gotta understand, Georgie—and I know you do, which is what kinda surprised me about what you were asking—is there's a lot of people out there who want to cause harm to the Gregorys. Sometimes it's for political reasons, sometimes it's just nutcases. People who want to make themselves famous at the Gregorys' expense. So, yeah, somebody all of a sudden starts asking about where family members were and what they were doing at certain times, the kids know that's when they have to pull the curtains, lock the doors, call for help. She had help there, Georgie. Did you know that?"

"The black guy."

"Yeah. Recognize him? Pierre Mumford. Used to be my teammate on the 'Skins."

"He wasn't exactly discreet in making his appearance."

"Nope. Wasn't supposed to be. Since the Gregorys have all kinds of issues, all kinds of things to be concerned about, if you will, they use different assistants for different reasons. Sometimes they want to make a show of being protected, they use someone like Pierre. Sometimes they're more subtle and you don't even know someone's watching out for them. Could be a little old lady walking her dog or something. You understand what I'm saying, Georgie?"

"I do, Chuck."

"So you can also understand that somebody like Cory doesn't necessarily know where everybody fits in. So when she finds she's being questioned by an assistant district attorney, it kind of freaks her out. And when she goes home and learns that a few years ago some detective was asking her brother and cousins questions about this same weekend you were asking about, well, that's when she calls me. You got something you wanna know about that weekend, Georgie, something that involves the family, you're better off asking me."

"I just want to know where Paul McFetridge is."

"Yeah, but why now? Why after all these years, you suddenly want to find him?"

It crossed my mind to tell him that it had recently occurred to me that I had no friends, that McFetridge was the last close friend I had had, that I just wanted to reach out and talk to someone about the way things used to be. I got rid of those thoughts in a hurry.

"McFetridge," I said, "came up in a discussion I had with a guy named Bill Telford, whose daughter was killed that weekend."

"We know about Anything New, Georgie. His name speaks for it-self."

"Yeah, but he keeps contacting me." And here I diverged from the straight and narrow. "I think he's got somebody talking to him."

"The girl in the store."

"Somebody else."

"So that makes you want to talk to Paulie?"

"Let me put it this way, Chuck. It reminded me that I knew him. Made me think that if I made enough calls to enough people, I'd find him."

"Yeah, but why?"

"Because I want to talk to him."

"About what?"

"About what he remembers happening that weekend."

"And you think that's important?"

"I think somebody does."

Chuck heaved a sigh. A big sigh. A two-hundred-ninety-pound sigh. "Okay, Georgie, I'll see if I can help you out there. Only thing is, you gotta stop bothering the family, all right? It's best for everyone that way."

## 11.

"MY FATHER IS HAVING A COOKOUT THIS SUNDAY," Barbara Belbonnet said. "Want to come?" She had never invited me to anything before. I looked across the room and wondered why she was doing so now. Once again, I was struck by the fact that this woman could be quite good looking when she was not stressed.

It was just that most of the time we had shared an office her face was turned away, bent between her shoulders while she talked into her phone, or focused on her computer screen while she tried to do in four hours work that she was being paid to do in eight. If someone had asked what she looked like, I might have said tall and athletic, light brown hair worn bunched on her head. If pressed for details, I would have said brown eyes, oval face, high cheekbones. Good shape, I guess. Hard to tell by the clothes she wore.

But now, as I studied her, I realized her hair was more blond than brown, her eyes were actually hazel, and her skin was virtually flawless. How, I asked myself, had I missed all that? Two people sitting in a room for weeks, each immersed in his or her own problems, barely looking at each other. Except now we were.

"Where?" I asked. Was that a good response to a personal invitation? I was still wondering why she was asking me, her office-mate, with whom she never so much as went to lunch.

"Oyster Harbors."

Yes. Of course. An island community, where you have to go over a drawbridge and be cleared for entry by a man in a booth. Eight years on the Cape and I'd never been there.

"It's the family home," she said, as though embarrassed.

"Sure," I said.

I BROUGHT WINE. Nickel & Nickel cabernet. The guy in the wine store on Route 28 acted as though he was selling the Romanov jewels. I told him I wanted a good wine and he pulled it out from behind the counter, cradled it like a baby, looked both ways, and said it would cost me $80 but be well worth it. I figured Barbara's parents were likely to know their wine and made the purchase. *Who's this young man, Barbs? Oh, and such exquisite taste. He must be one of us!*

I made it across the drawbridge well enough, but then had to wait several minutes while the guard searched for my name on a list.

"Ah, here it is," he said at last. "Straight ahead. Bear left, then second left on Indian Trail. Go to the end of the road. You'll see the cars."

Indeed, I did. Mercedes Benzes, BMWs, Jaguars, Cadillacs, convertibles of all makes, including a Bentley. Luxury vehicles filled the crushed-shell driveway and lined the road in front of a twenty-first-century version of a sea captain's home. The real thing, only better. With a widow's walk on the roof.

I heard the sound of a steel band and multiple voices from the backyard as I walked onto the property, and so I steered directly there without going through the house. Men and women were clustered in little groups, maybe clustered closer than usual because it was not that warm, even though the sun was shining. Men wore polo shirts under sport coats or golf sweaters; women wore slacks and light jackets. All looked as though they were gritting their way through the brisk weather because it was worth it to have drinks and be in such august company.

A few people looked up as I entered the backyard, but no one acknowledged me. No one even stopped talking. I glanced around, thinking there had to be someone I knew, someplace where I could at least point myself to deliver my wine. An outdoor bar was located at the far end of the patio, manned by a bartender in a waistcoat and bow tie. I did not think he would fully appreciate my gift, so I stood there holding it by the neck, figuring sooner or later at least Barbara was bound to see me.

A tall man with a full head of perfectly brushed gray hair was leading the discussion in one of the groups. He watched me as he spoke, kept his eyes on me to the point I had to nod at him. Nod and smile and raise my shoulders in admission that I did not know what to do, where to go. I saw him say, "Excuse me," to those he was with and make his way over to rescue me. Or confront me.

It could have been either.

His manner was a little brusque.

"Hello," he said in a way that was impossible to interpret as welcoming, "I'm Hugh Etheridge."

"George Becket," I told him. "I work with Barbara."

Only then did he extend his hand. I think he was glad to see that I was bringing wine and not pilfering it. I offered the bottle and he held it out from his chest and read the label closely. "California, is it? Oh, yes, Napa. Fine, fine. I'll have it opened." His admiration was at an end and he lowered the bottle and scanned the crowd, looking for someone to carry out the assignment or, perhaps, for someone to whom I could talk.

"Are you alone?" he asked, and I told him I was.

I could see a slight change as it occurred to him that his married daughter had invited a man of about her age to a party where he knew no one else.

I quickly explained that Barbara and I shared an office. "We kid that we're cellmates. Down in the dungeon."

Mr. Etheridge stopped scanning and looked at me out of the corner of his eye. "The what?"

"That's what we call it." I was beginning to sweat. Sixty-five degrees and I was overheated. "Because we're on the bottom floor."

I wished what I had said had been funnier. My host did not smile. He just went back to scanning. I had an impulse to tell him that I had been married. That I was a lawyer. That I had gone to prep school. That I knew the difference between *that* and *which*.

"Ah, there she is, playing croquet. Come."

He strode off in the direction of the water, which I could see in the distance. There was a patio, where we were standing; then a border of outdoor grills, where men in aprons were busy flipping sizzling hunks of meat; and then a broad green lawn rimmed by great bushes of light blue hydrangeas. On the lawn holding mallets were several people of various sizes, but my attention was distracted.

As we walked across the patio I could see that the largest cluster of people was around a tall, thin woman with white-blond hair and a fixed smile painted in red lipstick on her face. I knew that woman. I had seen her face before. I slowed my step, not enough to let Mr. Etheridge get away from me but so I could get a closer look and see that she was hanging on to the arm of a shorter man with a distinctively floppy hairstyle, a white shirt, a blue blazer, a pair of khaki pants. The woman, I realized, was an actress. The kind of actress whom everyone knew but whose movies were not likely to come readily to anyone's mind. And the man she was with was none other than Jamie Gregory.

He looked up, looked through the crowd of admirers right at me. Or right through me.

Didn't he?

Wasn't he grinning at me? Not the same God-awful grin I had seen in Palm Beach, but it was a grin just the same, and it chilled me.

"George."

Somebody was annoyed. Mr. Etheridge, still with my bottle of wine, his hands inverted on his hips. I apparently had stopped, since I was not moving. And I most definitely was staring.

"Yes, yes, that's Darra Lane. She's with Jamie Gregory and I'm sure you'll get to meet them later. Come along now because I want to get you to Barbara."

Five minutes into the party and I had already incurred the ire of the host. Perhaps he was not going to like it so much when I confronted Jamie, when I knocked him down, tore off his runt punk bastard lips and fed them to the seagulls while I danced around his prostrate body, delivering kicks to his ribs and an occasional stomp to his head. Yeah, I would do that. But in the meantime I had to hurry after Mr. Etheridge.

BARBARA WAS WEARING a white jacket over a black-and-white striped jersey top that appeared to cover only one shoulder. Her slacks, too, were white, and they hugged her long legs, something I had never seen any of her other clothes do. I had thought that white was not supposed to be worn until after Memorial Day, but this was her house, her family's party, and she could clearly wear whatever she wanted.

With her mallet gripped mid-shaft, she held out her arms to greet me, calling my name.

In all likelihood, I had never done more than shake her hand, and now here I was, hugging her in front of her father. Hugging Barbara Belbonnet, who had let her hair down and whose skin was as smooth and cool as silk. I did my best to hug deferentially, positioning myself slightly to one side so as not to make too much contact. She kissed me loudly, exuberantly, on the cheek. When, I wondered, had she become so radiant?

"Pop-pop, this is my very best friend in the office, George Becket!"

Pop-pop? Intimidating old, steel-haired Hugh Etheridge?

"Yes, we've met," he told her, with just the slightest flutter of irritation. "You might have noticed I brought him over. Now if you'll excuse me, I have to return to the other guests." And with that, he turned his back on us.

"Oh, don't mind him," Barbara said as we watched him walk away. "Do you play croquet? You can take my place. Here."

She thrust the mallet into my hand. Three other people stared at us. A Gatsbyish man and woman, obviously a couple, were introduced as Grace and Parker. Maybe they weren't Gatsbyish. Maybe I was just thinking that way. Except the man was wearing a white hat with a brim and a thick black band around it and the woman was wearing a sailor-type dress that went to her ankles. The third person was a boy of about eleven, introduced as Malcolm. Grace and Parker said hello. Malcolm did not. He squealed something about "Gwa!" and ran awkwardly to swipe at a ball.

"Malcolm's different," Barbara whispered unnecessarily.

FIVE MINUTES INTO THE PARTY, I had annoyed the host. Ten minutes after that, I had ruined the croquet game. Without Barbara, Grace's play became desultory. Parker made a cutting comment and then suddenly announced he was going to get a drink. That made Grace stop playing altogether and start whispering to Barbara. Only Malcolm wanted to keep going and it fell to me to keep going with him. Then the patrician tones of Hugh Etheridge wafted over the lawn, calling to Barbara, telling her one of the guests was leaving and she had to say goodbye and all of a sudden both she and Grace were gone and I was left alone on the back forty to play croquet with a boy with Down syndrome.

Over the next twenty minutes I made several efforts to extricate myself, but Malcolm would have none of it. I had no idea to whom he belonged, but he wanted to play and nobody, not Barbara or anyone else, came to rescue me. It was only by convincing Malcolm that he won and enticing him into the ritual of exchanging high fives that I was able to lay down my mallet and scurry away.

I arrived back at the patio looking more or less like an escaped prisoner with the sheriff after me. I tried to blend in, but I knew no one. I could not see Barbara, Hugh turned his back on me, and as best I could tell the guest who had departed was Jamie, taking with him, of course, the movie star. People were forming a buffet line to pick up their meats and salads and spring vegetables and hot rolls. I contemplated getting in line with them, but then I would be a sitting duck for Malcolm, who was pushing his way through the crowd, mallet still in hand.

I would get my food and then what? Sit with Malcolm? Sit by myself?

Georgie Becket, all alone. Georgie Becket hit the road.

# 12.

THE FIRST PHONE CALL WAS FROM BARBARA. SHE WAS SO SORRY. Her fourteen-year-old daughter had had a meltdown. "You know what it's like with fourteen-year-old girls," she assured me. "Everything is a life-ending crisis."

I pretended I did.

"Anyhow, by the time I got back outside you were gone and nobody knew what had happened to you."

Nobody, meaning Pop-pop, Malcolm, and Mr. and Mrs. Gatsby.

"I hope you'll forgive me, hope you'll let me make it up to you."

Oh, sure. Yes. No problem. Don't give it a second thought.


THE SECOND CALL came from Chuck Larson. He wanted to know if I had had a good time at the party.

How, exactly, did you know I was there, Chuck?

Did Jamie tell him? Did Jamie recognize me? Chuck wasn't saying. His job was only to tell me things he wanted to tell me. He did, however, tell me what Jamie was doing there. He was thinking of producing a movie for Darra.

"I thought he was a Wall Street banker."

"Banker? Sort of. Right now, Jamie's making a lot of money for a lot of people in nontraditional investments."

"What's that mean?"

"Something to do with mortgages. Sub-prime mortgages. Don't ask me, but folks at that party all want to invest with him. So now he's thinking of branching out."

"Into the movies."

"People say he has the magic touch."

I recoiled at the image.

"In any event," he said, "Jamie was more or less showing off the product."

That got him several seconds of dead air while I tried to figure out why he was telling me this.

Chuck Larson sighed. "You still looking for Paul McFetridge?"

"I am."

"Try Stanley, Idaho, Georgie," he said. "Two Rivers Whitewater Rafting Company."

I wondered if I had passed some sort of test. You saw Jamie and you behaved yourself. Here's your reward, good boy.

## 1.

I T WAS A SMALL PLANE, A TAIL-DRAGGER WITH NO WHEEL IN THE
front. It held the pilot and would have held five passengers if one of
the seats was not filled with gear. We landed on a dirt runway that required a very sharp left bank in which the pilot seemed to exult. I had
the feeling the whole flight up from Boise to this pinprick on the map
known as Indian Creek had been worth it to the pilot just so he could
make that bank.

The first three passengers who disembarked were greeted with a
smile and a welcoming handshake. I got an "Oh, shit."

It did not come right away. Initially I got a smile, then the smile
faded, replaced by a look of confusion, then recognition. Then, "Oh,
shit."

We shook hands nonetheless. I wondered if he would hug me, as I
think we had done when we last saw each other. But Paul McFetridge
was raised an Episcopalian. In my experience they don't like to touch,
preferring to sing boldly instead.

"Paul."

"Jesus."

"Not quite."

"The hell you doing here?" He was still holding on to my hand.

"Came to go rafting."

"So is this, like, a coincidence?"

Paul McFetridge's hair was very long and pulled back into a ponytail. Curly and springy hair does not fit well in a ponytail, and his was no exception. He could have been carrying a pillow on the back of his head. His features had grown lean and hawkish over the years and he had developed something of a stoop, so that his neck seemed to project forward and his shoulders curled slightly inward. His was no longer the look of a college tennis player with a hundred-twenty-mile-per-hour serve.

"I called your mother."

"She knew where I was?"

"She said you were a"—I did my best to imitate her voice—" 'river . . . guide.' "

He let go then. He searched my eyes.

"I got divorced recently," I said. "I'm on my own. So when she said that, I thought, 'What the hell, I'd like to go whitewater rafting,' and I figured if I was going to do it, especially by myself, I'd try to do it where you were. At least I'd know somebody."

I had practiced all of this. I thought it went off well. But McFetridge kept waiting for more. And then, finally, he asked, "Where you living?"

I told him I was a lawyer on Cape Cod, and he thought about that before clapping me on the back and telling me we'd better get my gear down to the river and meet the others. This was not his company. But he was the senior guide on this trip. The one who knew the river best. It was up to him to get things going, keep folks organized. Don't worry, though. We'd have plenty of chances to talk. Catch up. Remember old times.


WE WERE SUPPOSED TO have put in twenty-five miles upstream and done a series of class IV rapids, but the snowfall the previous winter had been heavy and the roads that the outfitters needed to get in their equipment were still blocked and so we put in at Indian Creek and had a short and leisurely run on the first day. There were twenty of us paid participants and about seven crew members, two of whom floated down ahead of us each day to set up camp.

We were given a lecture before we started. The river, we were told, was exceptionally high and the water flowing exceptionally fast. There were few rocks sticking out and even fewer drops. The danger was getting caught in a hole, a depression formed by subsurface boulders, where the raft would tip on its side and stall, perhaps dumping paddlers out. If we got dumped, we were told, it was necessary to get out of the hole any way possible. Do not allow the swirling water to circulate you. If you are pulled down, form a ball and try to drop all the way to the bottom, then spring back up again at an angle. The guides will get you a rope as quickly as they can.

I got into a raft with five other folks and McFetridge sitting in the stern with a pair of oars. We paddled when he told us to paddle, stopped when he told us to stop. There was little to it on that first day, little danger, little required output by the paddlers, so little that I had the feeling he did not really need us to propel the boat as much as he wanted us to think we were.

McFetridge talked to everyone in the raft as we went forward, me no more than anyone else. I was confident he knew what he was doing. As a student and an athlete he had always known what he was doing, and he had never acted as though anything required particular effort or concern. Things would work out for McFetridge. They would work out for his friends . . . unless he and his friends wanted the same thing, in which case his friends' interest was of no consequence. I pictured myself going over. I pictured myself going into one of those holes. I pictured McFetridge continuing to guide the boat right on down the river.

WE CAMPED FOR the night at a place called Marble Ledge along the left side of the river. I was given my own tent, for which I was grateful. First day on the voyage and most people clung to whomever they came with, which left me on my own. I climbed a very steep hillside that was covered with thousands and thousands of yellow flowers known as arrowleaf balsamroot. I got about halfway up the slope, sat down on a rock that gave me a good view of the river, and wondered what I was doing there.

# 2.

ONCE, SHORTLY AFTER MARION AND I GOT MARRIED, WE WENT to a party at Mitch White's house. It was the only time I was ever there. He lived in the town of Dennis and it was a perfectly nice home, the kind you might see in suburban Boston, with a two-car garage and a manicured lawn. It was not the type of house that could be found on the Cape prior to the latter part of the twentieth century, but Mitch and his wife did not know that.

Mrs. White's name was Stephanie, a sharp-featured woman who wore pointy eyeglasses and was possibly hiding an impressive figure under a consistently dowdy wardrobe. Like her husband, she was mid-forties and seemed slightly bewildered by the rush of time. She knew things were supposed to be done a certain way and that was the way she did them. Utensils were wrapped in napkins and set out next to a stack of small plates at the end of the dining room table, which was covered with a tablecloth that sported images of lobsters and clams. The real things were not among the array of hors d'oeuvres that were carefully arranged on the table, but the tablecloth images paid homage to their place of origin.

Stephanie, despite her seeming lack of savoir faire, scared a lot of people. She had an edge to her, and while she did not say much, she tended to stare at other people rather intensely, as though she was waiting for some criticism that she knew was probably justified and for which she was already planning a response.

She and Mitch had a son, a broad-shouldered twelve-year-old with a toothy smile. One could only assume that Stephanie had large brothers, because the boy had a lot bigger frame than either of his parents. They dressed him up in a tie and one of Mitch's short-sleeved white shirts and had him serve nonalcoholic drinks on a tray. There were local wines, one red and one white, but they were on a card table in the backyard and partygoers had to go find those themselves and then pour them into plastic cups.

It was Marion's first introduction to the attorneys in my office and when they discovered where she worked she became the most popular person at the party. Later, she would tell me she couldn't understand why I didn't have more friends among my co-workers. Such fun people, she said, so convivial.

Shortly after 9:00, when Marion had drunk most of what was available to drink and pried herself away from those desperately craving a Boston job with a prestigious law firm, she sidled up to me and asked me to come with her. I had been thinking it was time to leave, but she wanted me to accompany her to the second floor. People had been going up and down the staircase all evening because there was only one bathroom on the first floor and I figured she wanted me to guard the door so she could use the facility upstairs. I didn't think that was necessary, but I had nothing else to do, so I went.

Once on the second floor, however, Marion wanted me to go into the bathroom with her. She looked up and down the hallway, determined no one was watching, and pulled me by the wrist. "Here," she said, locking the door behind us. The same look was in her eye that she had shown after she had fooled the cops in Old Town.

"What?" I said, hoping she didn't really mean it.

She turned, positioned herself over the sink and in front of the mirror. She did not touch the faucets, she just pointed her hands outward, placing one on each side of the sink, and grinned mischievously into the reflecting glass.

When I did not react, she leaned farther forward, moved both hands to her hips, and slowly raised her skirt all the way up until it exposed her ass. She was wearing a satin thong. A skimpy, cherry-colored thong. Her mouth opened, her teeth flashed in the glass. "You like?"

"Marion, we can't do that in here." But I was staring at the thong, the way it disappeared between the rounded mounds of flesh.

"Fucking in your boss's house," she whispered hoarsely, looking over her shoulder. "What could be better?"

"Put your skirt down, Marion." But I was still looking at her ass, still imagining where that tiny piece of cloth was going.

"Come on, Georgie—it will be fun." She leaned even farther forward. She began to grind her hips one way and then another.

"Jesus, Marion," I said, my heart beating, sweat forming on my lip. "Get dressed. I've got to work with these people." I put my hand on the door handle, looked into the mirror, and saw the disappointment on her face.

It was, I recalled as I sat on the hillside above the Middle Fork of the Salmon River, the beginning of the end for my wife and me.

## 3.

I EXPECTED WE WOULD TALK THAT FIRST NIGHT ON THE RIVER, but a makeshift bar had been set up and the booze kept flowing after dinner and everyone, clients and crew alike, sat around the campfire as a group, telling stories and staring into the flames. McFetridge was as friendly to me as he was to everyone else, but he stayed on the other side of the fire. A woman crew member named Bonnie sat next to him. They didn't talk, didn't touch, but I sensed an air of possession on her part in the way she positioned herself, the way she looked at him.

Bonnie was five-feet-ten and sturdily built, with long, dark hair and a muscular stomach, which she made constantly visible: a bikini top in the morning, a cutoff T-shirt in the evening. In the outside world she might have been a landscaper, a physical education teacher, a UPS driver. Here, there was no doubt she was the belle of the river.

THE NEXT DAY I was told I was in Bonnie's boat. There was a rough stretch of rapids, McFetridge said, and she was going to need some strong paddlers. As before, the water was running swiftly, and in the morning I was never sure if she really needed me or not. But I sat in the key paddling seat, right front, and when she told me to go forward, I went forward; when she told me to backpaddle, I backpaddled; and when she told me to dig, I dug, setting the pace for the five other paying guests.

We broke for lunch and had elaborate sandwiches that we put together from an extensive smorgasbord of meats and cheeses and condiments, chased down by cans of beer, and then in the afternoon we hit the rapids. There was an oar boat ahead of us being manned by one of the paid crew, then our boat went next. We watched the oar boat bounce around and oohed and ahhed as it readied itself. Bonnie said to go forward, and suddenly we were skimming downstream twice as fast as we ever had before.

Bonnie shouted to paddle hard and we did, or at least I did, as a four-foot wave smacked the front of the boat and washed over us. She screamed, "Left back!" and the three of us on my side stroked forward while those on the left were supposed to backpaddle. Something went wrong. We turned too sharply and took a wave broadside. "Right back!" she screamed, and I planted the oar on my hip and pulled backward with all my might. The bow swung and all of a sudden the other side went vertical and one of the paddlers went flying over the gunwale as the raft shuddered to a halt, caught on a huge sloping rock just beneath the surface. "High side!" Bonnie yelled, as water poured in on us and the two of us remaining on the right abandoned any effort to do anything other than scramble up to where the others were. The raft shifted, the stern went clockwise, and we shot off backward, dropping almost straight down, Bonnie frantically pulling at the oars, her head turned about one hundred eighty degrees over her shoulder, searching for her lost rafter, her voice beseeching everyone to get back to their stations.

We hit something hard and it jarred all five paddlers into the middle of the boat as another huge wave hit us like a car crash. I crawled back to my position in the front and tried to paddle, tried to get a rhythm, but I seemed to be the only one doing it. Wave after wave rolled into and under us and in between swells my paddle was grabbing nothing but air. We were up for an instant and then plummeted down into a depression as suddenly as if we were on a roller coaster and once again the left side caught and snapped straight upright. There was a cry behind me and first one paddler and then another flew out of the boat. "Grab them," yelled Bonnie, but they were gone. It was all I could do to hold on myself as someone from the left side smacked into me and went overboard. There was a scream of panic and a fifth rafter went out as the boat continued to wobble on its side. It was a man, the only other good paddler, the one who had been in the left front. I reached for his life vest, but the water wrenched it out of my fingers the moment I touched it. I threw my head back and looked for Bonnie to tell me what to do. It was just her and me. She was still holding on to the oars, even though only one of them was in the water, and she was looking directly at me without the slightest indication she knew what came next.

## 4.

IN MIDAFTERNOON WE FLOATED INTO CAMP NEAR LOON CREEK. The five people who had gone swimming weren't sure they wanted to go on. McFetridge had his hands full, trying to convince them how difficult it would be to get them off the river.

I watched from afar, impressed with the way McFetridge was handling the situation, not denigrating the guests' fears but trying to assuage them, make them seem unreasonable without being unfounded. It must have been hard for him; McFetridge had never been a sensitive guy.

The rafters who had not done the inadvertent swim had set off on a two-and-a-half-mile hike to some hot springs. McFetridge, when he was done wheedling, cajoling, promising, looked up and saw I was there, waiting for him. After a while, he made it over to me, shaking his head, speaking quietly. "I guess now you see why I wanted you in Bonnie's boat."

"Because you wanted to see me drown?"

McFetridge had not expected such words to come out of my mouth. "Bonnie's a damn good rafter," he said. "Things just got away from her on that one. It happens."

"She been guiding long?"

He looked as though he was thinking of lying and then changed his mind. "It's her first time. Although I'd rather the others not know that."

"She your girlfriend?"

McFetridge hesitated. "I guess. Things are kind of different out here." He glanced back at the distraught rafters, his excuse for getting away. They were sitting up now, speaking quietly to one another. The man who had been positioned across from me and his wife were leaning forehead to forehead, and every now and then the two of them glanced up. From what I could tell, they were glancing at me. As if I were somehow to blame because they went out of the boat. As if I were at fault for not going out.

The husband seemed to be doing his best to convince his wife of something and she was resisting. In my married experience, it was usually the other way around. But I recognized the dynamics.

"We really should talk, Paul," I said.

He sighed and cast one more longing look back at the unhappy guests. "If we're gonna do that," he said, "I'd rather not do it around camp. Most of the people will be coming back from the hot springs in a little while so they can get ready for dinner. So here's what I'm thinking. I've got to finish up with these folks, take care of them, convince them everything is going to be okay. You head on up there now and I'll join you as soon as I can. I'll get the kitchen crew to set aside a couple of plates for us. Okay?"

Can't talk here. Go 2.5 miles into the wilderness and wait for me there. Got it, George? Sure, Paul, no problem. I just walk straight until night and then turn left, is that it?

TO GET TO the hot spring, I walked along the Salmon on a narrow dirt path that bore the footprints of my colleagues and went up and down little rises and around bends that opened into groves of Douglas firs and lodgepole pines. Most of the way I was accompanied by a pair of yellow-and-red-and-black western tanagers, who constantly zoomed ahead of me and then dashed back as if they were border collies out for a walk. Then I went up a somewhat sharper incline and found myself in a big meadow filled with blue spruce–like bushes that stood about five feet high and were spaced far enough apart to make me feel I was at a Christmas tree farm. And it was then that I first heard the Loon, sounding vaguely like a great wind or crowd noise emanating from a giant stadium, growing louder with each step I took.

The trail bent to the right as I left the Salmon and headed along the tributary and the noise took on a crushing tone as if it were a waterfall. I would have had to raise my voice to be heard, if anybody had been around to hear.

There was a footbridge leading to what looked like a small ranch, which I figured must be some sort of fishermen's retreat. It had a wind-sock, indicating an airstrip, but I saw no indication of aircraft. As I passed the bridge my fellow rafters were coming back in the other direction. "Hey, George, you just getting here?" called one. "It's still a quarter-mile," shouted another, cupping his mouth. "You're going to miss cocktails!" cried a third.

I counted them: thirteen. I made fourteen. There were at least four who stayed in camp. Who else was there?

After what seemed to be considerably more than the allotted mileage I had been given, I encountered two more rafters coming up from a steep path that dropped down to the creek. "Right down there, George. You'll love it."

At the creek's edge, someone had built a stone box at least twenty feet long and six feet wide. A pipe projected from the hillside, and a constant stream of hot water flowed into one end of the rectangle. It was a lovely setting, with Loon Creek swirling by, and I had it all to myself.

I wondered if I should get in naked. It was just me and the great outdoors. But of course McFetridge would be along soon and it would be weird, me waiting for him like that, so I kept on my bathing suit. I sat in the hot water and I waited.

# 5.

I DON'T KNOW IF THE WORD "ELOPE" IS STILL IN USE. YOU DON'T hear it much anymore. But that is what I convinced Marion to do. She had friends, relatives, even co-workers she wanted to invite. I had my mother. I told Marion that it would be more fun, more romantic, just to run off.

We went to the Berkshires, stayed at the Red Lion Inn in Stockbridge, which was fun but not particularly romantic. We saw the Boston Symphony at Tanglewood, saw the Alvin Ailey dance troupe at Jacob's Pillow, saw an obscure Tennessee Williams play at Williamstown. I talked her into renting bicycles with me, but her idea of riding was to stop at every art gallery and antiques shop, and so that did not work out particularly well.

We returned home and she did not leave her job. She was supposed to leave, but she had not yet secured anything on the Cape and there was a big project her firm had going, a class action, and they needed her. We moved into the house in Centerville, but she kept her apartment in Boston. It would just be for a little while, she said. A month or two. Three at the most.

Three grew into six, and six into a year. They gave her a big raise, she said. They promised she wouldn't have to work weekends.

Okay, I said, and a year grew into two before she told me she wasn't coming down anymore.

# 6.

IT MAY HAVE BEEN 6:00 WHEN I GOT TO THE HOT SPRING. IT definitely was closer to seven when I heard McFetridge, walking in river sandals, step down the path. He was carrying something over his shoulder that looked like a small canvas mailbag. He looked at me, looked at the creek, and placed the bag carefully on the ground. Something inside it clinked metallically as though two heavy objects had bumped against each other. He took off his T-shirt and sandals and stepped into the box in his rafting shorts.

"Hey."

"Hey."

"How those people doing?"

"They're going to stay."

"Good. You handled them well."

He cut me a quick look to see if I was serious. Then he glanced around as if he had never been in this place before. "Pretty nice, huh?"

"Awesome."

He laughed. "Wicked awesome. You're beginning to talk like a Cape Codder."

"I've been there awhile now."

Of course, I had also been *here* awhile. Forty-five minutes is a long time to sit in a box of hot water, even if the setting was as superb as this one. My skin was beginning to pucker. The water was no longer as warming as it had been.

McFetridge swirled his arms, leaned back, closed his eyes. "You said you called my mother," he said. "What was that all about?"

"Just wanted to know how you were doing."

"Bullshit."

I didn't look at him. I kept my eyes on the river.

"Look," he said, "my name's not on any letterhead, in any brochures, on any website. You'd have to go to a fuck of a lot of trouble to find me. But here you are, not even pretending it's a coincidence. So what's going on? That's what I'm asking."

"You remember a girl named Heidi Telford?"

I would wonder later if it was good to have come right out with it like I did. I had planned subterfuge, sneaking up on the subject, working around from college days to the Gregorys to the Cape, to the race, to the party, and then to the missing girl. *Hey, how about that girl with the golf club in her head? Remember her?* Somehow, sitting in a pool of water in the middle of the wilderness with a guy with whom I had shared houses, rooms, vacations, parties, countless bottles of beer, I ended up skipping all the preliminaries.

When McFetridge didn't answer I turned my head to look at him. He, too, was staring at the river and what I saw was a rather grizzled profile, causing me to wonder what had happened to the handsome preppie, the sophisticated master of country-club sports, the young man who at one time had known all the right people, all the right places in New York, Palm Beach, Cape Cod. As I watched, he sank beneath the water.

Perhaps he thought he could stay down forever. But I was still there when he surfaced. He spit water, gasped, blinked. "She's dead," he said.

I nodded.

"Why you asking me about her?"

"I've got the case." It wasn't quite true, but it was close enough.

"You told me you were a lawyer. Didn't tell me you were a D.A."

"Assistant."

"Senator get you the job?"

"Yeah. Pretty much."

He nodded, putting something together, not sharing it with me.

"What's that guy's name? Marshall? Marshall Black? White?"

"Mitchell White."

"Yeah, that's him. I always thought he was a nerd."

"Still is."

"Yeah. Used to be a staff member on the Senate Judiciary Committee in D.C. Figured he must have had something on somebody. What did you have, Georgie? Was it that girl down in Florida?"

I wondered if sitting in the water all that time had made my testicles shrink into nothing.

McFetridge waited for an answer.

"I guess."

"And now what? Senator sends you to check on me?" There was a sneer in his voice, the kind he might have used if we were brothers and he was talking about Mom.

"He didn't send me. Fact is, outside of meeting him that one time you introduced us at the party in Palm Beach, I've never even talked to the Senator."

McFetridge thought. He apparently had a lot to think about because it took him a long time. Then he said, "It was Chuck-Chuck, then, wasn't it?"

"Chuck Larson? Why do you say that?"

"You're in the circle now, Georgie. They obviously want to know if I'm still in it. Who better than you to find out?"

McFetridge went under the water again. He did not stay down so long this time, but he did come up wiping his eyes. "Senator gets you a job in the D.A.'s office. D.A. puts you to work on the Heidi Telford case, and Chuck-Chuck tells you to come talk to me." His mouth was set somewhere between a smile and a smirk. "Well, you can tell them I'm good, Georgie. Tell 'em all I'm good, just living out west, river-guiding in the summer, ski-patrolling in the winter. *La dolce* fucking *vita,* baby." He went under the water again.

This time when he resurfaced I said, "Your name is on a list, along with Peter Martin, three of his cousins, and a guy named Jason."

"Stockover."

"That's right."

"That isn't news, Georgie. We were the crew on *The Paradox* that weekend. Cops wanted to know if we saw Heidi Telford."

"What did you tell them?"

"Never did. I was out here by the time they got around to asking. But I heard they talked to Peter, Jamie . . . Ned."

"If they had talked to you, what would you have said?"

Paul McFetridge put both his hands to his head and pulled his hair back. I was struck, once again, by how different he appeared now, how foreign he seemed to be from the guy I once knew. "Who's asking?" he said, and his question conveyed very much the same displacement I was feeling.

Somehow, in whatever half-assed planning I had undertaken for this journey, I had not prepared for this moment. And now two men who had been possibly best friends in a different place at a different time sat in a makeshift hot tub in the middle of the wilderness, miles from any other human being, trying to figure out who each other had become.

I looked at the Loon as it bubbled and frothed and raged past me. "I talked to Cory Gregory," I said. I wanted to let him know he wasn't the only one being singled out.

"What did she say?"

"Said there was some kind of party after you got back from Nantucket."

"She wasn't even there. She took off for school."

"That's what she told me."

"So that's it, then. She doesn't know anything, none of the rest of us know anything."

Except he did. He knew that Heidi Telford was dead.

The silence became palpable. I wondered if it was possible for the two of us just to stay in that little pool and never move on, never exchange another bit of information about the Gregorys and Heidi Telford and what the two of us were doing in Idaho twelve years after we had last spoken, hugged our goodbyes. I wondered if we could start talking about Quaker basketball, Fiji Island parties, whether Ellis had ever gotten into medical school.

"Do you know something different, Georgie?" he said at last. "Is that why you're here?"

"Apparently Peter's been linked up with Heidi that day."

"Linked up how?"

"Linked up like maybe inviting her to a party at the Gregory house." I was surprised by my courage in saying what I didn't know to be a fact, surprised by my cowardice in using the word "maybe."

McFetridge could have been considering the many different possibilities for using that word. He was trying to get me to look at him, trying to read my eyes. "So you're what, just doing your job, Georgie? Going around talking to possible leaks?"

I didn't answer.

"That sucks, Georgie."

"I know it does," said George Becket, who was not just doing his job, who didn't even have an assignment, who had come across the country to exploit a friendship, quiz his old roommate about his possible involvement in a murder.

The silence grew oppressive again. I wanted one of us to say something reassuring to the other. It didn't happen. I wondered if I could just get up, tell McFetridge it was good seeing him, slap hands, ask what the rafting was going to be like tomorrow.

"Look," he said after about three very long minutes had passed, "I think I'm gonna stay here a little longer. Why don't you go back now, catch your dinner, let those guys clean up."

The message was clear: Fraternity brothers or not, my company was no longer desired.

At this point, I didn't even desire it myself.

# 7.

*I* PUT ON MY SHIRT AND SHOES AND WENT UP THE HILL TO THE trail, hiked the trail along the creek, past the bridge that led to the fishermen's camp and the airstrip, and was so occupied with my thoughts that I barely even noticed the ground under my feet. I tried to remember what Paul McFetridge could ever have possibly liked about me. He was the guy who made things happen; I was the guy who tagged along. And now I had used everything he had ever given me, done for me, shown me, to put myself in a position where I was making him hate every moment he had ever been nice to me. And why was I doing it?

Nobody wanted me to investigate the murder of Heidi Telford, nobody except her father. I could have done as everyone else had. Told Bill Telford there was nothing new, told him I had other things to do. *Do you know how many drunk drivers there are out there endangering our streets and highways, Mr. Telford?* I was sorry his daughter was dead. Everybody was. But it wasn't up to me to investigate my friends just because they happened to be in the area at the time the girl was killed. Just because they happened to like girls and girls liked them and things came easily to them and people protected them.

I thought about the grin on the Senator's face as he looked back over his shoulder at us when he was dancing with his sister. So different from Jamie's grin, and yet so much the same. Each was the grin of a man who could do anything he wanted and be praised for it. The Senator, at least, had earned his pass, but what had Jamie ever done to deserve a grin like that? Was that what I hated most? Was that why I was doing what I was doing? *You have broken my heart . . . please go a-way!*

I reached the bend in the trail, the turn where it angled away from the Loon and headed upstream on the Salmon. There was a hill on my left, but I paid no attention to it. I was only aware of it because I had to circumnavigate it. Go around the hill and enter that field of small blue spruces that had reminded me of a Christmas tree lot. There was water on the path ahead of me, the runoff from a trickle of a stream coming down from the hill. The trees to the left of the trail seemed slightly smaller, the ground slightly more sloped than to the right, where the field of spruces went all the way to a ridge and then dropped precipitously to the river. I was vaguely aware of all these things simply because there was water ahead of me on the trail and a part of my brain was wondering where it came from and why it seemed to gather where it did, and while I was wondering about the water and thinking about the Senator's grin there was an enormous bite taken out of the ground near my foot and an almost simultaneous cracking sound.

How does one's body know it's being shot at before it even registers in the mind? All of a sudden I was diving into the spruces.

Something whizzed by my shoulder, whizzed through tree branches. Did it come at the same time as the second crack? It made no difference. I was already facedown. I was on my chest, crawling on my elbows, trying to get as deep into the little spruces as I could, cursing them for being so far apart, for having so much space between them. Spruce needles, rocks, sharp leaves, all dug into my skin as I sprint-crawled over the ground. None of it mattered because there was a third crack and I was absolutely certain I was never going to be able to get away. I was the only thing moving in a field the size of a football stadium, trying to get protection from skinny tree trunks and even skinnier branches. I needed to get back to my feet, I needed to run, I needed to zigzag, to get all the way to the ridge and then jump as far out as I possibly could.

I pushed to my hands and knees and took off with my legs driving and my upper body parallel to the ground. I made it to the first tree to my right, cut sharply to one on my left, cut back to the right, and then dove into the dirt and rolled. I was on my feet again, trying to outsmart the shooter as I went from side to side, using no pattern but what appeared in front of me as I ran, my heart pounding, my breath searing my lungs. I was yelling my name as I dove, tumbled, got up again. Except I wasn't yelling. That wasn't me. Somebody else was yelling. And coming after me. Coming hard and fast in my direction.

I looked toward the river. It was still thirty yards before I could get to the ridge, before I could jump, and I saw now how high that jump was going to be. I looked back. There was a flash of color, a ball of hair, and I realized it was McFetridge. Coming to kill me. He couldn't run and shoot at the same time. Not accurately. So I made the dash. I didn't bother going from tree to tree anymore, I just bolted to the ridge and launched myself off it in full stride.

I was probably less than a second in the air before I realized the mistake I had made.

# 8.

"GOTCHA, MAN. I GOTCHA."

The voice was McFetridge's. It was straining, but it was comforting, too. It kept saying the same thing over and over.

I opened my eyes. The trees above me were at a funny angle. They were growing out of my feet. It took me a moment to realize I was looking at their tops, from the bottoms up. Blood was in my head. But it wasn't loose blood. Not wet blood. I blinked and listened to McFetridge cooing to me. I listened to him grunt, curse, reassure me all over again, and I realized I was upside down. I was on a steep slope and my head was lower than my feet. But where were my arms? Where were my hands? What was holding me?

I remembered now. I remembered jumping, seeing I wasn't going to reach the water, trying to find a place to land. I had hit feetfirst and then pitched forward, head over heels. I had gone back into the air, seen the boulders below me as I flipped, and grabbed for whatever I could. And now I was lying upside down, not feeling anything in my limbs. Except I could feel my feet. I just didn't want to move them because they were caught on something, holding me in place.

"Hang on there, buddy. I gotcha. I gotcha. I'm almost there."

I could sense McFetridge more than I could see him. He seemed to be swinging from one handhold to another. I concentrated very hard on moving my left arm. It moved and I had a rush of exultation. I tried my right arm and it moved as well.

"I'm okay," I said. I meant it only in terms of how bad I might have been, but it was enough.

McFetridge stopped his descent. I could hear him breathing hard. I could hear despair. Why despair? Because he hadn't killed me right away? Or because I was broken?

How broken could I be? I could feel my arms. I could feel my feet. If I could feel my feet and I couldn't move them, what did that mean? I began to hyperventilate. Noises were coming out of my chest. They weren't noises I had ever made before. They weren't noises I had ever heard any human being make before.

"It's okay, buddy, I'm gonna get you."

He was going to get me.

"You sonofabitch," I said, because I was scared, because I did not want him to see how scared I was. "Come near me and I'll fucking kill you." I did not explain how I was going to do that and McFetridge wasn't listening anyway.

"Wait, wait, wait, buddy, don't move!"

But I wasn't moving, was I? If I couldn't move my legs that meant I couldn't dig them into anything. Which meant I would slide. Plummet. Go headfirst into the boulders, ricochet into the water and get carried downstream. I lay very still for a moment, trying to get my thoughts under control.

"Look," I said, "if I sit up, am I going to dislodge anything?"

"I got nothing to haul you up with," he said, which wasn't really an answer.

I tried again. "If I swing my legs around, am I going to be all right?"

"Do it slowly. Move them one at a time, just a little to your right. You're on about a forty-five-degree pitch, Georgie."

Except I couldn't move my legs. Unless, possibly, I swung them from my hips. I pictured it in my mind. A right angle—forty-five degrees was half a right angle. I could swing my legs as a unit.

I groped with my left hand and found something long and thin and secure—a shoot off a tree root, in all likelihood—and I held it as hard as I could. I dug my right hand into the dirt and it gave way, sending a mini-avalanche of stones tumbling down toward the water, scaring me all over again, making me think the whole hillside was going to collapse beneath me.

"Move it up higher, Georgie. Move your hand a little higher. Reach, buddy. Reach!"

My fingers closed around a branch of some kind, something that bit into my palm but was anchored to the ground. I started the swing. My legs moved, but not together.

Slowly I worked each one around like the hands on a clock.

"That's it. Keep going, guy. Keep it up." McFetridge's voice had dropped to an encouraging whisper. "You're almost there."

The idea was to spin my body, get my head uphill from my feet.

I inched around until I could see him. He was hanging off a bush himself, hanging with his right arm, reaching down toward me with his left. If that bush pulled out of the hillside, he was gone. All of his weight would propel him like a missile into the boulders below.

Was McFetridge risking his life to save me? But he wasn't saving me, was he? He was there and I was here, and at least ten feet of sloped earth was between us.

I had to let go of the root if I was going to get to him. Did I want to do that? He wanted me to. Why? Because he knew I couldn't.

I tore into the dirt with my fingers. I balanced one foot on a rock that I had to trust would stay in place. I pushed the side of my face into the hill and tried to dig it in as though somehow my skin would create some adhesion, and I spun slowly and deliberately, and all the time McFetridge kept calling to me, telling me I was almost there, that I was going to make it.

He reached, I reached. I touched his fingers. Our hands crept over each other and I grabbed his wrist.

# 9.

THE TWO OF US LAY ON OUR BACKS. STARING STRAIGHT UP AT THE sky. What we could see of it. In between the branches there were swabs of gray growing ever darker. Night had not completely fallen, but it was close. We could not stay here any longer, but we could not move, either. At least I couldn't.

"Why did you jump, George?"

"Because you were shooting at me."

"Me? Shoot at you? With what?"

"What did you have in that bag you brought? I heard metal clunking around."

"What did you think it was, a gun? I brought fucking beers, you asshole. Then you pissed me off so much I forgot all about them."

"So where are they now?"

"Where? I imagine they're where I dropped them when I heard the shots."

"You heard the shots? All the way back in the hot tub?" I meant to sound cynical. I was probably too spent to pull it off.

"I was on the trail, coming after you. Because I was sitting there after you left, thinking why the fuck would you do this to me? Be the family's little errand boy, run out here to check on me, see if I'm still being loyal? And I'm saying to myself, hey, you're loyal to anyone, it should be to me, for fuck sake."

Loyal to him. Guy who hadn't so much as called me since the day we graduated from college.

"And then I keep thinking about it and I realize, wait, you're not really accusing me, so why am I acting the way I am? I mean, it wasn't as though you lied to me or anything about what you're doing here. And suddenly it all started making sense."

It didn't to me, whatever he was saying, and I didn't have the energy to piece it together. I was thinking about the beers, how much I would like to have one.

"I mean," he said, apparently wanting some reassurance, "it's like that Florida thing, right?"

What was? Did I get that question out? I must have, because he was answering it.

"Somebody makes a claim against them, it's not as though the family's going to hire a hit man or anything. That's not the way they do things. They got a problem, they put someone in the right place to take care of it."

He meant me. Being put in the right place.

"It's just that this one, you know, I thought this one had been taken care of a long time ago. And then I'm thinking, okay, so something must have happened besides that stupid list of crew members the girl's father was waving around a few years back. Something's come up and Mitchell White has got to act like he's doing something about it. So he sends you. I mean, that's the reason the family's got you working where you are, in case a problem like this came up."

I lay even stiller than before. A man in the dirt in a faraway place, having just been told his function in life.

"Which means I shouldn't be treating you like you're the fucking enemy or something."

I'm not the enemy. I'm the Gregorys' errand boy. I'm one of the beagles they keep in their kennel.

"So that's what got me out of the tub, running after you." He shifted his position, lifting himself up onto his forearm.

"I was just trying to apologize for getting defensive like I did. Because all you're doing is what you're supposed to be doing. Talk to Cory, talk to the boys, to Jason, to me. Check things off. Everything's fine, everybody goes on about their business. I didn't have to get all pissed off like I did. That's what I was coming to tell you."

He was telling me something else, as well, although he didn't seem to realize it. He knew something; he assumed I knew it, too. If I asked him what it was, it would show I didn't really know it, and then he wouldn't tell me. It was all very complicated, staring up at the sky, still feeling blessed just to be alive.

"You know where Jason is?" I asked.

"No. Doesn't Chuck-Chuck?"

"He seems to have disappeared." I felt that was a safe thing to say, given how long it would take for McFetridge to prove me wrong. Assuming I was wrong.

"I haven't seen him since that weekend. I went back to New York. He went, I don't know, wherever he came from. Connecticut, maybe. I didn't really know him that well. He was Ned's friend, and Ned was, you know, tied up that night with his au pair. The only reason Jason and I ended up together was that we were the ones who met those girls."

Girls. The boys on the boat met girls on the night Heidi died. I tried to formulate a question that wouldn't get me a question back. "You ever hear from them again? Those girls?"

McFetridge snorted. "We never even got their last names. Candy was the one I was with. Candy, Taffy, Cindy. Something like that. All they cared about was they got to go to the Gregory compound. I don't think we had any in-depth discussions."

"Yeah," I said. I tried to snort, too. Dirt came out of my nose. It landed somewhere on my shirt.

"It was like, 'Okay, here's the Senator's house. There's his brother's house. His sister's house. Wanna take a walk down the beach?'" McFetridge was quiet for a moment. "He got the better-looking one, I remember that. She was all over him, so I just took the other one, the one with the big tits. Kind of a squishy ass, I think, but she was great doing it in the sand. Cynthia, I'm pretty sure her name was."

Age and responsibility, I saw, had not completely changed Paul McFetridge.

Out loud, I said, "You don't think she could be the one who's talking, do you?"

"Oh, man. She didn't know anything. Jason and I screwed her and her friend on the beach and then I was hoping we were gonna switch, but Jason kind of liked his, so that didn't happen. In the end we just brought them back to the house and when we got there nobody was around. We knew where Ned was, of course, but the rest were just gone. So we said, 'Whoops, party's over. Gotta go.'"

"And they left?"

"They had their own car, so it wasn't hard getting rid of them. They were going back to Boston anyhow, I think. Roslindale, does that sound right? I really don't remember. That might have been somebody else. I mean, these were just a couple of skanks down for the weekend to party. They ran into us and extended the partying a little longer. That's all."

"But, you know, Heidi's picture was in the paper, wasn't it?" This was pure guesswork on my part. I had never checked.

"Was it? I don't know. I mean, I didn't even know there was a problem until we weren't able to get on the golf course the next morning. But I didn't want to play anyhow. That was just something Peter was insisting on, fuckin' seven o'clock tee time. So we didn't get on, and I just said, 'Screw it, I'm outta here,' and I left. And as for those girls, they had such stars in their eyes, you'd think they were in Hollywood or something. I don't know what they saw, who they saw, I just know they never came forward."

McFetridge was silent for a moment. "Unless, like you say, they're doing it now."

"I didn't say that. I was just asking."

McFetridge thought about it. "You know, Chuck-Chuck's gotta know who they are."

"Why do you say that?"

"Because the guard, every car that goes in the compound, he's got to write down the license number. So if he thinks that's who's doing the talking ... though I can't imagine after all this time ..." He stopped. "You don't know anything about that, huh?"

"No."

He said "Huh" again.

I lay very still and abandoned plans to ask anything else. I could hear McFetridge moving, getting up on his side. I sensed him looking at me. "What *do* you know, George?" he said.

"I know somebody was just trying to kill me, Paul. That's what I fucking know. Who do you suppose that was?"

"This is Idaho, man. It's filled with wackos, isolationists, crazies living out in the woods."

"You guys run a commercial rafting operation. You send people to walk miles up that trail. Up and back. And you've got crazies shooting guns at them?"

"It's never happened before."

"So why me, Paul? Why's someone trying to kill me?" It felt good to be aggressive. It gave me a use for the leftover adrenaline.

"I doubt he was trying to kill you. More likely just trying to scare you. Scare all of us. I don't know. Maybe he's got a pot farm or something he doesn't want us to find. But I'm guessing, the way rifles are these days and the way some of these gun nuts are, that if he really wanted to hit you, he could have . . . especially if he was on that hill and you being in an open field and all."

Was I in an open field? I was in the spruces, the five-foot spruces, and the hill was behind me, where McFetridge was. McFetridge who had had the bag that clinked.

"What I'd like," I said, "is to get one of those beers you dropped."

"Go back there after you know somebody's been shooting at you? I don't think so."

"You said yourself he wasn't trying to kill me. If he was, he would have followed us here. Don't you think?"

McFetridge certainly acted as though he was thinking. "You're right. Let's get the hell out of here. Get back to camp. We can get beer there." He pushed himself to his feet.

I did the same. "You going to tell the others?"

It was now dark enough that I could barely see his features, but I was pretty sure he was biting his lip. "I'm going to tell the crew because I don't think we're going to be coming up here anymore. But I'd appreciate it if you didn't tell the other rafters, Georgie. I mean, all it's gonna do is scare them."

"Like *Deliverance*."

"Yeah, like that."

"Anything else you don't want me to tell people?"

"Yeah, don't tell 'em anything that's going to make them think it's not wonderful living out here in the fuckin' woods."

## 1.

Barbara Belbonnet said I looked tanned, relaxed. "Mellow," she said.

I had nearly drowned, nearly been shot, nearly fallen to my death, and she thought I looked mellow. I dropped my head, said nothing.

"Was it wonderful?" she asked.

She was wearing a copper-colored silk blouse that showed a little décolletage, and form-fitting tan slacks, the likes of which I had never before seen her wear in the office. She was standing at my desk, which she almost never did. She had no pockets and her cell phone was not in her hands, which made me wonder what was going on, why she was not fretting about her kids.

"Yeah," I said, "it was great."

She waited for details. She was smiling at me. She seemed to have done something to her hair, highlighted it, made it even more blond; and to her eyes, made her lashes longer, made the whites stand out and the color of her irises more vibrant. Maybe that was why she was standing so close, so I could see what she had done.

"That is something I would love to try," she said. "I'd like to go down the Colorado."

I gave her a half-smile that left her free to imagine eagles flying overhead, happy prospectors waving from the shore.

"There's whitewater rafting up in New Hampshire, you know. We should organize something, get some of the people from the office to go."

Barbara, as far as I knew, had no more friends in the office than I did. But I nodded and said we should look into that.

"Or maybe get some of your crazy buddies there on the defense side. They'd probably be more fun."

I wondered what she knew about my crazy buddies. I never talked about those guys, never saw Barbara when I was out drinking with them. Before I could ask what she meant, she said, "One of them called while you were gone. Buzzy Daizell." She put an extra twist in her voice when she said his name. "He said he hadn't been able to reach you on your cell, so I told him where you were. I hope that's all right."

Her face scrunched a little, her eyes narrowing, as though she really was worried she might have done the wrong thing. It was, surprisingly, a rather becoming look; it made the imposing, intimidating Barbara Belbonnet girlish and almost vulnerable. "He wanted you to call him as soon as you got back."

I thanked her and told her I would get to Buzzy later. I had a calendar call at 9:00 and a half-dozen files that I had to review before then.

IN FACT, I FORGOT. Buzzy had to track me down, call me again at the end of the day. He said he needed to see me. He sounded anxious.

When I told him I had just gotten back from vacation he suggested we catch a Cape League baseball game. "Hyannis is playing Cotuit at home tonight and the Kettleers supposedly have this great catcher. Next sure thing for the majors."

I had not been to a Cape League game in years, didn't care about Cotuit's catcher or Cotuit or even the local team, but I agreed to go simply because he seemed so intent on getting me to do so.

"I'll bring a couple of lawn chairs and a couple of beers," he said. "We'll sit on the grass down the left-field line."

Away from the crowd in the stands, in other words. Buzzy clearly had something to tell me.

BUZZY DAIZELL WAS a multigeneration Cape Codder. He was an off-shoot of the ubiquitous Bangs family and could trace his lineage all the way back to Edward Banges, who arrived in Plymouth from England on the ship *Anne* in 1623 and moved onto the Cape in 1645. This was generally the source of much humor to Buzzy, who got to refer to virtually everyone else as a "wash-ashore."

He had graduated from Barnstable High School, gone off to Bates College, where he had not done particularly well, gone to the same law school as I did in Boston, and then ended up back on the Cape because he was not in high demand by the big-city firms after not doing particularly well in law school, either. Because his family knew so many people, he was able to open his own practice and make a go of it. Because of the nature of the natives, particularly those with whom he had tended to socialize, he specialized in criminal law.

I had tried three drunk-driving cases against him and he had lost them all. That did not make him a bad trial lawyer. I was supposed to win those cases. What set Buzzy apart was his willingness to try most anything that came along. He thought it was fun.

He was not, however, having fun with me at the Hyannis Mets baseball game. He wanted me to drink the beer that he gave me. Then he wanted me to drink another. He put away three to my two before he said, "I gotta talk to you about something."

"I figured that."

"It's really kind of hush-hush. Confidential."

"Does it have anything to do with work?"

"Sort of."

"Then maybe you better not tell me."

"It has to do with Mitchell White."

I gave that some thought. I rather liked hearing stories about Mitchell White, although there generally were not many to tell. Mostly people just made fun of him.

"All right," I said, "tell me."

The crowd roared off to our right. One of the Hyannis players had just stroked a double into the gap between center and right. The game was scoreless and the double was the first exciting thing that had happened since I arrived.

Buzzy waited till the noise died down. "I've been asked to run against him."

I had been about to sip the last of my second beer. Instead I lowered the can. "Nobody runs against a sitting D.A."

"Yeah, I know, but it's not as though Mitch has a real constituency."

What Mitch had was the Gregorys. What the Gregorys had was anybody and everybody. I asked Buzzy what was in it for him.

"A real job," he said, "with a real paycheck. A chance to maybe put my life together. I'm pushing forty, you know."

He was, I was pretty sure, thirty-eight. Buzzy was a good-looking guy with what might be called *joie de vivre*. It made him a great person to share a night on the town. I wasn't sure that qualified him for being a district attorney.

"What about some of the cases you've handled, some of the clients you've represented?" I asked.

"The people who want me to run, they think I can use that as a positive. I know the way the other side works."

"Fox in the henhouse and all that stuff," I said back.

"Well, it's not as though I have a political agenda about getting *the man* or freeing the people or anything like that. It's just the business that comes to me. And I do know criminal law."

A long fly ball to left caused the guy on second to tag up and sprint to third. The left fielder had a strong arm and made a perfect throw, nailing the runner just before his foot reached the bag. The third-base coach didn't like the call and began arguing with the ump. A lot of people came running down to the fence to support the coach, tell the umpire how blind he was. Buzzy and I had to wait until the fans finished expressing their opinions and moved away.

"Look, Buzzy, Mitch is one of those guys that just kind of goes along, and most people in the community couldn't even tell you who he is. If he's pissed somebody off, I don't know who that could be. So

I'm just kind of wondering who's come to you, who has decided it's time to take on and kick out a sitting D.A.? And more important, why?"

"If I tell you, I've got to swear you to secrecy." He didn't look at me when he said this. Most people, they swear you, they look you right in the eyes.

"Swear," I said.

"It's the Macs," he said.

I watched his face. He still didn't look at me. His Adam's apple went up and down. "You want another beer?" he asked, and busied himself in his cooler getting one for each of us.

"Okay," I said, taking the cold can so that now I had a beer in each hand, "what's their deal? Why do they want him out?"

"They're not telling me. They just say it's time for a change and they'd like to get a local guy in there. They've got plenty of financial backing, they say."

I finished the old beer, cracked the new one, sampled it. "If you're asking me," I said, "and I assume you are, I wouldn't do it. There's something funny about this, at least the way you describe it. I mean, the Macs are small businessmen. What do they care who the district attorney is?"

"Don't know. I just know it's an opportunity for me."

I decided to give him advice. I decided that was what he really wanted from me. "Listen, Buz, running for D.A. is not like running for any other office. For a D.A. to get voted out he has to have really screwed up in some way. Nobody in our office likes Mitch, but they're not going to come out against him."

"I've already agreed to do it, George."

The batter at the plate got hit by the pitch. He was gesturing at the pitcher and the pitcher was stomping down off the mound, gesturing back. The about-to-be-famous Cotuit catcher got between the batter and the pitcher. The umpire tried to get between the catcher and the batter. Players, coaches, and managers poured from both dugouts, and the crowd loved it.

"You know," I said, "my job sucks bad enough already. I really can't do anything to make it worse. I mean, I'll give you money, vote for you, obviously. But I'm not going to say anything quotable or let you use my name on your literature. So, great, you've got me and the Macs and your high-school buddies showing up at a fund-raiser for you, and Mitch has Senator Gregory showing up at a fund-raiser for him—who do you think's going to get the short end of the stick on that one?"

Buzzy shifted in his lawn chair as if to get a better look at the brouhaha on the diamond. But he was not really watching it. "What I wanted to speak to you about, what I asked you to meet me for, was to see if I could get you to not make my campaign any worse."

"By what, holding a press conference, telling everyone what a lush you are?" I was making a joke. I didn't really know anything bad about Buzzy. He drank no more than anyone else, from what I could see.

Only he drank now. He drained the whole can of beer in one long gurgle.

Out on the field, the umpire was having a high old time throwing people out of the game. He would point at someone, then turn half a turn away and sling his arm up in the air as if he were casting a fly rod. Each time he did it the crowd cheered or booed.

"These guys are saying, and it's mostly McBeth, he's like the spokesperson, that if there is anything bad in my background . . . anything unsavory, then Mitch White's going to come up with it. Maybe not Mitch so much, but the people who want him around, the people who support him."

I waited to see if he would say it. When he didn't, I did. "The Gregorys."

"Yeah."

"So you're going to throw in with some anti-Gregory faction. What are they, Republicans?"

"Fuck no, and that's not what I said."

Buzzy's anger startled both of us. He dragged his hand across his mouth to calm himself down. The combative baseball players and coaches were still milling around. Cotuit was going to have to get a new pitcher. The game was going to be delayed for a while.

"Look, George, I want this job. I seriously would like to get my life together and be somebody, get on track for something. And these guys, they came to me. I didn't go to them. They say they want me because of my family, my roots. They say I'm personable. The other thing they're saying is that I'm telegenic, although I don't know what good that does me in this race. They just want to know if there's any shit in my past, anything that the Gregorys could dig up that would, you know, make me look . . . less than honorable."

"Like representing Colombians?"

"They don't have any problem with that. I was just doing my job there."

"Getting paid in cash."

"Yeah, well, I had enough other people paying by check. I've never had any problems with the tax folks."

"So that's not what you're concerned about."

"No."

"It's something personal."

"Yeah."

"Something you think I know about."

The Adam's apple went up and down again. It had now been several minutes since Buzzy looked my way. "Something other people know about. Something I don't think you do."

There was a little fluttering in my heart, a cold bolt that went down my spine. The things that went through my mind were all things that should not have affected Buzzy Daizell in any possible way.

The words burst out of his mouth as if he could not wait any longer. "I had an affair with Marion," he said.

I looked at the top of my beer can and wondered if I should drink some more. "We've been divorced for some time," I said.

"It was while you were married."

"I see." I could trace my finger all around the top of the beer can, let it follow the inside of the rim, fall into the hole, pop out again.

"Sometimes I would go up to see her in Boston. Sometimes, toward the end of when you guys were together, when she didn't come down on weekends, it was because she was seeing me up there."

"In her apartment."

"Yeah."

"When she said she had to work."

"Yeah."

"Well," I said, "things were coming apart anyhow." Except I wanted to crush the beer can.

Order had been restored on the field. The new pitcher was heading to the mound to start his warmup tosses. A pinch runner was trotting out to first base.

"This is like full disclosure, George. I mean, if this stuff comes out, you're going to hear about it and, well, I didn't want that to be the way it was."

"You didn't want the *Cape Cod Times* calling me up and asking for a comment, huh?"

"I don't know."

"I mean, you're not asking my permission or anything. You're telling me you're going to do this and I should be prepared, is that it?"

"Well, you might say you were separated."

"You want me to cover up the fact that you were having sex with my wife by saying we were separated?"

"She told me things weren't going particularly well for you guys in that department."

I may have stopped breathing for an instant. There was a constriction in my chest and my entire body went very cold and then very hot. I wondered if my friend had just offered me an excuse or issued a quid pro quo.

"Except we weren't separated."

"Not all the time," he said. "Except, you know, for her being in Boston—"

I tried to absorb all this information. Tried to parse it out. I kept coming back to the part where she told him things weren't going particularly well between us sexually. "Anything happen between you two when I was around?"

"One time."

"When?"

"You guys had us over for dinner."

" 'Us?' "

"Me. Jimmy Shelley and his girlfriend. Alphonse and his wife, Caroline." He took a breath. "You were out in the backyard barbequing and we did something in the bathroom."

"Who did?"

"Marion and me."

I didn't know if I wanted to ask another question. I didn't know if I wanted to sit there one instant longer. Everything around me was a blur. The only thing I could sense distinctly was the spinning blade churning its way through my stomach.

"Well, *she* did something, really."

"Jesus fucking Christ, Buzzy."

People hanging over the fence turned to look in our direction. Buzzy covered his face. He may have done it because he was ashamed, or maybe because he didn't want the people to recognize him, remember this blasphemy when he started his campaign.

"Did they know? Jimmy and Alphonse?"

"Jimmy, man." Buzzy spoke from behind his hands. "He saw her follow me in. He opened the door. He saw it."

I leaned over. I tipped the lawn chair so it was up on one side, nearly touching his with the other. I wanted to hurt him. I wanted him to hear how rotten this really was. "You're telling me Jimmy saw you screwing my wife while I was barbequing?"

"We weren't screwing."

I waited, hoping I had misunderstood his confession, hoping this was not going to be so bad as I had thought.

"She was . . . you know . . . down on her knees."

"Jimmy Shelley saw my wife giving you a blow job?"

"It wasn't my idea, Georgie," he yelped, his face still hidden. "I think she liked the risk, man. I think she liked the possibility she might get caught."

I slowly eased my chair back into its former position. I had gone from wanting to hurt Buzzy to wanting to say something in my own defense, something to overcome my inadequacies. "She usually liked doing other things in bathrooms."

Sensing a reprieve, Buzzy lowered his hands. "Tell me about it, man. She wanted to do it in the restroom of the fucking Locke-Ober restaurant one time."

I sat very still, thinking of Buzzy and Jimmy and probably Alphonse knowing what my wife had done. Not telling me. Just knowing. "Well, thanks for letting me know," I said softly.

"I'm sorry, Georgie."

I stood up then. Play had resumed on the field, but Buzzy was watching me, his face in total disarray, as if he had no idea what I was going to do, what he should do: stand up with me, beg for forgiveness, ask for another affirmation of loyalty from me, his cuckolded friend.

"Thank you for the beer," I said, and left him looking like one of those people who are always at the foot of the cross in Renaissance paintings, gazing up in total mystification, wondering what is to become of them.

# 2.

COULD NOT BLAME MARION FOR HAVING A MISIMPRESSION. THE first time I had sex with her was in the front seat of her Audi, the front passenger's seat, while we were parked at a curb on H Street in D.C. She was giving me a ride home even though I lived only a few blocks away because we had been at the library studying late for finals. We were giddy from effort and lack of sleep, and I am a little vague as to how it was that she happened to fall into my lap after I was seated. I know only that we started to kiss, then touch, then move about. I know there was a sense of danger, a need to hurry, and that she got one leg out of her jeans and underwear and straddled me as I partially reclined in the seat. It was dark and I enjoyed it. From the sounds she was making, she enjoyed it every bit as much as I did.

The second time was on the National Seashore, a public beach, where anybody walking in the dark could have come upon us. After that, she could well have thought I wasn't just kinky but an exhibitionist.

I am sure I was an incredible disappointment to her.

## 3.

CHUCK LARSON WAS WEARING A SPORT COAT WITH ENOUGH material to house a family in the Sudan. It would not have been an attractive sport coat even in a smaller size on a much slimmer man. It did, however, project a certain good cheer, with its faint yellow squares imposed on an olive-green background.

He was sitting on the couch in my living room. I had much nicer furniture than a bachelor should have, at least a bachelor like me. Marion had picked it out. Paid for it herself. Left it behind. Now Chuck was dwarfing it. His huge legs were spread apart, his hands clasped between his knees. He wanted to know how my visit with Paulie went.

I told him I was shot at.

Chuck's massive face crumpled. "By who?"

I shrugged. There was a certain amount of spite in that shrug.

"Paulie wouldn't have had anything to do with shooting anyone. Least of all you. You told me you used to be best buds."

"I didn't say it was McFetridge, Chuck." I let the silence build just to see if he would get uncomfortable. Chuck Larson was, after all, the one who had sent me to Idaho, directed me there, at least, and I still had no idea who had shot at me.

But the big man outplayed me. His expression stayed mournful for so long that I could not stand it anymore. "All I know is that it happened."

"Where?"

"On a path, when I was walking through the woods on my way back from a hot spring."

"And were there, like, other people around?"

"Only Paul. He came running up right after."

"And what did he say?"

"Said he couldn't believe it. It had never happened before."

"Oh." Chuck tilted his head back to give himself a full range of ceiling to survey. "Could you have, like, been somewhere you shouldn't have?" The marijuana-farm theory again. I wondered if they had talked, if Chuck Larson already knew what had taken place.

I could see only the underside of his chin, which was about the size of a dinner plate. I spoke to that. "I was just doing what McFetridge told all the rafters to do. Only I was alone and it was late and he was behind me and that's all I can tell you."

"Oh," Chuck said again. He continued to search the ceiling.

I was sitting in a recliner chair. High leg, country style, it was called. It did not match the couch. But the two items of furniture went together. The chair was "taupe"; the couch was "smoke."

Chuck's eyes came down with an idea. "You don't think he's gone crazy, living out in the woods and all?"

It was an interesting question, not because there was any possibility of truth to it, but because it indicated that Chuck was thinking McFetridge might actually have fired the shots.

"Chuck, I don't think he's gone crazy."

"All right, I'll drop it. It's just, you know, nobody in the family's heard from him in years."

"Not since he was here for the Figawi race."

Chuck spent a moment deciding how to react. He went for innocence. "Yeah. Did he say, like, why?"

"No."

Chuck was in a quandary. He needed information, but he also did not want it to appear that he was concerned about anything that had happened that last night McFetridge was at the Gregory compound. I wondered if he would examine the ceiling again.

"Did you get the feeling he was mad at the family?" That was his first foray.

"No."

"Well, to just disappear like that, never be in touch again, something must have happened." That was his second.

"I asked him what they did when they got back from Nantucket. And he told me he and Jason Stockover picked up a couple of girls and brought them over to the Gregorys'."

If a stranger came into the room he might have thought Chuck was in agony, that, at the very least, he had hemorrhoids. "Is this the party old Mr. Telford's been talking about?"

"He said they went down the beach behind the Senator's home. He and Jason and the two girls."

"One of life's two most overrated pleasures," Chuck declared. "Making love on the beach and reading in the bathtub." Immediately, he looked apologetic. "'Course, could be me. A guy my size doesn't always experience things the same way as other people." He pressed his hands down on his thighs as if he was going to stand up. "So, that was it? That was all he said? About a party, I mean."

I didn't tell him about the golf. I just nodded.

Now Chuck smiled in that way he had of making his whole face crinkle. The hemorrhoids were gone. The stranger who thought he had them might now have guessed he had just been given a new pickup truck, one with comfortable cushions. "Okay, then. You ready to report back to Mr. Telford that he's got to start focusing somewhere else?"

"I'd like to find those girls, talk to them."

Agony, happiness, apology, helpfulness, confusion. Chuck Larson had an expression for each of them. "Paulie give you their names?"

"He said you had them."

"Me?"

"Said they drove their own car and the Gregorys' security guy writes down the license-plate number of every car that enters the grounds. Said it's your job to know things like who is visiting. So, I'm thinking, why don't I go talk to them, see what they know?"

Chuck gave that suggestion a good deal of contemplation. "How about if I have somebody do that?"

"Well, Chuck, it's like this. You've got a couple of women who've never said anything for nine years because in all likelihood they don't realize they know anything. A private person shows up, an investigator, a friend of the family, whatever, starts asking questions about being at the Gregorys' house on a particular night when something bad happened in the area. You don't think that's running a risk as to who they're going to tell about this visit from the mysterious visitor? I mean, chances are they're married now, right? They're going to tell their husbands, husbands tell the boys at the bar, next thing you know it's in the tabloids."

Chuck's face was a portrait of worry.

"But me, I go up, show them my credential as an assistant district attorney for Cape and the Islands, tell them we are still looking into an unsolved event in our jurisdiction and it has just come to our attention that they were in Hyannis that night. Just want to know if they can tell me where they were, what they were doing, who they saw. I won't have to get into specifics. I'd just be speaking with the voice of authority."

Chuck Larson, for all his ability to get along with people, proved surprisingly easy to manipulate.

I wondered if that made me a worse person than I thought.

# 4.

ATTY, NOT CANDY. AS IN PEPPERMINT PATTY.

Patty Margolis of Margolis & Associates, CPAs, Center Street, West Roxbury, Massachusetts. She was not a CPA herself. That was her husband, Nick. She was the office manager, and a notary public.

I was there without a file, without a briefcase, without a familiar face. She thought I had come to get something notarized and gave me the welcoming smile that harried people bestow on customers whose business they really don't care about having.

She was in her early thirties, with a significant amount of black hair that was brushed in such a way as to add a few inches to her height. She was vaguely pretty, generously endowed on top, even more so on the bottom. I did not see her as McFetridge's kind of pickup, but her body fit the description he had given me.

I told her who I was and her eyes dimmed, even as she looked at my card. She asked what she could do for me, and I gave her the story about our ongoing investigation and her name just coming to our attention.

"That wasn't my name back then."

I had been expecting her to act perplexed, befuddled, confused. Why should she remember one particular night out of thirty-plus Memorial Days?

I said I realized she had gotten married, but that's why it had taken so long for us to locate her.

She looked behind her. There were two inner chambers with doors, a half-dozen open cubicles, a large photocopy machine. I saw no other people, but I had the sense they were there, behind the doors, inside the cubicles. She tapped my card on the reception desk. "Let's go outside," she said.

She walked around the reception desk, showing me a pair of not bad legs between wedge heels that were too high for the office and a skirt that was too short for someone with her figure. I followed her out the door to the sidewalk, where she squinted in the sunlight, studying the neighboring stores and businesses, before deciding that where she stood was as good a place as any. "All right," she said, turning on me, poking my card into my chest, "what's this all about? Why are you showing up at my office where my husband is?"

"Why?" I said. "Is there something you don't want him to know?"

She was more than up to dealing with a little cruelty. "You know damn well what me and Leanne were doing there or you wouldn't be asking me questions. Now, if you don't tell me who it was who told you, you can haul my ass into court and I still won't tell you a fucking thing. Get it?" And with that she squished the card into my chest and let it fall to the ground.

Ms. Margolis did not look even vaguely pretty now.

"A man named Paul McFetridge told me he met you that night."

"Fucked me on the beach and pushed me out the fucking door is what he did." This was a very angry woman. "And he didn't tell you because I never gave him anything but my first name."

"Ms. Margolis, who else has talked to you since then? About that night, I mean."

"I know goddamn well what you mean. And let me tell you, Mr. Junior District Attorney, I've got a deal, okay? So leave me the fuck alone or I'll call your boss and your next job will be selling newspapers at the T-station."

And with that, Patty Margolis left me on the sidewalk in front of Margolis & Associates, CPAs, Center Street, West Roxbury, Massachusetts.

# 5.

"IS THERE SOMETHING WRONG WITH YOU?" MITCHELL WHITE WANTED to know.

I said there wasn't, although in truth I could have spent the better part of an hour telling him the opposite.

"Who told you to go see that woman?"

"Chuck, Chuck Larson."

"Chuck, huh? Well, I can only imagine that he sent you there so you could learn for yourself there's no evidence to support the latest crap that Bill Telford's throwing around."

"So she went ahead and called you, huh?"

"Why would she call me?" Mitch demanded, his voice rising, his mustache flaring.

"Because you know I talked to her and I haven't told anyone."

This threw the district attorney into total discombobulation. He twisted sideways in his big rolling chair so he could put his left forearm on his ink blotter and look at me over his shoulder. "You know, this isn't your case, my friend. Your cases are operating under the influence and petty burglaries, and until you hear different that's all I want you working on."

"She told me she cut a deal."

"With whom?" Mitch White's little eyes popped behind his over-sized glasses. "Not with me."

"Oh, jeez, I knew that."

That seemed to temper him a bit.

"But that leaves open the question of whom she did cut a deal with and what kind of deal she cut." I felt a little bit like I had when I told Bonnie to throw the rope to the swimmers.

Mitch's eyeballs receded, but he kept me in his sight, not sure what I was going to spring on him next. I let him swirl in uncertainty for a moment, then said, "I'm thinking whoever it was had a reason for cutting that deal. I'm thinking the deal could have had something to do with seeing Heidi Telford that night."

"She say she saw her?"

"Nope." It was hard to tell if he believed me.

"What did she tell you?"

"Nothing. But she was angry I found her."

"She's not talking; there's nothing more we can do."

Strange thinking, I thought, from the man with the power of a subpoena. "There's one more person we can try," I told him.

Mitch's fingers were conducting a drumbeat on the pad. He was still sitting sideways. He hadn't blinked in an extraordinarily long time. Now he looked as though he wasn't planning on speaking again, ever. I helped him out.

"Jason Stockover. He was another guy who was there that night."

"What night?"

Oh, very good, Mitch. "The night somebody buried a golf club in Heidi Telford's head."

The district attorney sucked in his lower lip. "And where is he?"

"I was hoping somebody could tell me. Then I'd ask your permission to go talk to him."

"But right now you don't need my permission because nobody knows where this Jason Stockover is." Mitch was not stupid, just simple.

"Well, let's put it this way—I don't know where he is."

Mitch had the exit he needed. He repositioned himself so he was facing me directly. He squared his bony shoulders, set his eyes on mine, and said, "Therefore, you will have no problem getting back to what you are supposed to be doing, which is prosecuting OUIs, right?"

I knew the answer he wanted. It seemed best to give it.

———

BARBARA BELBONNET ALSO WANTED to know what was wrong. Her concern was different from Mitch's. Still, I told her nothing and set about arranging my files.

She came over and leaned her butt against my desk. She was wearing a sand-colored top that at first I thought was a T-shirt, but it was tightly woven material made to look more casual than it actually was. Once again she was wearing form-fitting slacks, black this time. She must have gone on a shopping spree.

"Want to tell me about it?" she said.

I looked down at her feet. She had shoes that matched the color of her top. "Tell you about what?" I wondered if women bought shoes to match their tops. Twenty tops, twenty shoes.

"Whatever it is that has you so worked up," she said.

"I'm not worked up."

"Oh." She didn't leave my desk. She raised her hand and brushed her almost-blond hair back from her face. For an instant the top that was not a T-shirt opened wide under her arm and I could see an expanse of smooth, fair skin. The hand came down. The skin disappeared.

I looked at my files again. I had a trial in the morning. A doctor had blown a .14 and thought he could beat it. I was supposed to wipe the floor with him. The doctor apparently didn't have friends in the right places.

Barbara pushed off the desk. "I think I liked you better the way you used to be," she said.

Which was funny not only because I didn't think I had changed, but because I never knew she liked me before.

*1.*

I KNOCKED ON MARION'S DOOR.

A male voice asked, "Who is it?"

There was something familiar about that voice, but I did not immediately place it. I was thinking about Buzzy, and I knew it wasn't him.

"My name is George Becket," I said, "and I'm looking for Marion."

There was a very long pause on the other side of the door. I was about to knock again, ready to explain my relationship with whomever was guarding her privacy when the door was pulled open and I looked into the taut face and cold eyes of Roland Andrews.

"Marion doesn't live here anymore," he said.

"But you do."

"You've been a busy boy." Roland Andrews came close to smiling. "Somebody has to look out for you."

I may have sworn at him then. I can't think of any other reason why Roland's eyes suddenly lit up, why he grabbed my wrist, jerked me into the apartment, flung me against the wall, and kicked the door shut in one continuous, fluid movement. I was bigger than Roland, taller, heavier, but there I was, my feet dangling above the parquet floor, his forearm across my neck. "What did you say?" he demanded.

I did not tell him. I didn't say anything else, either. At that moment I thought there might be a certain poetic justice in him hanging me on my ex-wife's wall. There was, from what I could see, nothing else on the walls—no pictures, no art. Just me.

Roland applied one last bit of pressure to my throat and then let me slide down the wall to my feet as he backed away. He had hurt me, but I was not going to let him see that. I did not touch my throat or my wrist. I stood still and waited for my functions to return.

"Figured you'd be here sooner or later," he said, as if now that he had asserted physical mastery we could move on to convivialities. He was wearing a gray T-shirt with a faded insignia over his heart that said Royal Regiment of Fusiliers. The T-shirt fit tightly, particularly over his arms, and it was tucked into jeans that seemed equally tight. Tight, tight, tight—the man radiated tightness. I wondered what would happen if my fist shot out and hit him in the nose. Probably my hand would shatter.

"Why?" I said, when I had enough air in my lungs to get the word out cleanly.

"Well, after you learned about Marion and Buzzy, I assumed you'd want to talk to her."

I looked around the living room. It was clear Marion was not living here anymore. There were no books in the bookshelves. Wherever Marion went, there were books. "You tell him to tell me?"

"No, sir. Never met the gentleman."

"But you have met the Macs, I'm guessing."

"And who might the Macs be?"

"Mike McBeth, Jerry McQuaid, Declan McCoppin, maybe."

"Ah, *those* Macs." He grinned in what was meant to pass for irony. Grinning did not become Roland Andrews. It made you want to cover his mouth with your hand. "Fine fellows, one and all. Would like to change the legal establishment down in your neck of the woods, from what I understand."

"And why are you involved? What's in it for you?"

"Why, I've got a job to do, Georgie. I told you that back in Philly when we first met. And here I am, lo these many years later. Still doing it."

"Screwing up my life, you mean."

"Hey, you screwed up your own life, son. Threw in your lot with the Gregorys." His eyes, small to begin with, narrowed into mere slits.

I had not moved from my position in front of the wall. I would have moved, but I wasn't sure where to go. The living room was not that big. It had black-leather-and-chrome furniture and all of it matched. Quite different from what she had bought for our house.

"What's your relationship with her?"

I didn't have to use her name. He knew whom I meant. That was why he smirked. Given how thin his lips were, it came more naturally to him than a grin. "You might say employer to employee."

My knees wobbled. I wanted very much to sit down. No, I wanted to run. Run right at Roland Andrews. Run through him and then through that window that ran the length and breadth of the wall behind him, get myself up in the air six floors above Storrow Drive, pumping my legs and swirling my arms just as I had when I'd leaped off the cliff in Idaho. Run, leap, fall.

"You shouldn't be surprised," he said. "I told you that things were going to happen that never would have if you hadn't done what you did." Somehow Roland had gotten his hand on my arm. He was not gripping it like he was going to break it this time. He was guiding me into a seat, into one of the black-leather-and-chrome chairs.

"You want some water, Georgie?"

I didn't answer and he didn't get it. I think he was afraid of what might occur if he left the room.

When Marion lived here she had African masks, Tibetan prayer rugs, a photograph of a hillside village in Italy that she said was her ancestral home. She had . . . stuff. Now there was nothing personal at all. It could have been a hotel room.

"Where is she?"

"Gone back to Washington. She wanted to do it long before she did. We convinced her to stay on for a while, that was all."

Looking out the window I could see the Charles River and Cambridge on the other side. I could see sailboats on the water and cars on Memorial Drive. People enjoying themselves, driving home, going on errands, living normal lives. Not me. I couldn't even marry normally. "So this whole thing was just work to her?"

"I didn't say that, Georgie. I think there was a time she really liked you."

Until when? The Berkshires? Until she didn't move down the Cape? Until she met Buzzy? Out loud, I said, "Until she met you?"

"Well, you gotta figure, Georgie, here you were, right in the Gregorys' home base, right in their nest, so to speak. But you don't join any clubs, don't go out partying; you don't even date. The only thing you ever did was ride your damn bike. Hard to make contact with someone on the road cruising by himself. So we made contact with her, instead."

I was fumbling with the math. Twelve years since I had witnessed Kendrick Powell being violated. Eleven and a half since I had last seen this evil little creature in front of me. Eight since I had joined the D.A.'s office.

Andrews read my mind. "Mr. Powell is a patient man, Georgie. He's had to be. He tried to act quickly once, and that's when you let him down."

Five years since she reappeared in my life.

"So you sent her down the Cape to hook up with me, huh?"

"No. We just saw her with you, recognized her from that little stunt she pulled with the police in Old Town, Alexandria, and thought, well, she might be game."

Spring of my first year of law school. Nineteen ninety-seven. Eleven years ago. They recognized Marion from then. My breath was coming in short spurts. I looked at Andrews. I looked past him to the window. I wanted to run again.

Roland had been standing the entire time. Now he took a seat on the black-leather-and-chrome couch at right angles to my black-leather-and-chrome chair. It was a good place for him to sit. He could block me if I moved. Tackle me if I bolted.

"She did have a job up here," I asked, my voice tight. "Didn't she? With a law firm?" I didn't want to sound as though I was pleading, but I knew I was.

"Oh, yes. Got the job, contacted you, came down to see you all on her own. At first, we were just watching, hoping she'd loosen you up a bit. Talk you into going to some of those Gregory soirées."

Of course. The ones to which I had never been invited.

"But you proved to be a tough nut to crack, Georgie. As far as I can tell, you've never even been in the Gregory compound. With or without Marion."

"What good would it have done you if I had?"

"Who knows? But there would be something. With the Gregorys, there always is."

"So it all proved to be a big waste of time, didn't it?" I was trying to be smug. "All that watching, all that scheming."

"Not really. We're here now, aren't we?" Andrews smiled. It was an ugly thing. A fissure in a glacier.

"We're here because you paid my wife to spy on me."

"No, George. We're here because the Gregorys murdered Heidi Telford."

My head was suddenly too light to stay upright. It wanted to fall forward onto my chest. It wanted to drift away. It wanted to spin in different directions. Somehow I kept my eyes on Roland Andrews. I wanted to search his face, look for clues as to how one thing had led to another, but for several moments I could not quite get it in focus.

"I'm not going to help you," I said at last. It was a statement of desperation, a claim more of spite than of purpose.

"Oh, but you already are. I mean, you just led us to Patty Margolis, didn't you?"

Sometimes you get hit with so many things you become inured. You start looking for them, expecting them, almost not caring when they rip into you. "You followed me?"

"I'd say it's a safe bet someone's always following you, Georgie. Pull up at a red light, look at the guy in the car next to you. Think, Does he know Roland? Is he one of Roland's guys?"

Was it possible? Twelve years of watching me go to school, go to work, go home at night and watch television?

"How about the people on that airplane that flew you into Indian Creek? They legit rafters or they working for Mr. Powell? Tell me, Georgie, you see anybody on that raft trip that maybe shouldn't have been there? Any couple that struck you as maybe not being a couple or who didn't do the things everybody else did?"

"You had me followed to Idaho?"

Roland Andrews laughed. At least that is what I think he was doing. It came out in a gruff barking sound, like he was spitting up a hairball. "Maybe I was there myself. You check out that little landing strip at Loon Creek?"

"You shoot at me, Roland?" It was the first time I had ever used his Christian name. It was meant to reduce him to my level. To show that he was every bit as venal as I was.

"Do you really think I'd miss if I shot at you?"

No, I didn't think that. But maybe his henchmen would. The couple that had been blown off the raft, the ones who had declined to go to the hot springs.

Except why would they want to shoot me? Josh David Powell wanted me to do something for him, and that wasn't going to be accomplished if I lay dead on a trail in the Idaho wilderness. "You would," I said, "if you wanted me to think it was McFetridge."

"Yeah? And why would I want you to think that?"

Why, indeed. It was something more complicated. More complicated and yet more obvious. The Powell faction was watching me; they knew where I was going, what I was doing. Perhaps they knew it was Chuck Larson who had sent me to Idaho, directed me at least.

I threw it out there. "The Gregorys send me into the wilderness, you make it look like they're trying to kill me because I'm getting too close to the truth about Heidi Telford. Is that it? Do I have it right, Roland?"

He said nothing. He didn't move.

"Then what? Then I'm supposed to hate them, give you whatever you want?"

Roland Andrews appeared more than willing to let me work this out.

"I mean, that's what it's all about, isn't it? Everything you're doing? Using me to get to the Gregorys? You pay Marion, that doesn't get you anywhere, so you start digging around, discover old Mr. Telford and his idea about the Gregorys killing his daughter. You put him onto me, then you follow me around, see what I come up with, hope it's enough for you to give to some muttonhead like Buzzy to use in a campaign against Mitch White. 'Senator's Protégée Covers Up Murder Investigation,' is that it? And of course you don't care about Mr. Telford or even about defeating Mitch, no matter what you may have said to the Macs. All you care about is hurting the Gregorys."

I was getting somewhere. That much was clear from Andrews's continued silence, from his failure to scoff at me—to put out his hand and make me stop.

"Couldn't you just get somebody to write a book? *Murder on Old Cape Cod,* how about that? Get some police detective or one of those guys who likes to do exposés on the rich and famous. Let him write up Telford's theory, speculate on who did what and why."

"Then we wouldn't be able to have so much fun with you, would we?"

"Fun? That's what this is all about, fucking with me because I got manipulated by some paid-off prosecutor when I was a kid?"

"No. The fact is we're on a mission here, Georgie. Fucking with you is just a side benefit."

"Well, fuck all you want, Roland." I practically spit out his name. "But I don't know shit. I haven't learned shit. And I'm not going to do shit. Not anymore."

"What did Patty Margolis tell you?"

"Nothing. She wouldn't tell me anything."

"At least you found her," he said calmly, using his voice to emphasize how out of control I was. "Tell you the truth, we hadn't been able to do that."

"So what? She's not talking."

"Let me tell you what we've learned in the few days since you uncovered her. Patty Margolis, born Patricia Afantakis in Roslindale. Age thirty-three. Earned an accounting degree at Babson two years before Heidi Telford was killed. At the time of the murder, she was working for a Big Eight accounting firm as assistant to Nick Margolis, a CPA who she was screwing after hours. Mr. Margolis was looking to get out, start up a firm of his own. Three months after the Telford murder, he did just that. Opened his own shop with Patty as his office manager.

Within a year they were married. Now have two kids. Homely little suckers, but I'm sure their parents love them."

Andrews sat forward, the better to hold me in his sight, the better to keep me from thrashing around and looking away from him. "Most interesting thing we've learned is that the office lease is in Patty's name. Patty pays the extraordinary low rent of three hundred dollars a month to a company called Arrangement Property that is located in the Cayman Islands and seems to have no other property anywhere that we can find. We're still tracing Arrangement Property's ownership, but we have every confidence that it will lead, sooner or later, to the Gregorys. Now, why would the Gregorys do such a nice thing for a hunk of blubber like Patty? Could it have anything to do with where she was on Memorial Day night 1999?"

"I . . . don't . . . know."

"Sure you do." He slapped my knee. "And it's the very reason why she wouldn't tell you anything."

"Well, I'm done now. I led you to her. You can take it from there."

"We want to know who she was with that night, Georgie."

"She was with McFetridge."

"I'm talking about girlfriends. A girl like Patty wasn't going to be McFetridge's date, and she didn't go off to the Gregorys' all by herself." He paused long enough for me to catch up with him. "We've narrowed down the people she could have been with to about ten in number. Girls from high school, college, work. What I need from you now is a name."

"She didn't give me one."

Andrews put on his hard eyes.

"Suppose she did. What do I get for telling you?"

"What do you want?"

"Tell me why Marion did what she did."

Andrews actually looked away for a moment, a rather un-Andrews-like action. "I think," he said when he looked back, "she was very unhappy, Georgie."

"What's that supposed to mean?"

"It means she had a job she hated, working sixty hours a week, and you weren't making it any better, like she thought you would."

"She was supposed to quit."

"And she didn't, did she?" For a moment the man almost looked sad.

Roland Andrews, who hated me, whose job was to make my life miserable, felt sorry for me. What a poor, pathetic creature I was to have my enemy look at me the way he was.

"She was . . . rather a free spirit, wasn't she?" he said, and I couldn't tell if he was speaking in solace or not.

"So." I cleared my throat because the word did not come out clearly. "What are you saying, you asked her to cheat on me?"

"No, didn't ask her to do that. Like I said before, we knew who she was. We saw what was happening, saw she was getting ready to leave you, and approached her. Told her she didn't have to do any more than what she'd been doing. Just keep her eyes and ears open for anything that had to do with the Gregorys."

"And she agreed?" I was skeptical. Marion was a good liberal, and good liberals didn't do things to hurt the Gregorys.

"I think she liked the idea of being a mole, a spy." Andrews flicked his fingers. "And of course we made it worth her while."

"How?"

The finger flick became something more, a sweep of the room in which we were sitting. "This apartment, for one thing. We took over the lease, paid her a salary on top of what she was making at the law firm. She actually did quite well for herself. Too well, probably, because as soon as she had enough to buy a house in Chevy Chase we couldn't hold her anymore."

Once again, I felt sapped of breath. A man thinks he's one person, he finds out he's somebody else altogether.

"And the . . ." I struggled with the words. "Buzzy thing?"

"All I can tell you about that is once we came up with the idea of using the Telford case to take on the district attorney we needed a candidate. Mike McBeth suggested Buzzy, and since we were paying Marion anyhow we asked her to find out a little about him, make sure he was worth our investment."

He spread his hands as if I should understand what happened next. I stared back, making him say it.

"That was all we expected, that she would do a little reconnoitering for us. I guess she liked what she saw." Andrews gave a twitch of his shoulders. "Actually, I can't even tell you that. We didn't tell her to start an affair with him. It just happened and we let it go. No telling when we might need something on Mr. Daizell."

I wanted out of the room, out from under the humiliation his every word was inflicting on me. But Roland Andrews had inched even farther forward on his chair.

"You see where your actions have gotten you, buddy?" He was still looking sympathetic. "You think you're in control of your life? You're not."

The look wasn't sympathetic after all. It was mean and conniving, like everything else about Roland Andrews. "Mr. Powell can make every aspect of your life miserable," he said, "make you suspicious of every good thing that happens to you, make you so afraid that you won't want to commit to anything, anywhere, anytime. You understand?"

I wanted to look out the window at the river, the boats, the cars going by on Storrow Drive, the people whose lives were their own to do with as they wished.

"This Marion thing is just an example, Georgie. He's rolling over you. Just like he's going to do to the Gregorys." Andrews tapped my knee. In Philadelphia he had made my leg go numb. But this was just a tap.

"The only difference is," he said, "you can still get out."

"Leanne," I said. "She didn't give me a last name."

## 2.

GOT IN MY CAR TO DRIVE HOME. IT WAS A STIFLING HOT DAY, THE
first really hot day of the year. I was parked at a meter on Charles
Street and there was a great deal of activity going on around me. The
merchants and restaurateurs were getting ready for the big Fourth of
July fireworks celebration at the Hatch Shell on the mall next to the
river, just a few blocks away. Tens of thousands of people would be
coming. They would line the riverbank waiting to hear the Boston
Pops and whatever celebrity singer was going to join them this year.
They would sit wherever they could, on lawn chairs and blankets, arrive early in the morning to get the best possible spots and then wait all
day for the music and the colorful explosions. They would be there
with family and friends, and the only people by themselves would be
losers and perverts and weirdos, wandering around staring at everyone
else having a good time.

I didn't love Marion and I never had. I just felt so foolish.

## 3.

M Y PHONE RANG, BUT I DIDN'T ANSWER IT. THE MESSAGE MA-
chine picked up and Barbara Belbonnet's voice came on.

"George, hope everything's okay. You missed a court call today and
one of the other guys had to cover for you. He apparently reported it
because Dick O'Connor's been looking for you. I didn't know what to
say, George. So, anyhow, if you could give me a call back I'd really appreciate it. Just tell me what to tell him. Okay. You've got the number."

I stared at the ceiling and wondered why I should get up, why I
should go in to work, go to court, risk running into all the people who
knew what Buzzy and Marion had been doing behind my back. The
Macs knew. If they knew, then Cello DiMasi knew. Cello, who didn't
like me in the first place. Or maybe that was why he didn't like me. A
guy like Cello wouldn't have put up with his wife cheating on him
with his friend. A guy like Cello wouldn't have had that happen to
him. And once he knew about me, he would tell everyone else, all his
cops, all the assistant D.A.s. Maybe even Barbara.

I didn't return the call.

An hour later she called again.

"Now I'm really worried," she said. "Dick has actually come down
here himself. He wants to know if I've heard from you, when was the
last time I saw you, if you left early for the holiday. All that stuff.

Please call me back, George. Even if you're too hung over to talk. Just let me know you're all right."

She showed up at my house at 5:30. It was about a fifteen-minute drive from the office and she had somehow managed to get herself squeezed into a pair of jeans that would have impressed me if I had been in any condition to appreciate them. Barbara had never been at my house before, but she knew enough to park in the carport and go to the kitchen rather than walk around to the front, where the door was always locked. She knocked; I didn't answer. She opened the door from the carport, called my name, came inside. She passed through the kitchen and came down the hallway to my bedroom. I knew she was coming and pulled the covers to my chin.

"Jeez, George!" she gasped, as though I had scared her, as though she had not really expected to find me there. "What is going on?"

"Nothing."

"Nothing? You've been lying in bed all day, not going to work, not answering your phone, and nothing's going on?"

"That's right."

The jeans made her legs look startlingly long. She was taller even than she usually was and I saw she had some kind of sandals with spike heels. White heels to match the white peasant blouse she was wearing. Her nearly blond hair seemed longer than it ever had been. Women and their hair: How can they make it disappear and reappear like they do?

She looked around. She walked to a window and forced it up. "You need some air in here."

Her eyes went to the clothes I had thrown on the chaise longue. Then they went to the open closet, where a week's worth of dress shirts lay in a pile on the floor. What passed across her face was more a look of exasperation than disgust. She came and sat on my bed. For one brief instant she had to turn those incredibly tight jeans in my direction. I had not realized Barbara Belbonnet was in such good shape.

She reached out and took my left hand away from its grip on the sheet and held it and didn't speak for a long time.

Neither did I.

"Do you like cigars?" Of all the things she could have said to break the silence, that was not in the top thousand.

"I guess," I told her.

"You want to go smoke one?"

Smoke a cigar. I was lying in bed. I hadn't gotten up all day. I hadn't gone to work or even called in to say I wasn't coming, and she was asking if I wanted to go smoke a cigar. "Okay," I said.

"I picked up a couple of Gurkhas at The Magic Dragon."

I knew the place, a cigar bar at the east end of Main Street in Hyannis. I knew Gurkhas. I was surprised she did.

"We can sit out in the backyard," she said, "keep your house from getting all stinky."

*Stinky.* A woman's word. I hadn't heard a woman's word in my house for a long time. "Okay," I said.

"But you're going to have to move," she told me.

"I don't have anything on but a pair of boxers."

She looked bemused for a moment. "Then," she said, giving my hand a squeeze, "I'll go outside and wait for you." She stood. She did it slowly. She let me look at her while she did. "But you have to get up."

GURKHA ASSASSINS. Pretty good cigars. We sat in the Florentine chairs that were part of the Brown Jordan patio set Marion had bought once upon a time. The patio set made me sad. Barbara noticed that. She patted me on the knee. I had put on a pair of shorts, and her hand seemed cool on my skin, palliative. I tried to smile.

"What did you do all day?"

"Nothing."

"Didn't go out? Didn't see anyone?"

"No."

We smoked and watched a gray squirrel scamper across the lawn, leap, hit a tree a couple of feet off the ground, and scoot up the bark to the branches. So many important things for a squirrel to do.

"Yesterday? After work, I mean."

"Boston."

"See Marion?"

Pretty good guess, Barbara. "She wasn't there. She's moved back to D.C."

Pause. Smoke. Think about it. "And that's what has you upset?"

Think about it. Think about it. Think about it. "She was having an affair with one of my friends."

"Which one?"

"Buzzy Daizell."

"That asshole."

I raised my eyebrow, looked over the burning Gurkha. "I didn't realize you knew him so well."

"Buzzy Daizell has hit on every woman on the Cape. There's a reason he's never been married, George."

Yeah, I thought. He's not a fool. Or a sucker.

"I went to school with him until eighth grade," she said. "He was the kind of kid who used to set off firecrackers in the boys' room."

The conversation died out. I didn't mind hearing Barbara talk. I had opened the door about the affair and I didn't mind hearing what she had to say about the man who had been with my wife. The man I thought I knew. "Then what?" I asked.

"Then I went off to Tabor Academy and he went to Barnstable High."

"Tabor, huh?"

"I liked to sail. Thought I was good at it. Turned out a lot of people were better."

A picture of Barbara Belbonnet sailing came into my mind. The perspective was all wrong. She was sitting straight up in the cockpit of a Laser. Half as tall as the mast. "Ever sail with the Gregorys?" In my vision they were little people. Lilliputians. But there were hundreds of them. Scattered all over the deck of the Laser.

"I've done it, sure. We were all members of the yacht club."

"Sail with Ned?"

"I have."

"Peter Martin?"

"I know Peter. I don't think I've ever sailed with him."

"Done the Figawi race?"

"Every sailor in these parts has, sooner or later. But I haven't done it with the Gregorys."

"But you've partied with them. Figawi parties, I mean."

"I have." She inspected the ash, tapped it, made sure the tobacco was still burning. "Tyler, my almost ex, used to work on their boats. The Senator would sail someplace like the Caribbean and then he'd fly home or to D.C. or wherever, and Ty would sail the boat back for him."

Barbara's almost ex was all things nautical. That, she told me one time, was the problem with him. He loved the sea more than her. More than the kids. I thought about my ex and what she loved more than me. Apparently everything.

I heard a voice in the neighborhood, a mother shouting at her son. I heard a car door slam shut. An engine gunned to life. The car took off. Barbara and I exchanged looks, but said nothing.

"How did you find out about the affair?" she asked, after we had smoked in silence for a while.

"Buzzy."

"He told you? Why would he do that?"

"There are people who want him to run for D.A. against Mitch. He's afraid the affair will be exposed." I had not expected to come right out and tell her. I heard the words and wondered why I had. I wondered if it had anything to do with her being friends with the Gregorys. Run home and tell them, Barbara. Let them squish Buzzy like a bug.

But "Huh" was all she said. She put the cigar in her mouth, did it expertly, and squinted her eyes against the smoke. And then she added, "Why would somebody pick him to run?"

"From what I understand, it has to do with his family connections."

She took out the cigar, waved it around, and said, "Then why not come to me? My family is as established as his. My background is probably a lot cleaner."

Probably, I thought, because your family is established a little differently than Buzzy's.

"Maybe they're sexists," she said. The idea seemed to get her worked up, made her suck hard on the cigar. "Who are 'they'?"

"McBeth, McQuaid. Those guys."

"Get out!"

"No. Why?"

"McBeth and McQuaid want to take Mitch down? What on earth for? So they can build stuff without permits? Wait, wait, wait, wait." She held up one hand, the non-smoking hand. Her eyes brightened. "This have anything to do with the Indians over in Mashpee? The ones who are trying to get a casino?"

"I don't think so."

"Why not?" Barbara turned in her seat. She had lost interest in her cigar.

"There are people out there," I said, not looking at her, "who are convinced the Gregorys were involved in the murder of Heidi Telford." Take that back to the compound, Barbara.

I tapped my cigar ash, watched it fall. "They think that Mitch is protecting the family rather than investigating them."

Barbara bounced. Her cigar apparently was in her way because she threw it onto the pavers. "You're talking about old Bill Tel—"

"No, I'm not, Barbara. If anything, Bill's become a pawn for these people."

Her chin tucked into her neck. "Is this, like, a political thing?"

I said no, it was more of a personal thing.

"How do you know them? These people?"

At almost any other time I probably would not have told her. But I had been lying in bed for about twenty hours, feeling miserable about myself and my life and the world and everything in it; and now this woman, this gorgeous woman, had come to see me and brought me a cigar and was sitting on my back patio acting as if what I had to say really mattered to her.

"Barbara, did you ever wonder how I got my job?"

"No. Yes. Well, I sort of figured it was like me. You had someone who pulled a few strings—"

"Yeah. The Senator. Because I had once done him a favor. Well, not him so much, but one of his nephews. Him, too, I guess, if you really get right down to it."

"Which nephew?"

"You already mentioned him. Or one of us did, anyhow."

"Ned? Peter?"

I motioned with my head, probably tried to raise my eyebrows in affirmation. "Peter."

"Oh, my God . . . you're talking about the thing down in Florida?"

"I helped cover it up."

"He really did it? Peter the doctor? Peter, who works with AIDS patients out in San Francisco?"

"He did some nasty stuff, Barbara, and I was there, and a few months later the girl was dead."

"Oh, God."

I wanted her to understand the depth of my depravity. Of the Gregorys'. Maybe even of her own for being friends with them.

For a long time we just sat there, me smoking, Barbara staring off into the yard. Then, very softly, she said, "Why did you ask about the Figawi race?"

"Heidi Telford was killed the night the race ended in 1999. Bill Telford thinks she was at the Gregorys' that night. I think he's right."

There, Barbara, what are you going to do with that information? Perhaps you could pass it along to Cory, or Jamie, or whoever else comes over to your father's house for big hunks of meat grilled by hired help. Then they could send Chuck-Chuck by to have a talk with me. Better yet, Pierre Mumford. He could squeeze my head between his fingers. Make it pop like a blister.

"You think it was Peter?" she said, jerking my thoughts back to the moment.

"I think Peter is a sick, twisted misogynist. I've seen what he can do."

"So . . . like . . . are you helping these people? The ones who want to get the Gregorys?"

Yes, you would like to know that, wouldn't you, Barbara? Let your hair down, pull on a pair of tight jeans, give me a cigar, and I'll tell you anything and everything. Because that's the kind of guy I am, the kind who can be bought for a cigar and a glimpse of paradise.

"I'm not sure what I'm doing," I told her. "I'd like to help Mr. Telford, I know that. And these people, as you call them, they're using me just like they're using him and even poor dumbass Buzzy to get what they want."

"And is that so bad? If it's going to lead to the truth, I mean."

Wait. That wasn't what she was supposed to say.

I had a sudden, terribly cold feeling. The idea came into my head that Barbara Belbonnet, my office-mate with a world of problems of her own, had shown up at my house without her kids and her cell phone not because the Gregorys had sent her, but because Roland Andrews had. My breath caught in my chest and I turned my head slowly to look at her.

Barbara's eyes were on me. Big yellowish-brown eyes. She didn't look devious, nefarious, manipulative. She didn't look anything other than beautiful. "Isn't that what we're supposed to do?" she asked. "As prosecutors? Go after the truth?"

"I'm not prosecuting this case," I answered. "As Mitch has taken pains to remind me."

"Mitch, who has his own interests to guard."

"So what are you saying, Barbara?" I spoke carefully, deliberately. "You think I ought to do what these people want?"

"I think"—and then she took her time telling me what she thought. She did it by watching me intently, making sure I really was listening. "I think you ought to decide what's right and then go ahead and do it. No matter what."

No matter if I lost my job and never worked again. No matter if I was vilified throughout the country, the world, for betraying the Gregorys. "Yeah?" I said harshly. "Well, these people we're talking about want me to track down everyone who could have been at the Gregorys' that night."

"Hasn't anyone done that yet?"

If she was with Andrews, she would know they hadn't. If she was with the Gregorys, she would know they had . . . sort of. Chuck Larson had said a detective had talked to Cory Gregory's brother and cousins. A detective who had put nothing about the Gregorys in his file.

I lofted a cloud of cigar smoke straight above my head. "That's one of the great unresolved questions," I said.

"Nobody's investigated Peter?"

"It doesn't appear they have."

She thought about it. "Tyler still sees him, you know."

Tyler, the ex. The almost ex.

"He's living in Sausalito. Tyler, I mean. Peter still sails out there on San Francisco Bay. He gets Ty to crew for him sometimes. If you want, I could get Tyler to put you in touch. He's more than happy to do little things like that for me. As long as I don't try to get him to come home, help me take care of the kids."

It was time to stop this dance. I tossed my cigar next to hers on the pavers and sat up straight. "You realize you're telling me I should be going after your old friends."

"What I'm telling you is what I said before. Decide what's right and then do it. And as for going after old friends, well, they're friends because I know them. Because I grew up with them. Not because they've ever done anything for me."

"And if they had? If they had done something great and wonderful for you?"

Barbara threw up her hand. "Look, George, I don't know what more to tell you, but you're obviously torn up by this. So what I'm suggesting is maybe you ought to stop worrying so much about other people and what their motivations are and just do something because it's the right thing to do. That's all."

I did not agree or disagree. It was easier just to stare at the tree where I had seen the squirrel go. Try to figure out where he was hiding, when he would come out next.

# 4.

MITCH WAS NOT EXACTLY SANGUINE ABOUT MY DAY OFF. "You think I can't fire you?" he screamed at me.

"I think it would be awfully awkward if you did."

"What's that supposed to mean?"

"It means you would have some explaining to do." I was not being forceful or even cocky. Half of me did not care if I was fired; the other half just wanted to inflict a little damage on Mr. White. "It means it just may be that the card I'm holding is worth more than the one you have."

Mitch was unnerved. His eyes did the bulging thing behind his glasses. "Are you threatening me?"

"Not at all."

"Because I'm still the boss here."

The boss whose butt had come out of his chair, who was now leaning across his desk, his weight on his bare forearms. Once again, he was wearing a short-sleeved shirt that severely impaired the authority he was trying to exert.

"You think you're already at the bottom doing OUIs, Becket?" he bellowed in his little man's voice. "Well, I can make it even worse for you. I can put you in juvie. I can have you going after deadbeat dads. I can give you nothing whatsoever to do if I feel like it."

"Or the two of us can work together in what you might call our common interest."

Mitch's face had gone blotchy. Like his pipe-cleaner arms, it was not a pleasant sight.

"This Telford thing isn't going away," I told him. "In case you don't know it, there's a movement afoot to get someone to run against you. And the main platform of your opponent is going to be that you've been covering up for the Gregorys."

Mitch came even farther across the desk. His next move would have to involve putting his knees on it. Then he would crouch like a porcelain cat. "Who?" he demanded. "Who is it?"

I did not give him an answer. I had something I wanted from him and that was my only bargaining chip.

"You?" His voice soared to the point of cracking.

"Not me, Mitch. I'm the Gregorys' friend, remember?"

Mitch did not know what to say to that. Little gurgling noises came out of his mouth and spit rolled down his chin. After a while, he sat back. I have never felt so hated in my life. Not when Roland Andrews confronted me in my apartment in D.C. Not even when I was being shot at. I gestured to my own chin, pointing with my index finger. That made him even angrier, but at least he wiped the spit away. He did it with his bare forearm.

I told him that Bill Telford had raised enough questions about whether his daughter was at Senator Gregory's house that night that people were out there now, combing the country for information.

He gurgled again, but held his saliva.

"One of the questions being asked is why you and Cello DiMasi didn't follow up on the leads you had. I talked with Cello and he told me the police investigation was conducted by a certain Detective Landry, a guy who took early retirement and moved to Hawaii shortly after he didn't find any connection to the Gregorys. You see where this is leading, Mitch?"

He didn't tell me. He was too busy trying to reduce me to cinders with his eyes.

"We have no reason to want the Senator besmirched, do we, Mitch?

He's had enough problems over the course of his life. And he's been good to us, to the people of this state, good to the entire nation. But you know as well as I do that there are folks out there who will seize any opportunity to tear him down. So I see us, you and me, as being in a position where we can do something about this whole mess. A unique position. Wouldn't you agree?"

Mitch was not agreeing to anything. It is possible that the movements I saw his head make were simply the result of his body shaking.

"So what I propose is that you send me to visit former Detective Landry and see if we can't come up with an explanation as to why certain things were or were not done. Why there are things that don't seem to be in the police investigation file. That way, if he's questioned by reporters or one of those pseudo-journalists on TV, or even, God forbid, the U.S. Justice Department, we can have a little more control over the situation."

"You want me to send you to Hawaii."

"I do."

"So you can talk to Landry about the Heidi Telford investigation."

"So I can straighten out the Heidi Telford investigation. Before the whole world gets the wrong impression."

"Before some guy can use it against me in next year's campaign."

"Yes."

"And you still haven't told me who that guy is."

I told him.

"You've got to be kidding," said Mitch White. But he knew I wasn't, and he seemed to be just as worried as he had been before.

# 5.

SEAN MURPHY.

I didn't know Sean all that well. He was younger than I was, had been in the office only two or three years, but he was already doing felonies. He had gone to law school at Northeastern and interned at the Suffolk County D.A.'s office in Boston. That was a big deal to our guys. Reid Cunningham, in particular, loved him. He called him Murph-Dog and treated him like a hound, to be loosed on the most deserving of criminals—the home invaders, child molesters, wife beaters.

"George, old buddy," Sean said. He had something under his arm. A clipboard and some papers. He was smiling at me. He appeared to have been waiting for me to come out of Mitch's office.

"Sean," I said. I was prepared to walk past him, but he put out a hand.

"You're the only one I haven't got yet," he said.

"For what?"

He untucked the clipboard and held it in front of him as if it was self-explanatory. He had now smiled at me for longer than he had done so in all the time we had been in the office together. "The Pan-Mass Challenge. It's a bike race across the state. Well, not a race, exactly. One hundred and ten miles one day, ninety the next. Sturbridge to P'town, and I'm doing the whole thing. Got to get four grand in sponsors. You in?"

"You want me to sponsor your bike ride?"

All I had to say was that I was doing the ride myself, but I didn't. I looked down the hallway instead, hoping someone else would come along and demand my attention.

"Well, not you by yourself. I've got every prosecutor in the office to put up a hundred bucks."

"Everyone?"

"Everyone except Mitch. Got Cunningham and O'Connor, though. I just haven't seen you around for a few days. That's why I'm getting to you last."

"You got Barbara Belbonnet?"

"Sure. It's for a good cause, George. Children's cancer fund." He was beginning to falter in his bonhomie, as if he had known all along that I wasn't going to do what everyone else had done.

I signed the form he held out to me. Pledged $100. I was now into the ride for $2,600.

## 1.

FLYING FROM BOSTON TO HAWAII CAN BE A VERY LONG JOURney if you don't like the person you are with. Especially if that person is you.

Things did not improve once I arrived. Perhaps I thought it would be like Bermuda: hop on a motor scooter and cruise the entire island in an hour.

The airport was small, one story, and there seemed to be a dearth of walls, but there were plenty of people, and while most were in tropical clothing, virtually everyone was too intent on finding someone or someplace to help out a stranger who apparently thought he had landed in some Polynesian Mayberry.

It took me more than an hour to rent a car because I had not thought to reserve one, being under the illusion that I was going to take a taxi into town. "Which town?" the first cabdriver asked in response to my question, and I knew I was in trouble.

I told him I was staying in Princeville.

He shook his head as if there was something wrong with me. "Long way, man. Cheaper to rent da car than take da cab."

So I did.

At least the hotel was nice, and it had a concierge named Ki'anna, a dark-hued, zaftig young woman with waist-length black hair, who assured me she knew everything that was worth knowing about the island. One thing she didn't know was the whereabouts of a man named Howard Landry. She did the logical thing and looked him up in the phone book. No Howard Landry was listed. She went to her computer and found no reference to Howard Landry there. I would have despaired except I was beyond that point. I just stood in the open-air lobby and wondered what I was going to do next.

It was three o'clock in the afternoon. I had the option of walking a quarter-mile down to the beach, which, from where the hotel was, perched on top of a cliff, did not look as nice as a Hawaiian beach was supposed to look, or going to the pool and having a waiter bring me drinks.

I went to my room, changed into a bathing suit, and walked back to the pool, which had various arms and inlets and vaguely Asian-style pedestrian bridges and which dominated the grounds. I dove in, swam a half-dozen laps without disturbing the water for the wild children and passive adults who were using the pool for everything but swimming, then climbed out and dropped onto a lounge chair. I was in Hawaii and someone else was paying for it. I should relax, take my time. I didn't have to do everything in an afternoon.

I closed my eyes and tried to think of Barbara Belbonnet in those long-legged, incredibly tight jeans. It did not work. My eyes would not stay closed. And the noise around me was cacophonous. Kids, swarms of them, were trying to climb on inflatable floats, an activity that seemed to require shrill yelling that cut out only when their heads went underwater. I heard parents laughing as they hung on to the edge of the pool, holding exotic drinks with straws and umbrellas and chunks of fruit impaled on little plastic swords. Everyone seemed happy but me.

I ordered a mai tai, hoping it would make me feel better. The glass came filled with ice and the drink disappeared in a matter of seconds. I ordered a Primo beer because I figured the bartender couldn't water that, and I kept right on ordering them. I was on my fourth and thinking about Barbara without employing half as much effort as before when Ki'anna the concierge appeared at my side with a lovely smile.

"I found your guy," she said, the smile growing even lovelier. "Whyn't you tell me you looking for Cap'n Howie?"

# 2.

THE PROBLEM WITH LOCATING CAPTAIN HOWIE WAS THAT HE was no longer where Ki'anna had known him to be. Not to worry, she assured me. She had gone to school with some of the island's policemen and she would make some calls.

It took more than a day to find him in Poipu Beach, on the opposite side of the island, about as far away from Princeville as he could be. He had been a boat captain once. Now he ran a small condominium complex that provided units as vacation rentals.

The Hana Palms was three stories high, built of nondescript stucco and situated directly above a rocky beach. It had a parking lot in front and a small fenced-in swimming pool with a concrete deck between the lot and the building. Although there were a few cars in the lot, there did not appear to be any people around at all.

A breezeway led to the ocean side, where a green lawn looked nicer than it felt on bare feet. I retraced my steps and saw what I had missed on my first pass, a living quarters off the breezeway that doubled as an office. I opened a screen door in which part of the screen was separated from the frame. A bell tinkled above my head and a minute later a shirtless man appeared at a counter set up in the front room.

"Aloha," he said, as if he was challenging me to a fight.

I figured I had my man. I asked if he was Cap'n Howie, just to make sure.

"Some call me that."

"You also known as Detective Landry?"

The man's eyebrows rose as slowly as an elevator.

I went right to the point. "Chief DiMasi told me I could find you here."

I showed him my card. He inspected it and said, "You wanna rent a condo?" There was just a bit of hope in the question.

"No. I need to talk to you about a case you worked on years ago."

The man put his hands on the counter and tilted back like a water skier. He had a long, lean torso, with white hairs sprouting from his chest and a few from his shoulders. He was clean-shaven, but the hair on his head was sparse and blown about at various angles. He could have been seventy. He could also have been no more than sixty. "Got telephone service. Got email. Even got teleconference things these days. No need to fly all the way here just to talk to me."

"This is a special case."

Howard Landry could have done a lot of things at that moment. My own options were limited. If he had told me to get lost I probably would have had to go back to Princeville and drink whatever Primos were still available at the bar. But he spared me that. He asked if I wanted a beer right there.

WE SAT ON LOUNGE chairs facing the ocean. The lawn chairs had plastic cross-straps, some of which were broken. Ahead of us, the water was rough and sapphire blue. I wasn't used to the color. On the Cape the water tends to be green when it isn't gray. And if it ever is blue, it is only from a distance and more cobalt than sapphire.

Landry didn't give me a Primo, he gave me a Sam Adams. "Taste of home," he said, as if Sam Adams was a treat for me, and we clinked bottle necks because I was still being polite.

"How long you been here?" I asked, settling in.

"Seven years," he said without looking at me.

"Like it?"

"It's fuckin' paradise, isn't it?" He didn't sound like it was paradise. I took a diversionary approach with my next question, trying to make nice with a statement that clearly wasn't true. "You look pretty young for a man who's been retired seven years."

"Took it early. When I was fifty. I'd put in twenty-five years. Figured that was enough."

"Your last big case was the Heidi Telford murder, huh?"

"That what you're here about?" He still hadn't looked at me, not since we'd touched bottles.

"Remember her father?"

"Anything New."

"That's right. He's still looking."

"Must be a nutcase by now."

"Why do you say that?"

"You dwell that much, let it take over your life, wipes out everything else. I know. Believe me, I seen it happen." He took a long pull on his beer. "What's he come up with now?"

"A girl who was at the Gregory compound on the night Heidi died."

Landry held the bottle to his lips. Without lowering it, he said, "You talkin' about the babysitter?"

"I'm talking about one of the girls who went to the Gregorys' to party after the race."

The bottle stayed. Landry talked around it. "There wasn't no party."

"But you checked it out, didn't you? I was told, I was told by the Gregorys themselves, that you were asking them questions."

That threw him. Like McFetridge, he had to figure out if I was friend or foe. "I asked questions of everybody I could find."

"Thing was, I looked in the file. Didn't mention the Gregorys. Didn't say anything one way or the other about a party."

Landry lowered the bottle. He had his answer now. He turned his head and leveled his eyes on me. They were more or less a washed-out blue, and I doubted they were ever used to show merriment. "I didn't put down every false lead I had."

"It seemed to me you started off chasing every possible lead, whether it was false or not. Then all of a sudden you stopped."

"I stopped because I wasn't getting nowhere."

I gave him a number of nods, each one meant to be a strand of false hope. I said, "It's unusual, though, to see that much diligence up to a point, and then almost nothing after that. Wouldn't you agree, detective?"

He obviously had not been called detective in a long time. It brought him up short. Made him blink. "You wanna tell me what in particular you're complaining about?"

"What I just said. Looking through the file, it was almost as if something happened somewhere along the line and you decided to close down the investigation."

"I didn't close it. I handed it off to Pooch."

"Detective Iacupucci."

"That's right. Pooch."

"Did he do anything with it?"

"Don't know. I left."

"And no one ever got in touch with you after you left?"

"That's right."

"That strike you as curious?"

"I don't know. I never been retired before."

I smiled, as if he had made a good joke. He did not smile back. He was looking at me warily. It was probably the look he had developed when he was about to arrest somebody and was thinking that a weapon might get pulled. I stopped smiling. It wasn't doing me any good.

"File lists every friend, friend of friend, waiter, shopkeeper you talked to, but you never so much as mentioned the Gregorys. Why was that, detective?"

"Case as serious as that one," he said, "you wanna be careful what you put down. Never know who's gonna read it."

"You thought the wrong people might read the police file?"

"I think, counselor," he said, dragging out the last word, paying me back for calling him detective, "things work in funny ways back in the Bay State. The Cape, in particular."

"So you were doing a little preventive maintenance, is that it? Deciding what should go in the file and what shouldn't."

"Something like that."

"And the chief, did you tell the chief what you didn't put in the file?"

"Depends. After a while you don't keep reporting that you got nothing to report."

I tried to keep the questions coming. Hit him with another as soon as he was done answering the one before. It was a basic courtroom technique. "You tell him what the people at the Gregory compound said?"

"Don't recall."

"He told me you couldn't find everyone who was there that night."

"So?"

"So you couldn't find everyone; you must have found someone."

Landry drank his beer, staring along the barrel of his bottle while he followed the logic.

"Who did you find?" I pressed.

"Gimme some names and I'll tell you."

"Peter Martin; Ned, Jamie, and Cory Gregory; Paul McFetridge; Jason Stockover."

"That it?"

"A girl named Patty Afantakis."

He didn't ask who she was. He asked if I had talked to her. I said I had.

"What did she tell you?"

"Nothing. She wouldn't tell me anything, except it was clear she was there."

He nodded. "Anybody else?"

"Patty said she was with a girl named Leanne."

"You talk to her?"

"Nope. Haven't found her yet."

Landry finished off the bottle and threw it on the lawn. His own lawn. I looked at mine and saw I had barely gotten beyond the first sip.

"All right, counselor," he said, his voice suddenly very taut, "you want to know what was going on? Fine, I'll tell you. Ned Gregory was fucking his babysitter, that's what. His whachucallit, his au pair. Eighteen-year-old beauty who happened to be the daughter of a guy who owns a nationwide chain of movie theaters and contributes a zillion bucks a year to all the Gregory campaigns. And Ned's got a wife and three kids and being groomed to run for some office himself and there he is, layin' pipe with the girl who's supposed to be watching his children while his wife's away. You get the picture now, pal?"

"So you were covering up."

"You wanna call it that. It didn't have nothin' to do with the investigation. So you put something down in writing, all it does is embarrass the people who pay for the Little League fields and the skating rink and underwrite the summer Pops concerts, what's it gonna get you?"

"You don't put it down, maybe it gets you retirement in Hawaii."

We were dangerously close to a physical confrontation. I was pointed toward the ocean, but out of the corner of my eye I could see his fist balled. I tensed. If the fist came flying, I was going to hit him over the head with the bottle I was still holding. Until then, I was going to keep looking at the water.

He elected to keep glaring at me.

I made an effort to change the subject, see if I could temper him a bit. "Sounds like there are things you miss back there," I said.

"I miss the fucking Red Sox, that's what I miss." And with that, Howard Landry got up and left me.

## 3.

DROVE ALL THE WAY BACK TO PRINCEVILLE ASKING MYSELF IF I had posed the right questions, if I could have handled things better than I did, what I was going to do next. I drove past my hotel and continued to the end of the highway, where the pavement stopped and a dirt track began. Cars were parked under the trees, and I could see a smooth golden beach and water that was a much clearer blue than it had been on Howard Landry's side of the island. I got out and found a seat on a log in the shade at the edge of the open sand.

I had made a copy of the file and brought it with me, hoping I could get Howard to go over some of the details. But I had been too direct, too confrontational, and I had learned nothing. So now I sat by myself, hugging my knees, weighing my options: try again, go home, call Barbara Belbonnet.

I looked up and down the beach and wondered if everyone there was as content as they appeared. The local families tended to keep to the shade. The mainlanders lay out in the sun and baked. Everyone went in and out of the water. Some just splashed about. Some rode waves. A few actually swam. I wondered if this was what life was supposed to be all about: a day at the beach. You lay on the sand until you got too hot to lie there anymore and then you went in the water and cooled off. Then you did it all over again. The people who were doing it seemed happy. Why wasn't I? Lie on the beach, go in the water, go back to my room and drink beer until I passed out. Go back to work and sit in the dungeon. Hope Barbara wore those long, tight jeans again.

I stared at the water. I opened the file.

The first thing that should have been there was a crime scene log to document the arrivals and departures of personnel. There was none. By the time Landry arrived at 6:42 a.m. it was impossible to tell how many people had been there and who had done what to alter or preserve the evidence. That, I supposed, was a point he could argue. Except he could have asked; he could have tried to do a reconstruction.

I looked at his description of the body. Heidi Telford was partially hidden under low-lying branches when he first saw her, lying on her stomach, her arms pulled up, her hands clenched. There was no mention of whether she was rigid or cold, so I gathered he had not touched her. He described her dress as bunched beneath her buttocks. He described her hair as soaked with blood so thick it was like jelly.

No other blood around the body. Just in the hair. And on the back of her dress.

I flipped pages, looking for some other description. Rinaldo DaSilva said he had moved her hair, but he did not say what the wound looked like. I had to look at the pictures to see for myself how the skull had been sliced open, wider at the surface, narrower as the slice went deeper through the bone and all the way into the dura.

Sitting where I was, on a beach half a world away, more than nine years after the fact, it was easy for me to agree that the girl had been killed because she was struck with some metal object from behind. Why it had to be a golf club, I couldn't say, but I had to presume it had something to do with the entry wound.

Hit with a golf club, found on a golf course. Except she was wearing a dress. And she had not left home to go golfing. She had left home in the evening and been found just after dawn. Whoever had killed her may have been thinking, but was not thinking too clearly.

Where is someone going to come up with a golf club as a murder weapon? If not on a course then it would have to be at home. Or at a clubhouse, maybe. Possibly the trunk of a car. But a killer wouldn't be likely to go stalking with a golf club. No, more likely it was the weapon that was available when the killer got angry, went into a rage, lost control and picked up what was handy. What was lying around.

Heidi's eyes were closed; her hands were clenched. Was she running away? There was no mention of any defensive injuries, no indication she had fought back. She had not tried to scratch or punch, had not even put up her hands or arms to protect herself. Someone was coming after her and she had tried to flee and that someone had crushed her to the ground. Peter Martin could do that. He was a big boy. And he played golf. And he had insisted McFetridge go out to the golf course with him at 7:00 the next morning.

And here was Howard Landry, a decent cop if not a great one, but at least good enough to get the heavy cases in Barnstable County, assigned a murder in which there was no evidence of the killer at the scene. At least none as of the time he arrived. Okay, Howie, what do you do? You try to retrace her path from the moment she left home. You talk to every possible bartender, waitress, shopkeeper. You go all through Hyannis and then as soon as you get outside Hyannis you give up. At least, the file seems to indicate you gave up.

Except he did talk to people in Osterville. Five miles from Hyannis. Six miles, at most. Chuck Larson told me so. Howie had gotten that far. And it wasn't reflected in the file.

Howard Landry, age forty-eight, maybe burned out, two years from possible retirement, with a dream of going off to the South Seas. There were things you could do for a man like that once he got a little too close to the truth.

No wonder he wanted to punch me.

## 4.

Ki'anna wanted to know if everything had gone all right.

The question startled me. I was eating papaya with lime squeezed on it and drinking Kona coffee, and I had been lost in thought.

Now I told her she had done a great job and I had indeed found him where she said I would.

"You know," she told me, resting a hand on my table, a hand with a coral ring but no wedding band, "it really bother me. I *know* he was Cap'n Howie because sometime I book fishing charters for the guest on his boat."

I told her all he seemed to be doing now was renting out condos.

She shook her head and looked regretful. "He musta lost his boat. Bad economy, you know." And then Ki'anna wandered off, leaving me to reflect on what she had just said.

I had little more than one day left to make something happen, about thirty hours before my flight back to the mainland. I had to make another go at Landry. I had to do it without expecting him just to confess. *Oh, yeah, I tanked the Telford investigation when I saw the Gregorys were involved. That's what got me this lovely place here in the islands.*

Except it wasn't exactly a lovely place. It was a rectangular box in need of repairs. And I had not seen a single guest while I was there. This man, this early-retired police detective, had come to Hawaii to run a charter boat service, spend the rest of his days fishing for sword-fish or marlin or whatever they caught in these waters, and here he was renting out other people's condos by the week and apparently not doing a very good job of it. What had gone wrong? Ki'anna said it was the economy, but we had had a bad economy ever since George Bush had tried to run two wars without raising taxes. And that was, what, five years?

If, in fact, the Gregorys had financed his getaway, why hadn't they come to his rescue? Their crisis wasn't over. Their crisis wasn't ever going to be over because there was no statute of limitations on murder. An unhappy police detective who knew too much was a threat to them and would stay a threat.

Unless, of course, he didn't really know too much. Or anything at all. Except what he had put in the file. Which didn't include anything to do with the Gregorys because that would just distract everyone's attention. Some people get their mitts on the file, all they're going to see is something to shame the Gregorys. What are the Gregorys up to now? Sailing boats, getting drunk, having sex with the au pair. Letting their friends screw skanks on their beach.

*Skanks.* That was McFetridge's term. That was what he had called them.

McFetridge had probably played wingman that night because, horny a guy as he was, he just wasn't likely to go after a girl like Patty Afantakis.

A hand closed on my shoulder. Ki'anna had come up behind me. "You sad man, you," she said.

I told her I wasn't really. She didn't believe me.

"You not s'pose to be sad in Kauai."

Which was pretty close to what I was thinking about Howard Landry.

She stuck her finger in my cup. "Your coffee cold."

"I'm all right." I forced a smile.

"I wish I could do something for you."

My smile got more genuine. "Would you? Do something, I mean."

She sucked the coffee off her finger and put her hand back on my shoulder. "Oh, can't date guests. But you like to snorkel? I can show you secret place. Can't be unhappy with all the fish and coral, you. Too pretty."

I stumbled a bit, trying to tell her that a date wasn't what I meant. "What I would like you to do, if you could, is put in a call to one of your connections and see if you can find out what happened to Captain Howie. Why he went bust. Why he lost his boat." I closed my hand on hers. "Could you do that for me?"

"I try." She squeezed my shoulder in a way that she could not possibly do to all the guests. "But only if you snorkel while I doin' it."

## 5.

N THE MORNING, KI'ANNA LAUGHED AND PUSHED ME PLAYFULLY in the chest. "What the matter? You didn't like snorkel?"

"It was the best snorkling I've ever done." In truth, I had not gone. I had spent the day in the town of Hanalei at a bar called the Tahiti Nui, drinking beer and worrying.

She raised her eyebrows, but let the lie pass. "I got something good for you," she said, and handed me a piece of lined paper with hand-written notes on it.

I read: "Princess Lea, Bertram 38 Twin Diesel bot January 2001 by L. Sullivan title trans. H. Landry June 01 taken by bank September 2005. Sold auction February '06."

"See," she said, pointing with her finger, "Princess Lea. Like the lady in *Star Wars*."

"That was Leia, with an *i* in there somewhere."

"Boddah you? L. Sullivan. *L* for Lea. Thing is, he bought wrong time." She moved her finger to the purchase date. "Summer's pau here. Then Nine-Eleven, you know. Not so many people come after that. See, I been knowing him maybe five years." She counted off her fingers. "Two t'ousand t'ree. And the reason I know him is when we couldn't get nobody else, I would call him and he always there for me. You know?"

"Wasn't he a very good captain?"

"Fishing boats. Not hard. They all have sonar, go same place. T'row the lines in the water and fish jump on board. Tourists go home happy."

She pulled my face down close to hers and kissed me loudly on the cheek. "Now you go home happy, my friend."

# 6.

PRINCESS LEA. LIKE *STAR WARS*. ONLY HOWARD LANDRY DID not strike me as a *Star Wars* kind of guy.

And as it turned out *strike* was the operative word when he saw me at his door. He looked like he was going to attack me, put his head and shoulder down and bull-rush right through the screen. He also looked like he had already had his daily ration of beer, even though it was barely 10:00 in the morning.

"Get the fuck outta here, you moron," he bellowed.

"I want to know what really happened, Howie."

"What happened is I'm gonna punch your teeth down your throat."

I didn't laugh, although I could have. If he tried to carry out his threat, the only thing the American Dental Association could look forward to was Howard falling over, hitting his mouth on the floor. "Shouldn't say such a thing to a district attorney, Howie. Not when he's on official duty. You know that."

"You're not on jack-shit duty, pal."

"You obviously didn't call my boss."

"Fuck your boss."

"Did you call Chuck Larson?"

His rage stalled. His expression clouded. "Who?"

And then I knew. He had not been sent into exile by the Gregorys.

Or at least not directly. I had an initial clue of somebody who bought a boat for him. Somebody named L. Sullivan, and the *L* was probably for Lea. It all came together almost without me thinking about it. "What happened to Leanne, Howie?"

He did not ask me who Leanne was. Instead, he waved his arm. He was still a good ten feet and a screen door away from me and he had not gotten his body focused enough to mount the charge he had been intending. "Gone."

"She left you?"

The former detective was swaying. He had to grab the counter to make his next pronouncement. "It's not just she left me." He held on tighter. "It's how she left me." His voice rose a couple of decibels. "It's who she left me with." And then his eyes opened wide in surprise at what he had just said. "Or for."

I guessed again. "She leave you for Jason Stockover?"

"Yeah, right," he howled. He put his hand under his chin and began flapping it up and down. "That twit," he said, and I realized he was simulating an ascot. "Mr. La-de-da."

"Who was it, Howie, that she left you for?"

"That's my point. Who? A fuckin' exterminator, that's who." He thumbed his chest. Unlike the last time I saw him, he was wearing a shirt, but it was made of burlap, like an old flour bag, and his thumb got tangled in the cloth. "My exterminator," he said as he struggled to extract it. "That I hired. Coming to my house all the time while I'm out on the water. Supposed to kill the bugs. What's he doin', really?" His eyes grew even wider than before. "Killin' bedbugs?"

He was expecting a reaction to his line, his little joke, and was going to keep looking until he got one. But then he started to topple over.

I opened the door just as he caught himself and yelled at me to stop. "I used to shoot fucks like you," he said, pointing a shaky finger in my direction.

I told him I didn't want to hear that. I was just there to learn about Leanne Sullivan.

"So you know," he said, as if we had not just been discussing her. And then he busied himself holding on to the counter again. He appeared to be riding waves. "Cutest angel you ever seen. But inside? Inside she's the fucking devil." His voice took off again, soaring until the last syllable was almost deafening.

"Why don't you come out here with me, Howie?" I figured that was the safer alternative to me going inside. There were fewer things he could throw if he were outdoors. More room for me to maneuver. "We'll sit like we did the other day."

"Fine," he said. "And then I'm gonna bust your head open."

"Fine," I agreed. "And bring me a beer when you come, will you?"

He said fine to that, too.

I waited until he came out and negotiated a position in one of the broken lounge chairs before I sat down myself. He did not have Sams this time. Sams were probably too expensive for the type of binge he was on. He was holding two cans of Miller and I had to pry one from his hand.

"You know what the worst part is?" he asked, just as if our conversation had not been interrupted. "Worst part is it makes me feel so fuckin' old. I never felt so old in my life."

"How old's Leanne?"

"Leanne's . . ." He tried to count. "Thirty-three, maybe. But it started before that. Started like when she was thirty, or gonna be thirty. I think that's when she felt she was old. She was old and I was older. She used to like it I was older. She used to like it I was a big-shot detective."

"You met her on the investigation?"

"Yeah."

"Who told you about her?"

"The fat girl."

"Patty? Patty Afantakis?"

"Yeah." He managed to get the top of his can open. It was a struggle. It nearly cost him his seat in the chaise longue.

"How did you find Patty?"

"I was a local cop. You think I'm stupid?" This was not a question to be ignored or sloughed off.

"No," I said, and Howard grumped his acceptance.

"I knew about the post-race thingamajig. The girl walks into town, makes sense she's goin' there, right? But she brings a change of clothes. You know what I'm sayin'? Why's she do that? You can wear anything you fuckin' want to that party. Some people, you know what? They wear costumes." He elongated his face, emphasizing the strangeness of the world in which we live. Then he negotiated the beer can to his mouth.

I drank from my own can and waited for him to get back on track.

"So she's got a change of clothes, means she's expectin' to go someplace. I can't find she got a boyfriend, so I'm castin' around. Know what I mean?"

It was tiresome to keep reassuring him, but we were getting somewhere and it did not require much more from me than a nod or a single word of affirmation.

"Who's at the party? Who's at the party she might know is gonna be at the party? Huh?" He drank. "Huh?"

I tried to move things along. "The Gregorys."

I got rewarded with one finger raised from the hand holding the beer can. "There you go. They're the obvious ones. So I go check 'em out. No reason other than that. Go to the house, talk to the gatekeeper. The security guard, whatever. He's just a kid. Knows somebody, so he gets the job. Black kid. Nice kid."

Howard had gotten distracted. I had to bring him back. "What did you learn?"

"What did I learn? I goes, 'Was there a party here the other night?' I'm talkin' about a party after the party. Black kid goes, 'There wasn't a party, but there was people here.' This is early in the investigation, so nobody even knows I'm lookin' at the Gregorys. Why not answer the question? Nobody's told him not to. I mean, all I'm lookin' for is where did Heidi Telford go? Is it possible she ended up here?"

"And what did he tell you?"

"He gets out this list. Like I said, nobody's tellin' him shut up, don't talk to the cops. I think all anybody cares about at this point is don't let nobody know Ned's rammin' the babysitter."

Once again, Howard Landry stretched his face in a show of amazement.

"Except you didn't know that at the time, did you?"

The face-stretching ended. "No. I didn't know nothin' except here's something I might as well go check out. The black kid goes, 'Here's the people was here.' Blah, blah, blah, and the fat girl."

"Patty Afantakis."

"Yeah, got her name and car registration, both. But there was no party. And he don't remember seein' Heidi. Don't mean she wasn't there because, look, the Gregory kids are drivin' in and out and they don't keep a record of that. She coulda been in one of their cars. I mean, this isn't like Stalag Thirteen or anything. The kids wanna bring friends in, nobody asks who they are. They're friends, right?"

I didn't get the Stalag reference, but I told him right.

"So that's all I got. Wait, no." He had to take a long drink before he could continue. "There were a couple of guys had cars, but they had been there all weekend. The only car come in and out that night was the fat girl's."

"Patty's."

"Yeah. So I get the number and I track her down."

"But you didn't report this anywhere."

"Nah. Because all I'm doin' at this point now is I'm castin' pearls before swine."

"What?"

"It's a sayin'. It's like . . . I don't know, maybe I got the wrong one. I'm just castin' about. I'm just fishin', that's all I'm doin'. Maybe I wanted a trip up to Boston. What time of year was it?"

"Heidi was killed the end of May."

"Right. So maybe I wanted to go to a game. The team any good that year? Probably not. They sucked until '04. Anyhow, I goes up there, I talk to Patty. At this point, you know, she's another one got no reason not to talk to me. Well, she's got a reason, it turns out, but she's willin' to tell me some stuff. Yeah, her and her friend went to the Gregorys' that night. They met these guys, the guys with the cars I was tellin' you about. Met 'em at the after-race party, and the guys told them there was another party at the Gregorys'. So they go there and there wasn't no party, so they left. That's what she tells me. Just to be sure, I get her friend's name, because I can tell, like, this Patty's holdin' back. Holdin' something back."

"So you went to see her friend and the friend turns out to be Leanne Sullivan."

"Best-lookin' girl you ever seen. Got this red-blond hair, goes all the way down to her waist. Little freckles on her nose. Body that won't quit." He sighed, probably inadvertently, then started up again. "And she tells me the truth. Her and Patty met these guys, went to the Gregorys', had sex with them on the beach, went back up the house. Just comes right out and admits it. She says there were other people there, all kinds of commotion, she says. Couple of the Gregory boys were having a fight with each other, but the guys the girls was with kinda whisked them outta there before she could learn what that was all about. I show her the picture of Heidi and she can't remember one way or another whether she seen her."

Howard's beer was gone. He looked at the can regretfully. I gave my own can to him and he gurgled it for me.

"Thing was," he said when he was done, which took about two seconds, "thing that was different was that Leanne was still in touch with the guy she was with."

"Mr. La-de-da."

"Yeah, him." Howard crushed the can. "I mean, it wasn't him wanted them to leave after the beach thing. He knew a good thing when he seen it. It was the other guy, wanted to get rid of the fat girl. So Leanne gives La-de-da her phone number and the fucker calls her. Wants her to go down to New York to visit him."

"I thought he lived in Connecticut."

"She tells me New York," Howard said, "and I tell her, next time he calls, I'd like to talk to him."

He stopped then. He looked at the crushed can and dropped it on the grass next to his chair.

"And did you?" I prodded. "Talk to him, I mean."

"Well, first I go back to the Gregorys', start askin' questions for real, because now I know there been at least a couple people at their place that night Heidi Telford gets killed."

"Who did you ask?"

"I asked whoever was there, okay? The one with the babysitter, definitely him. And one other."

"Could it have been Peter Martin?" I was surprised that my heart raced when I said the name.

"That little shit."

"Peter's a big guy."

"He's still a little shit. Mr. La-de-da's friend, Mr. Ha-ha-ha."

"He laughed at you?"

"Fuckin' wise guy. Thinks he's a fuckin' duke or something just because he's a fuckin' Gregory."

"But you didn't put anything in the file about talking to him."

"Okay, here's the thing. Ned, that's the guy with the babysitter, he admits to what he was doing. Asks me to keep it quiet unless I really have to use it. Obvious reasons, he says."

"And you agreed?"

"Well, I talked to the chief. And the chief talked to Mr. Fuckhead, and everybody said all right, keep it quiet unless you need it. And then, like, nothing else came up so it went like, *pfft,* under the door."

"Who's Mr. Fuckhead?"

"The other guy there." Howard closed one eye to help him concentrate. He put both arms on the arms of the lounge chair to ride out some particularly bumpy waves. "The real D.A., Mr. White."

All right. So both Mitch and the chief at least knew the lead investigator was talking to the Gregorys. And both had to know there was nothing in the file about such talks. *Pfft,* as Howard had just said.

"So was this when you stopped writing everything down?"

"Pretty much."

"Because nobody wanted to get the Gregorys in trouble."

"That wasn't really the order. It was more like, don't put anything in writing unless you really got something."

"And you didn't."

Howard thought about it. At least that is what I assumed he was doing, because he was quiet for a long time. "Here was the thing," he said at last. "By this time, we're like weeks afterward, you know? I'd talked to everybody I could. And there still wasn't anything tyin' Heidi Telford to the Gregorys, which is why, I'm guessing, nobody wants to mess up Ned."

"Who did you talk to besides Ned and Peter?"

"I don't know. The girls, I talked to the girls."

"How about Jason Stockover? Ever get hold of him?"

"Leanne never gave me his number."

"You were staying in touch with her?"

"Yeah. I was. I mean, it was supposed to be about the case."

"Only you started having an affair."

"I . . ."

"With a witness."

". . . yeah."

"Were you married?"

"Yeah." Howard's mind was drifting and I had a good idea where it was going.

"And you decided to take off together for Hawaii?"

"It wasn't like that. Look, we both knew it wasn't a good thing to do and she told me she was gonna put an end to it, get away as far as she could."

"And she had enough money to do that?"

"All I know is she did it. Moved to fuckin' Hawaii."

"And you followed."

"Not right away."

"But you stayed in touch."

"What she told me was"—his sad face re-formed into an expression that could have passed for pride—"I should come over and see her."

I nodded encouragingly, but he wasn't looking.

"I mean, it wasn't like things were goin' so good between me and my wife. And the kids, they were outta the house by this time, so this was like, wow, I can go to Hawaii, say it's part of an investigation."

"The chief gave you permission to do that?"

"I told DiMasi I was goin' on vacation. Told my wife I was goin' on an investigation. Fucked up, I know. But that's what I did."

"And you came here."

"Nope. Went to Maui, because that's where she was. Had a great time. Time of my life, as a matter of fact. And I'm lookin' around, I'm lookin' at the fishin' boats in Lahaina Harbor, and I'm thinkin' this'd be the perfect life." He stared out at the water in front of us. There were no fishing boats there. Just rough waves and water that stretched on forever.

"I mean," he said, "I had a boat back on the Cape. Wasn't licensed to do fishing charters or nothing, but I was pretty damn good at it, and I figured if you can fish off the Cape you can fish anywhere, so I start lookin' into it. Gotta get a master's license, get some time on the water out here, take a course, take a test, but I can do all that because, what the hell, my retirement's comin' up if I want it. See how everything was coming together?"

"Sure," I said.

"Only problem was, Maui's pretty developed by this time. Not exactly in need of any more mainlanders coming over and cutting into the existing guys' operations. I tell all this to Leanne and then I end up goin' home without doin' nothing. Next thing I know, she's callin' me on the phone, tellin' me all about Kauai, how it's just perfect for what I want to do, how she's gone over and checked it out already, and I'm thinking, You're doin' that for me?" Even telling the story this many years later, Howard Landry still seemed overwhelmed by the wonder of it all. "I'm thinkin'," he said, "I'm in fuckin' love."

"Information I have, Howie, is she bought you the boat."

"Bought me the boat." The man's face went back to looking worn and weathered. He made a spitting sound through his teeth. "Got me to leave everything I had, move here, and then, boom, all of a sudden it's Nine-Eleven and there's no more tourists. Nobody wants to get on a plane anymore, and I'm out on the water, tryin' to catch fish, and this girl I'm livin' with is stayin' on shore, runnin' around with a crowd half my age. God knows what she's doin', because she ain't working, that's for sure. Then one day she just takes off and I'm stuck with the boat, stuck on this fuckin' island, stuck with my thumb up my ass."

"And you can't go home."

"Burned my bridges there, didn't I?"

"Where did she get the money to buy the boat, Howie?"

"Same place she got the money to live here without workin'. I don't know."

"You didn't ask?"

"I asked." Howard Landry was still watching the ocean as it broke into little swells that lifted and flopped back down again in no particular pattern. "She told me it was something I shouldn't know about. Me being a cop and all. So I figured it was drugs and stopped askin'."

"You didn't care if it was drugs? You weren't worried that—"

Howard held up his index finger and I thought he was telling me not to say another word. But then he began slowly arcing it back and forth in front of him. "I didn't care because the woman, despite everything else, the woman had an ass like a Metrodome."

It took me a moment. "Metronome," I said.

He shrugged. "It was like the Eighth Wonder of the World."

I watched the finger continue its arc. I watched the smile break the corners of his mouth.

"Tell me, Howard, did it ever occur to you that the money she was spending might be coming from someone else?"

The finger movement stopped. So did the smile. "Like who?"

"Like the Gregorys."

"Why would they be giving her money?"

"Keep her quiet."

"About what? She didn't know nothin'."

"Maybe you did."

Howard Landry raised his hand, palm up, and then let it fall back onto the arm of the chair. He looked confused. "I didn't know nothin', either."

"Perhaps you did and didn't realize it."

"Realize what? I'm tellin' ya, in all the time I was on the case, I never found a single bit of evidence that Heidi Telford was at the Gregorys' that night. Not one bit."

He had raised his voice to tell me that. Now he turned his head away and let his chin drop. "This thing that happened with Leanne, that was something that just happened." He seemed to be staring at his stomach. "It was something else altogether."

I thought back over everything he had told me. I had to do it quickly because I could see his chin beginning to moor at his chest. I leaned toward him and gave him a shove. "Maybe they were trying to keep you away from Jason Stockover. I mean, Leanne was your connection there, wasn't she?"

Howard's eyes popped. "You keep bringing that guy up. How about you don't do it again, okay?"

"Okay. Leanne, where did she go? When she left you, I mean."

"With the exterminator." Howard spread his shoulders until his arms were almost akimbo. Then he made gorilla noises.

"What's his name?"

"Bob. Bob the Exterminator. That's all I know. I didn't pay the bills."

"Are they still on the island?"

"Nope. Gone to Las Vegas. Him and her were gonna set up a new business there."

"Exterminating business?"

"Far as I know."

"Well, if it's any consolation to you, they picked the wrong time to do that. Las Vegas has been hit harder than anyplace by the economy."

"Good. May they rot in hell."

"So maybe she'll come back."

Howard Landry's eyes closed and I assumed he was thinking about the prospect. When they did not open, I had to decide if it was worth trying to rouse him one more time.

I decided it wasn't and got up to leave. I took about three steps when something hit me in the back. I looked down at the grass. It was a crushed beer can, probably the very can I had given him. I turned and stared at the pathetic old bastard, still sitting in his lawn chair, daring me to do something about this insult he had just dealt me.

Except he was not all that old. He only looked it. And the lawn chair was broken and the cement-block condo complex he was running was either empty or virtually empty and it sat above a beach that was so rocky you couldn't even go in the water. I picked up the crushed can, retraced my steps, and gently placed it in his lap.

## 1.

WHAT'S THE PROPER PROTOCOL FOR GETTING THE ATTENtion of someone aboard a sailboat berthed in a slip? I stood on the dock and yelled—"Hello!" and "Tyler!" and even "Yo, anybody aboard?"—and people from several slips away poked their heads out of their quarters and regarded me as if I was pissing in the water.

Tyler Belbonnet's sailboat was about thirty-five feet long, white with teak decking, with the name *Pretty Hat* scrolled on its stern. The boat to its starboard side was much bigger, with a black hull, and a muscular, gray-haired woman in a cut-off sweatshirt looking at me with great concern.

"Tyler's not here," she said. "He's doing the TransPac." She spoke as if everybody should know that.

I gathered the TransPac was a race. I further assumed it meant Trans-Pacific. "When will he be back?"

"Well," she said, as if that was a most peculiar question, "he's on a fifty-two-foot Santa Cruz, which should get to Kauai in ten days if they catch the right winds. Then they'll have about an eight-day layover, and then he's one of the short crew sailing her back, which ought to take him a couple of weeks. So I'd say you're looking at about thirty-three, thirty-four days from when they set sail."

I was not sure I had heard right. "He's on his way to Kauai?"

"He'd better be. Race ends in Hanalei Bay."

I, of course, had just been in Hanalei Bay, had just left Kauai that very day. The fact that I did not know what to do next probably explained my hanging jaw. "And when did they set sail?"

" 'Bout three days ago."

Which meant it would be a month before Tyler Belbonnet returned.

"You look like that's a problem," said the muscular mistress.

"I was supposed to meet him," I said, as if somehow she could fix that, make him come back, do something so that my short time in California would not be wasted.

I had arranged my return flight to Boston so that I could have a stopover in San Francisco. Barbara had called Tyler and made the arrangements. She had told him when I would be arriving and he had said sure, come around. And he had given her directions. Explicit directions. Go to Sausalito, just across the Golden Gate Bridge; drive all the way through town to the last marina on the right; park where you can and look for the houseboat that resembles the Taj Mahal at the far end of one of the docks; walk straight down that dock till you get to slip 23B on your right. Which was where I was. Where he wasn't.

The plan had been for Tyler to put me in touch with Peter Martin. A friendly meeting. Between a couple of old pals. *Greetings, Peter. Good to see you, Georgie. I wonder, Peter, if you would mind telling me why you bashed in a young girl's head with a golf club?*

No, that wasn't how it was supposed to go. If I were just going to accuse him I could have set up the meeting myself. No, the idea had been to talk to him, gather what I could without arousing suspicion. And to do that I needed Tyler. "Hey, Peter," he would say, "look who I got here. My wife's office-mate. Just passing through town. Says you and he are old friends." *Why, Georgie, is that you?*

We would have drinks together, Peter and I. We would laugh about the fun times we had back in Florida. Remember Kendrick Powell?

And then we would go on from there, talking about all the things he had done to women over the years, including driving a golf club into the skull of Heidi Telford.

"I assume," I said to the woman watching me, "it takes some time to get ready for a race like that."

"Oh, Lord, yes. Six months, at least."

In other words, a long time before Barbara spoke to him, told him I was coming. Yet Barbara said he would be here, waiting for me.

"Are you all right, young man?"

I gave her half a wave. Sure, no problem. Set up an appointment from three thousand miles away, show up, and nobody's there. Happens all the time.

"Because you might want to check with his friend Billy."

I stopped.

"Why?"

"Well, Billy's boat-sitting for him." She gestured to the *Pretty Hat,* as if it was obvious.

"Where can I find Billy?"

The woman cast an eye up into the cloudy sky, as if that would tell her. "Well," she said without bringing down her gaze, "I'd say it's not too early for him to be at Smitty's."

I asked who Smitty was and she gave out with a hoot, as if she had misread me. "Smitty's is a bar over on Caledonia, darling," she said, pointing back the way I had come. "Walk two blocks inland, turn right, go two blocks down the street and you can't miss it." Then she added, as if she had her doubts about me, "At least I don't expect you will."

QUITE A PLACE, SMITTY'S. A big open room with a bar on one side and Formica tables scattered around the floor. It was obvious you could push the tables anyplace you wanted, either because you had a large group that wanted to sit together or simply because they were in your way. At three o'clock in the afternoon they were in somebody's way. The juke box was blasting Steppenwolf and two rough-looking men were dancing. Only their dancing looked more like fighting. Their legs were wide apart, their arms were swinging, and they were taking up lots of space as they kicked and flailed, first rocking toward each other and then much more forcefully pulling away.

I hoped neither of the dancers was Billy.

There were probably a dozen other people in the bar, most of them guys, a couple of females who looked like guys. Virtually everyone wore blue jeans. A few were in long-sleeved T-shirts, a few were in sweatshirts, a few in windbreakers. Summer attire, I gathered, for the fog-bound Bay Area.

I ordered a bottle of Anchor Steam and asked the bartender if Billy was around. He surveyed the room, which was bathed in natural light coming through large front windows and an open door, and said, "Billy who?"

I said, "Billy who's a friend of Tyler Belbonnet's," and hoped that sufficed.

"Ty's racing," he said, focusing someplace above my head.

"I know. That's why I'm looking for Billy."

"And you don't know what Billy looks like?"

"No. That's why I'm asking you."

The bartender nodded toward the dancers. "That's him," he said, with just enough cant to his head that I assumed Billy was the dancer on the right, the smaller one, a wiry guy who looked like the sort of person who would crawl through drainpipes or shinny up flagpoles for the amusement of his friends. I waited until the song was over and then stepped in between Billy and his buddy before they could start flailing about to Bachman-Turner Overdrive.

"You Billy?"

"What's it to you?"

It occurred to me that people were not as friendly in California as I had imagined.

"I was looking for Tyler."

"Ain't here."

"I know. He's sailing the TransPac. But I was supposed to meet him."

"Yeah, well, he ain't here." Billy wanted to get back to dancing. His buddy was playing air guitar without him. His buddy was making terrible faces, as though that was what was necessary to get the notes out of his imaginary instrument.

I wanted to put my hand on Billy's arm and steer him away, but I had the feeling that Billy, his joints warmed and his spirits fired up, would not accept physical maneuvering. "I'm a friend of his from back home," I said.

That earned me a squint. "You from the Cape?" he asked.

I told him I was. "You?"

"Nah," he said. Yet he obviously had some familiarity with it.

"Where you from?"

"Martha's Vineyard."

Martha's Vineyard, sitting about seven miles off the Cape, but not the Cape itself, according to Billy. I said, "You know him back east?"

He looked at his friend having all the fun. "Yeah."

"Then you must know his wife, Barbara." I had to stretch matters a little. "I got a message from her I have to give to him."

"From Barbara?" Billy's eyebrows went up.

"Can we go outside and talk for a minute?"

He said to his friend, "Be right back." But his friend didn't care. He was stuttering his way through "You Ain't Seen Nothing Yet."

Billy grabbed a bottle off the bar that may or may not have been his, chugged it, and led the way to the sidewalk, where a man was sitting with his back against the outer wall of the building, selling paintings that were spread around him. From what I could tell, he had taken several mass-produced pictures of sea and landscapes and then slapped great gobs of dark blues and greens and reds on the canvasses so that the otherwise peaceful or idyllic scenes looked as though they were being ripped apart by explosives shot from outer space. That was my only explanation.

"Hey, Taquille," said Billy, and threw the artist a couple of quarters. Then he turned to me. "'Sup?"

"I was supposed to meet Tyler to talk with him."

"He's—"

"I know, sailing. Look, my name's George Becket. Did he leave any kind of message for me?"

This gave good old Billy a chance to show how clever he was. "I thought you was s'pose to give a message to him."

"I was, and he's not around, and I'm trying to figure out why."

Billy looked at Taquille scrambling around on the sidewalk, trying to pick up the quarters he had failed to catch. Taquille appeared to be cursing his benefactor. I said, "I was wondering if maybe this was kind of unexpected, him sailing this race."

"Oh, man, if anybody could do it, it's Ty. He knows that boat better'n anyone."

"But he wasn't part of the original crew, is that it?"

"Well, man, the TransPac's got this whole social thing to it. All those dudes from the Saint Francis Yacht Club, the San Francisco Yacht Club, the Corinthian, they all want a ride. I mean, don't get me wrong, you get some good sailors comin' outta those places, man, but they're not like Ty and me. You know what I'm sayin'?" He slapped my arm with the back of his hand.

He apparently thought I was like Ty and him. Being from the Cape and all.

"They got eight people goin' over," he added. "Ty's bringin' the boat back with four. What's that tell ya? We're like the grunt guys, you know? The blue-collar guys."

"So what I'm asking is if Tyler got put on the race crew at the last minute."

Billy shrugged. "Coulda been, man."

"Well, when did he ask you to boat-sit for him?"

"Just, like, a week ago."

"So he wasn't planning on sailing before then?"

Billy was distracted. "Jumpin' Jack Flash" was playing inside. His buddy was getting all the good chords. "Look, fact is, you can have all the big-shot friends you want on board, but you want to win, you need somebody like Ty."

This was getting frustrating. I wondered if Billy was brain damaged. I wondered if his condition was contagious. "But," I said, trying to be patient, "doesn't the crew have to train together?"

"Damn straight. Captain gets his crew, then you train. Do short races. Take the boat up and down the coast, out and back, make sure it's gonna do the job. Make sure everybody on the crew's gonna be able to do his job. But guys like me and Ty, we're usually the ones givin' the trainin'." Billy flexed his arm, got it going like he was pulling the cord on a power saw. "I was doin' that, man, till I blew out my shoulder."

He kept working the shoulder until I realized that he was simulating winching. Then he grabbed his upper arm and grimaced to let me know he was not back to full strength. "That's why I'm not gonna be able to sail her back with Ty. Captain said I could do permanent damage and, well, he's a fuckin' doctor, man. So I did what he said. I'm trying to rehab it."

"Who we talking about?" I asked. "Who's the doctor?"

"Dr. Martin, man. Dr. Peter Martin."

"You mean Peter Gregory Martin?"

"I mean the fuckin' Saint of San Francisco. But yeah, he's a Gregory."

"Why would you call him a saint?"

"Why? He's the AIDS doctor, man. Works all those clinics doing shit nobody else will do. Doin' it all for practically free, too."

"But he's got enough to fund a sailboat and a crew on their way to Hawaii."

"Hey, man, even saints need vacations. Look at Jesus. Went up the Sea of Galilee in his time off, remember? Used to go fishing." Billy stopped messing with his shoulder and looked through the door longingly. It was time to go back and dance.

"Tell me, Billy," I said, "the people who are on Peter Martin's boat right now, other than Tyler, are they all locals? All people from the fancy yacht clubs here in the Bay Area?"

"One or two are, like, his old buddies from other places. He's a—"

"A Gregory, I know. I'm just wondering if one of those old buddies might happen to be a guy named Jason."

"I don't know. I could find out for you, I guess." He started his winching arm again. Had to keep up that rehab. He glanced sideways at me in the midst of his movements.

The guy was living on someone else's boat, drinking beer in the afternoon in a place like Smitty's. I offered him twenty bucks.

"Twenty, huh?" Billy stroked his chin, using his good arm. "Can you make it fifty?"

We settled on thirty.

# 2.

WE COULD HAVE MET AT SMITTY'S AGAIN, BUT BILLY WANTED to go to the No Name Bar on Bridgeway. I got the impression it was because he figured it was his chance to get fancy drinks and, indeed, he ordered an old-fashioned.

It was not ideal. The place was narrow and had a trio playing loud enough to overcome most efforts at conversation.

We were seated by the door, which was good because Billy was wafting both sweat and alcohol. He was holding a piece of white notepaper in his hand and he wanted to do a simultaneous exchange. I grabbed the paper from him and spread it out on the table. The handwriting was childish and I was trying to read by the light of a candle, but I could make out: Martin, Lipton, Todd, Turpie, Evans, Sherwood, Lally, Travis, Belbonnet.

"That it?"

"You look disappointed, man." And he looked worried. I suspected he was afraid I was not going to give him the thirty bucks.

It had been a long shot and now it did not seem worth the investment. Nevertheless, I handed over three tens.

Billy stacked the money and patted the edges till each of the bills was precisely in line with the others. He looked at the list, licked his lips, set himself, and asked, "That guy Jason, though, he's not on there?"

"No." I started to get up. Ten minutes was more than long enough to spend at a small table with Billy.

He spoke quickly. "What made you think he would be?"

"Nothing. He was just a guy who had sailed with Peter a number of years ago."

"Yeah? Where?" Billy's eyes were nearly crossed in concentration as he tried to hold me in place.

"The Figawi."

"Oh, man, I *owned* that race. Won it like five times." He pounded the paper with the side of his fist.

People at other tables looked at us. I made an effort not to look back.

"What's his last name?"

"Stockover."

Billy howled loudly enough that the trio actually missed a couple of notes. "I know that dude, man! I know him!"

I did not react right away. The trio was looking directly at us and Billy was waiting for me to acknowledge my good fortune.

"Where do you know him from?" I asked cautiously.

"From sailing, man."

"Back east?"

"No, out here. Remember I told you about training? We did a tune-up race, Newport Beach to Ensenada, and he was there. Him and Doc ran into each other down there in Mexico." Billy was smiling, but sweat was rolling down his face.

"He was racing, too?"

Billy busied himself wiping his eyes clear. He did it by using his shoulders. "I don't think so. I think he was just there, 'cause he was coming up from the other direction. He just sailed up from Tamarindo."

"Which is where?"

Billy looked doubtful for a moment. He also looked like he was losing weight by the minute. "I think it's Costa Rica, man."

"This meeting, did it seem to be unexpected?"

"Absolutely. It was like, real unexpected."

I let him know he needed to elaborate on that one.

"Like neither one of them expected the other to be there and all of a sudden there they both were." Billy gestured with his hand back and forth from his chest to mine, as though the same thing had just happened to us.

"Was it awkward?"

"Awkward?" Billy repeated. I was taxing him now. He had to talk it through, recite the facts to answer the question. "We were in a restaurant at this big table, I remember, and Doc was at the head of the table because he was buying—and all of a sudden this guy walked by and they recognized each other and Doc stood up. I remember that because I was sitting right there at Doc's end and I figured he was gonna start introducing everyone. So I was getting ready, you know?" He demonstrated how he was getting ready by placing both his hands on the edge of the table as if about to spring to his feet. "But the two of them just talked for a minute and that's where I heard the dude tell Doc he had come up from Tamarindo. And I'm, like, waiting the whole time." He relaxed his grip. "But then the guy just left."

"And you thought that was strange?"

"Well, what happened was, okay . . ." Billy pulled his upper lip as if trying to extract the memory from his mind, get it to come out his mouth. "Okay, after the guy leaves, Doc asks if I knew who he was. I wasn't sure, you know? So I ask what his name was and he goes, 'Jason Whatever, used to sail off the Cape.'"

"Stockover."

"What?"

"Jason Stockover, that's the guy I'm looking for."

"Yeah. That's him. Guy from Tamarindo."

He seemed very anxious that I understand that. At the time, I assumed it was because he wanted to make sure I got my money's worth.

# 3.

"He's gone," I told Barbara.

"He can't be," she insisted.

I explained the situation and she cursed Tyler's name. Then I told her about Billy, and about Jason. "Can you make up an excuse for me?" I asked.

"Like what?"

"Like, I don't know, tell Mitch I broke my leg."

"Except when you come walking in a couple of days from now, what are you going to say then?"

"That I went to Mexico for a miracle cure. I don't know. Tell him I've got the flu."

"And that you're still in Hawaii?"

"Let him think that, yeah."

"Only you won't be."

"Well, I'm in California now, so obviously not."

"Where will you be?"

"Costa Rica. Where else?"

## 1.

I FLEW INTO THE CAPITAL, SAN JOSÉ, YET ANOTHER MISTAKE BY a naïve traveler. I rented a car and drove for hours until the pavement ran out. Then I continued on a hard-packed dirt road until I was sure I had gone the wrong way. By this time I was in cattle country, and I was supposed to be heading for the coast. The red-orange dust swirled around me, making me keep the windows closed and limiting my vision to no more than about ten to fifteen yards ahead of me. And then all of a sudden there was an apparition, a barefoot man carrying a surfboard across the road. I hit the brakes.

The dust raced past me, back to front, and then it cleared and there was a bank on my left. An honest-to-God Bank-of-America type bank. And behind that was some mini–shopping mall. There had, indeed, been a surfer crossing my path. He had reached the far side of the road and was walking up a sidewalk with a board under his arm. I looked back to the side from which he had come, looked through trees and what were now wisps of dust, and I could see ocean water.

I drove on.

The city center was basically a fork in the road. Turn left, go slightly uphill, come to restaurants and surf shops and little businesses selling trips to see tortoises, sailboat rides, deep-sea fishing excursions, zipline and rainforest adventures; turn right and head down toward the water, where smaller, older shops sold trinkets, jewelry, Central American fast foods, bathing suits, T-shirts, skirts and wraps and blouses, and where the streets were made of cobblestones and men walked around hawking boxes of Cuban cigars.

I drove until I got slightly south of town, where I came upon a bungalow-like hotel that fronted the beach. For a hundred bucks a night I got a room in the Captain Suizo, directly on Playa Tamarindo. It was July, and the place was barely occupied because it was supposed to be the rainy season, off-season for tourists. Except there was no sign of rain that I could see. All I could see was dust.

The woman who checked me in was thin, with long blond hair that marked her as an exotic in Costa Rica. It turned out she was from Denmark.

"Oh, Copenhagen?"

"No."

It was that way with the whole process—no further information needed. Stay, don't stay . . . one night, two nights, three nights, whatever you wish. I tried to be just as laid back as I told her I had come down from California and, hey, you happen to know an American named Jason who lives in town? Her casualness reached the point of lethargy. No, she didn't know anyone named Jason. Here was my room key. Go around the back of the building, ground floor, third door. Goodbye.

# 2.

I WALKED THE BEACH. IT WAS AN EASY WALK AND PEOPLE SEEMED to be using it as the main means of getting to and from town. Most of the people I encountered were quite friendly, especially the older Anglos. They smiled at me as if we shared a secret, as if we each had discovered a place that was absolutely perfect but ought to be kept quiet. I didn't think it was perfect. Someone was building a high-rise within twenty-five yards of the water, and gray cement dust was mixing with the brown road dust and the noise of hammers hitting spikes and forklifts dinging as they backed up and cement mixers rattling and occasionally banging; and all of it was ruining the tranquility of the bay. Still, I nodded amiably at anyone and everyone whose eyes met my own, and I looked for an opening where I could say *Hi, how are you? You know Jason Stockover?*

It did not take long to realize that the people who weren't smiling were the younger ones, those in their twenties and thirties. If I got anything in response to my silent overtures, it was only a nod, a quick nod as they moved on, moved past. *Don't ask me anything, man,* they seemed to say. *I wasn't here, remember?*

The older people had a secret place. The younger ones just had secrets.

I got to town and found a bar at the edge of the sand. A restaurant-bar. I walked in off the beach and sat down at an outdoor table on a concrete apron. For a while, nobody came to wait on me, and then a waitress showed up, a local girl, a Tica, short, squat, with a dazzling smile when she chose to use it and the same attitude I had seen at the hotel. You want to eat? Fine. You want to drink? Fine. You don't want either one? That's fine, too. I asked her what was good and she said coconut pie. I looked at my watch, saw that it was only three o'clock and ordered coconut pie and a beer. It turned out to be the best coconut pie I ever had.

Then I sat and stared at the water and wondered what I should do next.

I EVENTUALLY HAD to notice the sailboats. We were on a big bay, a broad bay, and it had no marina as such. Sailboats were simply anchored, most of them about a quarter-mile off shore. There were nice-looking two- and even three-masted craft out there, flying flags of the United States, Canada, Australia, and other countries that I did not immediately recognize. Jason Stockover, my prey, was a sailor. He had sailed with the Gregorys. He had sailed to the finish of the Ensenada race just to be there when the competitors came in.

I called the waitress over and when she eventually made it I asked where the sailors hung out. She ran the question through her mind, probably translating it as she tried to understand what I was asking. "Here," she said.

I looked around. It was now about four o'clock and the only other customers at the restaurant were a table full of Germans pounding Imperial beers faster than I was. She saw me look and said, "Wait."

A minute later she was back with the manager. I had seen her before, seen her messing with napkins and things like that, moving in and out of the kitchen, but I had not paid much attention. Now I did. She was a jockish-looking woman whose short brown hair did not quite go with her complexion. She had a slight gap between her front teeth and a dusting of freckles that had more or less been faded by the sun. She wore a sleeveless blue shirt that showed off a pair of muscular arms and that was not intended to reach the top of her white cotton drawstring pants, from which a tattooed green-and-red bird was clawing its way upward to get to her magnificently flat belly. "Hi," she said.

"Hi," I said, trying not to look at her tattoo, not to look at her belly.

"You wanna go sailing?" She was clearly an American.

"Well, I was just asking. I see all the boats out there and I didn't realize this was a sailor's port."

"It's not, really. More of a fishing village turned surfer town. Those boats . . . mostly people who like to cruise the coastline." She put her hand over her brow and stared out to sea as if to confirm what she had just told me. I again tried not to look at her belly.

She was saying something about people who were sailing around the world sometimes coming in and anchoring for a week or two. But there was not really a sailing culture in Tamarindo.

She pronounced the word "cul-tcha."

I asked where she was from.

She told me all over.

I said she had a Boston accent and she blushed. "Yeah. Grew up around there," she said, "a long time ago. I been trying to lose it."

I told her I was from the Cape and a whole new look came over her face. It was as though she was inspecting each and every one of my features, making sure it passed muster. She wanted to know where I was staying and I took that as a good sign, a sign to keep talking. She listened attentively until I asked if she knew a guy named Jason Stockover.

No, she told me, didn't know him. And she really had to get back to work.

"Nice chatting with you," I said, but she was already gone, there was somebody at the front desk, somebody who could not pick out one of the twenty empty tables for himself.

I flagged the waitress and ordered another Imperial. Then I looked around. The manager had disappeared. More people came in. They simply sat down without the manager's help.

I got the waitress's attention yet again.

"Yes?" she asked, smiling as though I was becoming a pain in the ass, ordering my beers one at a time, not even giving her a few minutes . . . five, ten, fifteen . . . to go and get them.

"The manager," I said. "What's her name?"

"Leanne," she said.

"That's what I thought," I said.

## 3.

I WALKED BACK TO THE HOTEL AND TRIED THE DANE.

The waitress hadn't been able to tell me any more than Leanne's name and the fact that she was the owner's girlfriend. The owner whose name was not Jason, but J.T. Which was close enough. She did not know where they lived. But she had pushed her hand in the direction of the Captain Suizo.

"Yes," the Dane said when I asked if she knew the restaurant down the beach. She had been leaning on the reception desk, reading a newspaper. It was a tabloid newspaper, printed in Spanish, with lots of photos. She looked up, as if she actually were going to pay attention to me this time.

"You want a reservation?" Her tone said such a thing was unnecessary, maybe even unimaginable.

"No. I was hoping you could tell me something about the person who owns it."

"The restaurant?"

I nodded, tried to look as though it was a perfectly innocent question.

"You mean J.T.?"

"J.T. what?"

"What?" the woman said back. She folded the newspaper without looking at what she was doing.

"What's his last name?"

"You want to buy the restaurant?"

I was not sure why she cared, what business it was of hers, why she could not just answer my question. "Is it Stockover? Is that it?"

"Maybe." She was looking at me peculiarly.

"Is that his girlfriend who works there—"

"You mean Leanne?" A slow smile crept over the woman's face.

"You know her?"

She shrugged. The smile faded but did not disappear completely. "I know her."

"Know where she lives?"

Slowly the smile grew back. "You want to see her?"

I suddenly felt like a lug, an oversized American with wet feet and sand all over his shorts. "Well," I said, formulating excuses as I spoke, "I was just trying to figure out if I knew who her boyfriend was, if he was this guy I used to know named Jason Stockover. Back in the States."

Something was going on with this woman. Everything I said, every question I asked, was making her think thoughts that were not in keeping with mine. "You like her?" she said.

"Who? Leanne?"

She nodded once and waited for me to answer.

"Yeah. She's great."

"You like her hair?" The Dane touched her own hair, mimicked cutting it off.

What was she telling me? That Leanne had just changed her appearance? That the strawberry blonde of Landry's description had just become the nondescript brunette of Tamarindo?

I told her I didn't think one way or another about her hair. I just wanted to know where she lived.

She pointed down the beach, away from town. "Get to the big rock. Go over it. Then one, two, three, maybe four houses. Look for the big table under the big tree."

"Maybe I should drive there."

"Is better to walk. No *wachiman* ask what you are doing."

"I'm just going to visit a friend."

"Of course."

"I could just go and ring the doorbell."

"Only thing is," the Dane said, "it's got a big"—she demonstrated, sliding a hand up and down in front of her face—"gate. It's like a big door. You can't just go in there from the street. The door has to open up." She put the backs of her hands together and then drew them apart as if she was doing the breaststroke. "No. Better to go the beach."

# 4.

WAITED UNTIL WELL AFTER DARK.

I had showered and shaved, dressed in a black polo shirt and olive-green cargo shorts, my darkest clothes, and followed the directions the Dane had given me.

I didn't have to go back through the lobby to do that, didn't have to go past anyone. Just opened my door and walked straight down to the water. From there I was guided by moonlight. There was enough of a reflection to form a path on the water, and the path seemed to follow me as I made my way south to the end of the bay and over a huge rock that usurped the sand for one hundred feet or so and that had to be ascended and descended without help from anything other than the moon.

And then I was on the other side, with no one else around, no other signs of human life, no sound except the water rolling into the shore. I passed one, two, three hulking houses, none of which showed any lights. Then, by moving slowly and peering closely, I found the big table on a little rise just slightly above the sand. It was positioned to provide a view over the water while sheltered by large branches from a Guanacaste tree. I climbed up to the table to look around.

Again, the only sound was the water surging and receding.

The house was at least one hundred and fifty feet away. Up slope. It was a very large house, and it came out toward the water in two wings, with a patio in between. Stairs led from the patio down to a swimming pool that was glowing blue-green from an underwater light. A path meandered from the pool to where I was. Both wings of the house were lit up. The path was not.

I had no real plan. I mostly wanted to see what Jason Stockover looked like. I would see him and then I would find a way to confront him.

I never got the chance.

I had not even made it halfway up the path between the beach and the pool when something struck me across the shoulders so hard it drove me to my knees. Then a foot was delivered into my back, sending me sprawling into the dirt, and a huge body landed on top of me. It was all I could do to get my breath and all I could do to keep my head from being forced into a hood and then my arms were pulled together, something snapped over my wrists, the hood was cinched tight at my neck, and whatever sounds I made were those of a shocked and wounded animal.

I WAS PUSHED and pulled up the path, up a flight of stairs and into the house. I couldn't see and the best I could do was feel with my feet, try to guess where I was and where they were taking me. With my wrists cuffed behind my back, it was doing me no good to continue to struggle. I did anyhow. I shouted out my name and the fact that I was a district attorney. My captors went right on pushing and pulling.

I tried digging in my heels, but it made no difference. I was shoved across a floor and then down a single step and onto a much rougher flat surface. I was delivered smack into the rear of an open-doored van, and when I ricocheted off the van's bumper I was slammed in the back again so that my upper body catapulted forward and then someone grabbed both my legs and heaved me into the vehicle headfirst. The door slammed shut while I was still bouncing. I came to rest about the time the engine coughed to life. I started to get to my knees and the van surged forward. And nobody paid the slightest attention to the fact that I was being pitched from one side of the vehicle to the other.

THE VAN TURNED LEFT. It turned right. I would remember this, I told myself. We flew over rough road, potholed road, and I repeatedly went up in the air and crashed down again. The bed of the van was made of thin steel, and it was ribbed, so there was no place to seek any kind of comfort, even in those rare moments when the nonexistent shock absorbers let me lie flat. We turned left.

I told myself we were heading back to town. There should be lights, noise, something to indicate other people were around. As soon as we slowed I would start kicking the rear door. I would kick with both feet and someone would hear; someone would want to know what those sounds were.

The transmission shifted. We picked up speed. I bounced more, flew higher in the air, came down harder. My focus became trying not to move so much. The transmission shifted again. The driver was not doing me any favors.

We kept going. Only once did I get the sensation of light, but that was about twenty minutes into the drive, long after we should have passed through Tamarindo. And it was there for only a second. Something that streaked over my head. A single streetlight, perhaps. With no voices.

We slowed, we downshifted, and then we sped up again. It occurred to me that these men could do anything they wanted with me. Who was to know? The Dane? And when would she know? Tomorrow? The next day? I had taken the room for two days. Would she do nothing until I failed to leave? How long would it take the people at the hotel to search my stuff? To see that I had an airplane ticket to fly to Boston by way of Houston on the day after tomorrow? To realize that I was really and truly missing? And who would realize it? The very woman who had sent me to the spot where I got mugged?

I told myself I had to live in the moment, not think so much about what lay ahead. Bounce, recover, be grateful you're still okay.

It worked part of the time.

# 5.

ANOTHER TWENTY MINUTES PASSED BEFORE WE LURCHED to a halt. I slid forward, banging into the back of the driver's seat. I was sick from being tossed around. I ached. I tried to lie very still, as though somehow, if I was good, nothing bad would happen.

The engine was shut off. I could hear chirping and peeping noises. Doors opened and closed. Footsteps sounded, one set much heavier than the other. The rear door was unlatched, hands seized one of my ankles and hauled me toward the opening. I tried kicking with the other foot. I hit someone, but it did me no good. I was pulled so hard I dropped at least three feet from the floor of the van to the ground. It was soft ground, but it still hurt when I hit. It still made me groan and stunned me enough that I couldn't kick again before both my feet were grabbed and I was being pulled over rutted, uneven, rock-strewn dirt, and it was all I could do so my head would not hit all the things that were thumping against my back.

I thought of things to say. I said none of them. What kept going through my mind was the idea that the farther they dragged me the worse it was for me. I could see nothing through the hood and what I could hear was mostly the sounds of my body bumping and scraping. And then my captors began to argue.

The two men were going at it in a language that was not Spanish. One of them wrapped his arm around my chest and hoisted me to his hip as if I were a sack of potatoes. I tried to knee him in the back of his thigh and he rewarded me by flinging me away from him. I had the sensation of flying through the air and was certain I was being tossed off a cliff. The air surged out of my lungs and then almost immediately my shoulder hit something. My shoulder, my hip, my side. I had been thrown inside some sort of structure. I landed on my left side and slid across a wooden floor, but I did not slide too far because the planks of the floor were pitted and worn. Splinters stabbed into my arm and stung my leg. Once again I tried to keep my head up, my face away, and then I stopped moving.

I told myself this was good.

If they wanted to kill me they would not have brought me here, to a house, a cabin, a room, a shack. They would have just shot me and dumped me in the rain forest. Dumped me anywhere. Not here. Unless. Unless they were going to light the place on fire. Take the American to a cabin in the woods. Lock him in. Burn it to the ground. I wouldn't even be able to find my way out.

"Hey," I shouted. "Hey!"

Nobody cared.

# 6.

I TOLD MYSELF A LOT OF THINGS. GRACE UNDER PRESSURE. KEEP my breathing in control. Don't say anything more. Don't beg. What would it accomplish? These men obviously were just doing a job. Doing a job for someone. For Jason. Leanne. Peter Martin. All the people who got me here.

I could hear cans being opened. I heard cracking and crunching sounds, the sounds of teeth biting into chips. A radio was turned on and I could hear music that was fast and jittery and was overlaid by a male's voice singing happily, as though he and everyone who was listening were at a celebration.

No one made any effort to speak to me. Not in English, Spanish, or the language I had heard them using.

I wanted to tell them that I was not who they thought I was. That I was nobody. Nothing to anyone. Just a man trying to do another man a favor. A man who was not even my friend. I didn't owe him anything. I just was trying to do . . . *something*. Something that meant something. But I didn't have to do it. I could just go home. Say I couldn't find anything. My boss would actually like that.

Except my boss didn't even know I was here.

Nobody knew I was here.

Okay. That was okay. It meant I could go home without anybody asking any questions. Go right back to prosecuting OUIs. I'm good at that. In fact, I've never lost a case. Never lost a case and never been promoted. And I'm perfectly happy, how about that? Take off my hood and I'll show you. I'll smile.

But the hood stayed where it was, pressing into my nostrils every time I tried to inhale, sticking on my lips whenever I tried to breathe through my mouth. I thought if I could just get some water I would be all right. They wouldn't even have to lift up my hood. They could just pour it over my head.

And then I freaked at the idea of what they might pour over me and I said nothing.

# 7.

I T WAS HARD TO TELL HOW MUCH TIME PASSED. IT WAS POSSIBLE that I was becoming delirious. Or at least dehydrated. I heard a motor and was not sure it was a motor at all. But then I heard metal bouncing, heard the softer sounds of springs expanding and contracting, heard rubber tires slide to a halt.

This is it, I told myself. This is where someone is going to do terrible things to me. I will be brave as much as I can, as long as I can.

I heard footsteps. I heard the door open. I waited for the steps to quicken. I waited for a shot to my stomach, a blow to my head. I tensed my whole body, curved my shoulders, drew up my knees, did everything I could to make myself as small a target as possible.

I heard voices. I could not hear who was speaking or what was being said, so I stayed curved and prayed silently as though somehow I could be made so small I would be overlooked.

Something was scraped across the floor. A hand slid under my armpit and guided me to my feet. I was turned, repositioned, dropped onto a wooden stool.

A voice close to my ear said, "Boss want to know, who you are?"

Apparently Boss had not been listening when I was shouting in the house back in Tamarindo. Apparently my interrogator had not been, either.

"My name is George Becket and I'm an assistant district attorney in Barnstable, Massachusetts." I was pleased that I got that out. Pleased that I sounded calmer than I was.

The person went behind me. I tried to keep him from doing that. I tried to turn. His arm went around my throat and I realized it was the big guy again. Every fiber of my body went rigid, but he merely held me while he ripped my wallet from my back pocket. Then he let go. Then he was gone, fat-padding his way back toward the door.

He had left my passport, the one I had gotten in San Francisco for $200 and a claim of emergency, left it in the front pocket of my cargo shorts. I was absurdly grateful. I would need that when I was found. When my body was found.

There was considerable whispering. Voices going back and forth.

"Boss want to know what you do here."

I was not in a good position to lie. "I came to talk to Jason Stockover, to ask him questions about a party he attended many years ago."

There was more whispered conversation, just close enough for me to realize it was going on, just far enough away for me not to be able to distinguish any of it.

My captor spoke up. "Why you ask Jason about this party?"

Now I had to clear my throat, which was not good. I wanted to appear strong. At ease with a hood over my head, talking into the dark. "A young girl who was at the party died that night. I'm supposed to ask questions of everybody who was there." I paused, sucked in air as best I could, then used my trump card. "The government sent me."

There were more whisperings.

"Why you don't ask someone else?"

"I'm trying to ask everyone."

"You think Jason know how the girl die?"

I had to choose my words carefully. Show I was just Good Old George, doing a job. Gets his information, moves on. "No. All I want him to do is tell me what other people were doing that night."

Whisperings again.

Something may have gotten lost in the translation because the voice asked, "Why you don't think Jason know?"

Why I don't think Jason know—how the girl died? That was the question I answered. "Jason was with a girl of his own that night."

It is possible the whispering was a little louder; more likely my hearing was better attuned. I still could not make out what was being said or who was saying it, but I was part of the rhythm now. The whispering would occur, the Tico would speak, I would answer, we would do it all over again.

"Who? Who this girl Jason with?"

"A beautiful girl named Leanne Sullivan."

The rhythm picked up. The stream of words flowed faster.

"No Jason here."

"No reason for me to stay, then."

"Why you think he here?"

"He was seen at a sailing race in Ensenada, talking to Peter Gregory Martin, the man who was with the girl who died that night. He told Peter this was where he was."

There was a long pause, then a long exchange.

"Wha'chu know about Leanne Soolivan?"

"Leanne Sullivan and a friend got invited to a party at the home of Senator Gregory. When they got to the Senator's house, there wasn't much going on, so Leanne and her friend went down the beach with two guys, one of whom was Jason. By the time they got back to the house there was nobody around, so Leanne and her friend left."

"It's all?"

"Leanne liked Jason. He liked her. They wanted to get together again after that, but the Gregorys didn't want anybody talking about the girl who died. The Gregorys are very rich and very powerful people. To keep people from talking they found out what each of them wanted most in life and gave it to them. Leanne wanted to move to Hawaii. They made it possible for her to do that. Then, when she'd done what she had to do there, she came here to be with Jason."

There was a quick movement, too quick to come from the fat guy. Somebody grabbed my hood and pushed it down hard on top of my head. There was a sudden swooshing noise next to my ear, and something gave way. I tried to jerk my head to one side, but the hand held me in place. And then the hood was ripped off and I was left staring face-to-face with Leanne from the restaurant, Leanne wearing shorts and flat shoes and a man's dress shirt untucked and rolled up at the sleeves. Leanne with a vicious-looking knife in her hand.

# 8.

I BLINKED.

"How did you know it was me?" she said.

"I didn't." My eyes were on the knife. It was not the kind of knife that one brought to the dinner table, or even kept around the kitchen. It was very long, and its point was very sharp.

"You just go around telling strangers I'm beautiful?"

I moved my gaze and tried to focus on her face, tried to get past the bad haircut to the freckles, the brown eyes, the full lips, the teeth that were white and straight except where they gapped in dead center. "I thought you were Jason. I thought he'd agree."

The knife moved suddenly, as if she were going to thrust it into my eye. There wasn't anything I could do but throw my head back, try to take the knife on the cheek, the shoulder, anyplace but the eye.

"Fuck you," she said.

I had no response to that. I was feeling only relief that she had not actually stabbed me.

But she was still bent forward, still poised to strike. "He's got nothing to tell you."

He had nothing to tell me, he was hiding from me, and she was threatening my eyesight, if not my life. I slowly unclenched. I did it like a man balancing on a log, letting go of a branch, moving one millimeter at a time. "Heidi Telford was just a girl out for the night, Leanne. Just like Patty. Just like you."

The knife was pulled back enough to give me room to square up with her again. "Well, I was there," she said. "And I never saw her."

I couldn't just keep my mouth shut. I couldn't just nod and agree. I saw her backing off and I went after her. "Which explains why you're here now, hiding out with Jason Stockover."

She slapped me hard across the face. I didn't see it coming. I had been conscious only of her right hand, the hand holding the knife, and the slap came from her left. My head rocketed to my shoulder and I left it there, my cheek stinging, making it harder if she wanted to hit me again. Leanne Sullivan was a strong woman, and she hit like she had done it before.

"We're not hiding out," she said, spit flying through the little gap in her teeth. "We're just living."

"Living pretty well, too, it seems."

"Jason's got family money."

"And what have you got?" I tried to rub off the spit by dragging my face over my shirt, first one side, then the other.

"I've got the satisfaction of doing something good, of helping people who can do a hell of a lot for our country if everybody just leaves them alone and stops trying to screw them over."

The surprise must have shown on my face because her expression turned both righteous and contemptuous.

"You think the Gregorys have been set up?" I asked.

"I know they have."

"By whom?"

"There's a guy who thinks Peter Martin did something to somebody in his family. He can't get him on that, so he's trying to get him on something else."

"Josh David Powell?"

"I don't know who the fuck it is. I just know it's happening. That girl you're talking about, she was followed to the Gregorys', and somebody picked her up on the street when she left. The whole thing was arranged to make it look like Peter Martin did it."

"How do you know that?"

"Everybody knows that. The girl wasn't sexually molested, was she?"

I was trying to put this together. I seemed to be missing giant pieces.

"Oh, people like you," she said, as if she had known people like me all her life, been abused by people like me, wanted to inflict pain and humiliation on people like me. Her brown eyes drilled into mine. "You don't have any idea what it's like to be in the Senator's shoes."

"Jesus, Leanne, I owe my job to the Senator."

"Then why are you doing this?" The knife flicked, carving the air in front of my nose.

"This?" I said, backing my head away as much as I could. "Investigating a murder? It's what my job is."

"But everybody knows it wasn't any of the Gregorys. So why aren't you doing what you're supposed to be doing?"

I waited for her to tell me what that was. She didn't. She stayed bent, with the knife poised. I was thinking she was a big girl. With a long reach.

"Look, Leanne, I'm going to give you a name, okay?"

There may have been a slight nod of her head.

"Chuck Larson."

This time I did not even get the slight nod.

"He works for the Senator," I said, encouraging her to remember. "He's the one who got me my job. He knows what I'm doing. And I have to think that having me go around talking to everybody is exactly what I'm supposed to be doing. What the Senator wants me to be doing."

"I've never heard of any Chuck Larson."

Oh, God.

"No?" I tried to make my face convey that there must be some mistake. "Well, someone sent you to Maui and then gave you money to buy a fishing boat to get Howard Landry over to Kauai. I mean, you didn't just get Howard over there on your own, unless—"

I cut myself off, but I had said one word too many. It was not lost on Leanne Sullivan.

"Unless what?"

But it didn't make sense.

Leanne advanced the knife again until its point was pricking the skin of my neck. I raised my chin as much as I could. It was instinctive. It also gave her more access to my throat. She could cut my carotid and I would be dead in minutes. "Unless I was in on the killing myself, you mean?"

I had not even thought about that.

She pushed the knife into my neck nonetheless, making my skin fold around it, silently threatening to slice all the way through to my artery, my larynx, my trachea, my spinal cord.

She needed to understand what would happen if she kept pushing.

"There's a lot of pressure on the D.A. . . ." I said. It was difficult to get out the words, but I was trying. "Political pressure . . . and I'm the guy he sent to ease . . . that pressure."

The knife went through. I could feel the tissue give way. I could feel the blood start to gush down my neck.

"Aren't you listening to me? I'm a Gregory appointee." The fucking thing was inside my neck and staying there. And I was gasping. "The D.A. is a Gregory appointee. I don't have to go back with a right answer. Just an answer."

The knife was moving. I could feel it sawing through flesh.

"Nobody knows anything. That's all I have to report. So the D.A. can say he investigated, okay?"

The knife came out.

I tilted my head one way and then the other, trying to stanch the flow, but I was breathing hard and it wouldn't stop.

"Are you saying what I think you're saying?"

Who knew what this woman thought? She had run away to Hawaii, seduced a cop old enough to be her father, pretended to leave him for an exterminator. Cut off her hair. Stuck a knife in my throat. "What I'm telling you, Leanne, is either you deal with me or someone else is going to come along who's not a member of the team."

" 'The team'?" She said it mockingly. The knife bounced up and down, a ripple effect from the chuckle that went through her body. Drops of my blood fell to the floor.

I stared my answer as best I could: Sure, the team, Leanne. People like you and me. People who allow the Gregorys to do what they do.

The chuckle ended with a quick exhale through her nose. "Okay, *teammate,* so now you've talked to me and now you're done. You can go home now."

I could go home.

Which meant she wasn't going to kill me.

She was waiting for me to acknowledge that, waiting for me to agree, to do what I had been rehearsing in my mind ever since I had been thrown onto the floor of the cabin. But now that I knew she wasn't going to kill me, I didn't have to agree. I didn't have to go. Not at this moment.

I said, "I need to speak to Jason, too. The D.A.'s got to be able to stand in front of the microphones and say he did everything he could, interviewed everybody there was, and there's no basis for any claim."

"Fine. Tell him you talked to Jason and he doesn't know anything."

"I can't do that, Leanne, because I don't know if Jason's the one feeding the information to the Senator's enemies, to this guy who thinks Peter did something to him, to whoever it is who's causing all the political pressure that's on my boss."

She hesitated. I could see her replaying what I just said.

"Where is he, Leanne?"

"He's not around."

"Where is he?" I repeated, brave man that I was, sitting in the middle of the jungle with my hands tied behind my back, knowing that I wasn't going to die, wasn't even going to be left to rot, because I was supposed to be carrying a message home.

"Gone," she said. "The Osa Peninsula."

I knew the Osa Peninsula from guidebooks. It was down in the southwest corner of the country, a relatively undeveloped thumb of land made up of rivers and jungle. I wasn't even sure you could drive there.

"When's he coming back?"

Leanne shook her head. "He's not," she said, proving herself to be every bit as big a prevaricator as I was.

## 9.

LEANNE SULLIVAN DROVE ME DIRECTLY TO THE AIRPORT, WHICH, it turned out, did not mean driving several hours to San José. There was an international airport in Liberia, which did not take more than an hour to reach, even in the dark. She had the big guy—Pablocito, she called him—ride on the backseat of her SUV with me. The smaller guy, Israel, drove the van with no shocks.

I asked if we could go by the Captain Suizo so I could get my suitcase, my clothes, my toiletries, and she told me those things would be taken care of. Marika would pack everything up and send it to the address I used when registering.

I had a rental car, I told Leanne. That, too, was being taken care of, she assured me. The boys would get it, return it for me.

Everything, she said, would be taken care of.


I WAS TO BE on a plane bound for Houston at 7:00 a.m. The airport in Liberia was about the size of a bus terminal, and Leanne left Pablocito and me sitting in the SUV. She took my passport and credit card, and was back in a quarter of an hour with a one-way ticket. Then the two of them walked me to security. They could see me as I entered the waiting area, and I could see them, standing with their arms folded, not leaving their positions, watching me until I boarded the plane.

Something wasn't right. I show up to see Jason and he's not there but Leanne is. I tell her why I have to see him; she tells me I can't. And then she lets me go.

Something wasn't right with a woman whom Howard Landry had called the best-looking girl he had ever seen, but whose most salient feature was a gap between her teeth that he had never mentioned.

I had one last look at Leanne Sullivan before I walked out to the tarmac. She dropped her hand in front of her, back of the hand toward me, and then extended her fingers forward. *Shoo,* she was saying. Be gone. Run home to the D.A., Mr. Becket. Explain how Jason Stockover has disappeared. Left his girlfriend, his restaurant, his fancy house. Tell the D.A. to stand in front of the microphones and tell people that. And think about what can happen whenever you look at that scar that's going to form on your neck.

A U.S. CUSTOMS OFFICER NAMED MELINDEZ WANTED TO KNOW why I didn't have any luggage. I pointed to my neck, showed him the blood on my collar. The shirt was black, but he could still see it. "Girlfriend," I said.

He looked closely. Got halfway up from his seat. His eyes grew wide, then narrowed.

"I told her, 'That's it. You pulled that psycho stuff on me for the last time. I'm outta here.' "

"And you just took off?"

"Went right to the airport."

"Left all your things?"

"Wasn't worth it, man."

"Local girl?"

"Hell, no. Boston Irish."

Officer Melindez was unmoved.

"I figured, that's the way you want to be, you can just vacation by yourself."

"Oh," he said, as if everything suddenly made sense, and handed me back my passport.

## 1.

WAS IT POSSIBLE THAT THE BEACHES OF CAPE COD COULD be more beautiful than those of Hawaii or Costa Rica? Maybe some. Maybe for two or three months of the year. Certainly this one seemed to be.

I parked in the public lot at Craigville Beach. I had to pay because I had not gotten around to getting my resident's beach sticker. It was only eleven o'clock in the morning, but it was a Saturday, and already it was getting crowded. People had driven down from Boston—families, mostly. In the old days there would have been primarily Irish and Italian families. Now there were people from all sorts of places: Indian families, wearing their street clothes, the women going into the water with full skirts and dresses, a man sitting on the sand in a white shirt and pin-striped pants, dark socks, black shoes; Russians in teeny-tiny bathing suits, even the old men with big bellies; Brazilians, already in a party mood, already playing their music too loud.

I walked west, past The Beach Club, where rich people paid big money to sit with their own kind, have good-looking teenagers arrange their beach chairs and umbrellas. Then I walked past the private homes of even richer people, who had the advantage of Commonwealth laws dating back to colonial days when the government did not have enough money to fund docks and so encouraged people to build privately by allowing them to own the beach all the way down to the median low-tide mark.

The rich people were kind enough to let the rest of us walk across their property, twenty-six houses with at least half a mile of prime real estate that we had to cross until we got to the area on the point that the town owned. The town beach, with virtually no parking but clean white sand and clear blue water for those savvy enough to find it and energetic enough to get there.

I had a long towel over my shoulder, I was carrying a small cooler with green seedless grapes and a couple of beers, and I had a radio in my pocket in case I stayed long enough to listen to the Red Sox game. It was a precaution, really. I was not going to the beach to enjoy myself; I was going to think.

I had thought on the plane from Costa Rica to Houston and again from Houston to Boston and I had not liked my thoughts. Now I was hoping to sort them out.

After the last house there was a clear strand of sand extending all the way to a natural rock jetty. Behind the strand were long, waving sea grass and an occasional scrub pine covering rolling dunes, and on the far side of the dunes was the Centerville River, an estuary, really, seawater flowing in and out from the bay. If I went to the point there would be a hundred-yard channel and on the other side would be Dowses Beach in the village of Osterville. Land of the rich and famous. Home of the Gregorys.

I would not be able to see the Gregorys' compound from the point, it would be another mile along the coast, but I would be able to sense it, to feel it looming there, just beyond the trees, just around the bend of the shoreline on the other side of the channel. And I would be able to feel their presence: the Senator and his kids and his sisters and their kids and his late brothers' kids. All of them, leading the lives to which the rest of us aspired.

But I did not go that far. I ducked into a hollow in the dunes and set up my little camp. Others had found this spot before. There were the remnants of a fire, burnt black logs, and while I was clearing them out of the way I came across a used condom. I took a stick and flicked it into the sea grass behind me. A seagull thought it was food and made a dive for it, then rose again, squawking in indignation.

I took off my T-shirt and spread it on the ground next to my towel. I put my watch on top of it, along with my car keys, my wallet, and the little radio. I slathered on some sunscreen in a rather haphazard manner and then tossed the tube onto the shirt. It bounced and went into the sand, and I left it there. This little hollow was mine. I could sit here and look out over a berm of sand at the beach, the water, the boats on the bay, the people walking by, and no one would even know I was here unless they looked closely. George Becket, in a nice sequestered place. He's there and he's not there. I cracked a beer and sat on the towel with one arm around my drawn-up knees.

George Becket, watching the world go by. George Becket, filled with information about other people's lives. Lives lived in exotic places, lives that seemed good until you probed. Lives like mine.

Nine people had been at the Gregory compound that night in May many years ago. Peter, Ned, Jamie, Cory, McFetridge, Jason, Leanne, Patty, and, I had to believe, Heidi.

Cory left that night. Heidi was dead the next day. That left seven. McFetridge and Patty, I had learned what I could from them. I could not say the same for Leanne. I could not say anything about Jason.

I had gone to see Jason and he had fled. Why? Why not just talk to me, the way McFetridge had? And how had he known I was coming? I had gone there only by serendipity. I was supposed to see Peter in San Francisco. Supposed to see Peter through Barbara's estranged husband, Tyler. Who was supposed to be in Sausalito waiting for me. But who wasn't there after all. Who had been replaced by slippery Billy, who had sent me off to Tamarindo.

Maybe it wasn't serendipity after all.

Here, George, as long as you're looking, why don't you go to another country? I'm sure you'll see someone there. Except the guy who isn't there any longer. But look who you found. Someone else you were searching for. Someone who nearly killed you for asking questions.

Is that what really happened?

Sitting by myself, with nothing but the occasional sound of seagulls and the background noise of waves washing into shore, I tried to figure out Leanne Sullivan. Who, if it wasn't Chuck Larson, had tapped into her patriotic fervor? Could it be one of the other Gregory henchmen? Pierre Mumford? The monster of the muffin house? He had seemed more a protector than a manipulator. Had it been Jason himself? An assignation on the beach, a phone call—even a weekend together afterward—was that enough to cause her to give up her life in Massachusetts and move to Hawaii?

And what life? I didn't know. Was she a salesclerk? A Pilates instructor? A bank teller? A phlebotomist? An insurance adjuster?

And what was in it for Jason? Preppie Jason and the rough, tough girl from Roslindale. Leanne Sullivan, said by Howard Landry to be sporting the Eighth Wonder of the World, and I had not even noticed. Of course, she had been wearing baggy cotton white pants the first time I saw her and she had been covered by the tails of a man's dress shirt the second time. A muscular girl with a flat belly—could she have had hidden what Howard said she had? And what it did for Howard Landry, a small-town police detective whose passions were fishing and beer, would that have been enough for Jason Stockover, Mr. La-de-da?

Was Jason like Paul McFetridge, the Paul I used to know? Not so much Mr. La-de-da as Mr. I've Got Everything? Mr. Of Course You'll Do This For Me. Here, love, go off to Hawaii and live with Howard for a while. Then come back. I've got this nice little place in Central America, and I'll be waiting for you.

Hard to figure.

How do you get someone like Leanne to live with a man like Howard? For years. Was it possible she really did love him? Jason and then Howard and then Jason again. Maybe Bob the Exterminator in between.

Maybe she didn't love any of them. In which case, who was she doing all this for? The Senator? Was that possible? The Senator was rumored to have a ravenous appetite when it came to women, but I had never witnessed that myself. When would I have? I had seen him only the one time in Florida. And then I had spent the rest of my life doing his bidding.

Living in a nice place.

Sort of like Tamarindo. Or Kauai. Or Stanley, Idaho.

All nice places where the people involved never expected to live. People not guilty themselves. People guarding someone else's secret.

A leg appeared next to me. A very shapely leg attached to a small, very shapely foot. The owner of the leg had not approached from the beach, but from the dunes and trees behind me. It was possible. There was a path that led from the street, went through a thicket of pines and then forked, one way to the estuary, one way to the ocean. I saw the leg, I thought of the condom, I looked up.

Squinting into the sun, I did not make her out right away. A woman with a short white skirt, a yellow halter top, a broad-brimmed hat, sunglasses with sharp edges. The sharp edges gave her away. I leaped to my feet.

"Thought you were in Hawaii," she said.

I glanced around to see if her husband was with her, to see if anybody was with her.

"Just got back."

Why was she looking at me that way? And how did she get so short? Was her body always that compact? I tried to remember if I had ever stood next to her before. I certainly had never seen her when she wasn't wearing something frumpish, something designed to make her look like wallpaper.

It was possible, just possible, that she was not wearing a bra under that halter top. No, that wasn't possible. Not Mitch White's wife. I didn't know where to look. I tried the sand.

"He said you went to talk to Detective Landry."

Where had she come from? She lived in Dennis, to the east. They had their own beaches in Dennis.

"Hello?" She had a canvas bag over her shoulder. It dropped to the sand, exactly where my eyes were focused. Apparently she was going to stay.

"Yes," I said. "Well, it's because of that guy Bill Telford."

"Anything New."

"Yes." I tried looking at the sea. There were a couple of groups of people down at the water's edge. Maybe she had come with one of them. Except she had come up to me from behind.

"What did you learn?"

What did I learn? What did she know? What was I supposed to tell my boss's wife? "Not much."

She pushed me. She put her open hand on my bare chest and gave me a slight shove. "C'mon, George. There's some reason why you stayed as long as you did. By the looks of you, you must have been mauled by tiger sharks."

She was talking about my bruises, my splinter marks, my black-and-blues, and the cut on my neck.

Her hand went to my elbow and stayed there. It was a cool hand, and it was making me sweat. I went from looking at the sea to looking at the sky to looking at her. She was having no trouble looking at me. Jesus, Stephanie White was doing a woman thing on me. "You know," she said, her hand staying where it was, "you have Mitch quite worried."

"About what?" I wiped my mouth. I kept not looking at her yellow top. I wanted to sit down.

"He says your friend is going to run against him. Mitch is afraid you're not quite as loyal as he would like a member of his office to be."

"Mrs. White—" Her hand squeezed my elbow tighter and I stopped. Perspiration was beginning to bead along my hairline.

"Oh, it's Mrs. White now, is it? I'm not so much older than you that you have to call me that, am I?"

If she had enough confidence to play men like she was playing me, what in God's name was she doing with a dweeb like Mitch? "Stephanie—"

"That's better." She may have moved an inch or two closer to me. It was getting harder and harder not to look directly into her face.

"I don't know if you're aware of this, but your husband and I aren't exactly friends. He's stuck with me because someone called in a favor—"

"The Senator."

"Yes."

"And you know, of course, that Mitch owes his own job to the Senator."

"I'd say that's the common belief here on the Cape."

"Mitch was a staff attorney on the Senate Judiciary Committee down in D.C., did you know that?"

"I've been told that, yes."

"Were you also told he got the Senator out of a jam?"

"I figured it was something like that."

"Sort of like you did."

It was time for me to look away again. The wind, I saw, was beginning to pick up on the water. Tiny waves were being formed. I knew the pattern. They would get bigger.

"Which means"—her fingers moved, encircling my arm a little higher than the elbow and then pulling me toward her—"the two of you ought to be working in common interest, don't you think?"

"Stephanie, do you know what I do for your husband? Do you know how long I've been doing it?"

"What I know is that Buzzy Daizell used to sleep with your wife."

The touch on my arm was no longer cool. Now it was like the handcuffs that had been put on me in Costa Rica. "Maybe that's why we're no longer married," I said.

"Is it? Because I saw you and her go into the bathroom of my house that time. I thought, man, what kind of couple is this? They go screw in someone else's bathroom? They couldn't even wait till they got home?"

*Screw*. Stephanie White, my boss's wife, said "screw." I didn't know where she had come from, why she was dressed this way, why she was addressing me the way she was. I didn't know what to say.

"She had issues." I spoke over the top of her head. Over her hat. "She liked bathrooms."

"I started thinking about you differently then. I started wondering what you were really like, George."

I apparently gave something away because Stephanie's mouth twisted. Did her hand squeeze me again? I pulled my arm away, just in case. "You thought I liked my wife having sex with other guys?"

"I thought maybe you had an open marriage." From the way she tilted her head, I gathered I was to understand she was casting no judgments.

Stephanie, the sharp-featured ice queen, was open-minded about open marriages. Stephanie, who was married to a guy with a prepos- terous mustache and a wardrobe full of short-sleeved white shirts. What was she doing? What was she offering the swinger in her hus- band's basement? The perspiration rolled down my sides.

"And then it occurred to me that maybe that wasn't it at all. Maybe you didn't know what was really going on."

I felt a strange relief when she said that. My body temperature seemed to drop two or three degrees in an instant. "So you're telling me now in case I'm supporting Buzzy against your husband."

"Because if you are, George, his affair with your wife is going to come out. And I suspect it won't just be him who's embarrassed."

"Are you threatening me, Mrs. White?"

"I'm just saying, George, there are reasons why we should work together."

"You've got my secret. Tell me yours."

It was her turn to be surprised. Or at least to act it. "What makes you think I have one?"

"I think Mitch does."

She shook her head. "Well, if that's true, you're not getting it out of me."

She was still standing close, closer than a stranger would, closer than a boss's wife should. A sudden breeze came up and blew back her hat. She threw her hand to her head to hold it on and her back arched and there was no longer any doubt about what was and was not under her yellow tank top.

I had a moment, or maybe she gave me a moment, and then she took off the hat and spent some time straightening her hair before she put it back on. Hair that I always thought was mousy was now glim- mering in the sun. "You're a strange man, Mr. Becket," she said.

Not half as strange as you, I thought.

She went from straightening her hair and her hat to straightening her skirt. "I have a question for you," she said. She positioned herself directly in front of me again. She did it deliberately. Everything she was doing was deliberate. "What do you think is going to happen to my husband if he loses his job?"

"Get another one."

"Here? On the Cape? He's not from here, you know."

"Former D.A. He'll have criminal clients flocking to him."

"Let's not kid ourselves, George. Mitch is not a courtroom lawyer. And he doesn't exactly have a lot of friends in this area."

"Except the Senator."

"That's right. And the Senator wants Mitch to stay in his job. So why is it that you, as the Senator's other friend, are trying to keep him from doing that?"

"I'm not. I'm trying to find out who killed Heidi Telford."

"That's not quite what you told Mitch was your reason for going to Hawaii, was it?"

I was telling so many half-truths these days it was hard to remember what I had said to whom.

"Your reason for talking to Howard Landry wasn't so you could help Mitch and it wasn't so you could put to rest the rumors that he covered up for the Gregorys, was it, cowboy?" Her finger thumped my chest. It left a mark. First yellow, then red. "Don't think," she said, her finger lingering, "we don't know what's going on."

*We?* Who was we? She and Mitch?

Stephanie's hand came up and I flinched, remembering what had happened with Leanne in Costa Rica. But this time the touch against the side of my face was gentle. "So what I want to know is," she said softly, "what you've found out."

I let her hand stay. I looked directly into her sunglasses again and said, "I've found out that Heidi was at the Gregory compound that night."

Nothing changed. The hand did not move.

"That she was probably there with Peter Martin. That in all likelihood Jamie Gregory and Jason Stockover and maybe Paul McFetridge and possibly Ned Gregory know exactly what happened to her and how she ended up on a golf course with her head stove in."

Was there a change now? Did her fingers curl so that her nails were digging into my cheek ever so slightly?

"And I've found out that Howard Landry was just about to put this all together when he was whisked away to Hawaii with promises that his every fantasy would come true. Just, Mrs. White"—I took her hand away, let it drop—"like you are trying to do to me."

"You flatter me, George."

I couldn't see behind the dark lenses, but I imagined her eyelids fluttering. There was a hint of that in her voice. She laughed suddenly, and there was a hint of flutter there, too.

"I have a proposition for you, Georgie."

"No." I said it quickly.

She laughed again. "That wasn't what I meant. What I meant was, what if I could get you promoted within the office? What if I could get you promoted to felonies?"

"You?"

"Well, Mitch isn't going to come right out and tell you. It would look too much like what you think he's been doing already. But if you believe Buzzy Daizell has a better position waiting for you, maybe we could head that off. Get you the same thing without changing ad"—she touched my chest—"mini"—she touched me again—"strations."

"You're making me an offer?"

"It can be made to happen." She turned her shoulder slightly, moved her chin so that it was aligned with her shoulder. All edges and angles.

"In exchange for what?"

"In exchange for reporting to whoever you're reporting to just what you've found. Which is nothing."

I leaned down until my face was so close to hers that her lips opened in expectation, and then I said, "She was just a young girl, Stephanie."

There was a moment of complete stillness. And then Stephanie White spoke as if we were two adults trying to solve a problem, two adults who just happened to be inches apart from each other. "It was a horrible thing and nobody is trying to say it wasn't. But trying to pin it on the Gregorys is wrong."

"And is that because none of them did it?"

She heard the taunt and she understood it. "It's because all you're doing is playing into the hands of some right-wing extremist who's trying to get revenge on the Senator."

"You know who this extremist is?"

She hesitated. "You know who it is."

"Who?" I demanded.

"Josh David Powell. Isn't that who's behind Buzzy's campaign?"

I wondered how so many people seemed to know so much. I wondered, for a moment, what I was doing trying to be involved at any level. But my head was still tilted forward, my face was still nearly against hers, so close that I had only to whisper. "What do you know about Josh David Powell?"

"I know you're his stooge, George. You and all that guilt you've stored up over what happened in Florida. He's playing you, and I'm just telling you, if you allow this to keep going, everybody's going to get burned—you, Mitch, the Senator, the Gregory kids, your meat-head friend Buzzy. And none of it is going to result in the real killer getting caught."

"She was at the house, Stephanie. She was there the night she was killed."

"And then she was gone. Pushed out the side gate because she wouldn't put out, okay? It's not very nice, it's not very pretty, it doesn't look good for the Gregorys, but that's what happened. So yes, one or two of them have some responsibility because they put her in a position where she got picked up by someone on her way home. But they weren't the ones who killed her."

"And so we should protect them?"

"And so we shouldn't turn this into something more than it is, all right? Gregorys act bad sometimes, but they don't go around killing people."

She dipped her knees then, managing to do it without coming into contact with me and without ever taking her eyes off mine. She came up holding the canvas bag. "There are things my husband will do, George. You can say it's for the greater good. You can say it's for his own self-interest. But they're no different than what any of the rest of us are doing. Understand?"

Her hand went onto my chest one more time and pushed. I staggered back, not because I had to but to give us both some room. She twirled her finger. "Now turn around," she said. "I have to get dressed."

## 2.

MY EYES POPPED OPEN. I STARED THROUGH THE WINDOW THAT faced the backyard. Something was out there. Something was moving. A critter bigger than my friend the squirrel. But it was not the noise that woke me. It was the thought of Stephanie White. The suddenly sexual, suddenly direct, suddenly forceful Stephanie, who seemed to know so much about me and what I had done.

Who was informing her? Mitch could have told her about Hawaii, about Detective Landry, but if Mitch knew about Marion he did not need to send his wife to talk to me about her affair with Buzzy. And if Mitch knew about Palm Beach and Josh David Powell, why had it never come up before?

And those thoughts led to a question that would keep me up the rest of the night. I looked out the window, I looked at the ceiling, I buried my head in the pillow, and I asked myself over and over who she was really protecting.

# 3.

*B*ARBARA LOOKED SURPRISED. THEN SHE SMILED. SHE LIT UP the room with her smile. She came over to me, took both my hands in hers, and said, "You're back."

I was, of course, back. I acknowledged as much with a squeeze of her hands and then let go.

"Did it all work out? Did you get everything you were looking for?"

"I'd say so. Pretty much, anyhow."

"You saw Jason?"

"Oh, sure. He says hi."

"He did?"

"Absolutely. Asked about Tyler, too."

Barbara Belbonnet stood in front of me looking puzzled.

We didn't get any further because one of the secretaries came in and said Mitch wanted to see me right away. I was being called to the principal's office.

MITCH WHITE SAT looking lost in his big leather swivel chair. Reid Cunningham sat in one wing chair at the side of his desk; Dick O'Connor sat in another on the other side. It occurred to me that something had changed since I last appeared in this office; that maybe I was about to get fired, after all.

"How was the trip?" Dick asked. He was a heavyset man, fat really, thinner in the chest than around the waist. He wore black-framed glasses and a black-and-white checked sport coat. He smiled. Dick was a man who had perfected the art of smiling without meaning it.

"Very productive," I said. I was hoping to throw them off guard.

Mitch fiddled with the arm of his chair. Since the arm was covered with smooth leather, he had very little with which to fiddle. So his fingers just splayed and twitched. Dick continued smiling. Reid stared. I was not part of Reid's team and he and I had almost no relationship at all.

"Tell us what you learned," Dick said. He raised and lowered a hand, like he was inviting a third-grader to describe his summer vacation.

"I learned that on the night Heidi Telford died, Ned Gregory, then married and the father of three kids, was in bed with his eighteen-year-old au pair."

No reaction.

"I learned that Howard Landry found out about this and informed, at the very least, Chief DiMasi. I learned that he was told not to record that anywhere, not to tell anyone."

"Except he told you," Reid Cunningham said. He was a man with a military haircut and a military bearing. As far as I knew, he had never been in the military. He liked to swim long distances in the ocean.

"It's been, what? Nine years? And Howard Landry is a broken man."

"Broken in what way?" It was Reid again. He appeared to be assuming control of the interview. Or interrogation. Whatever it was.

"He ran off with one of the people he was investigating in connection with the Telford murder, one of the people who was at the Gregorys' that night, a young woman named Leanne Sullivan. That's who got him to take early retirement, move to Hawaii."

I was standing in front of Mitch's desk. Nobody had asked me to sit. Now nobody asked me anything at all. I stuck a hand in my pocket and continued.

"Then she dumped him," I said. "Went off to Costa Rica to join up with another one of the people who was at the Gregorys' when Heidi Telford died. Howard took to the bottle after that."

The ruling triumvirate of the Cape & Islands district attorney's office did not seem pleased by what I was telling them. Even Dick stopped smiling, although he looked as though he might take up the effort again if given even the slightest reason to do so.

"Who was this other person, the one in Costa Rica?" Reid wanted to know.

"Jason Stockover."

"Do you think he had something to do with Heidi Telford's death?"

"I think everyone who was at the Gregorys' place that night had something to do with Heidi's death."

Now the senior staff all looked at one another. It began with Mitch cutting a glance Reid's way. Dick looked at Mitch, saw where he was looking, and looked that way, too. Reid, who had gray eyeglasses to match his iron-gray hair, stayed stoic as long as he could and then slid his eyes to Mitch without moving his lenses.

"You mentioned nine years," Reid said, speaking to me. "People have been working on this case all that time and you've been messing around with it for how long? Three months? Most of it without authority. And now, what, you're ready to solve it?"

"Didn't say that."

Reid didn't like the way I spoke back. His mouth locked up. Then Dick asked kindly, "What did you say, George?"

"I said there have been a lot of people doing strange things since Heidi Telford's death."

It was hard to tell who was making the little growling noises. Maybe it was me.

"What I have discovered in my four months, Reid," I said, correcting him, "is that not only was Heidi Telford at the Senator's home that night, but so were Jason Stockover; Leanne Sullivan; a guy named Paul McFetridge; a girl named Patty Afantakis, who was a friend of Leanne Sullivan's; and three of the Gregory kids, Ned, Jamie, and Peter Martin."

Mitch spoke up for the first time. "You know some of those people, don't you, George?"

I turned my attention back to him, looking at him directly, seeing how far he wanted to go in front of his colleagues. "I know Peter. Jamie a little bit. McFetridge was my college roommate."

What I was admitting was not lost on the deputies.

"And you think," Dick said, leaning toward me as far as his stomach would allow, trying to divert me from Mitch, "that all these people were involved in Heidi's murder?"

"No."

Relief showed on Dick's porcine face. He thought we were ready now to end the discussion, get on to something more pleasant.

"But I do think, one way or another, they were all involved in hiding the fact that she was there."

The smile faded. Dick sat back, defeated.

"Landry, too?" Reid asked.

"Don't know," I answered. "The information I've gotten so far is that Ned headed him off, told him the big secret they were hiding had to do with the au pair. Asked him, in that very Gregory way, if he couldn't keep it quiet unless he absolutely had to let it out." I stopped then. I cut myself off before I related the fact that Mitch had been part of the decision to keep it quiet. Mr. Fuckhead, as Landry had called him.

Maybe Reid didn't know about Mr. Fuckhead, because he went right ahead and asked, "So Landry agreed? Is that what you're telling us?"

I nodded. "And he was rewarded with retirement in paradise with the luscious Leanne."

Dick tried to sum it up. He did it by moving his hand around in the air. "You're saying that the people who were at the Senator's house that night know how Heidi Telford died, but they threw Detective Landry off the track, and that somehow this Leanne Sullivan was, what, the bait they used?"

"You got it, Dick."

What Dick got was a lot of jiggles in his jowls as he mulled that one over. "But," he said, and then he said the word a few more times, "you're not claiming that they killed her? The Gregorys, I mean."

I gathered a line was being drawn, at least in Dick's mind.

Mitch spoke before I could respond. "The Gregory compound is within walking distance of where Heidi Telford was found," he said. "Not advisable to walk there in the dark, and it's probably especially not advisable if you're an attractive girl in a sexy dress."

I was about to argue that it wasn't all that sexy a dress when I remembered that Heidi had not been wearing a bra. Just like Mitch's wife had not been wearing a bra. The thought distracted me, made me miss something Mitch was saying. I had to ask him to repeat it.

My boss looked annoyed. "I said, I understand you may have learned something else the Gregory boys had to hide. Something about how she may have gotten out of the house."

Yes, of course, Mitch. You mean what your wife told me about them pushing Heidi through the side gate because she wouldn't put out for them?

"It seems," I said, looking directly at the district attorney so that he would know I was at least partially answering him, "that most of the people who were at the Senator's house that night paired up: Jason and Leanne, McFetridge and Patty, Ned and the au pair. That left Heidi, Peter, and Jamie."

Mitch White waited for me to get to what he wanted.

"The autopsy showed Heidi had not been sexually molested." That was Dick, still trying to ride to everyone's rescue.

"And maybe," I said, "that's the key. Two guys, one girl."

No one picked up on it.

"Peter Martin, that guy's a doctor now," Dick said, no doubt giving me one more sign of where this conversation should go.

"And the other one, Jamie, he's some big-time Wall Street guy now, isn't he?" This was Reid's line. Then his brow clouded. "Bundles up people's debts or something, then sells them to other investors, something like that."

"I heard he's making a fortune," said Dick.

And still nobody responded directly to the prospect I had put in front of them. Finally, however, Mitch sat forward. He actually wheeled his chair to his desk and dropped his forearms on the big ink blotter, a signal that he was about to take a new approach. "Look, George," he said, "you've done good work. But most of what you're telling us, we knew all along. Not the part about how Landry ended up in Hawaii, but, yes, we had information about Heidi being at the house. The Gregorys have been candid with us. And you're right, they behaved badly."

I didn't say they behaved badly, you craven piece of shit. That was something Stephanie had said.

"The kids were drunk and they were feeling their oats and this townie girl willingly came to their house looking for a good time—"

*Townie,* that's a good one, Mitch.

"And then she wouldn't play their little game, hide the salami or whatever—"

Oooh, another good one, Mitch. You must have been listening to a book-on-tape of colloquial expressions.

"So, yes, they did something they shouldn't have done. Kicked her out in the middle of the night. Told her to get home any way she could." Mitch brought his hands together and then opened them until they were shoulder-width apart, the universal sign of resignation, of what-can-you-do? "She was never seen again. They put her in a position of danger, and they feel terrible."

Who, I wondered, was talking now? The words were coming out of the district attorney's mouth, but who had put them there?

"Let me get this straight, Mitch. You knew Heidi was at the Gregorys' and you never told her parents?"

Mitch did the hand movement again, closing them and opening them, although he did not spread them so wide this time. "Who knows what Bill would do with it?"

Like go to the newspapers? I did not say it out loud.

"Thing was, it wasn't leading us anywhere," Reid said. "All right, you make the Gregorys look bad, but it doesn't get us any closer to the killer. Takes us further away, in fact. There was a whole mile along Sea View Ave. that the killer had to pick her up. Another quarter-mile along that pitch-dark street runs next to the golf course."

"West Street, which is really dark," agreed Dick.

"Which meant she probably would not have gone down it on her own," I said.

"No," said Reid, "she was probably picked up on Sea View and taken there. We figure once she saw where he was going, she"—he paused long enough to make his own little hand gesture—"jumped out of the car and tried to run away. The killer chased her, hit her with what he had."

"Reid, there was no blood on the ground, remember?"

He was ready for that. "We know she wasn't killed where they found her. She had grass stains on her knees and clearly had been dragged under the trees, hide her a little bit."

"If she was killed somewhere else on the golf course, don't you think somebody would have found the blood?"

"Didn't have to be the golf course," Dick piped up. "There's plenty of shoreline along there. Take her to the parking lot at Dowses Beach. It's just down the road, around the corner. She sees what's happening, jumps out. He chases her to the water." Now he demonstrated, clasping his hands and raising both arms over his right shoulder. "Hits her there, it all gets washed away."

"There's nothing in the autopsy report about sand on her feet, Dick."

The office's brain trust went silent. At least a quarter of a minute passed before Reid shook his head and said, "It's one of the things . . . no, it's *the* thing that's made this case so damned difficult. We just don't know anything other than where she ended up."

"Hey, guys, she was hit with a golf club. A guy driving around looking for pickups isn't likely to have a golf club in his car, is he?"

"Why not?" asked Mitch.

"Could have had it in his trunk," Reid said.

"Or maybe," I said, taking my hand out of my pocket, stepping a half-step forward and bringing it down so the tip of my index finger hit the surface of the desk, "she was visiting a house famous for its sporting family, a house that was in all likelihood filled with golf clubs, and maybe she angered someone in that house who picked up the first weapon available and hit her with it and then said, 'My golly, she's dead, whatever am I going to do with her now?' And maybe his cousin said, 'Well, she was hit with a golf club, let's leave her on a golf course.' " I thumped the desk again. "By fucking golly."

There was silence again, and again it was Reid who broke it. "We don't know she was hit with a golf club."

The three men were staring at me and I wondered if this was the end of the interview. The interrogation. Whatever it was. And since I was now certain I was about to be fired, I pushed. "Tell me, Reid, Mitch, anybody who has an answer, was there ever a subpoena issued to search the Gregory houses? Even one of their houses? Ever any attempt to check their golf clubs, see if there was any blood or tissue on any of them? See if any was even missing?"

People in my position were not supposed to talk to people in their positions that way. The moment sizzled, then faded.

"You done?" Reid asked.

I nodded. I didn't put much effort into it.

"Like we said earlier, the Gregorys have been very candid. They've also been very cooperative. Let Detective Landry in their home without a search warrant. Let him look at anything he wanted. You say he got thrown off the track and maybe he did. But after he was off the case, someone else was on it—"

"Pooch," Dick interrupted.

"Detective Iacupucci, that's right," Reid agreed. "They gave him free rein, too. Talk to any family member he wants. Look at whatever he wants. The only thing they asked him, the only thing they've ever asked any of us, is not to report anything that just gratuitously embarrasses them. If it's important in the murder investigation, fine. But otherwise, please don't just say something that's going to end up on Fox News, being blabbed about endlessly by Rush Limbaugh. And we've tried to hold up our end of the bargain, George."

"Until I came along, is that what you're saying?"

"We're not saying you've done anything wrong, George," Dick told me. His expression was very sincere.

"Like Mitch said, the Gregory family feels terrible about this." Reid tried to sit up even straighter than he had been, which was probably not possible. "They've offered to do what they could for the family, offered a scholarship to the other daughter—what's her name?"

"Stacey," said Mitch.

"Arranged for her to get into UMass, even though she didn't have the grades."

"That's our alma mater," said Dick, sliding his hand back and forth between himself and Reid.

"It was all done as a civic gesture," said Reid. "She didn't want to go. But I'm telling you this to show how the Gregorys have let it be known that anything they can do to help the family, they will."

"As a civic gesture," Dick repeated.

"Concerned members of the community," Mitch elaborated.

"Puts us in a difficult position," Reid said. "I mean, if we have something on them, they have to face the law the same as anyone else. But if we don't have any direct evidence, if we have only a suspicion, or a rumor, or a funny feeling, well then we need to be careful, don't we?"

"More careful with them than others," I said, goading him.

"I don't have to tell you that, George." And then Reid went on just as if he had not waved a personal flag of any sort at me. "Take Ned. Why, Ned's running that nonprofit that provides heating oil for free to seniors and indigents. Peter's treating, what's he treating, AIDS patients out in San Francisco. Jamie's handling a lot of serious money for a lot of important people whose philanthropy keeps Cape Cod going. We don't want to be unmindful of all that."

The word *hypocrisy* was just being rolled into a sentence in my mind when Mitch shocked me with a word of his own, one that changed the whole tenor of the meeting.

"Except—"

My mouth was open, but I gave him the chance to finish.

"None of us wants to be involved in the cover-up of a murder."

My mouth stayed open. Only my eyes moved.

"You've done a good job, George," said Reid. "We're all very impressed."

"Shown a lot of initiative," said Dick.

"We'd like to reward that," said Reid.

I remained on guard. But I at least closed my mouth.

"If you really think," he continued, "that one of the Gregory boys . . . Peter, Jamie, Ned . . . killed that girl, then we want you to pursue it. We've told you all the reasons we don't think it's one of them, but, Lord knows, we haven't solved the murder doing it our way. So this is what we propose." He looked to his left. "Mitch, want to tell him?"

"We're going to put you in charge of the case. We've already told Chief DiMasi, told him to give you complete cooperation. We've also decided tentatively to budget one hundred thousand dollars for the investigation. Whether you use it to go to Costa Rica, find these people you're talking about—who was it?"

I made no attempt to help him out. I left that to Dick. "Leanne Sullivan and Jason Stockover."

"Whatever," said Mitch. "It's entirely up to you, but we're giving you a chance to run your theory to ground."

"You want me to go to Costa Rica?"

"If you think it will provide us some answers."

"Because you don't want anybody to say you're not following up on my leads, is that it?"

Mitch went a little whiter than he usually was. Which put him about the color of snow.

"Try not to be nasty, son," cautioned Reid Cunningham.

"We thought you'd be grateful," Dick O'Connor said, his head slowly rotating in disbelief.

It took a while for anyone to speak again.

"We're moving you up to an office next to mine," Reid said. There was reluctance in his voice, as though, now that I had spoken, he, for one, might change his mind. "You'll be under my direct supervision, but I don't plan to stand in your way. The only governor on this whole thing, and this is something you have to accept—"

He waited, letting me absorb the importance of this provision, perhaps trying to decide if he should even bother going through with it. ". . . is that there's to be no publicity. Not until you've really got something, and not until you've cleared it with me. Understand?"

I don't recall agreeing. I just recall standing with my hand still on Mitch's desk.

"One more thing," Dick added. "You'll need an assistant. We assume you'd like Barbara Belbonnet."

This time I was the one who shocked them.

# 4.

"**W**HAT DO YOU MEAN YOU'RE MOVING UPSTAIRS?" BAR-
bara was not even pretending to be happy for me.

"They've got a project they want me to work on."

"Let me get this straight." She rose from her chair and stared at me over her computer screen. She did not look particularly alluring. Of course, she had not known I was coming back today. "Ten days ago you went off to Hawaii because some people planted an idea in your head that Mitch tried to cover up the Telford murder in order to protect the Gregorys."

I dumped all the contents of one of my desk drawers into a cardboard box without trying to sort things out.

"And you didn't want to see the Gregorys get away with that kind of thing anymore, wasn't that it?"

I was surprised to see how many pennies came out of that drawer. Pennies mixed with business cards, pencils, rulers, receipts, unused tax forms, explanations by insurance companies as to why they were denying benefits.

She was standing stalk still.

I poured the contents of another drawer into the same box, covering the detritus that was already there. The stuff in this drawer looked more promising. Some brochures from places I once thought I would like to visit, records of my pension plan. Bizarrely, a picture of Marion floated out and landed faceup. In it she was posed, with one knee raised, her elbow on the knee, her fingers pointing down. She was smiling broadly, almost laughing, as if thinking of a big joke.

"Hey, George, I'm trying to talk to you."

"And I've got nothing to say to you, Barbara."

"George, why are you doing this?" Her shoulders curled, her hands clenched. "Have you sold out, George?"

"You, of course, wouldn't have to sell out, would you, Barbara?"

"What's that supposed to mean?"

"Why don't you ask your husband?"

"Hey," she said sharply, "is that what this is all about?"

I was getting out a third drawer, jerking it from the desk. "Is that what *what* is all about?"

"You coming in here like you have this morning, acting like I'm the enemy or something. I don't know what anybody said to you, but there's only one reason Tyler and I are not divorced, and that's because he won't sign the damn papers."

"I guess you haven't talked to him lately," I said to Barbara while looking at the face of Marion.

"Of course I haven't. He's still out on the ocean somewhere."

"Yes, he is, isn't he? Sailing in one of the biggest races in America. One that takes six months to prepare for. Sailing with Peter Martin, as a matter of fact."

"So?"

"So it was going to be awful hard for Tyler to hook me up with Peter when he was going to be hundreds of miles out to sea."

"I didn't know that—"

"But he would have. Tyler would have said Peter wouldn't be there if you actually told him I was coming to meet him."

I dumped the third drawer into the cardboard box. One of the staff had gotten me a two-level push cart and I shoved the box onto the lower level.

"Remember all those arrangements you made for me, Barbara? All those directions and everything that were supposed to lead to Tyler, but actually led right to his pal Billy?"

She grabbed my arm. She had made it all the way across the room while I was busy not looking at her. "I didn't know anything about Peter being in any race," she said. "Ty told me he would be there. And who the hell is Billy?"

"Billy knew you, Barbara. Why, his cute little elfin face lit up like a Christmas tree when I said I had a message from you. Almost like it was code. Oh, yeah, Tyler was gone, Peter was gone, but wouldn't I really like to go to Costa Rica, see Jason Stockover? Only, guess what? When I get there, a woman named Leanne Sullivan, who just so happened to be Jason's date on the night Heidi Telford was killed, had me kidnapped and handcuffed and stuck a fucking knife in my throat."

I grabbed Barbara's hand and jerked it to my neck. "See this? Feel this? I was about one half-second away from being dead."

She fought me at first, tried to hold her fingers back, then let them touch the ridge that had formed. "Oh, my God, George."

"Yeah, 'my God, George' is right." I pulled away from her and went back to jamming books and files onto the cart.

She watched me until I could no longer think what to gather up.

"You believe I planned to send you to Costa Rica to get you killed?"

Her voice, I noticed, had gotten very soft. Her legal training was coming through, asking me a question I could not answer without either backing down from what I had said before or making something up to justify it.

"No, I don't believe that's the way the Gregorys work. They don't kill people, they control them with their wealth, power, influence. Only, things are spinning out of control on this particular nine-year effort because they never really did control a key guy, the Barnstable police detective who was in charge of the case. They relied on Leanne Sullivan to do that and Leanne has turned out to be a loose cannon."

"The Leanne who stabbed you?" Barbara looked like she was gamely trying to follow me.

"The Leanne who, like I said, was at the Gregorys' that night as Jason's pickup date. The Leanne they got to move to Hawaii and the Leanne that got Detective Landry off the case by convincing him to move to Hawaii with her. And finally, Barbara, the Leanne who left Landry a broken-down old drunk in Kauai and returned to Jason Stockover in Tamarindo, Costa Rica."

"And?" She took a stand. "So what's my connection in all of this?"

"Your connection, Barbara, is that there are only two people on the planet who knew I was going to Costa Rica, you and that little boat rat, Billy, who seemed to be waiting for me to show up in Sausalito and mention your name. Your connection is that your family and the Gregorys have been intertwined since birth. And so when the Gregorys found out that Chief DiMasi had told me about Landry living in Kauai, they realized there wasn't anything they could do to keep me from talking to him."

I looked directly into her eyes for the first time. "So, Barbara, that's when you came into the picture. Showing up at my house, telling me to right the wrongs, do whatever is noble, go to Hawaii and talk to Landry—the very thing the Gregorys knew I was going to do anyhow. But your role, Barbara, was to make sure I stopped off in California on my way home so I could be directed down to where Jason and Leanne were."

She was confused. That was what her expression was meant to show. "If the Gregorys really were involved in a murder, why would they send you someplace where two people who aren't part of the family could tell you what actually happened?"

"Well, there are a number of possibilities, Barbara. One is that they knew Jason and Leanne wouldn't tell me the truth because they've made good lives for themselves off the Gregorys' largesse. But given the fact that Jason wasn't there when I arrived, I'm not thinking that's the most likely answer. I think it's entirely possible that his absence means I'm supposed to suspect him."

"You're not making sense, George." Now Barbara's expression was sad. It said she was concerned for me, that maybe she should get me an aspirin and a blanket and have me lie down.

"Oh, I'm making perfect sense," I assured her. "The noose is closing on the Gregorys and somebody's head has to be stuck in it so that Peter Martin's isn't. Whether it's mine or Jason Stockover's, it really doesn't make any difference, as long as it's not Peter's."

She continued to look concerned. "George, don't you think you're being paranoid?"

"Oh, I am, I absolutely am. In the past couple of months I've been shot at and knifed and learned that my wife was a plant. I also found out that I've been followed for twelve years, so don't you think I have a right to be paranoid, Barbara?"

"Who . . ." The hands came up, the fingers stayed together. Like me, she was finding it hard to keep this conversation on a civil level. "Who's been following you?"

"The father of the girl down in Florida. And his minions. Or at least one black-belt, Green Beret, Special Forces, show-up-anytime-anywhere minion."

"So . . . couldn't he have . . . you know, down in Costa Rica?"

"He wants me to prove the Gregorys' guilt, not steer me to some-one else."

"And you think that's what's been going on, that you're being steered—"

"What would anybody think in my position? First I'm told not to do anything, then, when I do it anyway, when I start learning things that I wasn't supposed to learn, all of a sudden my job is changed and I'm put in full-time charge of the investigation. Find the real killer, George. And, hey, make sure it's Jason now, okay?" I pointed to the ceiling. "Mitch White practically directed me back to Tamarindo a few minutes ago."

"Well," Barbara Belbonnet said, and then she waited a moment. "Good luck, George."

# 1.

WAS NOT PREPARED.

I probably had not ridden a hundred miles in the entire calendar year. I needed to get to Sturbridge and had made no arrangements for transportation. I needed a place to stay the night so I could be there for the 5:30 a.m. start time and I had made no reservation.

It was possible, I realized, to call Sean Murphy, see if I could catch a lift with him, sleep on his floor, if there was nothing else. I sat at my desk in my new office surrounded by unpacked boxes and thought about it. Pledge a hundred bucks to Sean's ride, don't tell him I'm riding myself, wait till the day before the ride starts and then tell him I need help.

Weird George. Wacky George. The guy they just moved upstairs. Can you believe it? Can't even plan a bike ride.


I GOT OUT OF BED at 4:30, ate a banana and an energy bar, drank some orange juice, and began riding at 5:00. I had to go five miles just to reach the starting line from the motel I had been lucky enough to get at the last minute. The motel wasn't much, but the owner agreed to let me leave my car. I would ride five miles to the start, ride one hundred and ten miles to the finish, and then catch the bus back to Sturbridge at 7:00 p.m., pedal five miles back to the motel, and drive home.

I would ride, and then ride, and ride again. Up at 4:30, be home on the Cape by midnight. It didn't make any difference. I wasn't sleeping much these days, anyhow.

WE STARTED OUT FAST, the sun not yet up, several thousand riders bunched together, chattering excitedly, feeling good about what we were about to do. I had begun close to the front, and for half a mile I was in sight of the leaders. I hit the first hill too hard and wasted a lot of energy. There were no hills to speak of on the Cape and I was winded by the time I reached the first crest.

People began passing me in droves. I concentrated on what I was doing, knowing the hills would keep coming, forty-five miles' worth, none of them killers . . . well, maybe one, out in farmland, but I kept pushing, telling myself to take my time, locking onto those other riders who didn't look to be in riding shape, trying to stay at least with the older people, the women with large bottoms and the men with big bellies, those whose gears clanked as they tried to downshift lower and lower as the road took us higher and higher.

Older people passed me. Women with large bottoms got away from me. Men with big bellies discussed the Patriots as they cycled along.

I couldn't have done that. I couldn't have talked even if I had the chance.

I thought of giving up, but then what would I do? Walk? Wait by the side of the road for the race marshals to come by and load my bike and me into a van? The van of shame. It would be like riding to jail in the back of a police cruiser.

One of the great things about cycling is that even when you think you can't do something, you're in the process of doing it. I told myself that's what I was doing. What I was doing on the road, what I was doing in the Heidi Telford case.

I won't quit the race.

I won't quit the search for Heidi's killer.

I know who killed Heidi.

I won't give up till I prove it.

Till I nail him.

Fat bastard.

Gets away with everything.

Just because he's a Gregory.

Not even a Gregory by last name.

Only by middle name.

Has to go around telling everybody.

I can make it halfway.

I can make it three-quarters.

Rape a girl. Lie about it. Let her life be ruined. Beautiful girl. Used to ride horses. Rich. Beautiful. Could have done so much. I could have said something.

Get up, get up. Over the top. Now you can coast.

He didn't ask, though, did he? Fucking Ralph Mars. Fucking state attorney. What's he now? Congressman Mars. And I was just a kid. A college kid. Who kept his mouth shut.

I didn't lie.

Peter lied. And probably Jamie.

I just kept my mouth shut. Answered what I was asked. No, the Senator wasn't there. He stuck his head into the library, that was all. Saw we were there. Peter, Jamie, Kendrick, and me.

No, he didn't come in.

No, he didn't say anything.

Drunk? I don't know.

I was drunk. I know that.

We all were.

Peter, Jamie, Kendrick, and me.

I told him what I was doing.

Looking at the Homer. The Winslow Homer. The boat with the big fish. Covered with dust. *Fucking Winslow Homer. Fucking big fish.*

Kendrick. On the couch.

Reclined. Did I say reclined?

Peter. Just standing there. Next to the couch. When the Senator looked in.

I didn't lie.

I answered what I was asked.

*Fuck you, George. You fucking wimp.*

WE TURNED ONTO a shaded lane in a rural town. There had been people all along the route cheering us on, sometimes offering water, clanging bells, blowing air horns. But this street was different. Cherry Street. Families were gathered out in front of their homes, displaying poster-size pictures of cancer-stricken kids. Big-eyed kids, hairless kids in nightgowns, kids who had terrible things happen to them that never should have happened to anyone.

The families clapped as we went by. They called out encouragement. They yelled, "Thank you, riders!" They made us feel like heroes.

If only they knew.

I WOULD RIDE. I would ride until I fell off. Until I blacked out. I would never give up. I would never surrender. I will push the investigation. I will go wherever it takes me. I will ask all the right questions. *All* the right questions. Of anyone and everyone. Even if I have to go back to Costa Rica. Back to California. I will go wherever I have to go. Do whatever I have to do.

IT WAS ABOUT 3:30 by the time I arrived at the Massachusetts Maritime Academy on the west bank of the Cape Cod Canal, the end of the first day's leg. The end of the ride for me.

A huge tent had been pitched, and inside was all the free food a person could possibly want. I went right for the beer. Harpoon Lager. Poured by people who thanked me for what I had done.

I sat down at a long picnic table that happened to have an open space and listened to the others at the table talk. Some were eating burgers, some clam chowder, some ice cream. Some, like me, were just drinking beer. Those guys, the beer drinkers, wanted me in the conversation. We all agreed that nothing in the world could possibly taste better than a fresh, cold beer after one hundred and ten miles of riding in the midsummer heat.

Where was I from?

What did I do?

"George?"

Somebody had heard me identify myself. I turned. It was Sean Murphy, a large cookie in one hand, a beer in the other, staring at me as if I were an apparition.

"Hey."

He looked at the rest of my table, searching for a familiar face. He didn't find one.

"You rode?"

"I did."

"I didn't know you even— Hey, can I talk to you?"

The Murph-Dog, with a cookie and a beer, in tight Lycra shorts, a colorful Pan-Mass riding shirt, and click-clackety bicycle shoes, wanted to talk to me in private.


WE FOUND A TABLE off by ourselves. Sean sat without using his hands. He was looking at me in a way he never had before. I assumed it was because he was impressed at my performance, my accomplishment, the mere fact that I was here in the beer tent at the finish line.

He said, "Pretty good gig you got there on the Telford investigation."

I drank because it gave me a chance to lower my eyes to my plastic cup.

"Office next to Reid Cunningham's, huh?"

He knew it was. I just nodded.

"I saw all those uniformed officers delivering files, so obviously something big is going on."

"It's been going on for a while, Sean."

"Cold case suddenly heats up, something new has happened."

Sean was leaning forward, his wrists resting on the edge of the table, his hands still holding his beer and his cookie.

"You taking it before the grand jury?"

"Taking what, Sean?"

He smiled as if he recognized that a certain code had to be used, certain protocol had to be followed. "Rumors are going around that there's new evidence the Gregorys might have been involved."

I did not respond. This did not bother Sean in the slightest.

"Is the Senator going to testify?"

"Sean, tell me exactly what it is you're hearing."

He looked left and right. He lowered his voice. "I'm hearing there might have been an orgy going on at the Gregorys' that night the girl was killed. I'm hearing she might have been there and seen too much."

There was something childish about the way Sean was addressing me. Maybe it was the cookie.

"You believe that?" I asked.

"What I believe," he said, his eyes sparkling, "is that Anything New Telford has been making the rounds for years telling people the Gregorys had something to do with the death of his daughter. What I hear is that he's got your ear now. What I see is you've suddenly got prime office space and stacks of files. And I want in."

"Want in how?"

"To assist you. To co-counsel with you. Whatever you'll give me. I heard you turned down Barbara."

He took a big bite out of the cookie, what I thought was a rather vicious bite. Crumbs shot all over the place.

"Guys are talking," he went on, his mouth full. "They're saying, 'Why would he do that?' People are saying, 'Well, she doesn't have enough experience.' But me, I looked at it, I figured something else out altogether."

He washed the cookie down with beer, dropped his voice even lower, and said, "I figure, Barbara, she's from around here. She's tied in with those people. You can't have her going after them like you and I could."

"By 'those people,' you mean the Gregorys?"

"Damn right."

"And you wouldn't care which Gregory might be involved, as long as it's one of them. Is that what you're saying?"

Sean Murphy looked at me as if I had just spoken a profound truth, one that was going to make us great friends now that we shared this understanding. "You got it," he said. "Case like this, fucking career maker, I'd go after the Senator's mother. Fry her ass, if I had to."

# 2.

SEAN WASN'T THE ONLY ONE WHO WAS EXCITED.

On Monday I got a call from the *Cape Cod Times,* then one from *The Boston Globe,* then *The Wall Street Journal,* and finally the dreaded Fox News. I referred them all to Reid, who repeatedly denied that there had been any developments. He said the matter had never been closed, and praised Bill Telford for his diligence in never letting them forget that the killer was still at large.

There was other news in the office, too—news that was not worthy of journalists' attention, but that was of some significance to me. Barbara Belbonnet had unexpectedly announced she was taking a leave of absence. This threw operations into a tizzy because nobody wanted to cover her caseload. "Domestic relations?" a woman said to me as she was trying to talk her way onto my project, "*yuck.*"

THERE WAS PRECIOUS little in the police files that I had not seen already. I read them and reread them. I interviewed the officers who had responded to the crime scene and who either were still with the force or lived in the area. I explored the possibility that Heidi had been chased across the golf course and tried to get someone, anyone, to give me information about a drag path. There wasn't any. Not even the last few feet, as Reid Cunningham had implied. Which meant that she had to have been killed somewhere else and someone had to have carried a hundred-and-fifteen-pound dead girl at least from West Street across a fairway to where she was found in the trees. Someone. Or some two.

Pick her up, put her over your shoulder in a fireman's carry. Peter Martin was big enough to do that. Or one person could hold her under the arms, another hold her feet. Peter and who? Not Jamie, they were fighting. Not Ned, he was occupied. Not Cory, she was gone. Which meant it would have had to be either McFetridge, who spoke to me, or Jason, who ran from me.

I MET WITH DR. PARDEEP, the medical examiner. He was reluctant to say anything at first and kept telling me it was all in his report, but I got him talking about his role as a scientist and how really what he was doing was solving mysteries, and he got excited and told me that was what people did not understand about his job. It was all about hunting for clues. Finding them, assessing them, putting them together to come up with answers as to what had happened. He examined bodies to find clues and, yes, that was what he had done in this case.

As for the conclusion that it was a golf club that killed Heidi Telford, he pointed out that he had said only it was most likely a golf club. The reason? Well, the entry was obtunded, which meant it had not been made by anything sharp, like an ax. Also, it was clean. No dirt, no bark, no foreign organisms, as might be seen if it were made by a rock or anything organic. Could I, he wanted to know, think of any other object that would cause such a wound? He was more than willing to consider any proposal I had. I offered the possibility of a fireplace poker, and he grew animated and told me he had considered that, but that the geometry of the entry wound, deeper toward the top of the skull than the bottom, did not comport with a completely straight object.

He was lecturing me on the dynamics of blows inflicted by pokers, but my mind had gone back to the idea of a golf club being clean. The only times the heads of my clubs were ever clean were when I was a guest at a private course and the caddies wiped them down before loading them into my car.

I wondered if that ruled out a transient. Not likely to find one of those driving around Osterville late at night with a bag of clean clubs in his car, looking to pick up young girls walking home. Young girls leaving the Gregory compound. Having been pushed out the side gate. As the Gregory boys were wont to do. A family tradition.

I MET WITH DETECTIVE IACUPUCCI. He was more than happy to come to my office. He stopped and talked to three different female staffers between the front desk and my door. Pooch was about six-feet-three, devilishly handsome and dumb as a box of rocks. He could tell me nothing that he had learned since taking over the case from Detective Landry. But he was delighted to talk about the Barnstable High Red Raiders football team, for which he was the defensive line coach. They were starting their workouts now. I looked like I might have been a player at one time. Maybe I'd like to come out and give the DBs a hand.

I gave him a list of the people known to be at the Gregorys' on the night Heidi was there and told him no, I wasn't available to lend the boys a hand.

He held the list and asked why not.

I told him I wasn't in shape.

He said he heard I had just ridden a hundred-mile race, and my first instinct was to tell him that it was one hundred and ten miles. Instead I told him it wasn't a race. I pointed to the list and asked who he had interviewed. He studied the names for a longer time than should have been necessary for a man with fluency in English. Then he said no one. Although he wouldn't mind interviewing Cory Gregory if I wanted.

## 3.

HAD A VISITOR AT HOME. IT HAPPENED RATHER LATE AT NIGHT. I walked into the kitchen, shut the light in the ceiling of the carport, shut the kitchen lights, and started along the hallway to my bedroom when there was a tapping on the carport door.

It was an insistent tapping, as though the tapper had waited until I shut the lights, was sure I was going to respond and that I would share his or her interest in discretion. Given the fact that my last visitor had been Barbara on the day I had stayed in bed, I could not imagine who would be hitting my door like that.

I walked back, flicked on the carport light again, and opened the door. It was deep summer on Cape Cod. It was somewhere after 10:00 p.m. The crickets were chirping, the bullfrogs were croaking, and a man dressed entirely in black bolted past me and into my house.

He looked around, his eyes sweeping the room, then sat down at the kitchen table.

It did not register with me that the man dressed like Johnny Cash was actually Roland Andrews until he was seated in my kitchen. I made a silent promise to be more careful about how I opened doors in the future.

I asked if he wanted a drink. He laughed, as if men like him didn't drink. At least not with men like me. They probably drank only like the Martin Sheen character in the beginning of *Apocalypse Now,* by themselves in hotel rooms, drank till they got totally wasted, then stripped off all their clothes and karate-chopped the stranger they saw in the mirror.

"There's been a change of plans, Georgie," he said.

I went to turn on the overhead kitchen light. He told me not to. He glanced out the sliding doors to the backyard and gestured that I should draw the drapes closer together.

I sat down in the gloom with him. There was enough light from the hallway behind me to make out his features. I said I wasn't aware of any plans.

"We're not going with Buzzy anymore. Too many complications."

I nodded, giving him time to tell me what they were.

"Now that they've renewed the investigation," he said, waving his hand as an indicator of how obvious it should be, "put you in charge. Brilliant move on their part." He was leaning in my direction. He wasn't whispering, but he might as well have been.

"On whose part?"

"The Gregorys', who else? I mean, you don't think Mitch White makes decisions like this on his own, do you?" Roland Andrews inched his chair closer to me. "Look, we go ahead and put Buzzy up, what's he going to say now that the office has you working full-time on the Telford case? That you're not investigating it? His buddy? The one he's been cuckolding? You see? See what I mean?"

I thought, not for the first time, how much I would like to punch Roland in the face.

"I know how the Gregorys operate. I should, I've been watching them all these years. They let Buzzy announce his candidacy. If he says you're not investigating, they immediately call in their journalist friends and tell them about the animosity between you two because you caught him hosing your wife. That's the brilliant part. They dirty up both of you. He's a cad and you're an unmanly guy, bitter at everyone who seems to have a better life than you."

He sat back. He smiled as if he expected me to share in his appreciation of the diabolism at work.

I played it out. I would swing, hit him directly under the chin, lift him out of his seat. If he didn't get knocked cold he would be back at me in an instant. He would no doubt beat the hell out of me. But so what?

I would wear my wounds proudly. Use my face as a platform to talk about how I had been attacked by Josh David Powell's henchman because of something that happened a long time ago in Palm Beach. Something involving an attractive young woman who had gone to a party at the Gregorys' house to have a good time and who had ended up dead. Just like Heidi Telford. Two girls, used, abused, and cast aside. One figuratively, the other literally. I liked the idea. I didn't take the time to think it all the way through; I just went with it.

I started down low because I was sitting, because my hand was already at my thigh. I shifted my weight onto my left buttock, dropped my left shoulder, and fired with my right fist.

Roland Andrews caught it in midair.

He twisted my wrist back, bent it until my fingers almost touched my forearm. I swung with my left. The two of us were still sitting in chairs and I couldn't get much leverage.

"Oh, ho!" Roland cried as I made contact with his cheekbone and then he laughed and bent my wrist farther. He kept bending until I dropped to my knees on the linoleum.

I was screaming in pain and he cuffed me on the ear. The sound inside my head was as if a cannon had gone off. I went over. He let go of my wrist and I found myself lying on my own kitchen floor in a near-fetal curve. It struck me that no man should be in that position and I tried to do something about it. I could hear nothing, but I spun as best I could and made a dive for his legs. He kicked me away and then rabbit-punched me on the back of my neck. This time when I hit the floor I couldn't spin, no matter how foolish I felt I looked. I was paralyzed.

"You done now, Georgie?" he asked, looking down. And I was surprised because I could actually hear him over the roaring in my head. I could hear, but I couldn't feel. I was numb from fingers to toes and couldn't answer.

Then, before I could get panicky, my wrist began to throb and for the first time in my life I felt joy at being in pain. I tried moving my feet and they did as I asked. I wanted to cry out in happiness.

"All right," Roland seemed to be saying, "I went too far. I admit it, and I don't blame you for attacking me." He touched his cheekbone where I had hit him. "Surprised, maybe, but you showed more balls than I thought you had."

He extended his hand to help me up, warrior to warrior, but I shook him off, figuring it might be a trick. I rolled onto my noninjured wrist and pushed down until I could kneel. Then I pushed again and staggered to my feet. I took a step or two to the refrigerator, leaned my forehead against it for a moment, then opened the door. "Want some water?" I asked.

"Nah. I'm good."

I got out a small bottle, took the cap off with my teeth, spit the cap, and drank about halfway down. "You don't have much time," I said when I had enough breath. "Find another candidate."

"Kind of campaign we have in mind, less time the better. It's a non-partisan election for D.A. All we have to do is go in at the last moment, blitz Mitchell White with the bad news."

"Which is what?"

"Whatever you've got."

"I don't have anything."

Andrews laughed. He thought that was great fun to hear me say that. "You've just come back from Hawaii by way of California and Costa Rica, my friend. You've got something."

More evidence that I had been followed. Or somebody had talked. And I had a pretty good idea who it was. I already had seen Roland Andrews's ability to plant women in my life. I finished off my water. "Who you thinking of putting up?"

"You've got two other buddies. I want to ask you about them."

I pressed my back against the refrigerator and let my feet slide out in front of me. "Who?"

"Jimmy Shelley, Alphonse Carbona. I need to know which one's better."

My chest ached. Everything about me ached. "Jimmy's a screwup, like Buzzy. Al, well, I don't see him as being political material."

"Jimmy kept his mouth shut about seeing Buzzy and Marion together, didn't he?"

"Al keeps his mouth shut about everything."

"Still, Jimmy, having seen what he did, never made jokes about it in front of you, did he? Never told anyone else, as far as you know?"

"You're right. What's your slogan going to be? 'He Won't Tell'?"

"You like Alphonse better, huh? As a candidate, I mean."

"Al's married, got a nice wife. Does a good job in court. Talks to juries fine. Just doesn't say much in social situations. Far as I know, he's never been in trouble."

"I see." But it was not clear he did. He seemed to have his heart set on Jimmy.

I shrugged, not really caring. "What do the Macs say?"

"The Macs will do what I tell them. As long as it doesn't interfere with their agenda."

"Which involves building a casino for the Indians in Mashpee."

Roland's head came up rather quickly. "Smart boy," he said. "Who told you that?"

I didn't answer.

"Seriously," he said, "who was it let his mouth flap?"

I said, "McCoppin," for no other reason than he was the one who had turned away from me when I went into Muggsy's that time I was trying to talk to the chief. And that reminded me of something else.

"What's in this for Cello DiMasi?"

"Who says there's anything in it for him?"

"Well, he's a friend of the Macs. If they're plotting to overthrow the D.A., he's got to be aware of it—yet the thing they're going to have the candidate say, that Mitch White protected the Gregorys, couldn't the exact same charge be leveled against the chief?"

"Let me tell you what I've learned about the chief. Except for the fact he's not a native, Cello DiMasi is your quintessential local guy. That's who he identifies with, the blue-collar people who've been here all their lives and all their parents' lives and who took him in when he was a kid playing ball in the summer. Like them, like the people who work on the summer residents' septic tanks and sell them lobsters, he'll do whatever the job requires, then go home and smirk about it with his buddies. But first he does the job that the powers that be want him to do. And if they don't want him going after something, he won't do it."

"But," I insisted, not sure if I was getting an answer, "if Mitch is thrown out, doesn't Cello have to go, too?"

"If we put up a candidate against the sitting D.A. and our candidate wins, the chief will no doubt keep his position by telling everyone Mitch White held him back. Made him put a clown like Iacupucci on the case."

"You said 'if.' "

"What?"

"You said, 'If we put up a candidate.' "

"Well, we may not need to, depending on what it is you've come up with."

"I told you, I haven't come up with anything."

Andrews's chin lifted. He dropped his eyes, wanting mine to follow them, wanting me to look at the floor. To remember I could be there again.

I said, "The whole reason they've promoted me, moved me upstairs next to them, is so they can monitor me, stifle whatever it is I might learn."

"Which is why we probably will need a candidate."

When I didn't speak, he added, "And that's why we want you to feel comfortable with whoever we put up to run against Mitch."

And then I understood. "Because when Mitch doesn't use what I give him, you want me to give it to his opponent, is that it?"

Roland Andrews clapped his hands in reward of my perspicacity.

"And the moment I give it to his opponent, Mitch'll fire my ass."

"I think you'll find that's not going to happen, Georgie."

"Why not? He'd know I was working against him."

"Oh, he'll head you off if he can. But if you turn around and give information to us, I can virtually guarantee you he won't do anything about it. He doesn't want any more spotlight on his relationship with the Gregorys than he absolutely has to have, and he knows that if he fights back the next step is for us to make this personal."

"Personal in what way?"

Andrews laughed. It was not the kind of laugh most human beings use to express mirth. It was more like a puff of air escaping from his lungs. "Ever seen his kid?"

I was not sure I had heard right.

"Look at the kid next time you're wondering how a simple staff attorney on the Senate Judiciary Committee got to be district attorney in the Senator's home district. And if that picture doesn't do it for you, I'll show you a few of Stephanie White when she used to dance at the Gaslight Club in Washington, D.C., where the Senator has been known to take a lunch or two over the years."

# 4.

I T WAS ALL SET. I WAS TO DO WHAT JOSH DAVID POWELL HAD WANTED me to do all along. I was to do what I had wanted to do ever since I hadn't done it. Absolution from Mr. Powell, redemption for me. Sort of.

We would expose Peter, the Saint of San Francisco, because he deserved to be exposed, because no matter how many lives he was saving now, he had to pay the price for the one he had ruined a dozen years ago, the one he had taken three years after that. He deserved it. He deserved to be punished. Mr. Powell was entitled to closure. I was entitled to closure. I would get it, I would move on, leaving heads bobbing in my wake. Peter's. The Senator's. Mitch's.

I thought I might leave Barbara's, too, until she appeared in my office ten days after she had abruptly disappeared. She had her hair brushed long again, the way she'd had it the day she had come to my house. She was more tanned than she was when I had seen her last, but not so tanned as to indicate she had been lying on a beach somewhere.

"Got a minute?" she asked.

I rose to my feet. "Of course."

She came in and shut the door behind her. She was wearing a pale blue blouse over a black silk sleeveless top. You could see through the blouse and I had the feeling she had just put it on for propriety, because she was coming to the workplace and wearing a sleeveless top would not be appropriate, not even a silk one. Her pants were white and clung to her legs and purposely did not reach her ankles. The pants had little zippers at the bottoms. Then there was bare skin. Then black woven sandals that matched her belt. I watched as she walked to a chair in front of my desk.

"May I?" she said, putting her hand on the back of the chair.

I nodded and she sat. She arranged herself gracefully, one leg over the other, and then inclined slightly forward. "We didn't part on such good terms. I'm wondering if you're still mad at me."

I took my own chair. It wasn't as big as Mitch's, but it was leather and it swiveled. "I wasn't mad at you, Barbara."

"Suspicious, then. You doubted me."

I admitted as much by flexing my fingers. Then I shrank into my chair, put my elbows on the arms, and clasped my hands in front of my stomach. I was acting like Mitch did sometimes. I wished I wasn't.

"I was hurt by the things you said. By what you were thinking. That night, the next day, I wanted to come see you, try to make you understand how wrong you were about me. Then I had to ask myself why you should believe me. And so I decided to prove myself to you."

"I heard you went on leave."

"They wouldn't give me a vacation. Not on short notice. So I just said I had a family emergency and I had to go out."

"But you didn't. Have a family emergency, I mean."

She shrugged. "My daughter, Molly, is on a tour of Canada with her soccer team, and my parents, for once, agreed to take Malcolm. So, no, I didn't."

She might as well have thrown boiling water on me. "Malcolm is your son?"

"Whose son did you think he was?"

"I didn't think."

"Why do you suppose I had to take the job I did? Why do you suppose I have to spend so much time dealing with kid problems?"

I probably stammered. If I didn't, I might as well have. Barbara tilted her head and held my eyes while she talked. "I used up a lot of favors this time, George. I told my parents I was going to San Francisco to have it out with Tyler once and for all. To tell him I wanted a divorce. It was the one thing I could say that would get them to help me."

I nodded, because it was what she wanted.

"I got on a plane and flew out there. I found that guy Billy, the one you said knew me. It wasn't hard. He was living on my husband's boat. And"—she hesitated before she brought up an old wound—"of course, I had those explicit directions I had given to you."

I nodded again. It was a conciliatory nod this time.

"I didn't know him, George. In fact, I think, when he found out who I was, I rather scared him."

I could see that happening. I couldn't imagine Billy ran into many women like her at Smitty's bar.

"It took me all of about twenty minutes to get the truth out of him."

The truth. I felt a tingle go up my spine. It made me bristle. She was going to tell me the truth. Something I didn't know. Something I hadn't been able to find out on my own.

"Did you have to buy him a couple of beers?" I asked. I was only partially joking. I was still chagrined by my misreading of the Malcolm situation. And I was uncomfortable because of the intensity with which she was looking at me.

"Sushi," she said. "Over a hundred bucks' worth. We went to a place on Caledonia Street with outdoor tables. Found out later it had a Michelin star. My mistake, I let him order whatever he wanted. By the end of his first tiger roll he had told me that Peter Martin had known you were coming all along."

All along? Since I had questioned Howard in Hawaii? Or since Barbara had suggested it? But all I asked her was, "How?"

"I don't think Billy was in a position to know that, but I can pretty much tell you from everything else I've learned that someone you talked to earlier was in touch with Peter."

She waited while I counted off the possibilities in my mind: Cory, McFetridge, Patty, Howard. Her.

"Only thing was," she said, "nobody knew when you might be coming, and Peter was sailing in the TransPac, and when I called Tyler to tell him about you, well, I guess Ty saw it as a way to get on the boat. To get into the race itself."

"And you know this because . . . ?"

"I just know Ty, that's all. He would have done anything to get in a race like that."

"Including lie to you?"

"Oh, like he's never done that before."

Barbara smiled at her own failings, inviting me to smile with her. Barbara Belbonnet. It was hard to see her as a victim.

"Don't ask," she said.

"You want me to believe you."

"What I want is for you to understand what happened." Her voice had suddenly grown taut. Just like that. As though I, somehow, was making things more difficult than they had to be.

I gestured, indicating she should go ahead, that I wasn't going to interfere anymore.

"When I told Ty you were coming, he must have gone to Peter and claimed he was the one you were coming to see."

"Had you told Ty that I wanted to talk to Peter about Heidi Telford's death?"

"Yes, probably. Yes, I did. Yes, and I'm sorry." Barbara Belbonnet wasn't looking so intense anymore. Her eyes were wavering, blurring, and suddenly she was in tears.

It was so unexpected I did not know what to do. For a moment, I fought the urge to get up, go around the desk, take her in my arms. Tell her I was sorry. For everything. I could not hold off beyond a moment.

"No," she said, sticking her hand out, making me stop, sending me back into my chair. "I want to tell you why." The one hand stayed up. The other went to the back of her head so that her elbow was aimed at me and her face was hidden. "I wanted to help you. I wanted to do something for you, George, something only I could do. When Ty asked why I wanted him to set up a meeting between you and Peter I should have made something up, but I didn't. He knew about Heidi. Everyone on the Cape knew about her, and I thought . . . I thought . . .

I don't know what I thought. I thought it would help you get what you want. That's what I'm sorry about, George."

"So Peter got him out of there. Took him on the boat."

The hand stayed behind her head, the elbow stayed pointed. Her hair seemed to be going out in every direction. "Billy told me that when Ty asked him to boat-sit he also told him you would be looking for him. And he said when you got there he was to call a certain number, find out what to do next."

I looked at the hair. Looked at the elbow. Looked at the person who had set this in motion.

"That story Billy had about running into Jason in the restaurant in Ensenada, it wasn't true?"

"I don't know. I just know that if you asked about Jason Stockover, he was to tell you he was in Tamarindo."

Six people have a party of sorts. Four of them Gregorys. Something goes terribly wrong. First bury it, then deny it, then, if somebody has to be thrown under the bus, pick one of the non-Gregorys. Send me to Tamarindo. Where Jason is.

Except Jason's not there. Jason has been tipped off. Run, Jason. Run, and he'll think it's you. Except we won't tell you that part. Because you're not one of us and you're not even a friend from childhood. Like McFetridge. You're only a friend from college. Which puts you in an outer circle, Jason.

First the family. Then lifelong friends. Then other friends. Then all those who want to be friends. Like George.

Oh, and by the way, do you need anything while you're running away? A new sailboat, perhaps?

Barbara was speaking. She was telling me she was sorry she didn't have every detail right as to what little Billy said and did. "But I didn't stop there," she said.

I looked up, shifting my attention to her again.

"I went to Tamarindo myself."

Another piece that didn't fit. If she was part of the scheme to get me to go there—Barbara to Ty to Peter to Billy—why would she go after I left?

Barbara was waiting. She clearly had expected a different reaction from me. I did the minimum. I murmured, "You've got to be kidding."

And then she, nearly six feet of long-limbed powerful female with big yellow-brown eyes and just possibly the disposition of a sadist, said she wasn't.

"You went to California, then continued right on to Costa Rica." I was thinking that meant she had brought her passport, which meant she had been planning to do that all along.

"I had my mom's ATM card."

"Your mom financed this whole trip?"

"My parents," she corrected. Then she unwound her legs. Then she rewound them, switching the one that had been on top. "Remember, they thought I was going to California to have it out with Tyler once and for all."

Still, she needed a passport.

"I get to Tamarindo," she said, her tone telling me I was going to hear this whether I liked it or not, "and it's a strange little place. It's kind of like being at the far end of the universe."

She paused, perhaps to see if I would say no, no, no, it's perfectly normal. Like Orlando or Las Vegas.

"The other thing is, and I don't know if this happened to you, but it rained most every day. I mean, what are you supposed to do in a beach town when it rains? I end up going from one bar, one shop, one restaurant, to another, and whenever I see anybody who looks like an American living there, I try to strike up a conversation."

"Hi. How are you? You know Jason Stockover?"

Her eyes flicked, rolled; her mouth grimaced. "Pretty much. Until I get to this one man, owns a restaurant on the beach."

"Wouldn't be the place with coconut pies, would it?"

"You've been there, I see."

"That's supposed to be the place Jason owns."

"Well, the real owner's name is J. T. Bauer. Balding guy, pretty muscular, about forty-five. He comes from Key West."

"Doesn't sound like Jason." I remembered what Howard Landry had said. I had a flash of Howard flapping his hand under his chin.

"Nope. What's more, he claimed never to have known any Jason in

Tamarindo. What he admitted, and this is what I've been trying to get to, George, is that he did know Leanne."

She clearly thought this was going to detonate, bring me flying out of my chair. She was disappointed when it didn't.

"Leanne couldn't have been there by herself."

"J.T. said she came into town, met him, hooked up with him, as the kids say these days. Stayed a couple of weeks, even helped him run the restaurant. Then she moved on."

It was possible. If someone had told Peter what I was doing enough time before I got to California, he could have called Leanne, gotten her to go down to Tamarindo knowing I would be coming.

I swallowed.

"What is it, George?"

"How do you know it was the real Leanne?"

"Well," she said, the word coming out slowly, lingering, "that's kind of hard for me to say, never having met or seen Leanne."

I had to agree and was about to tell her that when she added, "But this much I do know. The girl moved in with J. T. Bauer. He paid her in cash, never saw anything with her name on it, came home one day and she was gone."

"No note? No message, no forwarding address?"

"Nothing. And J.T. didn't seem all that upset about it, tell you the truth. He says that kind of thing happens down there sometimes. He said same thing used to happen in Key West. People come in, shack up, move on."

Barbara's legs crossed again. The upper one began to bob up and down expectantly. The woven sandal dangled from her foot. I had the feeling she was remembering something that I didn't. I tried to think what it could be.

"Key West is kind of a big sailing town, isn't it?" I asked.

"Oh, yeah."

"This J.T., he didn't happen to know Peter, did he?"

One eyebrow went up. Barbara looked at me approvingly. "Bingo, George. You win the prize. What he didn't know, what he couldn't tell me, was whether the Leanne who worked for him, moved in with him, had any connection with Peter."

"Except they were both from Massachusetts."

Barbara shrugged. "I'm not even sure about that. J.T. seemed to think the Leanne who was there was from Rhode Island. And that at some point she had been a cop."

It was making perfect sense. Go to another country, look for a man who isn't there. Get threatened by a woman who isn't who you think she is. Heck of an effort, George. Keep up the good work. Want a new office?

# 5.

WAS BEING PLAYED BY PEOPLE WITH A LOT MORE RESOURCES THAN
I had. I asked myself if that was the message Barbara had come to
deliver. Barbara Blueblood Belbonnet. The game was between the
Gregorys and Josh David Powell, and you're just getting batted back
and forth across the net, George.

Except Barbara had cried, hadn't she? And what was in it for her,
protecting Peter, running around the country, two countries, like she
was? If, of course, she actually had been doing that. I had no proof that
she had. No proof that anything she said was true.

I called Buzzy. It had been a long time since we had spoken and he
seemed to jump when he recognized my voice.

I told him I needed a favor.

"Anything for you, buddy."

I had to choke back my first reaction.

"Georgie? You all right?"

"What can you tell me about Barbara Belbonnet?"

"Your dungeon-mate? Used to be Barbara Etheridge?"

"She told me she grew up with you."

"Well, she did, sorta. I mean . . ." Buzzy wanted to be helpful; he
was looking for ways to do that. "I mean, she was one of the rich kids.
Into sailing and all that shit, and I wasn't. She was like Hyannisport

Yacht Club and I was, like, the public golf course. She was also, I'll tell you, about the best-looking girl around, so I knew who she was and everything. But as far as us hanging out together, no."

He stopped then, thinking he had answered my question.

"But you did go to school with her, right?"

"Up to about, I don't know, age fourteen, maybe. Then she went away to boarding school and, like, next time I saw her, she was married to Tyler Belbonnet. Or at least living with him."

"Did that surprise you? Her and Tyler?"

"Okay, I gotta back up. When we were little, Tyler was, like, legendary. Like I said, I wasn't into sailing, but everyone knew who he was. His picture was always in the paper, winning this or that race, and he was most definitely not a yacht-club kid. His father was a sailor, and Ty had his own boat and he only competed in the open races, but you'd hear people asking each other all the time, 'How did you do compared to Ty?'—that sort of thing. And then you'd see him at parties and it was always a big deal for him just to be there. Of course, all of us watching him, admiring him, wanting to be like him, weren't thinking so much about the fact that he didn't seem to have any plans beyond sailing and partying. What we were thinking, back then, was that he was the one who had all the girls."

"Including Barbara?"

"Oh, yeah. Early, early on. In fact, I think that was why they sent her away. It was pretty much common knowledge she was banging him."

"Sent her away to prep school, you mean?"

"Yeah, Tabor, I think. Then four years to Sarah Lawrence or someplace like that. I'd see her around in the summers and we'd say hi and stuff, but that was all. And then, what I heard was that she was going to law school at B.U. and she ran into Ty again. By this time he'd been all over the world, and once he starts telling her about Saint Bart's and the Greek islands and Tahiti, and it was like—fuck law school. That's, I guess, when it happened."

"When what happened?"

"She got knocked up. Preggers."

"But Ty did marry her." It was a question, really. I was trying to find out if anything she said was true.

"I don't know if it was that time or the next. What I can tell you is he signed on to a crew that was competing for the America's Cup and he was gone to Australia for a year while she was here by herself. Then he returns and everything starts up all over again. I think she and Ty were living in some dump down in Harwich while he was working in a marine supply store, and she was back trying to go to law school at night and you just knew that wasn't going to last. She has the second kid and the kid turns out to have Down syndrome and Ty sails off to the Azores."

"Before or after they had Malcolm?"

"I don't know, George. From what I understand, the syndrome is something you can find out about during pregnancy, so they must have known. Or at least she must have."

"You think it's possible she didn't tell him because she wanted to keep her hold on him?"

"Jeez, I don't know, George. I'd like to think she's not that stupid. I mean, I know she's not stupid, but sometimes people do things . . . you know?"

"I know, Buz."

"Look, I was shocked as hell when you told me she was working in your office. She was, like, one of the great tragedies of my lifetime. My lifetime—what am I talking about? Of the Cape . . . of . . . of . . . I don't know, of all time. Here was this beautiful girl, rich family, has everything going for her, and she lets her life get all fucked up by the local cool guy who doesn't give a rat's ass about anything but himself."

"I've heard about people like that."

"I don't know if I've talked to Tyler Belbonnet in twenty years, but I could sort of understand his appeal back then. He had this romantic pirate image, but, Jesus, you can't let some guy like that ruin your life. Especially when he keeps going, doing whatever he wants, and you're left behind to pay the consequences. You know what I'm saying?"

I told him I did.

"So I'm just sorry about the number he did on Barbara because she really could have been somebody." Buzzy caught himself. "Not that being in the D.A.'s office isn't being somebody. I mean, I'm obviously trying to do it myself . . . so to speak."

"Yeah."

"You still with me on that, Georgie?"

"Yeah, Buz, just as much as I ever was."

# 6.

MESSED-UP LIFE. A LIFE AS MESSED UP AS MINE. MORE SO, because she had responsibilities beyond herself. Were those responsibilities enough for her to sacrifice me? Why not? If they led to a better job, better security, better daycare.

Still, it made no sense. Fly to California, fly to Costa Rica. What for? I had already been to those places. Why would she retrace my steps? Why would she go before I had a chance to go back?

I decided I would call her. Ask her to come in again. Meet me someplace else if she wanted.

SHE WAS WEARING A DARK blue belted sheath top that dipped very slightly at the neck and slacks that were more or less the color of oatmeal. Her purse, which was big enough to carry a notebook, a change of clothes, and a frying pan, was in her lap. She had been glad to come in. She had something to tell me and wanted to get through the preliminaries as quickly as possible.

From my seat of power on the other side of the desk I waved her into whatever she wanted to say.

"Tell me, George, of the people who were at the Gregorys' that night, how many have you actually interviewed?"

I held up two fingers. "Not counting the woman who may or may not have been Leanne, only McFetridge and Cory." Then I remembered and held up a third. "Patty the pickup."

"You've tried to find Jason, Peter, Leanne, I understand that. But why haven't you tried to find the rest?"

"Who's left?" I said. "Jamie, who's never done anything but follow Peter around, and Ned, who had his own thing going on. Think either one of them is going to tell me anything about cousin Peter's adventures with his date that night?"

"First of all," she said, her hands on her purse, her back straight, her words quick, "what you're describing is not the Jamie I know. The Jamie I grew up with was the most conniving of the bunch. Maybe it was because of his size, I don't know, but the way he competed was to try to outsmart everyone else. And it's certainly not the Jamie I see these days, who's probably the most popular of all the Gregorys of his generation because he's making everybody a fortune." She paused. "You know about these mortgages they're giving away?"

"The Gregorys?"

She made a face. It wasn't a bad face. It probably wouldn't have been possible for Barbara to make a bad face. "Not the Gregorys. The banks. Something about they figure housing prices are going up so fast that as soon as people move in they've already acquired some equity. And then apparently the banks sell off the mortgages to somebody who bundles them all up, the good and the bad, and then offers them as a commodity that other investors bid on. Which I guess is where Jamie comes in. I don't understand how it works, but that's why Jamie was at my parents' party that turned out to be such a disaster for you."

"I thought he was there to raise money for a film for that girlfriend of his."

"Well, that was what was going on, yes. But Dad didn't know that ahead of time. See, that crowd, they've all been making money hand over fist through Jamie. So he shows up at the party, everybody wants to talk to him anyhow because he's been doing so well for them, and he's got this glamourous actress with him so he can let it drop how he's raising money for her next picture. He doesn't have to ask, which you don't do at a gathering like that. But as soon as the party was over you can bet they were all calling him, see if they could get in on it."

"Including Pop-pop?"

"That's what I call my father."

"I know."

Barbara's shoulders lifted and fell as if she did not quite understand me. It was a quick and graceful movement, and when it was over she was done with Jamie. She turned to Ned, and asked why I hadn't talked with him.

I explained about the eighteen-year-old au pair.

"Well, there was someone else who was there that night, too, George."

"Ned's children?"

"I'm talking about the gatekeeper. The guard."

"The black kid."

"Chris Warburton, that's his name," she said, chiding me. "Sound familiar?"

I shook my head, feeling more wary than excited that I was about to learn something I had not figured out already.

"He's the chef at The Captain Yarnell House in Brewster. You know it?"

Of course I knew it, a restaurant fashioned out of an old sea captain's home off Route 6A. I just had never been to it because it cost about a hundred bucks a person to eat there and because I had not had a dinner date since Marion left me.

"I've known Chris since he was about six years old. His father used to do my parents' yardwork, and he's one of the sweetest people I've ever met. All his life he wanted to cook, and the Gregorys gave him the chance. They sent him to culinary school. Then they made sure he got jobs until he proved to be so talented he didn't need them anymore. I went to Chris, George."

She went to Chris, who had spoken to Landry, and whom I had never even considered interviewing. I looked over the head of Barbara Belbonnet at the walls I had yet to decorate and wondered how long I would be here. In this room. In this office. On this job. Probably 2.5 months. Till the election. George Becket, my letter of recommendation would read, wonderful boy. Forgets to locate an occasional witness from time to time, but that's all right. He fit in just fine with Detective Iacupucci.

I looked across my desk at my former dungeon-mate and wondered not for the first time how I had managed to share a room with her for so long without really knowing her. Barbara Blueblood, with the pirate husband and the Down syndrome child and the daughter who was already fourteen years old. Friend of the Gregorys, second circle, taking a leave of absence from work so she could prove something to me. Was that possible? Didn't she need the job, the security, the life the Gregorys had provided for her when she had screwed up everything else?

"Chris confirm that Heidi was there?" I asked, half hoping that was all she was going to say.

"He remembered something about Jason Stockover, George. He remembered he wore a green hat with a white *D* on it."

Cory Gregory had remembered that, too. Dartmouth or Deerfield, she had said.

Now Barbara Belbonnet said the same thing. Such are the ways of people in a certain class in a certain place. She didn't think Drew, Drake, Drexel, Duquesne, DePaul, Davidson, Dickinson, Denison.

"Chris said he thought Jason and Ned had been friends in college."

She wasn't thinking Duke, whose color was blue, or Delaware, whose team nickname was the Blue Hens.

"Thing is," she said, "I know Ned went to college at Trinity and not Dartmouth, so I figured the *D* must be for Jason's prep school, and I took a chance and drove out there." She pointed. Nice, smooth underarms. "To Deerfield. In the western part of the state."

I nodded. I knew where it was.

"I went to the school library, examined yearbooks from twenty years ago, around the time a college classmate of Ned's would have been there, and was rewarded with a picture of Jason Stockover, a list of his school activities, and his home address in Cos Cob, Connecticut."

"And let me guess, that's where you went next."

"Yep."

Sure, of course. Barbara Belbonnet doing my job better than me. Or maybe *for* me. I still wasn't sure.

"I got there," she said, "only to find the Stockovers no longer live at that address. The family had some sort of falling out, the current owners said, and there was a divorce. They couldn't tell me where any of them went."

"Do you think the school would have a—"

She was way ahead of me. "So I drove back to Deerfield and visited the alumni office. They were so sorry, but they were not at liberty to give out addresses." She lilted the words "at liberty" as if she were imitating the Queen.

"But that didn't stop you, I assume."

"No," she agreed, "it didn't. I went back to the library, back to Jason's yearbook. I had the idea that maybe he was on the sailing team and I could find a picture of the team, see if I recognized any of his teammates, people I could contact about him. It was a long shot, I know, but there are only so many races in the northeast, and, hey, I was at plenty of them."

"Except you're older."

Barbara's recitation came to a standstill. "I'm thirty-seven, George."

"Oh."

"You're what, thirty-four? You think that's such a big difference?"

"No."

"You do, don't you?" Her chin moved, her hand moved, her leg moved, the corner of her mouth squeezed shut, and I realized that I had actually hurt her. It seemed like such a small thing. I wanted to tell her that. I wanted to tell her that I hadn't really noticed a difference, that it was one of a thousand things I hadn't noticed, that I hadn't noticed because my own life was so screwed up, such a mess, such a total disappointment, that I wasn't even aware of things that were right in front of me.

But Barbara was not waiting for my explanations. "Ned's at least two years older than I am," she said. "Which means, since Jason was in his class, he's about two years older as well."

"Thirty-nine," I said unnecessarily.

Was there a wince? It was hard to tell in the midst of my own embarrassment.

"The only problem with my idea was that the school didn't have a sailing team."

I told myself there could have been a lot of reasons for her new tone of voice. She could have been commenting on the incomprehensibility of a landlocked school not having a sailing team.

"What I found instead," she continued, "in the listing of activities beneath his yearbook picture, was that Jason had been a member of the cross-country team, the Outdoor Club, and the French Club. I asked the librarian about those things, not expecting they were going to get me anywhere, except, it turns out, Monsieur Weber, the faculty member responsible for the French Club, is still at the school."

"Great. That's great, Barbara." I may have gone overboard in my enthusiasm.

"That wasn't the end of my good luck, George. Monsieur Weber is still in touch with Jason because, it turns out, Jason is actually living in France. In a *bastide*." She got a shot in on me. "Do you know what a *bastide* is?"

I knew, but I didn't tell her.

"It's one of those fortified towns built during the Hundred Years' War, when France and England only fought when the soldiers weren't needed in the fields."

"Ah."

"They're all over the Bordeaux region, and what Monsieur Weber said was, the one where Jason lives is the most beautiful *bastide* of all."

A slow smile crept over her lips, enough to make me question whether my punishment was over. It was a smile of promise, one that invited me to smile along with her. "So," she said, as I watched her lips part, her teeth sparkle, her tongue flash, "I guess it's no wonder that a guy like Jason Stockover would own a bed-and-breakfast there. Don't you think?"

## 1.

CARTE BLANCHE TO MONFLANQUIN.

I still did not know about Barbara. My heart told me to believe everything she said. My head told me I had to watch out, because
she didn't need me; if Josh David Powell could employ a woman to
stay married to me, the Gregorys could certainly insert a woman into
my office. I was clearly susceptible. The cost of doing something like
that meant nothing to these people. Years meant nothing. I certainly
meant nothing, except as a tool. A pawn.

A denizen of the fourth circle.

Get out of town, George. Go to France.

I didn't go for any of the reasons she gave me. I went because I had
Mitch's $100,000 to spend. And because I had the time to do it. That is
what I told myself.

# 2.

I FLEW INTO CHARLES DE GAULLE, TOOK A LONG AND EXPENSIVE taxi ride into Paris, and boarded a train south to the city of Bourdeaux, where I rented a Renault with a stick shift and drove east. It was a sunny day, the air was warm enough to go without a jacket, and I was almost enjoying myself. I stopped in Saint-Émilion for lunch and drank wine because I was in the heart of one of the great grape-growing regions of the world and felt I should. The bottle I had was a merlot from the Médoc region, and I was disappointed. Perhaps I ordered from the wrong château, or the wrong vintage, or didn't let it breathe sufficiently. Or maybe I just was not sophisticated enough to appreciate what I was having, but I did not finish the bottle.

From there on, however, the drive seemed even prettier and more interesting than it had before.

I arrived at Monflanquin late in the day. "At" because one gets to the town well before one gets into the town. It is a walled city built on top of a hill overlooking a broad valley. I had to find the motor vehicle entrance and then wend my way around and around until I got to the top, where there was a large open square flanked by homes and shops and restaurants. For all that, it was surprisingly easy to find my destination on a side street leading off the square, and, miracle of miracles, a place to park directly in front of it.

My surprises only grew from there. The address Barbara had given me was a gray stone building sharing common walls with the buildings on either side of it and housing not just a bed-and-breakfast but a gift shop on the ground floor. Inside the gift shop was a large man wearing an apron and shorts. The apron I could accept. The exposed knees, shins, calves, and ankles were a shock. Then the man greeted me and I realized he was not French but English, which made the sight a little less shocking because it is a well-known fact that the English tend to do strange things when they see the sun.

I must have been dressed peculiarly for the region as well, because the first thing the bare-legged man did was greet me in my own language. He wanted to know how I was doing.

I told him I was fine and that I was interested in renting a room for the evening. He said that I appeared to be an acceptable lodger and it took me a moment to realize he had made a joke. It took another moment after that to laugh.

Barbara Belbonnet had used her cell phone to take a picture of Jason Stockover's photograph in his yearbook. While more than twenty years had passed and the camera image of a boy in sport coat and tie had not been ideal, this large man making jokes to me was most definitely not the same person. The boy in the photo had dark wavy hair and rather delicate features masked by an expression of smugness that promised cheer to those he liked and misery to those he didn't. This fellow in front of me not only had a British accent but a bald head and a wide-open face. The accent could have been affected, the hair lost, the smugness decimated by the realities of life beyond prep school, but this man, clearly, had never had delicate features.

"All alone, are you?" He posed the question as if being alone was an exciting thing to be.

I told him I was.

"Would you happen to have a passport?" he asked, getting out a hardcover register book and opening it to a page that contained the day's date and handwritten column markers that read *nom, adresse,* and *nombre de passeport.* The way he asked, I had the impression that not everybody who stayed there did have one. Or perhaps he was just being friendly. In any event, I handed mine over. He noted where it had been issued. "San Francisco!" he said with genuine enthusiasm. "I have had some adventures there, *mon ami,* I can tell you that."

"Yes," I said, not wanting to know. "Actually, I'm from Boston."

"Boston." He was busy writing things down.

"Cape Cod, really."

"You don't say. Could I have the address, please?"

I gave it to him. He transcribed and then handed back the passport along with a key attached to a heavy brass fob that would no doubt rip a hole in my pants pocket if I tried walking the streets of Monflanquin with it. "Number four, just at the top of the stairs behind you, two flights up. Need help with your luggage?"

"No, no. I've just one bag, and I can handle it."

"*D'accord,* as the locals say." He smiled.

I glanced around the shop. Knickknacks, mostly. Some framed vintage photographs and some paintings that had probably hung on walls for years without being noticed until their owners died and the estates were liquidated. But there was some fun stuff, too. Carafes and wineglasses and boards with comical renderings of various aspects of life in wine country. Posters and coasters and little figures made from pewter or blown glass. Chess sets with medieval warriors carrying French and English flags. Postcards, games, scarves, a display of tour books, and a rack of flamboyant sunglasses.

He saw me looking at the sunglasses. "Very Posh Spice, don't you think?" And I had to go through various mental synapses to realize he was referring to Victoria Beckham, formerly of the Spice Girls. "Oh, yes, very much so," I said, as if I knew what I was talking about.

I turned to go to the door, to go out to the car for my bag.

"You know," he said as my hand went to the handle, "my partner spent some time in the Boston area. Back in the halcyon days of his youth. You'll have to talk."

"Oh, good," I said. "I would like that very much."

THE PARTNERS LIVED TOGETHER on the second floor. The door to their apartment was open when I walked past with my suitcase. A short hallway led from that open door to a darkened sitting room, where a soccer game was on television. I could not see who was watching it, but I assumed someone was. I put down the suitcase and knocked.

"Hello," I called.

There was movement. A figure appeared at the end of the hallway. A lean man, a little less than six feet tall in bare feet, wearing a T-shirt and jeans. A man whose hair, if not wavy, was at least still on his head.

"Yes?" he said. Like the man on the first floor, he did not bother with French.

"Are you the fellow from New England?" I asked.

He came forward, out of the darkness. It was the boy in the prep school yearbook, two decades along. I felt a surge of elation and held out my hand even before he finished telling me he was from Connecticut.

"Massachusetts," I said.

He took my hand. I remember thinking it was not the shake of a sailor. "I went to school in Massachusetts," he said.

"Yes, I know." I did not release my grip.

"Oh, did Toby tell you?" The inquiry was friendly enough. There was no subterfuge to it. He did not even try to pull his hand away.

I said, "No. I know because I've come all the way here looking for you."

"Me?" He smiled, as though I might be a talent scout.

"I'm George Becket, from the Cape and Islands district attorney's office."

The handshake, minimal before, now went as soft as pudding.

"Oh, shit," he said, and the words came out partly in dejection, partly in alarm. He tried to step back, but I would not let go of his hand. I wondered if he would call for Toby. If the big man would come charging up the stairs. If I would end up grappling with both of them, tumbling around the second floor. Georgie Becket, punching his way across the Western Hemisphere. You see this scar? Tamarindo, Costa Rica. This one? Monflanquin, France.

But Jason did not call for Toby and he did not keep up the struggle. He left his hand, his arm, hanging in my grip as if I were a doctor taking his pulse. "What did I do?" he said.

"If you want me to guess," I told him, "I'd say you really didn't do anything. But there are those who would like me to think you did."

He did not respond. He just looked at me with eyes that contained none of the confidence of the youth in the yearbook photo.

"You are Jason Stockover, aren't you?"

There was an instant when I did not know what he was going to say or what I was going to do if he denied it, but then he nodded and I was so relieved I almost hugged him. I opted for dropping his hand, which immediately went into his front pocket. Both his hands went into both his front pockets. Because he was wearing jeans, and because they were fairly tight, he got only his fingers in.

"What do you want?"

"To talk. To ask you some questions. To get some answers."

He looked wistfully back into his apartment, no doubt wishing he had never come out. "About?"

"You know what it's about, Jason. It's about the night a young girl named Heidi Telford went to the Gregorys' compound on Cape Cod to visit Peter Martin and ended up dead."

I spoke brutally on purpose, letting Jason know there was no escape.

He made an attempt anyway. "I don't know anything about that."

"Let me help you, then. You sailed the Figawi race. You partied in Hyannis. You and Paul McFetridge picked up two girls and brought them back to the Gregorys. Once you got there you took them out to the beach—"

He glanced quickly down the stairs. From below came a deep voice. "I know all about your sordid past, Jason. Don't hold anything back on my account."

Jason looked at me as if it was really my opinion that concerned him. I tried to make sure my expression did not change one iota.

"You want to come in and have a glass of wine?" he asked.

## 3.

SANCERRE. A PECULIAR CHOICE FOR A MAN LIVING IN BOR-deaux, since it was my understanding that it came from the Loire Valley, but it was chilled and it tasted good and so I was grateful.

"Ned and I were just friends," he began. "We had been in Saint Anthony's Hall at Trinity together, and of course everyone knew who he was. Thing that was so amazing about Ned was that he never put on airs. I mean, certainly Saint A's was the elite fraternity at school, had its own part of the campus and everything, but Ned was friends with everyone. In the spring, just before exams every year, he'd have the whole frat up to his house for a party, and we had the run of the place. That's where he learned I'd been sailing all my life on Long Island Sound, and so he invited me to join in the Figawi race. After we graduated, I became sort of a regular. I was single, living in New York, it was a fun thing to do." He shrugged. He couldn't help it. Being single, living in New York. Fun things happened. They followed him around.

Jason sat on the very edge of the couch, bent forward at the waist, giving himself quick access to his glass whenever he put it down on the marble table that separated us.

"I got to know the family pretty well, even the Senator, who was incredibly nice. Thing was, nobody ever asked what you were doing there or acted like you didn't belong. Sometimes they didn't even ask who you were. And the Senator's house, the main house, it was like this seaside mansion where you could do whatever you want. The chairs, the couches, the dining room table, there wasn't anyplace where you felt you couldn't sit down in a bathing suit. And I don't want to say it was chaos or anything, but there were always people running around, going in and out, so, yeah, basically it was an exciting place to be."

It seemed important to him that I understand that.

"Can you tell me about meeting those girls? Leanne and Patty."

Jason drank more wine. He finished his glass and poured again. "I might have been mixed up about my sexuality in those days," he said.

I didn't think it was necessary for me to comment.

"I mean, you're hanging around with the Gregorys, so there's a lot of macho stuff going on. And we'd had this race and we're feeling pretty good and we're at the big post-race thingamajig in Hyannis and this girl starts hitting on me. She probably wasn't the kind of girl I would have chosen back in the day when I was into that kind of stuff, but she was good-enough-looking and, basically, she was doing all the work."

Once again, he seemed to be trying to explain things that were of no consequence to me. What did I care how he happened to be picked up by Leanne Sullivan? I asked him about McFetridge.

"Paul was just there. It was like, we were in a tent at this big table, and I think people recognized the Gregorys. Well, I'm sure they did. And I remember there was a whole crowd of guys around Cory, and I think she got a little freaked out and wanted to leave, and Ned, well, he wanted to get back to the house anyway, so he and Cory took off. And all of a sudden it was just Paul and me and I've got this redhead all over me and she's got a friend, kind of short and dark, I remember, and Paul said we should bring them back to the Gregorys' and have a party there."

Jason stared into his wine and thought about it, and then told me what he didn't think. "I don't think Paul had any particular interest in the other girl, but she was there, you know?"

"What was Peter Martin doing?"

"I don't know."

It was hard to believe a man staring so intently into his glass. It was even harder when he emptied the glass in one gulp and then almost immediately filled it again.

"Jason," I said, "this is the part where you get to save your own life, your own future. I know Peter met Heidi Telford at the Bon Faire Market that evening and I know she ended up at the Gregory compound later that night. I have to assume they got together at the post-race party in Hyannis during the time in between."

Jason shook his head.

I made things a little more difficult for him. "Heidi Telford was a wholesome-looking blonde girl with big breasts, wearing a blue dress with red rosettes."

Jason looked to see if I had anything more to keep him from saying he didn't remember.

"She was just twenty years old, Jason."

He stopped looking.

"She came into the tent where you were sitting at the big table." I was guessing now, playing his reactions. Even the smallest sign of acquiescence kept me going. "Peter saw her and jumped up." Peter had excellent manners. At least in public. "It was only you and Paul McFetridge and Peter left from your group and now that Heidi was there you all had girls, so you took them home."

"Jamie."

"What?"

"Jamie Gregory was there."

I had forgotten about Jamie. "Did he pick up a girl?"

Jason took his time answering. He placed his fingers on the base of his wineglass and then began moving the glass around in small circles, swirling the wine itself before he took another sip. Letting the wine go all the way down his throat before he answered. "No," he said.

No. But he had mentioned Jamie's name. There was something he wanted me to know.

"Did that cause a problem, Jason?"

"I'm not sure what you mean."

"Then let me make things as clear as I can. Nine years have gone by, and as long as nobody talked, as long as nobody acknowledged Heidi was at the Gregorys', everyone could just deny knowing anything about her death. Only now the story has cracked. You're keeping a secret that not everyone else is keeping, Jason. At this point, I know she was there. I know she got hit over the head with a golf club and never made it home that night. And I know one more thing, Jason, and this is the biggest thing of all. I know the Gregorys will not take the blame, no matter what."

I saw the color seep out of his face.

"First, they say it didn't happen. If they have to, they go the next step and say if it did happen it wasn't one of their people. Not the family, not the friends, not the hangers-on. Which one were you, Jason? Being a friend of Ned's and all, coming up once a year to go sailing. What do you think happens when they have to go to the step after that, Jason? Who do you think gets sacrificed?"

Jason's gaze suddenly went someplace behind me. His features twisted in surprise, alarm, possibly fear. I pictured big Toby standing in the doorway in his apron and shorts. I pictured him with a weapon in his hand: a cane, a hammer, a cricket bat. I debated whether I would look and decided nothing good would come of even acknowledging he was there.

"It's not going to be one of the family, Jason, you know that. Which just leaves you, the two girls, and Paul McFetridge. They can't blame it on the two girls, that just wouldn't make sense. And between you and McFetridge, well, you're the one who's in hiding."

"I'm not in hiding."

"The Gregorys would certainly like people to think you are."

Jason glanced past me again.

"If he's supposed to be in hiding," a deep voice asked, "how is it that you managed to find him?"

I had to answer this time, but I still did not look. "I've been searching for months. There are other people who supposedly have been searching for years. I believe, like me, they got misdirected."

A silent message passed between the housemates.

"The misdirection isn't quite so beneficial to you as you might think," I told Jason. I was looking directly at him, compelling him to look at me. "What the Gregorys are doing is making us think you've run away. Let me ask you this. What would you expect to happen when we're led to believe you're someplace you're really not?"

Jason lifted one hand and wiped his mouth. "Where do they say I am?"

"Costa Rica."

"I've never even been there."

"Pretty clever, then."

Jason must have gotten some sort of sign from Toby, some sort of affirmation, because he said, "What is it you want from me?"

"Tell me what happened to Heidi Telford."

"I don't really know anything, because I was—"

"On the beach."

Eyes to Toby. Eyes back to me. "I never so much as talked with her. So I don't see how I could possibly have anything to say, even if I were put on the witness stand."

I said nothing and Jason emptied his third glass of wine. He picked up the bottle and studied it. Then he looked at my glass with apprehension before pouring himself a fourth.

There was a big sigh behind me. Toby proceeded to walk past us, past me, through the room in which we were sitting and into the kitchen.

I was slouched in an armchair. I was holding my glass in both hands, holding it by the bowl because I wasn't really interested in the Sancerre and didn't care if it got warm.

"All I remember," Jason said, "is that she came with us when we left. She was sitting in the front seat of Jamie's Jeep while Pete and Paul and I were jammed in the back." He squeezed his shoulders together, demonstrating.

"And the girls?"

"Had their own car. Met us there."

"But there was no party, is that right?"

Jason drank. "Sometimes it was really kind of hard to say whether there was or not." He seemed to be thinking about what he had just said. "I mean, the music was blasting out the windows and people were going in and out doors and the closest person to being in charge was

Ned, who didn't give a damn what anybody else was doing." He glanced at me, did it quickly before going back to his wine.

"Because he was with the au pair," I said.

He raised his eyebrows as if the fact another person had been present gave him new hope. Another possible suspect.

Ah, yes, I felt like saying. And her motive would be what? Jealousy? But I only asked if he was aware what Ned was doing.

Jason took a roundabout way of answering. "We get to the house and Paul and I wait for the girls to arrive, and when they do we take them inside. We're walking around, showing them various things—you know the way you do—and we get to the kitchen and there's Ned. He's got his hair slicked back and he's bare-chested beneath this silk robe he's got on, and he's getting champagne out of the refrigerator."

Toby returned then, carrying another bottle of Sancerre and a glass for himself, both of which he carefully set down on the coffee table before dropping into an armchair of his own. "Do go on, Jason," he said.

But he didn't. I had to get him talking again.

"And you knew his wife wasn't around."

"She was up in Boston. Some charitable function."

"So the answer is yes, you did know what he was doing."

"It was pretty obvious. I mean, it wasn't just the champagne. He had the silver ice bucket, two glasses, and he's just standing there, like 'Oh, oh.'"

"Was anything said?"

"Yeah. Paul said to the girls, 'Hey, want to go see the beach?' Which meant: Let's get the hell out of here."

"So you did that, went down the beach."

"Yeah." He drank and held out his glass to Toby, who sighed loudly but got up to pour. "That's really all I remember."

"Except you came back to the house eventually."

"We were down the beach for a while. It was obvious what Paul was intending to do."

Toby said, "Emmm," but he was pouring when he said it and maybe he was commenting on something else.

The question as to what Jason himself intended hung over the marble coffee table.

He ran his fingers up and down the stem of his newly filled glass. "I mean, Leanne was willing enough, and the other two were pounding away and making all sorts of squishy noises, but she and I, well, we just sort of cuddled together. And that was all okay, but then, when they finally got done, Paul and the other girl, well, Paul wanted to switch partners and that was something I really didn't want to do, so I acted all, 'No, I really like Leanne, I'm really serious about her.'"

"And that's when you brought her back to the house."

"Yeah. All of us went back, because, like, with or without the switch, Paul was done with his."

"And what did you see when you got there, Jason?"

He looked at his glass as if it had betrayed him.

"Was Heidi Telford still there, Jason?"

He looked at Toby for help.

I figured it was enough. "And what was she doing?" I asked.

"She was trying to break up a fight between Pete and Jamie."

"A real fight?"

"It was real enough. They were pushing, shoving, slamming each other into walls. And there wasn't much she could do other than yell at them to stop."

"And you know what they were fighting about?"

Toby and Jason locked eyes. We were sitting in a triangle, with Toby's and my chairs pointed at Jason on the couch. But suddenly there was no room for me. I had to turn and look at the big guy myself.

"Toby," I said, "do you not want him to answer?"

"He's a free man," Toby said, but given the fact he was still looking directly at Jason, it was clear Jason was not completely free.

"Was it over Heidi, Jason?" I asked.

"The impression I had," he said slowly, never taking his eyes off Toby, pausing at each word as if it were a stepping-stone to the next, "was that Jamie didn't like the fact that he was the only one without a girl."

"And so he tried to put the moves on Heidi?"

"Exactly."

"And Peter didn't appreciate that."

Jason sat back, stopped looking at Toby, and offered me a chilly smile at the foolishness of Jamie's and Peter's behavior.

"You heard what was being said? In the fight, I mean."

"It was stupid stuff, for the most part. Pete kept yelling he had met her first and she had only come there because of him. Jamie was calling him names and saying he was sick and tired of his bullshit." Jason shrugged. "Pete, at least, had a point. Jamie was just being a brat."

"So what happened?"

"What happened, what happened, what happened," Jason repeated, looking around the room as though he might find something he could use to demonstrate. I could not imagine what it could be.

"What happened was I got rid of the girls," he said. "Walked them to their car. That was all."

"Except you didn't completely get rid of them. You stayed in touch with Leanne."

"I felt bad about what happened down the beach and asked for her number because I was thinking I wanted to make it up to her. I don't know what she was thinking, but she gave it to me and then she and her friend took off, and that's all I know."

To punctuate the conclusion to his story, he pointed to the hallway. "Do you need help with your suitcase?" he asked, and made a motion to get to his feet.

I stopped him. "Except you must have returned to the house after they left, Jason. What was going on then?"

Jason stayed where he was, one hand on the arm of the couch, ready to push himself up. "Nothing, really. Jamie wasn't there anymore. In fact, Paul told me to go find him."

"And did you?"

"I tried, but I couldn't." Jason shrugged one shoulder, the one that wasn't leading to the couch. "It's a big place."

"And the girl? Heidi?"

"She'd had enough. Said she was going home. I don't think she was enjoying herself anymore."

Heidi Telford, who had come in Jamie's Jeep, was going home without Jamie being around. And Peter, who had a night of pleasure planned, was already angry.

"Did you see her leave?"

"I just went to bed. I'll be perfectly honest with you, I was tired of the bullshit myself. It had been a long weekend and I was ready to go home."

He was also, it was obvious, ready for me to go home. Or at least go to my room. Instead, I asked the prosecutor's favorite question: "What happened next?"

Jason repeated himself. "Like I said, I went to bed."

"All right, what's the next thing you remember happening?"

"Going to bed."

Toby cleared his throat pointedly. One of us was supposed to stop. I decided it would not be me.

"You don't remember Peter waking you up about six or six-thirty in the morning to go play golf?"

"Is that what he said?"

"It's what McFetridge told me. You went to the course for a seven o'clock tee time and you couldn't get on because Heidi Telford's body had been found on the back nine."

I could hear Jason breathing. The room was not that big and we were not that far apart from each other, but I had not heard it before.

"I didn't know it was Heidi's body," he said softly.

## 4.

HE DIDN'T KNOW, BUT PETER DID. HE HAD TO. WHY ELSE WOULD he have gotten them out there so early to play golf if it wasn't to see if the body had been discovered, if it was being handled by the police the way he had planned?

I asked Jason if he had brought his own clubs and he shook his head. He said the Gregorys had a garage filled with clubs.

"Actually," he said, reflecting, "it was filled with more crap than you could possibly imagine. Jet Skis, sails, water skis . . . and the clubs were scattered all over the place. Not that there weren't bags. There were. And they were all, what do you call it? Callaways. Like somebody went out and bought ten sets of Callaways so nobody could complain that anyone else's clubs were better. Only it was like people took them out of the bags and never put them back, or put them back in the wrong bag. You'd be out on the course and you'd find three seven irons and no five."

I put my glass down on the marble, where Jason eyed it enviously because there was still wine in it. "Peter offer you a particular bag?"

"They were just out in the driveway. One for each of us."

"Three? Or four?"

"I don't know. Three."

"You, Peter, and Paul?"

"Pete said Jamie was still pissed off and wouldn't play."

"And were any clubs missing from any of the bags?"

"I wasn't counting. It was early. I was tired, hungover, I didn't want to do this in the first place."

"How about when you got to the course? You look then?"

"No, because we didn't get out. . . ." He waved his hand.

"Because Heidi's body was on the course." It was the second time I had said that and Jason no more wanted to hear it than he had the first time.

"I didn't know whose body it was," he insisted.

"What did you think when you learned that it was Heidi Telford?" I pushed.

Jason's head flared as if I had hurt him. "I didn't. I didn't know anything. All I can tell you is that we went back to the house, packed our bags, and left, which is what I had been planning on doing in the first place."

"But you found out eventually."

Clearly, I had become an irritant. Jason looked at Toby, wanting him to do something. Toby said nothing. He reminded me of lawyers I had seen watching their clients be deposed, listening to each word, weighing each one, waiting to jump in when there was one word too many.

"I got a call from someone who works for the Gregorys. He told me, what he told me was that something terrible had happened. The girl had left the house on her own, after the fight, and never made it home. He asked if I knew anything about it and I said no, she was very much alive when I last saw her. And he said that was a problem for all of us who were there. No one knew what happened, but everyone was going to be blamed. Curse of the Gregorys, he said."

"What did you tell him?"

Jason released his lifeline to Toby and returned to me. "I said, how can anyone blame me? I didn't do anything. And he said, I'll never forget this, he said, 'How do you prove a negative?' "

"Did you take that as a threat?"

"No, I took it as what the Gregorys have to go through all the time."

"You mean proving they didn't do things?"

"What I understood, okay, what I understood he was telling me was that the Gregorys are always being accused of something and it's not enough for them to say they didn't do it. The key for them is not to say anything at all."

"And you agreed to that." I tried not to let any judgment enter my voice. It wouldn't sound right coming from me. Not to my own ears.

Jason touched the hair at the back of his neck. The touch turned into a scratch. The scratch got harder, gave him an excuse to drop his head. "Yeah, well, it wasn't much he was asking."

"Just don't volunteer information."

"Yeah."

"Don't make yourself available if you don't have to."

Jason's head lifted. His expression asked how I knew so much.

"This guy, this caller, was it Chuck Larson?"

"No. It was a guy named O'Donald. He was a lawyer himself. Said he helps the family on cases like this."

"Did he want you to do anything else?"

"Just, you know, if I thought I could get the girls on board, Leanne and her friend. Get them, you know, to understand that, really, it would be best if they not admit they had even been at the house." Jason was having difficulty finding the right words. His hands were flailing.

"And you agreed to do that, too?"

"I thought I was helping Ned. I thought, people start investigating, it would be like opening Pandora's box. So what I agreed to do was invite Leanne down to New York, show her around a little bit, then introduce her to Mr. O'Donald."

"And were you there when he spoke to her?"

"All I know is, he asked her, okay, if she could go anywhere in the world, where would she want to go?"

"And she said Hawaii."

Jason turned down his mouth in silent commentary.

"But you of course drove a much harder bargain," intoned Toby.

Jason stared at him, but there was no rancor in the stare. "Lucky for you, I did."

"And I'd be luckier still, dear boy, if you would be so kind as to get us another bottle of *vin*. And none of that treacly stuff we've been making our friend drink. Look." He pointed disdainfully at my glass. "He won't even finish it."

Jason popped to his feet, happy to escape.

Toby waited until he left the room and then draped himself over the arm of his chair so he could capture all my attention. "He feels terrible about it, you know." Toby's eyes for some reason reminded me of moons. Big moons. Sad moons, like I used to see in cartoons. "All he was trying to do was protect his friend, his secret society friend from university days."

It was, I thought, a rather interesting interpretation of what I had just been hearing. I said, "But he wasn't. He was protecting his friend's cousin, who had murdered a young girl."

"I don't think that's ever been proven."

This information was delivered solemnly to me by an Englishman in France, draped over a chair.

"Think about it, George. You don't mind if I call you George, do you? We're not the least bit stuffy here in Monflanquin. I think it's what attracted me. I digress. Hear me out."

Toby dropped his arms so that they dangled almost to the floor. Interesting combination, this Toby, of a brute and an aesthete.

"He doesn't know how the girl died. The family, a famous family, a family who bring rewards just by having you in their presence, a family who have always been quite good to him, explain that she left, sallied forth from the garden gate or whatever, traipsed down the lane." He illustrated with rolls of his big hands and swirls of his thick fingers. "Is he to argue? Would you? Would anyone?"

"He could have told what he knows."

I said that. George Becket: voice of experience.

Toby stopped his display of theater and looked at me peculiarly. Did he know? About me?

"He sees her, she leaves, he leaves. Is that enough for him to talk about? With a family so newsworthy as the Gregorys? Do you really think he should have sold his story to the tabloids? Tell them all about randy Ned, doing a little shilly-shally on the side? That would have sunk Ned's career. Ended his marriage. And for what? It didn't have anything to do with the murder. No. No! Better to say Heidi Telford was never there. Better to say you were never there. Better even than that, not to be around yourself when questioners come knocking on your door."

"The same message this Mr. O'Donald gave Leanne."

Toby straightened himself out, then kicked his chair around so he could face me without the drape and the dangle. "Well, yes and no. The fact is, Mr. O'Donald liked Jason, and he had a project for which he thought Jason would be just perfect."

"Moving to France?"

"Not quite. As luck would have it, the family had a number of properties across the globe that needed checking on, make sure they were not being ripped off too basely. What the family needed was for someone to go to these properties, look them over, issue a small report that assured them, yes, this one's still standing, still functioning, not overrun by monkeys or wild goats or Arab seamen. Do a service and see the world. It was exactly the sort of thing Jason would love to do." Toby wanted me to appreciate Jason's good fortune.

"And there was probably no hurry to complete the task, I'm guessing."

"No hurry at all. Isn't that right, dear boy?"

Jason had come back into the room. He was holding a single glass and an opened bottle of very dark red. He didn't say anything.

"Is that what you've been doing for nine years, Jason?" I asked.

"Why, then he met me," Toby answered, his voice rattling the windows in the old stone building. "Trekking in Nepal. And when he explained about his job, how he simply had to dash about, we decided we should move here. Set down our stakes. Isn't that what they say in America?"

"Do you think, Jason," I said, trying not to let Toby distract either one of us, "the Gregorys are going to support you forever?"

Jason had put bottle to glass, but he stopped in mid-pour. Droplets of wine dribbled off the mouth of the bottle and fell onto the marble table. "What's that supposed to mean?"

"It means that after all this time, the search for the killer is still on. Whatever they may have done to try to hide you, it hasn't worked, has it?"

Jason's question lingered. I answered it another way. "I mean, I'm here, aren't I?"

"And," he said, handing the glass to his partner and then refilling his own, "I've told you I've got nothing to tell you."

"I think you'll have plenty to say if the Gregorys keep trying to make it seem that you're the one who killed Heidi Telford."

The pouring stopped again. "They're not going to do that," he said.

"Why not? You're the perfect guy to take the fall. You don't know anything about what happened that night other than Ned's little tryst, so you've got nothing to say in your own defense. And where, exactly, have you been all these years? You haven't been on the run, have you? I mean, suppose you get asked that. Do you have a record of your employment? No? Why do you suppose that is, Jason? Tell me, the money you get, it wouldn't by any chance get transferred into your account from the Cayman Islands, would it?"

Jason continued to hold the wine bottle almost but not quite parallel to the floor. He looked stricken.

"So now that everything's set up, what's going to prevent them from making you the scapegoat?" I asked. "Leanne? When was the last time you had any contact with her? McFetridge? He's known the Gregorys since birth. He's the next thing to family, and you, Jason, who are you to them? A now distant college friend of Ned's, and at this point nobody even cares that he was boning the babysitter a decade ago."

"She cares."

"What?"

"I said, 'She cares.' Her family cares. Her husband cares."

I was missing something. I struggled to sit up while I replayed that last exchange in my mind. "The au pair? You know her?"

"I know her husband. I went to Eaglebrook with him."

Eaglebrook, a pre-prep school. A boarding school you went to in order to get into a good boarding school. An institution for the country's elite. A place from which someone might grow up to be sensitive about his wife having once had an affair with a married Gregory.

"Who is she?"

Jason glanced at Toby. Words were not spoken, but there was plenty of message in the glance.

I was struggling to unravel that message when Toby's booming voice brought my thoughts to a halt. "I think, Mr. Becket," he said, "you will concede that you have no jurisdiction in this country."

"Yes, but—"

"And that it is highly unlikely you or anyone else would be able to obtain extradition from this country for Jason, because nothing gives the French more pleasure than to fuck with the American legal system."

I didn't need extradition. I needed information. And cooperation. I started to say that and was cut off.

"Those things being true, or at least unrefuted by you, I think you will agree that there is little reason for Jason to continue speaking to you on this subject."

But there was. I was almost there, within an arm's length of nailing Peter Gregory Martin for the murder of Heidi Telford. I needed only to reach a little bit farther.

But I was not going to get the chance, because Toby the protector was not done protecting.

"Which means, sir," he said, "your time as a guest in our home is at an end."

It is possible my mouth hung open.

"*Chambre Quatre* is at the top of the stairs. I suggest you find it now or you may discover that your time as a guest in any capacity in our establishment has ended as well."

"Then you—"

"*Au revoir, Monsieur Becket.*"

OUTE 6A FROM SANDWICH TO BREWSTER HAS TO BE ONE OF the most beautiful roads in America. It runs along the north side of the peninsula, past cranberry bogs and blueberry patches and small farms, and in early fall the small farms still have honor racks filled with corn and squash and tomatoes. It passes antiques shops, country stores, esoteric museums, cemeteries with flat, vertical gravestones that might date back to the 1600s, and tiny town centers with parks and gazebos. And all along the way are large eighteenth-century homes with huge lawns and stone walls and great, leafy trees. Some of those homes have been made into inns and restaurants. Like The Captain Yarnell House.

Sandwich, Barnstable, Yarmouth, Dennis, Brewster—each town has a slightly different look, a slightly different personality, far more obvious to the locals than the occasional or first-time visitor. Get to Brewster and the woods grow thicker and the spacing between homes and businesses becomes greater. Brewster, being at the end of the road, has a slight air of being pleased with itself simply because it is where not everyone can or will go. Pass Nickerson State Park, turn north on a small country lane and head toward the bay, where the water can recede a mile or more during low tide and people can go clamming with buckets and rakes or let their vizslas or Labs scamper across the flats in pursuit of seagulls. The Captain Yarnell House is set back behind a sickle-moon driveway filled with pebbles that splatter against the underside of your car if you drive in a little too fast. Which you might do if you're in a hurry, or nervous, or anxious because you have come a long way to get here and you know you are getting close to your goal.

At 3:00 on a post–Labor Day afternoon, I did not need to be in a hurry. Many restaurants on the Cape close for the season in September. The higher-end ones may stay open until November or even December, but you never know. The folks at Captain Yarnell could have packed it in and moved on to Florida or New Hampshire or Vermont, so I was glad to see a pair of vehicles in the parking lot: a small black BMW and a rather beat-up Ford pickup truck. I parked next to them and made my way around the back of the building to the entrance to the kitchen.

It was warm, somewhere between seventy and seventy-five degrees, and the screen door was still in place. By putting my two hands around my eyes I could lean my face against the screen and look inside. Two men were working. A short Latino was in a T-shirt and full apron, peeling vegetables. A tall, dark-skinned man wearing a white double-breasted chef's jacket was working over a gargantuan stove that must have had twenty burners. He was furiously stirring something in a heavy metal pot, and I thought it best not to disturb him until the fury subsided.

Minutes passed before the Latino noticed me. "Hey!" he said, and his eyes grew wide.

The chef looked over. He did not stop stirring. He returned his eyes to his task. "Help you?" he called out.

"Chris Warburton?"

"That's me."

"I'm George Becket from the D.A.'s office. I need to talk to you."

The job title works better some places than others. The smaller man stopped peeling and stood very, very still. Chris Warburton slowed his stirring, peered at his creation, lowered the flame beneath the pot and mumbled something to his assistant, who used a sidestep to take his boss's place at the stove without removing his eyes from me. Then Chris came toward me, wiping his palms against each other in quick, noisy slaps.

He was a handsome man with a confident smile. He gave me that smile because he, Chris Warburton, chef of The Captain Yarnell House, had nothing to fear from the district attorney's office, except perhaps the immigration status of his assistant.

I moved aside as he opened the screen door and came out of the kitchen. He looked up at the blue sky with its bright gray and white clouds rising from the horizon and said, "Nice day."

From the kitchen came a series of muffled noises. The assistant no doubt scooting off. I wondered if he would try to make it to the pickup truck or just hide in the main part of the restaurant. The cellar or the attic, perhaps. Maybe dash away on foot, head for the marshlands.

"I need to ask you about a job you used to have, Chris."

"Sure." Ask away. Look at my smile. Don't pay attention to what's going on behind me.

"With the Gregorys."

"The Gregorys?" Chris Warburton's smile got even bigger. "I was a kid then."

It was nine years ago. The man was not yet thirty.

"You used to, what, be a gatekeeper for them?"

"Yeah, pretty much. I mean, mostly I sat in a Jeep Wrangler and checked who came in, kept the gate closed to those who weren't supposed to be there. A lot of tourists would show up, try to peer through the bars." He showed me, holding his hands to the sides of his face, making his job seem both glamorous and boring at the same time. I had the feeling he could do that about anything, tell you how mundane his life was and make you wish you were doing it with him.

"When you were there, were there other people working at the compound? People who weren't just friends or family?"

"Oh, sure. Lots of 'em. Housekeepers, yard guys; they had caregivers for old Mrs. Gregory, the Senator's mom. And then she died, of course, so they weren't around after that. It was a group of Irish la—"

"You remember," I said, cutting him off, "an au pair that Ned Gregory and his wife used for their kids?"

The smile stayed. The eyes roamed. I wondered if I had gone too far. Chris may have been a beneficiary of the Gregorys' largesse, but he had gone out and made it on his own. Barbara had told me that. I was counting on that. Chris Warburton, chef, beholden to no one. Except, looking at him, it didn't seem like such a sure thing anymore. The Gregorys, Barbara said, had sent him to culinary school, got him his first jobs, put him on the path to success. How can you not be beholden to someone like that?

He was stroking his chin, thinking about how he could best answer. Au pairs? he could say. There were so many of them. They would come and go. Ned would give them a poke or two and they'd be on their way.

"This one came from a wealthy family," I said. "Her father owned movie theaters."

I heard an engine starting. It was a rough sound, not the kind a BMW would make.

"Lexi," Chris said, rather more loudly than he needed.

From the other side of the building I could hear pebbles being splattered.

"Lexi what?"

"Lexi Sommers," he almost shouted.

There were very tiny beads of sweat on Chris's broad forehead. I deliberately turned my own head in the direction of the engine and the flying pebbles.

"I heard she got married."

"That's right."

"You know what her name is now?"

The pebble sound was over now. The engine sound was fading. Chris moved just enough to intercept my long-distance gaze. "Why, Lexi done something wrong?"

"Just give me her name and tell me where she is," I said softly, "and I'll be on my way."

Chris heard the change in my voice. But with each passing second his task became less difficult. Stall, stall, say nothing.

"You were both about the same age, both working for the family. With them but not part of them. You must have at least gotten to know her, Chris."

"I did."

"So I'm expecting you stayed in touch."

The engine sound had completely disappeared. The fleeing Latino helper could be on 6A now. I looked at my watch. It was just a show. I didn't even note the time.

And Chris, for his part, simply let the time go by.

"Letters, pictures of the kids. Things like that." I was thinking about what Barbara had done at Jason Stockover's prep school.

When he still did not respond, I got out my cell phone. "You get invited to the wedding?" I asked.

He snorted. "We weren't that kind of friends."

He could have been saying any number of things. I didn't bother to work them out. I hit a button and put the phone to my ear.

"What are you doing?"

"Seeing if I need to stop that pickup truck, Chris."

"He's a good guy, just trying to support his family."

"Helpless guy, too, I imagine. Not like Lexi. She'll have all kinds of support. I talk with her, she'll probably have a lawyer sitting right there with her. Not that she did anything wrong or that she's going to be in trouble, but just to protect her against the things that all the rest of us have to deal with."

"Like you."

"Like me. That's right, Chris."

He shook his head. The drops I had seen at his hairline flew off. "I can't do anything to hurt the Gregorys."

"And I'm not asking you to do anything other than give me a name and address."

Chris Warburton cranked his neck back and looked up at the sky, which probably did not look as bright as it had when he came out of the kitchen.

"Hello, Sergeant?" I said into the phone. "It's Assistant D.A. Becket—"

"I might know where there's a Christmas card you could look at," the chef said, putting his hand out. And when I didn't lower the phone, he added, "Might still have the envelope."

"I'll get back to you," I said to the phone.

## 1.

CARRIED MY SUIT JACKET IN A GARMENT BAG. CARRIED IT ONTO the airplane. Carried it in the taxi on my way into Manhattan from LaGuardia. It was a light gray Zegna suit, purchased at a post-Christmas sale at Saks, tailored by a taciturn, chain-smoking Russian in the South End of Boston. My tie was a $150 red silk item from Louis Boston, a Christmas gift from Marion. At the time she bought it, I thought it was special because it was something I never would have bought for myself. This was the first I had worn it since she left.

I primped by marking my reflection in the passenger window of a Lincoln Town Car parked on the corner of 87th and Park Avenue. Then I walked a block north to an apartment building and presented myself to the doorman. Door*men*. An army of them.

"I'm here to see Lexi Trotter," I announced.

"Yoor name, sir," said the doorman sitting at the desk in pretty much the middle of the lobby. Behind him stood two others, both in doorman's uniforms with hats and epaulets. The guy seated didn't have the bandleader jacket, just a white shirt and tie.

"George Becket." I handed him my business card.

The man looked at it, fingered its edges, turned it over, looked at the front again.

Beyond him, behind his two buddies, there was a large atrium with a garden on the ground floor. The apartments rose up in two high-rise buildings on either side of the atrium. I resisted the urge to show the doormen what a regular, friendly guy I was by commenting on the attractiveness of the plants and the water features among them.

"I don't got you in the computah," said the man at the desk. "Was she expecting you?"

"No. I was just hoping she'd see me."

He looked at the card again. "Is this a legal mattah?"

"Personal."

The uniformed boys shifted their feet. One of them looked at a fourth doorman, who was sitting in an anteroom off the lobby watching a bank of television screens, perhaps getting ready to rush out and spray me with Mace.

"Do you have Ms. Trotta's phone numbah, sir?"

"Don't you?"

The seated man stuck out his hand. In it was my card. "I'm sorry, sir," he said with just a trace of menace in his voice, "you don't got an appointment, you can't see none of the guests. You wanna see Ms. Trotta, you got to call her beforehand, get her to call down to us or leave your name wit us."

I wanted to point out the quality of my suit, my tie, even my Bally shoes, but it was not going to get me anywhere. I thanked the man at the desk and said I would be back.

He didn't seem to care. Neither did the guys in the bandleaders' garb.

I HAD A PHOTOGRAPH. It was on the Christmas card. It *was* the Christmas card. A family shot of a mom and dad and what appeared to be twin girls, all of them lying on their stomachs facing the camera, all of them laughing, all of them quite handsome. From what the black-and-white picture showed, Lexi had dark hair, a dark brow, and a slightly rounded face. Only her face, shoulders, and one arm were shown in the picture, and it was not possible to tell how tall she was, but she appeared to be well proportioned. It would, I realized, be best if she came out of the building lying down, the way she was in the picture. Barring that, I would have to watch for a dark-haired, dark-browed, well-built woman in her mid-twenties.

Fair enough, except I had no place to stand at 88th and Park with my Christmas card picture in my hand. The apartment building was on the southwest corner of the intersection, and I particularly did not want to loiter there because one of the doormen had come to the entrance to hold his hands in front of his crotch while he stared at me. I went through a quarter of an hour pretending to make cell phone calls while I waited for something to happen. Nothing did.

I crossed 88th and looked back. I crossed Park and looked back. I had no place to sit on that side of the street, either. There was not even a shop I could go in. I went south across 88th and west across Park, and this time I had a little bit of luck because the doorman was no longer at the entrance. I did the circuit again. My feet were beginning to hurt. There are many things about detective work that should not be taken for granted.


AT 3:00 in the afternoon she emerged from the building. At least I had reason to believe it was her. A dark-haired woman wearing a dark blue sweat suit, white trainers, and a Yankees hat, pushing a double baby stroller. She came out the door, turned left, went to the corner of 88th and turned left again in the direction of Central Park. I caught up with her when she stopped at the traffic light at Madison.

"Hello, Lexi."

I got no hello in return. She stared at me, tightened her grip on the handle of her carriage, and looked impatiently at the light.

"My name's George Becket. I'm from the Cape and Islands district attorney's office in Massachusetts. Can I talk to you for a minute?"

The light turned and she flat-out ran across the intersection. On the other side of Madison she pushed the stroller up onto the sidewalk, looked over her shoulder at me walking after her, and kept on running.

I stayed back a block and watched her run all the way to the sidewalk on the far side of Fifth Avenue, turn north, and keep going. I crossed 88th, mingled with the crowd in front of the Guggenheim Museum and kept my eye on her as she ran to 90th, turned left, and entered Central Park. Then I ran, too: a guy in a suit sprinting along Fifth Avenue.

Enter Central Park at 90th and you come to a road, and on the other side of the road is the reservoir surrounded by a fence and a running path. I wondered if she could have gone there, thought it unlikely with her baby carriage, and looked to my right and left. There was another path, this one paved and just inside the park wall. Heading south, still running behind the carriage, was Lexi. Between us were at least a dozen people walking dogs. Purebreds, mostly. Airedales seemed to be extremely popular. I used the dog walkers as a cover, stayed back, wished I wasn't the only guy in the park in a suit and tie. People I passed shot me quick looks as if I must be a strange fellow indeed. I took off my coat and carried it over my arm. She went around a corner and I lost sight of her.


THERE WAS A CHILDREN's playground just south of the Metropolitan Museum. She wasn't there. No one was. I kept following the path until I got to a second playground below 75th Street. That was where I found her, sitting on a park bench in an area where young mothers and older nannies ruled. There were sandboxes and slides and fortresslike mazes with no sharp edges. Her kids, who looked to me to be about two years old, were still in their stroller, craning their necks to see what the older kids were doing while their mother pushed the stroller out and pulled it back, never letting it go more than a couple of feet. Mom was doing this while she talked to a woman dressed much like she and doing the exact same thing with her stroller from the other end of the bench.

I walked up and stood in front of them, halfway between them. "Lexi," I said, "can I just show you my identification?"

She was already getting to her feet.

"Here," I said quickly, "I'll hand it to your friend here."

Lexi hesitated just enough for me to get my D.A.'s card and my driver's license into the other woman's hands. The woman looked startled, as though I had just handed her a melting ice-cream cone.

"Read them out loud," I urged.

The woman held up the license, stared at the photo, and said, "All right. It says you're George Becket. And this other one says you're an assistant district attorney." She glanced at Lexi, as though she might not be the person she had assumed her to be, sitting on a park bench with adorable little twins. Not if an assistant D.A. was trying to talk to her. "You want to see?"

"I don't care about his ID," Lexi said. But she didn't flee.

"Look," I told her. "I'm going to stay back here, behind this crack in the pavement. What is that, about seven or eight feet away? I won't move in front of it unless you give me permission, okay?"

The other woman did not want my cards in her hand. She was waving them at me. I saw that with my peripheral vision, saw her put them down on the bench next to her, saw her start to stand.

"Please," I said, holding out my hand toward her, "just for a second."

Lexi was looking back toward Fifth Avenue, no doubt making escape calculations.

"I just need to ask you a few questions."

"About what?" she said, her head still turned.

"The night of May twenty-fifth, 1999."

"Nineteen ninety-nine? I was only eight— Oh, God." Her eyes sought out mine. "I've got nothing to say."

With that, the woman next to her was gone, racing away with her stroller at arms' length in front of her.

"Lexi," I said gently, "I can subpoena you."

"And I," she snapped, "can make your life miserable. My father happens to be a very rich man, Mr. Becket. You have no idea what he can do to you."

"Oh, I think I have an excellent idea what a very rich man can do, Lexi. Especially when his children are involved. I hope this won't come to that."

"You should be afraid, you junior shoeshiner."

It was not an insult I had heard before, but I got its meaning. I also understood she could say it because her anger was as great as her fear.

"I should be afraid. Ned Gregory should be afraid. But most of all, Peter Gregory Martin should be afraid. Don't you think?"

At the mention of the Gregory names, Lexi's chin shot up, as though questioning who I was even to mention them. The stroller began moving in and out twice as rapidly as before. "Seriously, do you have any idea who you're talking about?"

"I'm talking about what happened to Heidi Telford, and I'm almost there, Lexi. I am this close." I held my thumb and forefinger an inch apart. "I have been practically all over the world, and I know who was at the party that night. I know where Ned was and where his wife wasn't. I know about the fight between Peter and his cousin Jamie. I know what Peter did to her."

"Did to who?" she said, her voice dripping with scorn.

"To Heidi." I was bending forward at the waist, trying to keep my promise to stay behind the crack in the pavement, trying to speak so just she could hear. "Heidi Telford."

"You think Peter did something to her?"

"I know he did."

"Peter, the AIDS doctor? That's what you're saying?"

"It is, Lexi."

"Hah." She laughed a single sharp note, its meaning clear: You, George Becket, are an idiot.

"I know he saw her at the Bon Faire Market. I know they met up at the post-race party in Hyannis. I know he brought her back to the Gregory compound and things didn't work out the way he wanted, and I know he hit her over the head with a golf club."

"I am so out of here," she said, and this time she did get to her feet. She was already moving when I said, "She was just a young girl, not much older than you were that night. She was young and pretty, like you, and filled with promise, like you, and she was somebody's daughter, Lexi."

But not Lexi's daughter. She was getting into full stride and I had no choice but to follow. "Her parents were waiting for her, Lexi.

Doesn't that mean anything to you? They were just a couple of miles away and she never made it back to them. They could have been there in ten minutes to pick her up if she needed a ride, and instead the next thing they heard was that their child had been tossed onto a golf course like a bag of trash."

She kept going, her hands white on the handlebar, her feet a blur.

I was moving as fast as she, trying to keep my feet close to the pavement so I did not appear to be running. "It's all coming out, Lexi. It's been buried for a very long time, but I have tracked down everyone who was there and I know what happened."

"You obviously don't." She spoke as we were going up an incline. She was in better condition than I was. She was not breathing half as hard.

"I do, Lexi. I've found Paul McFetridge, Jason Stockover, the two girls they brought to the compound that night—"

Lexi braked. She did it so suddenly her kids began to cry and I nearly banged into her from behind. "If you knew so goddamned much, you wouldn't need me, would you?" she said.

"Look," I told her, holding my hands wide to show that the near contact had been a mistake, "I know what you're concerned about. The thing is, if you don't talk to me, it's all going to come out. If your husband and his family don't know already, they will. If your own family doesn't know, it will. And since it's the Gregorys, you can be sure they will not let Ned take the blame for having an affair with his babysitter. They will fight back, somehow, some way. And it will be in *Star* magazine, and *Us* and *People,* and it will be on the celebrity television shows, and men and women you never have seen before will be all over you wherever you go. Microphones in your face, taking pictures of your babies, disturbing your neighbors to the point where you might not even be able to stay in your building."

"Screw you," Lexi said. Her face was twisted. But she wasn't moving.

"The only way you can keep that from happening is to help me present a case behind the scenes that is so strong they won't fight us. We'll be able to arrange a plea bargain for Peter Martin. He no doubt deserves first-degree murder, but he'll probably get a deal for second-

or even manslaughter. And the most important thing will be that there will be some justice for Heidi Telford and some closure for her family."

I tried to speak with concern, care, reasonableness, even anguish. But I needn't have wasted my energy.

"You obviously don't know shit, Mr. Becket, and I, for one, am not going to help you. Okay? Now leave me alone before I start to scream."

"Lexi," I pleaded, "Lexi, I do—"

She was about fifteen yards up the path when she turned her head and shouted, "If you think it was Peter, then you clearly don't. You schmuck."

I watched until she disappeared and then I went back to the playground. My driver's license and district attorney ID had disappeared as well.

## 2.

I CALLED BARBARA'S CELL PHONE.

"I'm in New York."

"I know."

"I'm going to need some help."

"What kind of help?" Barbara had not hesitated before. Why now?

"An address, to start with."

"If I can, I will." Barbara, my collaborator, coming through again.

"And I'll need one more thing."

"What's that?"

"You to go there, to the address I want you to give me."

"Depends on where it is, doesn't it? I mean, I've got the kids—"

"It's here. In New York."

"When?"

"Tonight. Tomorrow night. When can you do it?"

"Oh, God. I don't know, George. I've only been back to work a few days."

"Please, Barbara." I took a deep breath. I forced myself to say it. "I need you."

## 3.

THE TOWNHOUSE AT THE END OF MORTON STREET WAS MADE OF red brick. Smooth red brick, neatly mortared. A brief walkway led in from the sidewalk to half a dozen concrete steps that rose to a small landing at the base of the front door, which was painted a glossy black and had brass fixtures. The face of the house was protected by a tiny yard filled with ivy plants and fenced off by curling wrought iron that matched the door in color and gloss.

It was dark when I rang the bell. It grew darker while I waited.

Out on the sidewalk, at the base of the railing, a figure in a soiled and ripped synthetic fur coat and a crushed felt hat sat down, hunched over, contemplated the gutter.

I rang again. And waited some more. I knew someone was inside. I could see the lights on the second and third floors. I could hear music.

I once again was wearing the Zegna suit and the red tie because it was all I had brought to New York. I had stayed at The Benjamin in Midtown, and the hotel had done a good job of getting my white shirt laundered, my socks and underwear cleaned—and for pretty much the same price I would have paid to buy them new.

I was about to ring a third time when the door was flung open.

The man who stood there had the long, straight hair that so many of those in his bloodline had, but he was short, like his sister Cory. Lexi Trotter had an army of men in uniform protecting her door; Jamie

Gregory not only opened his door himself, but he had come down two or three flights to do it. Come in his blue button-down shirt, his cream-colored slacks, his Gucci shoes with no socks. "Oh," he said. "It's you."

He recognized me.

And that empowered me.

"Heh, heh," I said. An expression of power.

"It's not a good day for me," he said, as if maybe I could come back another time to accuse him of murder.

"You got that right," I told him.

In Jamie Gregory's hand was a cocktail glass with a gold rim around its top. The liquor in the glass was floating several solid ice cubes. He dropped his eyes to the cubes and shook them a bit as if they, like me, were not doing what he wanted. "Maybe we could take this up later," he said.

Something about this encounter was wrong. I asked him why he thought I was there.

"You're the guy running for D.A., aren't you?"

I recognized the music that was playing. Aerosmith. "Dream On." Any guy my age would recognize it. There was an energy to it, a sense of frenzy that suited the moment.

"No," I said. "I'm the guy from Palm Beach."

"Of course you are. From the party at my family's home."

*Of course you are.* The sonofabitch. I thought of hitting him right then. How many people had I thought of hitting lately? How many times had I thought of hitting him, Jamie Gregory, in particular? All my adult life, it seemed.

"The party with Kendrick Powell," I said between clenched teeth.

"Yes." He sighed. He drank. He said, "And you want me to keep quiet about it."

Keep quiet? Did I say that, or did the question just bulge from my face?

Down the stairs came Steven Tyler's squealing, commanding voice: *"Sing with me, Sing for the years."*

"The party," I choked out, "where I watched you and your cousin molest her when she was too drunk to know what she was doing."

Why couldn't I make it sound as bad as it was? Make it sound as bad out loud as it did in my head?

The ice cubes in Jamie Gregory's glass swirled again. The drink sloshed over his fingers. "Is that the story you're expecting to tell?"

"It's the story that's the fucking truth," I said. But it wasn't even the story I wanted to talk about. I had come to tell him I knew he had killed Heidi Telford. Barbara was supposed to be here. She was supposed to hear his confession, his admission. Maybe come down the staircase right now. A slender foot, a long leg, a hand on the railing. I looked and there was nothing. All that was coming down the stairs was the music. *"Dream on, Dream on, Dream until your dreams come true."*

"You know, my friend," he said, as if I needed a lesson and he was resigned to giving it to me, "sometimes things happen. They might seem all right at the time, and then, years later, you're doing something else, you want to do something else, and all of a sudden you realize you have to explain this thing you did way back when." The glass went to his mouth. He spoke over the gold rim. "I understand that."

"Fuck you."

He looked disappointed at my argument. "I assume that's what's going on with you," he said, shaking the ice. "I mean, I know what you did. My uncle knows. He doesn't condone it, but he did the best he could to get you out of it because you were a guest in his house. In truth, he feels quite guilty about whatever little participation we had."

*Participation?* They were the ones who took her into the library. I just followed. I just stood there with a drink in my hand and a stupid half-smile on my face.

"He thinks, well, Peter and I should have watched you closer. Things happen in our house, anywhere near our house, anything to do with anyone who was at our house, and the whole family gets held responsible. It's the way it is, we realize that. We're supposed to realize that. And so we were responsible for you, and what happened is embarrassing all around. Especially embarrassing when someone tries to make a criminal case out of it."

What was he talking about? It *was* a criminal case. It was only because the Florida state attorney quashed the investigation that it wasn't.

Jamie was drinking again. It was not a matter of giving me time to say something so much as it was simply time for him to drink.

When he was done he put his cocktail glass down on what must have been a shelf or a table just inside the door. He let his hand stay there where I couldn't see it. He returned his eyes to mine. It had been time to take a drink, and now it was time to pay attention to me. Except his hand stayed out of sight. "Fortunately," he said, "that's all behind us now."

What was? The rape?

"I mean, you got out of it all right, didn't you?" he asked, as if he was inquiring about a sunburn. "All these years, you've been able to fly beneath the radar and everything's been fine."

Was he asking or was he telling me? No, I wanted to say. I've been in retreat, hiding, wasting my life while you went on to do whatever you wanted, wherever you wanted.

"And then one day you took a look at your boss and decided you should have his job." Jamie shook his head. His hair fell over his brow and he had to use his free hand to brush it out of his eyes. "So now you come here because you want to make sure I've still got your back. Do I have that right?"

Where had he come up with this? And who was he saying it for? Someone had to be behind the door or just up the stairs. Someone who was doing for him what Barbara was supposed to have done for me.

Unless it was Barbara.

Maybe he wouldn't know she was there for me. There to hear his confession. To be my proof.

"On Memorial Day of 1999 you hit Heidi Telford over the head with a golf club and killed her," I blurted out.

Jamie Gregory recoiled. "Hey, guy," he said, "you don't have to do this." Then, when I did not blubber anything else, he began to speak soothingly, the way people do to horses that are spooked. "You want to talk about how to handle the Palm Beach matter, that's fine. You don't have to go around tossing out wild accusations." His eyes left mine, traveled over my shoulder to the street, and seemed to get stuck there. "You want to come inside?"

Sure, go inside. And if Barbara was not there, what was I supposed to do then? Grab him in a headlock with one arm while I used the other to call the police?

Of course, chances were it wasn't Barbara I would find in there. It could be someone like Pierre Mumford, ready to snap my neck, say I fell down the stairs. The Gregorys probably had family boot camp, where they learned how to deal with adversaries, people who came after them, threatened them, wanted something from them. Never admit anything. Always have someone to back you up.

Jamie continued to look out to the street. I gathered his attention was on the guy in the soiled coat and crushed hat at the base of his wrought-iron fence, and then his hand suddenly came out from wherever it had been, came out with an ice cube and threw it. I turned in time to see the ice hit the person in the middle of the back. "Hey, you!" he yelled. But the figure took his abuse and did not so much as move.

Jamie shrugged at me, as though we had just done this together, thrown an ice cube at a homeless man. Then he stepped back, inclined his body slightly forward and did a mock sweep of his arm. "You coming in?"

I shook my head. "No."

"Well then," he said, pointing upward with his index finger, "I've got company."

He did not grin the way I had seen him in Palm Beach, but that grin was what entered my mind. Here I had just accused the man of murder and he was excusing himself because he had a date. I knew what that meant, having a date with Jamie Gregory, and I stomped my foot onto his threshold before he could close the door. "I've spoken to Lexi Sommers," I said.

For the first time, I got the reaction I was expecting. Jamie looked at my face, looked at my foot, then stepped back. "I told you," he said, moving away from the door, backing toward the wall of his foyer, creating space between us, "you don't have to do any of this. You want the D.A.'s job, there's plenty of ways we can help. But it doesn't serve anybody's best interest to go around threatening people. Someone hears you . . . they might even think you're engaged in blackmail."

Did his eyes flick to one side when he paused, or was it just my imagination?

"Lexi told me she was sleeping with your cousin Ned when it happened."

"Then she wouldn't be able to tell you anything, would she?" he said softly.

"She says they got woken up because something had to be done."

"And what was that?"

"Something had to be done about the dead girl downstairs."

It was unclear if I had guessed right, but his lips spread. It was still not the Palm Beach grin, just one that said I was nuts, didn't know what I was talking about, was profoundly mistaken. It was a grin that did not require his eyes to do anything at all.

Was I panting? Hyperventilating? Something was affecting my voice, making it tight and low. "She said it was Peter who woke them, Jamie. Because you were downstairs, trying to clean up the mess you had made."

"That's bullshit," he said. He didn't sound angry. I was certain now that there was someone in the room next to him, someone just beyond my vision.

"Something bad happens," I said, trying to speak louder, "no matter how mad you Gregorys are at each other, you stick together. That's the family code, right?"

"We do stick together," he agreed. "We stuck with you down in Florida, didn't we?"

"Peter was going to get the last girl that night and you were going to be the loser, weren't you, Jamie? Couldn't entice her to go off with you, so you decided to make sure he didn't get her, either. That's the way all you hypercompetitive Gregorys are, isn't it?"

"What we are is loyal to our friends and to those who are loyal to us. You took advantage of that girl down there; you wanted help. We gave it to you. Now you're afraid it's going to come back and bite you in the butt."

"Heidi Telford never left by the side gate, as you guys tried to make it seem. There was no motorist who picked her up while she was walking home. It was just you, Jamie, who screwed everything up that night."

"What I apparently screwed up was not turning you over to the police after catching you violating Kendrick Powell."

"You and Peter actually got into a fight over Heidi, and when Paul McFetridge broke it up, you ran off and got the first weapon you could find."

"So what you're thinking is that you can keep me from talking when you announce your candidacy by pretending you've got something on me. I talk about the rape and you'll tell everyone I'm a murderer, is that it?"

"Came back with a golf club. But you weren't going to beat in your cousin's skull, were you? That would tear the family apart if you killed your cousin. And your family doesn't tear apart. You're against each other only until it's time to be against everyone else."

Jamie Gregory looked into my face as if he were searching for something.

"So you snuck up on Heidi and hit her from behind."

"Fact is," he said, "a girl like Kendrick would never have had anything to do with a guy like you."

"How do you like your date now, Peter, huh? Like her with her skull split open?"

"And there she was, practically passed out on the couch, unable to stop you from doing anything you wanted." He moved to one side. Toward what? Toward a room that I couldn't see, toward whatever was going to get me if I actually went inside the house?

I stayed where I was. "Heidi Telford wasn't just passed out," I said, my voice pursuing him. "She was dead. And you and Peter were scared. You had to do something before the guests woke up in the morning and found the body, the blood, the little bits of brain and bone you had left scattered around."

"You must have thought you were in heaven. Seeing her lying on the couch like that."

"So Peter went to get Ned, get some help, while you started the cleanup."

"She couldn't even resist."

"One of you, one of the three, came up with the idea of taking her to the golf course, putting her out there in the trees along the fairway. It was dark, it was accessible, it kept to some kind of theme in terms of how she had gotten killed."

"What did you do with her underwear, anyhow?"

"It wasn't a good idea, but all three of you participated, and then the family machine started putting its spin on things, planting rumors, stories, buying off witnesses, just like you did down in Florida. Just like you always do."

"Put it in your pocket, was that it? Running off with a drunk girl's underwear in your pocket." He formed his fingers into a circle and made a pumping motion. And there it was, on his face, the same grin I had seen in Palm Beach, the one that had been in my mind for a dozen years.

The hand was pumping, the music was pouring down the stairs, the bastard was grinning at me, and I went after him. I took one lunging step, and Jamie Gregory's eyes went wide. Only they weren't looking at me. They were looking past me, behind me, and the hand, the one that had been pumping, went up in front of his face.

I spun and raised my arm to protect my own head from whatever was coming.

# 4.

THE POLICE WERE THERE WITHIN MINUTES. TWO MINUTES, MAYBE. Time was a blur. Everything was a blur except what was directly in front of me, which was Jamie's body, crumpled at the base of the foyer wall. He had a hole in his chest, right about where his heart should be, and blood was gushing out of it. I had both my hands over the hole, trying to keep the blood in, pushing down on his chest because I did not know what else to do; hampered in everything I tried by Darra Lane, who had come running down the stairs as soon as Jamie collapsed. She had dived on top of him, shaking his shoulders, beseeching him to wake up.

There had been a shot. A single loud, unnatural noise that had come from the street, overwhelming all other sounds for an instant and then swallowed up by accelerating engines and whirring tires and screeching brakes.

A car had appeared out of nowhere, right behind the figure in the old coat and battered hat. Right behind him because he was facing me. The hat did not quite hide the cold, narrow features beneath its brim. The loose sleeve of the coat most definitely did not cover the pistol held in the right hand.

It had happened so fast. I tensed, thinking I was hit, thinking that on the other side of me something had been punctured and was letting out air. There was a crash. Then a scream. All the noises started separately, then blended together, and Jamie Gregory, his arms flung over his head, dropped to the floor.

My head whipped back toward the street, toward the figure in the battered coat and hat. With an underhand toss, he flipped the gun into the ivy between the house and the wrought-iron fence. He looked at me. Our eyes held for a moment: He wanted me to know who he was. Then Roland Andrews jumped into the backseat of the car and was gone.

# 5.

THE FIRST COP TO ARRIVE WAS A BULKY FELLOW, OR LOOKED THAT way in his flak vest and his blue jacket. He recognized Darra immediately and believed everything she said, which, to the extent it was coherent, was that I had shot her boyfriend.

The cop pushed me back from the body and left Darra to flop around on top of it and do even less than I had to try to save Jamie's life. He was holding me against a wall, an arm across my neck, when reinforcements arrived. Two cops in uniform, two without. The guys without were detectives and they were not wearing suits, but they had plenty of comments about mine. While their colleagues tended to Jamie, they braced me, demanding to know why I was there, dressed like I was, on Mr. Gregory's doorstep. They fingered my lapels, told each other the suit must have cost a grand, must have come from Barneys, wasn't ever going to be any good again now that it had blood all over it. They wanted to know if Mr. Gregory had cost me a lot of money, if that was why I was at his house.

"Was it because of what happened in the market today?" said one.

"He lose you a shitload?" said the other.

An ambulance with lights rocketing in every direction arrived, and paramedics raced up the steps and into the house, pushing past us to get to what was now, clearly, a dead body on the floor. I told the detectives I didn't know what they were talking about, that I was an assistant district attorney investigating a murder on Cape Cod. We were being jostled this way and that and Darra had gone from screaming to wailing and I was half shoved, half guided into the adjoining room. It was sort of a den, sort of a breakfast room, with a fireplace at one end and a wooden table in the middle, and the detectives backed me into the table and demanded my identification.

They did a lot of smirking when I could not produce it. They got my Bar card out of my wallet, passed it back and forth, and decided I was an unhappy investor after all.

"Lost your ID but not your wallet, is that it?"

"What, were you trying to pick up girls by flashing it around?"

"Don't work for me when I show 'em my badge."

"Nah, they wanna see your baton instead."

They were really getting into it, throwing remarks back and forth, when one of the uniforms came rushing into the room shouting that he had found the gun.

The two detectives looked at each other, looked at me, and began shaking their heads.

"Bad enough you shoot a Gregory," said one.

"But doin' it in front of a movie star," said the other.

"Then throwing the weapon in the bushes. What do ya think, we're stupid?"

"Think you can get away with it because you got a fuckin' suit on?"

"Fuckin' Barneys suit?"

"You're up shit creek, pal."

"Suit's not gonna do ya much good at Rikers Island."

"You wanna tell us the truth now?"

# 6.

I WAS NEVER TAKEN TO RIKERS ISLAND. I SPENT THE NIGHT OF JAMIE'S shooting in a precinct, explaining how I happened to be where I was. I started with the rape of Kendrick Powell in Palm Beach, then talked of Josh David Powell's twelve-year quest for revenge.

The two detectives kept interrupting me. "Peter Martin, the doctor?" one of them said.

"Guy's devoted his life to helping other people, and you claim he's a rapist?" the other one mocked.

"And you, what, you sitting in some easy chair jerking off while all this was going on?" the first one demanded.

I reminded them I was now an assistant district attorney investigating a murder.

"Yeah, right," said the second detective. "In some piss-off fish-town famous for saltwater taffy."

"And for the Gregorys," said the first. "That just a coincidence? You bein' there, in their hometown?"

My failure to answer that only encouraged them.

"So," said detective number one, "you see the Gregorys rape a girl, you take a job in their hometown, then you're told to find a murderer, and lo and behold, it turns out to be one of them. That your story?"

It was my story. All it got me was eye rolls and guttural noises.

I tried to tell them about Bill Telford, about his theory of Heidi going to the Gregorys' house. They cut me off.

"Those Gregorys must be real bad people," detective number one said, "goin' around raping and killing."

"Especially Peter Martin," said the other. "Devotes his life to saving people, except when he's fucking 'em up."

"Dr. Jerk-Off and Mr. Hyde," said the first, who seemed to have a bit of a fixation.

"Sounds to me like you got it in for these guys, George."

"Something goes wrong, blame it on the Gregorys."

"Except now you're taking it one step further."

"Shoot one of 'em, blame it on someone they done wrong."

"Plenty people like that out there."

"Sure. Gotta be a million of 'em."

"There's a million Gregorys, aren't there?"

"Million times a million."

It was easy for them to keep up their witty banter because they knew I had killed Jamie.

Darra Lane had told them so.

EVENTUALLY THE DETECTIVES left me alone and I sat for a long time with nothing to do but stare at the table, the walls, the mirror through which I assumed someone was watching me. When they came back there was an entirely different cast to their faces. They looked like they had been taken to the woodshed.

They also were not alone. With them was another man, a captain, who appeared to have showered and shaved and dressed for the meeting. It was 1:00 in the morning.

I told the captain everything I had told the detectives. He didn't laugh, he didn't joke. He wanted to know Roland Andrews's phone number, where he lived, some way to track him down. I told him Andrews only contacted me. I had no way to get in touch with him, nothing to give but the address of Marion's apartment in Boston.

After that I was never even put in a cell. I was not fingerprinted, I was not photographed, the police did not so much as swab my hands to see if they could find any gunpowder residue. I was just left alone in the interrogation room. A few hours passed and one of the detectives stuck his head in and asked if I wanted to call anyone. I said I wanted to call Mitch White and he told me they already had. He said Mitch was sending somebody down. He asked if there was anyone else, a wife, a girlfriend, a buddy. I said there was no one.

THE SOMEBODY MITCH sent turned out to be Barbara Belbonnet. I did not know whether I was grateful or furious to see her. I probably showed no emotion at all. For her part, she was distraught. She had tried calling me, she insisted. Seven, eight, nine times, and I had never answered the cell phone.

The fact of the matter was, I had not come down to New York intending to spend the night. I had not brought my cell-phone charger, had not bought another, had not asked the hotel for assistance, and the phone had died in the afternoon without me even realizing it. If it had been on I would have known that Barbara had not been able to get a babysitter. Her parents were going to a dinner at the Wianno Club. She had no one else to watch Malcolm, not overnight.

But she had come mid-morning to take me back, keep me away from the press. I wasn't being charged, even though Darra Lane's agent had already arranged a press conference in which she told the world that a well-dressed man had come to Jamie's door and shot him dead right in front of her. There were a dozen television trucks outside the police station and a hundred reporters waiting to see who that well-dressed man was, who the police had taken into custody. The police weren't saying, were admitting only that they had a witness, and for security's sake they were withholding his identity. "When a Gregory gets shot," the chief of the NYPD declared at his own press conference that morning, "there could be all kinds of ramifications."

Meanwhile, I was being told by Barbara that Mitch had arranged things. If I was willing, the police would let me have a uniform to wear walking out of the rear of the building. They would put the two of us in a squad car and take us to LaGuardia. That was a problem, I told her, since I no longer had my ID and could not get through airport security. There were more negotiations. It was decided I would take the train from Penn Station. She couldn't, however. She was going to have to fly back. She had to pick up the kids.

# 1.

I T WAS AFTER 8:00 ON THE NIGHT FOLLOWING JAMIE GREGORY'S death when I got to South Station in Boston. The shooting was one of two major stories in the newspapers. The other had to do with the collapse of a pair of financial institutions, including the very one that had employed Jamie. It seemed something had gone terribly wrong with sub-prime mortgages. The newspapers thought the two stories were related.

There was a car and driver waiting for me when I got off the train. I did not know the driver, and he did not ask me any questions. If he knew what I had been through, he did not acknowledge it. We rode in silence for the hour and fifteen minutes it took to get from Boston to Barnstable.

The triumvirate were still in the office when I arrived: Mitch in his short-sleeved shirt, Dick with his belly hanging over his belt, Reid with his steel-gray eyeglasses. None of them was concerned with my physical or mental well-being. But they very much wanted to hear what I had to say. I did what I had tried and failed to do in New York, laid out the entire case against Jamie, laid it out painstakingly, starting in Palm Beach. Dick showed shock. Mitch looked uncomfortable. Reid was impassive.

"According to New York," Reid said when I was done, "they contacted Mr. Powell in Delaware and he claims not only to have never employed a Roland Andrews but never to have heard of him. NYPD says they have searched databases for the entire country and can come up with no one by that name who fits your description." He picked up a piece of paper, what appeared to be a faxed letter. "They tell me," he said, holding it by its corner, letting it swing back and forth between us, "there is no record of a Roland Andrews ever serving in the Special Forces."

"Check the fingerprints on the gun," I urged. "Andrews had to have served in some branch of the armed forces. There ought to be a match somewhere."

"There were no prints on the gun," Reid said. He did not act surprised or even disappointed.

"We think," said Dick O'Connor, his round face filled with innocent goodwill, "you might be best off going with the story that the shooter was a disgruntled investor."

When I didn't say anything, he went further. "Big collapse on Wall Street yesterday. A lot of angry people out there. People who lost everything."

I looked at the others. Reid appeared to be nodding, although with such economy of movement it was hard to tell. Mitch was neither speaking nor moving. He was just staring.

## 2.

I T WAS DECIDED I WOULD TAKE A LEAVE OF ABSENCE, WITH PAY. There would be no explanation and, I was told, if I was smart I wouldn't offer one myself. "Let the New York cops continue their investigation," said Reid. "They haven't disclosed your identity in any way. Leave it at that. The alternative, you know, the alternative is they parade you in front of the bimbo, let her identify you."

When I pointed out that it had been my job to find the killer of Heidi Telford and that I had done just that, Dick O'Connor shook his head until his jowls shimmied. "What you got is not enough to meet our burden of proof," he said. "You know how it is: We've got to show beyond a reasonable doubt. But here, what do you have, really? Some gal in New York says it wasn't Peter; you figure that means it was Jamie. You go to Jamie, try to beat a confession out of him. Only he doesn't confess. 'Least, nobody hears him confess."

He shrugged helplessly. "Which means, all we've got is you."

"And," added Reid, "you're tainted."

# 3.

I WENT HOME AND I WAITED. I WASN'T SURE FOR WHAT.

Every day I listened to the radio: the local Cape stations, WBZ in Boston, NPR. The airwaves were filled with talk about the economic crisis. Every day I read *The New York Times, The Boston Globe,* the *Cape Cod Times.* There were articles about Jamie's death, about the funeral, about his family. There continued to be speculation about the connection between his killer and the money that Jamie had lost for investors. Both the police and the FBI claimed to be investigating. "But," explained one NYPD spokesman, "there were just so many people who were wiped out, it may take years."

Every day I got out my bike and rode as far as I could, for as long as I could.

I HAD A CALL from Barbara. She wanted to know how I was doing.

She also wanted to tell me that with my office door closed and locked, there were rumors flying around the office about where I was and what was happening to me. Sean Murphy, she said, was telling people it was not just a coincidence that I had disappeared on the very day Jamie Gregory was shot.

I hung up with Barbara and immediately called Dick O'Connor. He told me I needed to lie low, let the process take its course. I repeated what I had heard about the rumors and Dick agreed that it was unfortunate. He said he would speak to Sean and urged me to be patient. "Things are being taken care of, Georgie," he insisted.

THE RESULTS OF the autopsy were released. It turned out Darra Lane had done me an enormous favor. In her press conference, in her stories to the police, on television and in magazines, she had insisted that a man in a suit had shot Jamie Gregory from just a couple of feet away. The autopsy confirmed that Jamie had been shot from a distance, at least twenty-five feet, said the coroner, who commented that it was a rather remarkable feat of marksmanship for a nine-millimeter pistol. The shooter must have been well trained, he said.

I waited for a call from Dick. It didn't come. I tried calling him. He wasn't available. His secretary said he would call me back. He didn't.

I placed three more calls: one to Dick, one to Reid, one to Mitch. Nobody took them.

## 4.

I RODE MY BIKE ALL THE WAY TO PROVINCETOWN. I HAD NOT MEANT to go that far. I had ridden the Rail Trail, taken the Chatham route, then continued on through Orleans until I got to the roundabout that marked the transition from Mid-Cape to Lower Cape. I could have gone one hundred eighty degrees around the rotary, then on to Rock Harbor, where I could have stopped and looked at the fishing boats, maybe bought a lobster roll at a place called Cap't Cass on the edge of the Harbor parking lot, then gotten back on the Brewster leg of the Rail Trail and returned to my car in Dennis. This time of year I wasn't sure Cap't Cass was still open, and so I decided to head east instead, go to Arnold's Lobster and Clam Bar along Route 6. It was closed for the season, so I kept going, through Eastham, with a vague idea that there were more roadside lobster shacks and one of them was bound to be open. I kept riding through Wellfleet, and by the time I got to Truro I decided to go all the way.

It was almost dark when I got to the end of the continent. I wasn't going to be able to ride back. I didn't have a light, didn't even have a windbreaker, and it was getting cold. I booked a room at a motel at the far end of town, out on a jetty, the very edge of the world.

———

IT WAS FOGGY WHEN I got up in the morning, and still cold. I had walked partway along Commercial Street the night before, looking for something to eat. I had gotten some catcalls from men who had enjoyed my spandex outfit, and now I was going to have to make the walk again if I wanted to buy something warm to wear for the long ride back.

I reminded myself that the catcallers were unlikely to be out first thing in the morning and left the dankness of the room to begin my trek. I had walked for no more than thirty seconds when a black vehicle that looked like a giant Jeep began blinking its lights. The clouds were at ground level and all around me. I could hear foghorns out on the water, and I could not see one hundred feet in any direction, but I could see those flashing headlights. I stopped, thinking it might be police or a national park ranger, somebody warning me it was dangerous to be trying to navigate on foot when visibility was this poor. Maybe warning me it was dangerous to walk through town dressed the way I was.

But this was P'town. People could wear anything they wanted.

The vehicle's door opened, and I realized it was not a Jeep but a Hummer, the smaller model, the one they called the Hummer 3. "Hey, Georgie!" a voice called. A male voice.

I squinted, trying to get a better look.

The man was holding something in his hand, something like a bag. I remembered the hood in Tamarindo and it occurred to me that I should run. Except there was nothing behind me but the motel and the long rock jetty. I stood my ground while the man approached. A big man, wearing shorts. Red shorts. Nantucket Reds, knee-length, salmon-colored, popular among the summer crowd on the islands. The object in the man's hand was a piece of dangling cloth, a blanket maybe, or a jacket. Below the shorts he was wearing Top-Siders; above them he had on a sweater and a polo shirt with the collar popped. The man was grinning. He was grinning because he knew me and he had not seen me in twelve and a half years.

He stopped when he got an arm's length away from me. He did not try to embrace. He did not even offer his hand. What he offered was the cloth, which turned out to be a sweatshirt. A crimson sweatshirt.

"Penn guy like you probably doesn't want this, but it's better than freezing your ass off." He tossed it to me.

I caught the sweatshirt in one hand, looked down at it, saw the word "Harvard" emblazoned with white letters and continued holding it, dumbstruck.

"Want some coffee?" He slung a thumb over his shoulder. "I got a whole Thermos. Got some Dunkin' Donuts, too, if you're hungry."

I was hungry. I did want some coffee. I said, "No, thank you, Peter."

He nodded. He looked as if he was going to try some other friendly acts, suggestions, gestures, and then he wiped the condensation from his brow and said, "I was wondering if I could talk to you."

"We're talking now, aren't we?" I still had not put on the sweatshirt.

"I guess you don't want to get in the car, huh?" Then he answered himself. "Yeah. I don't blame you. You've been through a lot because of us, and that's what I wanted to talk about. To apologize, really. Listen, can we go for a walk at least? You mind? How about out on that jetty?"

Go out on the jetty. In the fog. With Peter Gregory Martin.

"How about we go into town?" I said.

"Yeah." He nodded. "We could. Except you can never tell who's around." He looked around. "Always seems to be somebody with a camera when you least expect it." He inclined his head toward the jetty as if it were the only possible place for two men to walk if they wanted a little privacy.

"Which begs the question: What are you doing here, Peter? Outside my motel at eight in the morning? You follow me here?"

"Not really." He grinned some more, harder this time. It was still a friendly grin, not a sick one like Jamie's, but not a charming one like the Senator's, either.

I tried to think. Nobody had followed me. At least I had not seen anybody follow me. "Peter, I didn't know I was coming here. It's just where I ended up."

He waved his hand in the direction of Route 6, as if that was where somebody had seen me. Of course, it was also the direction of everything else in the country, everything except the motel itself. I looked at the motel office. He saw me looking.

"Nah," he said, interpreting. "What, do you think we have some big network of informers or something? You check in someplace and the desk clerk immediately calls us up?"

He acted like it was a joke, but that was exactly what I was thinking. It didn't make a lot of sense, but neither did the idea that someone could have been with me on a trail that did not allow motor vehicles and then tailed me all along Route 6, where I had not seen a single other cyclist. And then it came to me.

"You put a tracking device on my bike, didn't you?"

"C'mon, Georgie." Peter Martin swatted me playfully on the shoulder.

I recoiled. "Where is it? Under the seat?"

Peter stopped grinning. He looked away. There was not much he could look at. "I don't do these things myself, George."

"You wanted to talk to me, you could have come to my house. Called me on the phone."

"I wanted to see you in person. That's why I came across country. Didn't think it was going to be fucking winter." He wiped his brow a second time. The fog was so wet it was matting our hair into strands that plastered our skulls and created little follicular runways for drops of water. "I didn't want to come to your house because, like I said before, you never know who's around."

Peter Martin did not want to be seen with me. Peter Martin was standing with me in a fog so thick there could have been a troop of soldiers arrayed fifty yards from us and I would not have known.

"Could be anyone," I said.

He agreed.

"Could even be Josh David Powell."

"His people, yeah."

"All kinds of folks following me, aren't there, Peter?"

"It's part of what I want to apologize about. Look, can we please walk? Just in case Powell does have somebody around, can we not stand here like this?"

He wanted to go on that jetty. I looked and couldn't see anything.

Just the first few gray-black boulders that made up the riprap that curved its way into the ocean. A foghorn sounded again, warning me away.

*Prosecutor found dead floating off Provincetown jetty. He must have slipped on the rocks and hit his head. He was wearing bicycle shoes with metal plates on the soles.*

"No," I said. "This is as good a place as any."

*Prosecutor found dead in parking lot. Strangled, garroted, beaten to a pulp.* I would take Peter down with me. I would make him pay. *Hit me, motherfucker, and I will carve you up.* With what, I didn't know. My fingers, if that was all I had.

Peter sighed. He shrugged. "At least put on that sweatshirt if we're going to stand here. You don't need to freeze to death."

Prosecutors don't freeze to death in September on Cape Cod. Nevertheless, I draped the sweatshirt over my shoulders, crossed my arms, and waited.

"I know," Peter said, starting slowly, "that you were there when Jamie was murdered." He threw up his palm quickly to stop me from responding. "I even know what you said to him. I'm not here to argue about it. What I am thinking, however, what the family's thinking, is, okay, Jamie's dead, what good does it do to drag all this out?"

Now? Did he want me to answer now? No.

"Powell and his thug there," he went on, "they're not going to admit what they did, and we're asking ourselves if we really want to go after them."

Yeah, right. And bring into the open why Powell's man would want to shoot Jamie. I might have been sneering as I stood in the street at the end of the world.

"So," he said, "the next thing we have to consider is you, and how you feel about it. And we're thinking, you know, we've always been able to count on Georgie, count on his discretion. So what about now?"

"I've already talked, Peter."

"Yes. But you've talked to the police, to the folks in the D.A.'s office. That can all be taken care of. The question is, what do you really want to do?"

Peter, his neck extended, his head pointing toward me, seemed really to want to know. It took me a moment to understand he was not just asking my opinion, my preference, he was offering me something.

"What do you have in mind?" I said.

"You know," he answered, his eyes on mine, keeping contact, "Mitch White would like nothing better than to get out of here, go back to D.C. He's up for reelection in a couple of weeks and everybody figures he's a shoo-in, but the right job came along, he'd leave the Cape in a minute."

"Senate Judiciary Committee, perhaps?"

"Maybe even better than that. Democrat gets elected to the White House, a number of favors can be called in." Peter shrugged. That's the way things work, he was saying.

"And you're thinking perhaps I might like to take Mitch's place, be district attorney for the Cape and Islands."

"Somebody's got to. If the door's thrown open at the last minute, whoever is the best organized, has the best backing, is going to get it."

"Suppose somebody else is already out there getting ready? Somebody independent of the Gregory family?"

"That can be taken care of." Peter shifted his feet, moved in a little closer as if to make sure that nobody lurking in the fog would hear him. "You want the support of the Macs, all you have to do is come out in favor of the Mashpee Indian casino and they're yours."

"It's all arranged?"

"It could be."

"I just have to keep my mouth shut about Jamie."

"Look, George." Peter kept his eyes focused on mine. "I don't blame you for what happened there, in New York. Nobody does. You did what you thought should be done." He reached out to touch my shoulder.

Once again I twisted out of the way and he lowered his hand.

"Jamie was a difficult person," he said, a touch of sadness in his voice. "Brilliant, but he was missing a—I don't know, a moral compass, I guess you'd call it."

"Unlike you."

"Yeah, well, I know what you're talking about, George. I've got a lot of guilt built up in me about that."

"About Kendrick Powell, you mean." I wanted him to say it.

"I was drunk. I was young. None of that is an excuse, but it's true. And you pulled me off her, George, and for that I'll forever be grateful. I mean it." He once again started to reach out to me and then drew back his hand before I could move.

I said, "You guys raped her, Peter. And then you lied and insisted it never happened."

His face warped with confusion, as if he had misheard. "We tried to make it up to her," he said. "We really did. Offered her a great deal of money, in fact. Her father would have none of it. So that's when we had to ask ourselves—"

He hesitated, gauging what he should say, how he should say it. Small drops of water were making their way down his forehead.

"—what good was it going to do to confess? What, we maybe go to prison? At the least, the whole world was going to know. The family's name gets dragged through the mud. My uncle once again is kept from doing all the good things he could do for the country. Jamie and I are kept from doing all the good things that we, as Gregorys, could do."

"Like sell worthless mortgages to friends who are trusting you with their life savings?"

This was not going the way Peter Martin had envisioned. He shifted his weight, stuck his hands in the pockets of his shorts, moved his eyes from mine to the tarmac at our feet. "Yeah, well, that was Jamie."

"The one whose honor we're trying to preserve."

"Not just his, George. I mean, I tried, I really tried to dedicate myself to the betterment of humanity." His head lifted sharply, as if appalled at his own words. "I don't want that to sound pretentious, George. It's just . . . there were lots of things I could have done, but I chose to go to med school and to specialize in infectious diseases, and then I chose to go to San Francisco and work with AIDS victims. I didn't have to do any of that."

"You also didn't have to help Jamie dispose of Heidi Telford's body and pretend he didn't kill her."

Noises were coming out of Peter Martin. Noises that made me think of a steam engine. They were, I realized, rapid breaths of air. He was acting as if I had just punched him in the gut. Peter, the big bear, whose arm had been soft when I squeezed it in Palm Beach, who looked even softer now, did not know what to do. I could see him searching for words. I could see words starting to form in his mouth and then disappear.

"When you're in my family," he said at last, "and so many tragic things have happened, you learn from the time you're able to walk that you have to stick together. That's all we have—"

"That and money and connections and opportunity and rules that apply to everyone else except you."

Peter started to defend himself and I cut him off. "You and Jamie treated Heidi Telford the same way you treated Kendrick Powell. She didn't count. Not when it came to your pleasure, not when it came to your well-being. Justify it in your own mind all you want, you fat fuck. You molested and raped a young woman, then watched her life go down the drain because you didn't want people to know what you had done and because as far as you were concerned she wasn't worth what a Gregory was worth. Then three years later you let your cousin bash in the head of another young woman and you treated her like she wasn't worth anything, either."

I took the sweatshirt off my shoulders and threw it in his face. "You didn't care about Kendrick, you didn't care about Heidi, you didn't care about what you did to their parents. All you cared about was how you looked and when you tell me now about what a great humanitarian you are, I know the truth." I jammed my thumb into my chest. "Me, Peter. I know the truth."

The sweatshirt had slid the length of his body until he caught it somewhere around his stomach. Now he held it there while he stared at me in disbelief. His was the face of a man looking at the unknown; as if, standing here at the end of the continent, he had just discovered that the world really was flat, that the waters were rushing off the edge and taking him with them.

Very slowly, he began to back away.

# 5.

I T TOOK ME ALL DAY TO RIDE HOME. IT WAS WET ONLY THROUGH Truro. It was cold the entire way.

When I arrived, there was a message on my answering machine. Dick O'Connor. Good old Dick, who still used hardcover books to do his legal research instead of the Internet. Dick, who called me on my home phone and not my cell. Dick, who probably did not have my cell-phone number. Who might not have a cell of his own.

The message said he wanted me to come into the office that night. Any time after 6:00. He would be waiting. He would wait until midnight if he had to.

I GOT THERE JUST before 8:00, and as far as I could tell we were the only ones in the building except the jailers and the jailed, down in the basement, near where I used to be stationed.

Dick had the remains of a submarine sandwich in front of him. He glanced up at me, wrapped what was left of the food, and jammed it into a paper bag. He did not have the usual jovial Dick look.

"Hey," I said.

"Sit down," he said. Then he changed his mind. "Don't sit down, this won't take long."

I sat anyway.

The chief assistant grimaced. "We're not going to bring you back on," he said, speaking as if he had to rush in order to make sure the words all came out together. Dick was not good at this, being harsh, being direct. Dick would prefer to look at a jury in astonishment that some criminal could have acted the way he did.

After a moment of me regarding him in silence, he added, "Too much baggage."

"What kind of baggage are we talking about?"

"I could tell you it's the kind of baggage you accumulate when you're scheming to run against your boss, only I'm not going to say that."

"I'm not scheming to run against anyone, Dick."

"The Macs told us all about it, how you been talking with them, lining up their support."

He looked pained, hurt.

"That's bullshit, Dick."

He tossed his shoulders. He either didn't care or didn't believe me.

"Peter Martin called you today, didn't he?"

"All that time you kept quiet about the rape thing, George." He moved his eyes away from mine. It could have been out of disgust with either one of us. "Probably wouldn't look so good if it comes out that just before you were going to make your announcement you were present at the murder of the only guy in the world who knew the facts about that rape."

"He wasn't the only guy in the world. Peter Martin was there. What Peter did was worse than what Jamie did."

"And what Dr. Martin says, George, is that what you did was the worst of all."

## 6.

THE OFFER WAS FULL PAY UNTIL THE END OF THE YEAR. I WAS SIMPLY to leave. I could go to Hawaii, Costa Rica, France, anywhere that it looked like I was continuing my investigation.

Nobody would mention my involvement in Jamie's shooting or the Palm Beach rape. Six weeks from now, with Mitch safely reelected, he would prepare an excellent letter of recommendation, and by January I should have landed myself a new job, preferably quite far away.

There was no contract, nothing in writing. I was simply to tell Dick okay.

I told him.

It was hard to determine if he was disappointed.

I know we did not shake hands.

# 7.

CALLED BARBARA AND EXPLAINED WHAT WAS GOING ON. ONCE again, I asked for help.

This time, she said she couldn't do anything for me.

I reminded her what she had said that day on my patio about doing the right thing, and she agreed everybody should, but she had two kids and one of them had special needs. She had to put them first. I brought up what she had done already, going to Costa Rica, directing me to France, and she said yes, she had done all that, but that had been behind the scenes. Her position was different than mine. Her life was different. She couldn't afford to lose her job, she couldn't just leave the Cape, and she couldn't stay and be a pariah.

"My father," she said, and didn't finish the rest of the sentence. Then she added the words "My son," and I was supposed to understand.

## 1.

BUZZY HELD A PRESS CONFERENCE THAT WAS SURPRISINGLY WELL attended, proving that all you had to do to get the attention of the news media, at least in the northeast, was mention the Gregorys. A notice had been blasted by email to more than one hundred newspapers, television and radio stations, networks, and news outlets. The notice said an important announcement was going to be made regarding the Cape & Islands district attorney and his investigation into the Gregory family's involvement in the 1999 murder of Heidi Telford.

Mitch White, when he got wind of it, immediately issued a denial that there was any new development in the investigation, which, he said, was not only ongoing but now spanned three continents. Mitch did not identify the three continents, but I gathered he was counting Costa Rica as being in South America.

His denial managed to make it onto the 6:00 p.m. news on all the major television stations in Boston and Providence. I was biased, but to me he did not sound convincing when he said he knew of no involvement of the Gregory family. And he looked worried.

## 2.

BUZZY DELIVERED HIS ANNOUNCEMENT ON THE STEPS OF THE rear entrance to Town Hall, facing a broad expanse of lawn that extended all the way to Main Street, where anybody who happened to be walking could inquire why scores of people with cameras and recorders were bunching behind the old red-brick building.

Chief Cello DiMasi was there, standing to one side with half a dozen of his officers. But Buzzy had obtained a permit to hold a rally to announce his candidacy, and so the primary thing that seemed to have Cello fiddling with his thick black belt was whether Buzzy's email had created an event that exceeded the bounds of the permit. Clearly, he wasn't sure.

And because this had originally been billed as Buzzy's declaration of intent to run as a write-in candidate for district attorney, the incumbent could not very well line up with Cello, nor send him and his troops wading onto the lawn to disperse the crowd. There were too many cameras, too many of Buzzy's buddies from high school ready to start shouting about the First Amendment to the United States Constitution.

So Mitch himself did not even go. He sent Reid and Dick instead. They stood next to Cello. And next to them stood Sean Murphy, holding a legal notepad and a pen.

At exactly the time he said the event would begin, the double doors at the top of the stairs opened and Buzzy somberly walked out of the building with a very conspicuous sheaf of papers under his left arm. Friends offered good-effort cheers from scattered spots on the lawn. Buzzy acknowledged them with a wave of his right hand. He strode to a portable lectern that had been set up for him. He tapped the microphone to make sure it was working. He said, "Hello."

Those who knew him expected a joke, some lighthearted remark. But the closest Buzzy got to that was a half-smile as he announced, "I'm Frederick Daizell, known to my friends and family as Buzzy, and I am running for district attorney as a write-in candidate."

Friends and family put up another cheer and got a second wave of acknowledgment. But then Buzzy stopped even half-smiling.

"And the reason I am doing this very unusual thing, coming in at the last moment with no party backing and no official status as anything other than a citizen who happens to be an attorney, is that I have uncovered some very disturbing information about the incumbent, Mitchell White, his relationship with the Gregory family, and the effect of that relationship on his office's investigation of the 1999 murder of twenty-year-old Heidi Telford of Hyannis."

Some of the media people, the well-dressed men and women who were standing around with their cameramen, put down their coffees and bottled waters and started pointing fingers and issuing orders.

"To help me explain this," Buzzy went on, "I have asked Heidi's father, Bill Telford, to join me."

With tufts of white hair blowing in the breeze, Mr. Telford laboriously mounted the stairs and took his place next to Buzzy, who put his arm around him.

"I'm Bill Telford," the guest of honor said, squinting at the audience. "Most of you who live around here know me. The way I go around asking questions, some no doubt wish you didn't."

There were titters from those who understood what he meant, but they were short because nobody wanted to be disrespectful to a man who had lost his daughter.

"For nine and a half years I been going around asking these questions, trying to find out who saw Heidi last, where she went after she left our house on Memorial Day, 1999. I'm not senile. I'm not crazy. I been getting some answers, and I been steadily passing them along to District Attorney White, only to find out what I been giving him has gone straight from his hands to the wastepaper basket."

Bill's voice cranked up with indignation.

"I tell him, the very day she died Heidi met Peter Gregory Martin at the Bon Faire Market over there in Osterville. I tell him she went to a party down the street here, in the harbor, where the Gregory kids were after the Figawi race. I tell him the Gregorys had another party back at their house on Sea View Avenue that a bunch of people went to, and I give him names."

He paused just long enough to put on a pair of glasses, pull a list from his pocket, and begin reading. "Patty Afantakis, formerly of Roslindale, now Patty Margolis of West Roxbury; Leanne Sullivan of Roslindale, who I understand is now in Las Vegas; Paul McFetridge of New York City, out in Idaho now; Jason Stockover of Cos Cob, Connecticut, New York City, and now some town in France that I can't pronounce, but I got right here." He waved the list over his head but barely broke cadence. "And there were four Gregory kids: Ned, Cory, Jamie, and Peter Gregory Martin."

He turned the list over, as if there should have been more names. He leaned into the microphone and said, "There was also an au pair named Lexi Sommers, who is now married and living in New York City, and there was a young man on the gate who's now the chef at the Captain Yarnell House down there in Brewster—and every one of those people knows my daughter was alive at the Gregory compound that night."

There was a stirring in the crowd, a murmur that became almost a clamor. Someone shouted out a question. Bill didn't hear it.

"District Attorney White has all that information, he's had most of it for years, and he not only hasn't questioned the Gregorys, he hasn't hardly talked to any of the people who were there."

"Mr. Telford!" a woman journalist shouted.

"The question is why?" Bill said, and now he was shouting because everyone else was.

The woman's voice was the most persistent. I recognized her. She was from WBZ-TV in Boston, the CBS channel. "Mr. Telford! Mr.

Telford! Are you saying the Gregorys had something to do with the murder of your daughter?"

"Damn right I am. It was Jamie Gregory, hit her with a golf club. Then he and his cousin Peter dragged her body out to the golf course and left her there. And Mitchell White's been covering up for them ever since."

And with that, Buzzy totally lost control of the proceedings. The crowd was in an uproar, and he never got to talk about the Indian casino or the local drug problem or the illegal immigrant problem or any of the other points in the outline I had prepared for him to use in his campaign announcement.

# 3.

I HAD BEEN WATCHING FROM INSIDE THE BUILDING, LOOKING THROUGH a tall, eight-paned window on the first floor, with a good view of the backs of Buzzy and Bill. I did not want to present myself because I was supposed to be away, out of state, carrying on Mitch's investigation. Anyone, however, could have seen me enter Town Hall from the South Street side or, for that matter, seen me over the past several days going in and out of Buzzy's office in Bass River or in and out of Alphonse and Caroline Carbona's house over in Sandwich, where I was staying in their spare bedroom.

So it was not a complete surprise when a hand slid under my arm and seized me by the wrist. It could have been Chuck-Chuck, Pierre, any one of the Gregorys; it could also have been Roland Andrews or someone else in Josh David Powell's employ. It could have been Josh David himself. The hand was very strong, the fingers long, but the touch was more comforting than threatening.

I took a chance. I didn't try to pull away. I didn't even turn. I just said, "Hello, Barbara. I'm glad you're here."

The hand squeezed.

"All right," a voice whispered in my ear, "I'll go along with you. I don't want to work for those bastards anyway."

B UZZY GOT TROUNCED. BUT NOT BY MITCH.
Two days after the debacle on the lawn outside Town Hall,
Buzzy made the announcement that if Mitchell White did not drop
out of the race, he was going to issue a press release detailing the full
extent of Mitch's "personal and historical" relationship with Senator
Gregory.

Mitch and the Gregorys released their hounds to bay in the newspapers and on the local radio about the impropriety of making personal
threats in a campaign. The most prominent bayer of all was the very
same talk-show host who had been playing the piano at the Senator's
Palm Beach house on the night of the rape of Kendrick Powell.

Jimmy Shelley responded to one of the host's most vitriolic dia-
tribes about Buzzy's intention by phoning in and asking the host if it
was true that he was there on the night of the rape. The host went
wild. He could barely contain himself, shouting over the airwaves that
the caller, "Jim from Hyannis," was nothing more than a provocateur
and reminding listeners that there had never been a conviction, a prosecution, even a finding of probability that there was a rape.

"It's easy to attack the Gregorys," he screamed. "Easy to blame
them for anything and everything if you're some extremist reactionary
who doesn't like the idea of universal healthcare, after-school programs
for our children, and equal tax burdens for all. Oh, sure, blame the

Gregorys because they're always out there in the public eye. They don't run, they don't hide. And if you need a boogeyman, someone to fault because your own relationship is falling apart, you've lost your job, or your kid doesn't make the soccer team, there they are—the folks who seemingly have everything and are the antithesis of losers like you, Jim from Hyannis, and anybody else who spreads these vicious, unfounded rumors.

"Because let me tell you, *Jim,* you sanctimonious, supercilious sultan of slop, I *was* there, as were scores of other people like me. And I heard nothing, saw nothing, and the first I knew that anybody was even alleging anything was days later, when a girl, a young woman, who maybe had way too much to drink, apparently told her very rich daddy that something had happened. And the local prosecutor investigated and found nothing. Nada. Zip. Zero. You hear that, Jim? So how about you just stuff your nasty rumors and get on to something important? We're taking a break."

But Buzzy's promised revelation had its effect. Mitch, no doubt cognizant of what Buzzy meant by "personal and historical," or maybe Stephanie, or maybe even the Senator himself, made the decision not to run the risk that Buzzy would expose the full extent of the relationship between the Senator and the Whites. Mitch held a press conference in which he announced there was nothing to Mr. Daizell's reckless accusation, but it was the very fact that such accusations could be made that had soured him on the whole political process. Yes, he could win in the upcoming election, but why would he want to subject himself and his family to such personal attacks? He was sick of this kind of damning by innuendo, and he had other ways of serving the public. He had been offered and was accepting the post of deputy general counsel to the Health Resources and Services Administration in Washington, D.C.

Mitch did not depart without a final act, however. He urged all citizens, all voters, all right-thinking people, to get together and support his chief assistant, Reid Cunningham, a dedicated public servant with impeccable credentials and unblemished character. And to show the public what Reid could do, Mitch was appointing Reid acting district attorney while Mitch himself was going to use his accrued vacation time to take immediate leave.

Reid accepted the reins and promptly denounced Buzzy as a one-note candidate. "That young fellow may be running against the Gregorys," Reid declared, "but I'm no Gregory. I'm a career prosecutor, and I'm here to do a job, not stir up tabloid publicity."

Shortly thereafter, Reid came out with a program that included increasing prosecution of drug dealers, working with the federal government on rounding up illegal immigrants, and endorsing the Mashpee Indians' plan for a casino.

WITH THE CANDIDATES now fully squared off, both campaigning for write-in votes, I gave an interview to the *Cape Cod Times* in which I identified myself as the deputy district attorney whom Mitch and Reid had put in charge of the Telford investigation. I explained I had started with Bill Telford's list and tracked down anyone and everyone I could until I had come to the ineluctable conclusions that the murder had been committed by Jamie Gregory and the disposal of the body had been carried out by Jamie and his cousin Peter. I admitted that I was in the process of confronting Jamie when he himself had been shot. The shooter had been a man, I said, dressed as a homeless person, firing from the sidewalk and fleeing in a car that had pulled up behind him.

The Gregory forces struck back immediately. A spokesman named Larry O'Donald, a lawyer in New York, declared that the family was saddened to hear such unfounded accusations. The dead cannot defend themselves, he reminded everyone, and perhaps that was why Jamie was being singled out as a target by those who might be attempting to further their own careers.

Mr. O'Donald agreed with me about the shooter, however. All evidence pointed to a disgruntled, perhaps even deranged, investor, he said, and the family felt that should be the focus of law enforcement's attention. As for Dr. Martin, there simply is and never has been any reason to involve him, a good man, a private man, who has not tried to capitalize on his family name but who has devoted his adult life to the betterment of others. He read a statement allegedly written by Peter in which he expressed sorrow for the Telford family and compared it to the sorrow his own family felt at the loss of Jamie. He asked the public to extend the Gregorys, all the Gregorys, the courtesy of allowing them to grieve; and as for him, he was going to continue to focus his energies on his practice and his attention on creating brighter days ahead for everyone.

Meanwhile, Sean Murphy, who had been appointed by Reid to take his former position as first assistant district attorney, informed the press that yes, indeed, George Becket was present when Jamie was shot, and that, in fact, George Becket remained very much a suspect in the shooting. He described me as a run-amok, a man who had been banned from the office while the investigation was taking place.

It was then that Barbara came through for me. She spoke to the same reporter I had, and explained that she had been the assistant D.A. sent to New York to conduct the investigation to which Sean was referring, and she did not know what Sean was talking about, since she could confirm that I had been cleared by both the New York Police Department and her own office of any involvement. She pointed out that the actress Darra Lane had seen and heard me confronting Jamie Gregory from only two to three feet away, and the New York City coroner had unequivocally determined Jamie to have been shot from at least twenty-five feet away. "George Becket was not only nearly killed himself," she said, "but he tried desperately to save Jamie Gregory's life until the paramedics got there. My findings, as reported to and accepted by the office, were that George was a hero."

The office waited until two days after the election before it suspended Barbara for insubordination and me for misuse of funds.

*B*UZZY MAY NOT HAVE GOTTEN ALL THE VOTES HE WAS SEEKING, *but he got a lot of publicity, and the publicity has produced a fair amount of work. He has taken me on, even calls me his partner, although he continues to own the entire practice. I get paid half of what I bring in, which is almost nothing, and a third of whatever he gets for the work I do on his cases.*

*Mostly what I do is arraignments and preliminary hearings, which means I am in the courthouse a lot with my old colleagues. Protocol seems to be to ignore me, to pretend not to know me, never to use my name. I don't see Reid, but Sean tends to glare at me, as if we might get into a fistfight at any time. Once I ran into Dick, but he looked away.*

*As for Barbara, well, her daddy came through. To an extent. He gave her the funds to open her own office in a little complex down by the harbor, where she has hung out her shingle among those displaying the services of insurance agents, realtors, and accountants. She is specializing in family law matters: divorces and custody proceedings. But like me, she gets little work. The people her parents know tend not to have those problems.*

*Little work gives us lots of time to lie around in bed on cold winter mornings, pulling the covers to our chins and talking about whether it is time for us to go off-Cape.*

*"Rome, Paris, London" are places she has thrown out when feeling particularly giddy and impractical.*

*"New Hampshire, Vermont, Wisconsin," I say.*

*"Florida, California," she counters.*

*"Buckthumb, Maine," I suggest.*

*Her choices are fueled by romantic visions; mine by the desire for security and anonymity. Still, it is exciting to lie naked next to her, to be able to reach out and touch her anytime I wish, to know that she is here next to me because she wants to be. And so I encourage the thought that all things are possible.*

*"Maybe way up in Northern California," I offer. "Eureka, someplace like that."*

*When she doesn't respond, I improve the offer. "It's beautiful at Lake Tahoe," I say. "Truckee, Tahoe City, they're good places to live."*

*Of course, we are hampered by the fact that we can only practice law where we are licensed, which means Massachusetts, plus, in my case, New Jersey. Barbara does not want to go to New Jersey.*

*I tell her there are nice towns in Jersey: Short Hills, Saddle River, Princeton, Morristown.*

*She lists nice towns in Massachusetts: Newton, Wellesley, Weston, Sudbury.*

*All are places we cannot afford.*

*We discuss the various district attorney's offices around the state and acknowledge we will probably be blackballed from all of them.*

*"Maybe not Worcester," she suggests. "Or Framingham. There's a great little town between those two places called Ashland, where I understand they have services for people like Malcolm."*

*I am doing my best to get to know Malcolm. I try not to freeze when she mentions his name. I know it will be hard, but I am convinced I can do it. Not because I am paying dues like Peter Martin, but because I am getting stronger, becoming a better person. It may take a long time, but I am committed to trying.*

*Which is why I am listening to Bill Telford. He comes around now and then, usually right to my house because I don't go to Pogo's anymore now that I see Barbara at night. He is disappointed that his announcement, his speech, did not change things.*

*"The Gregorys have gotten away again," he tells me. "They are still denying Jamie killed Heidi and the rest of them just go on living their lives the way they always have."*

*He wants me to write a book.*

*I remind him of what Dick O'Connor said, that I don't really have any hard* evidence, any admission, any eyewitness testimony that constitutes proof beyond a reasonable doubt.

He tells me the Gregorys won't do anything about it except get some family spokesman to deplore the crass innuendos being peddled for money by some failed attorney, some would-be, wannabe socialite. Those aren't the exact words Bill uses, but it is what he means.

What Bill Telford wants most of all is for everyone to know.

I remind him that not everyone wants everyone to know, that there are people besides the Gregorys who could take legal action: Jason Stockover, Leanne Sullivan, Howard Landry, Lexi Sommers Trotter, just to name a few.

He thinks about it. "In that case," he says, "change the names."

PHOTO © JAY BLAKESBERG

WALTER WALKER is a San Francisco trial attorney, specializing in catastrophic personal injury matters, and the author of five previous novels, including the award-winning *A Dime to Dance By*. Originally from Massachusetts, he has homes on Cape Cod and in Marin County, California. He is a graduate of the University of Pennsylvania, and the University of California, Hastings College of the Law.